Justine Elyot's kinky take on erotica has been widely anthologised in Black Lace's themed collections, and in the most popular online sites.

She lives by the sea.

On Demand

JUSTINE ELYOT

BLACK
LACE

3 5 7 9 10 8 6 4 2

First published in 2009 by Black Lace, an imprint of Virgin Books
This edition published in 2012 by Black Lace, an imprint of Ebury Publishing
A Random House Group Company

The Random House Group Limited Reg. No. 954009

Addresses for companies within the Random House Group can be found at
www.randomhouse.co.uk

A CIP catalogue record for this book is available from the British Library

The Random House Group Limited supports The Forest Stewardship
Council (FSC®), the leading international forest certification organisation.
Our books carrying the FSC label are printed on FSC® certified paper.
FSC is the only forest certification scheme endorsed by the leading
environmental organisations, including Greenpeace.
Our paper procurement policy can be found at:
www.randomhouse.co.uk/environment

Printed and bound by CPI Group (UK) Ltd, Croydon, CR0 4YY

ISBN 9780753541364

To buy books by your favourite authors and register for offers visit
www.blacklace.co.uk

Contents

No Reservations

(Do you have a reservation? Then this isn't the hotel for you!)

Welcome to the Hotel.

All baggage is to be left at the door.

Please sign in, under whichever name you have chosen, at Reception.

You are now free to explore. Enjoy your stay!

I have always been drawn to hotels.

Call me commitment-phobic, but I love their eternal temporariness, their anonymity, their fluidity and flux. They seduce you without expecting your heart and soul; your home expects time and attention, but your hotel only wants your money, and only for as long as you care to give it. You can walk up the steps as plain Jane Smith and enter the lobby as Lady Furcoat-Noknickers; the hotel does not care what you do, or with whom.

A luxuriously appointed building full of people escaping reality can brew a heady atmosphere – I should know; I've worked here for four years now. Few of the comings and goings here pass me by. Especially the comings.

It all started so innocently.

A delayed train, an hour to kill. I was halfway to the queue for styrofoam-flavour sludge before I stopped myself and the idea sparked. I could spend my dead minutes on a spit-drenched platform staring at time ticking by on the 'Next Arrival' screen. Or I could spend them in the hotel across the road, drinking half-decent coffee and reading a complimentary magazine.

It was almost one o'clock, so I wouldn't stand out too much amidst the lunchtime rush – if I could find a comfortable chair in a quiet corner, I could pretend to be a bona fide businesswoman meeting a client or something. It would be fun; a tiny masquerade to enliven a dull wait.

This particular hotel was of the swankier variety; a row of international flags flapped above the plate glass, and uniformed doormen stood on sentry duty either side of the revolving entrance. I wondered if they had to remain impassive and still, like Beefeaters, but one of them unbent and smiled at me when I trotted past, intent on getting through the revolving door without a pratfall of some kind.

Sophie Martin, bored office drone and unsuccessful photographer, pushed her hand against the glass.

Sophie Martin, supercharged business bitch, stepped out on the other side.

Not that there was any telephone-box-whirlwind-style action going on in the revolving doors – all it took to turn from drab to diva was exposure to the seductive particles of the hotel lobby air, weighted with possibility and chance and choice and an undertone of wickedness.

My heels click-click-clicked on the marble lobby floor, passing the curved Reception desk, catching a haughty lip-curl from its pointy-nosed custodian. She wouldn't be looking askance at me once she knew exactly who I was, I told myself grandly. I would have her lilac-rinsed head on a platter.

I strutted into the bar, carpeted now so that my heels were muffled, found a corner with an armchair and a copy of some style glossy and sashayed straight over.

Within seconds, a waistcoated waiter was taking my order, hovering and fawning in a manner I could imagine myself getting quite used to. The prices were steep, but when you considered that a morale-boost came with your cappuccino, perhaps they were worth paying.

He was a few years younger than me, maybe twenty or so; the rude whiff of barely post-adolescent testosterone clung to his white shirtsleeves and poorly shaved chin. I wondered what he would do if I flirted with him.

'Do I get anything extra with my cappuccino?' I asked him, dropping the level of my voice a notch or two and hoping it would make me sound like Lauren Bacall. I raised one eyebrow, a forefinger tapping my lower lip to pull it down to a pout.

He coughed slightly. 'A biscotti, Madam,' he said, the tips of his ears reddening. 'And chocolate or cinnamon sprinkles.'

'Oh, cinnamon, I think,' I drawled, striving to keep my voice on the sexy side of forty-fags-a-day. 'I always prefer spicy to sweet, don't you?'

I almost laughed at my own cartoon vampishness, but it seemed to be doing the trick for him. He flushed beautifully and scurried away, leaving me to terrorise him with my eyes over the rim of my magazine until the coffee was ready.

The room was filling up with conference attendees on a lunch break: lots of men in suits talking loudly into mobile phones and gesturing over to whoever was getting the round in at the bar. Mmm, I thought, stretching a leg beneath my table and rotating my ankle slowly. I do like a good suit. Some of these were very well-cut indeed; I wondered what the conference was about. Were they bankers? IT consultants? Estate agents even?

My question was met with a question.

'What did you think of that session? Not enough

statistical evidence, I thought; bit too much reliance on the anecdotal.'

A man slid into the armchair opposite mine, placing a plastic wallet of papers on the table between us. Through the green shade of the cover, I could just make out the words 'Probate Law'. *Ooh, a lawyer*, I thought; *I've never met one of those before. Though if this one is anything to judge by, I should get myself arrested more often.*

Everything about him was top-of-the-range, from the haircut down to the polished Italian leather that peeked from the crossed trouser-leg. The voice was warm and smooth; an asset if he was a barrister. Even as I looked up and smiled back, I tried to picture him in one of those horsehair wigs and a black cloak; it proved to be a surprisingly sexy image.

'Oh, I'm not here for the conference,' I said, flicking the page of my magazine.

'Really? Meeting someone? Am I intruding?'

'No, no.' I waved him back down to his sitting position. 'Just taking a breather,' I told him.

'Right. I thought I hadn't seen you in the meeting room. My attention was wandering a bit from the flipchart, and I'm sure it would have rested on you.'

Wow! He was flirting with me. A man who knows how to wash and earns a wage flirting with me! Unheard-of in the annals of my experience. I had to wonder what all that pure new wool would smell like. Not to mention that subtly tanned skin, from which a hint of expensive aftershave was drifting over, activating my saliva glands.

He had beautiful hands as well; I could picture them gesturing in court. I could also picture them on my hip, my belly, my thigh. All in all, the effect he had on me was instant and acute. I found myself leaning forward, crossing my legs so that my skirt rode a little higher, just to the point where the elasticated part of my hold-up stocking might be a teensy bit visible.

'What's the conference?' I asked. 'Charm school head-masters?'

He laughed, throwing his head back, oh, Adam's apple, oh, deep, rich laugh, oh. I took advantage of his moment's lapse in eye contact to slip open my top button and put aside my magazine. I wanted him in the most sudden and violent way. I wanted to touch the fine cotton of his shirt, open it wide and see if what lay within was as luxurious as its cladding.

'No,' he said eventually, his bright blue eyes damp with mirth and ... something else. 'Solicitors. I specialise in soliciting.'

Now it was my turn to laugh. 'Clearly,' I purred.

Some form of conversation followed, of the kind you might hear between Mae West and Sid James, predicated entirely on smutty innuendo. I don't remember what we said, but I do remember the feeling of being involved in a dirty-minded game of verbal tennis: serve, volley, lob, smash, grunt, new balls please. Just like our more athletic fellows, we were getting sweatier and hotter with each point scored.

Much as we pretended to wit and sophistication, the real gist of what was said was:

Him: Get your kit off.

Me: Work for it.

Him: Look at me like that and I'll have you up against the wall before you can say 'No win no fee'.

Me: Sounds good; prove it.

Before the cinnamon sprinkles of my cappuccino had melted into the froth, he had a proposition for me.

'Listen,' he said, eyes now piercing blue laserbeams of seduction, body wide open in a pose at once relaxed and

5

predatory. 'How long do you have? Do you have to rush back to work?'

I bit my lip and smiled inscrutably.

'Come on, help me out,' he said. 'Do I have to issue a summons?'

This made me laugh again. I can't resist a man with a sense of humour. I also can't resist a man who looks as if he could be in the running for the next James Bond.

'What do you have in mind?' I asked. If he was James Bond, I was pretty close to Pussy Galore at this stage. 'Does it involve handcuffs?'

'Would you like it to?'

My mouth watered.

'You've got me on a technicality,' I told him, standing and taking his proffered pinstriped arm. The warmth and scent of him tripped my switches; I wanted that, just that, just for now.

'What's your room number?' he murmured, sweeping me past the potted plants into the lobby.

Ah.

'Can't we go to yours?'

He stopped smartly, frowning down at me. 'I'm afraid not; the conference finishes today.' He shook his head. 'You aren't staying here?'

I chewed the inside of my cheek, blushing. 'Well, no. Just came in for a coffee.'

'Just a coffee? You aren't another kind of solicitor, are you?'

I breathed in sharply. 'Fuck, no!'

He breathed out for me. 'I'm sorry. I didn't think you . . . OK. "Fuck, no," you say, but I'm still thinking, "Fuck? Yes!" If you're with me. Still with me?'

I giggled, a little bit hysterically. It wasn't the first time I'd been taken for a member of the oldest profession, but certainly the least opportune.

6

'We don't have a room,' I pointed out.

He manoeuvred me behind one of the substantial palms, pulled me against him and patted the seat of my skirt. 'I do have a car,' he growled.

The feel of him, hard chest, taut shoulder, large crotch-bulge, was enough to chase away my doubts. I wanted that, on me, above me, in me.

'Reclining seats?' I asked.

'Of course.'

'Good.'

In the underground car park, he bent me backwards over the bonnet and mashed his lips into mine. That well-cut cloth was covering my feeble manmade fibres, rubbing them up and down, sparking them into static cling. My nylon stockings nudged at his trousers, slinking up beneath his jacket and around his hips, wrapping around his back and clamping that central hardness right into the open maw of my skirt.

I ground my mound around it, enjoying the sensation of the fabrics pressing into me, while his tongue plunged downward and his hand excavated the hidden depths behind my blouse. His fingers plucked and sneaked under the lacy cups; there was pressing and kneading and hot breath and jammed pelvises and mock-thrusting, and all beneath the spotlit concrete ceiling of the public car park.

'Do you want it then?' he asked, holding my wrists pinned to the cool shiny paintwork.

'Maybe *in* the car?' I whispered, moving my head sideways to check for CCTV cameras and irate attendants.

'My command is your wish,' he said, pulling me up as if preparing for an energetic jitterbug and spinning me around to the side of the vehicle. He ducked inside the door, pressed the button to recline the passenger seat and bundled me on to it. I was a little confused when he shut the door, leaving me supine on the chilled leather, but he soon reappeared on the driver's side, kneeling on the seat and looking ravenously down at me.

'Get your knickers off then,' he prompted.

Thrilled at his excellent grasp of the command tone, I wriggled them down my thighs, past my knees, and brought my still-shod feet up in the air to release them from the legholes.

My escort put a steadying hand on one leg, indicating that he wanted them both kept up in that position, and moved his other arm down for a good feel of my newly exposed parts.

'Now that's wet,' he said, impressed. 'A good fuck is what you need.'

I couldn't argue with him. The speed, the suddenness, the rudeness, the wrongness of it all was the turn-on of my life. It was dirty and slutty, but I like dirty and slutty, and so, it seems, did he.

In his haste to mount me, he lost a button from the placket of his trousers, swearing as it pinged into the distance, then he slipped swiftly and efficiently between my knees, levering me up by the bum in order to skewer my dripping centre in one move.

We groaned in chorus as it stole inside so easily, so satisfyingly, filling the hole in perfect proportion.

'Do you do this often?' he asked, beginning to thrust.

'Mmm?' I replied absently, lifting my hips towards his, grabbing his bottom to push him greedily as far in as I could.

'Pick up strange men in hotels for dirty sex? I bet you do it all the time.'

It was on the tip of my tongue to protest, to say no, that I'm not that kind of girl, but before I did, my imagination stepped in front of my indignation and I realised that I liked this idea. I imagined him as one of a string of anonymous men, using my body, day after day, week after week, in the hotel bedrooms, the toilets, the car park. I'm not a whore, but I felt like one, letting this man whose name I didn't even know slam his cock up me within quarter of an hour of meeting.

'Yes,' I said. 'I do.'

'Thought so.'

The windows had steamed up now and I had to spare a thought for the expensive upholstery, which was getting the pounding of all time. I pushed my hands down, clutching at his belt, the buckle end of which slapped lightly against my bottom with each forward motion. These were becoming more frantic now, the jingling urgent, his loosened tie flapping over my face until I sank my teeth into it, irritated by the tickling effect. I could feel the quake, shuddering seconds away, and I accidentally kicked the dashboard quite hard, so that he stopped for a second and turned around to assess any damage. Luckily there was none.

All the same, 'I'll make you pay for that,' he vowed, ratcheting up the force of his thrusts, body-slamming me into a new realm of fierce sensation. The more I pretended to be a hooker, concentrating on servicing my client and avoiding orgasm, the more orgasmic I felt, until the wave crashed and I yelled until I was hoarse.

For a while, it was as if our bodies had melted together; the sweet glue of our exertions filled the air and stuck us to each other. The car seat was slippery now and my thin summer blouse drenched. He unpeeled himself shortly before I had to pass out, crouching between my sore thighs, which were chafed to bits by that pure new wool I had so admired in his trousers. Thank God they hadn't been made of cheap stuff; I would have been skinned alive.

'Nothing like a mid-conference knee-trembler,' he opined, taking a wallet from the glove compartment and stuffing a wad of twenty-pound notes into my cleavage. 'Get yourself something pretty. Off you trot then.'

Eyes on stalks, I removed the money – a hundred pounds – and tried to give it back, but he simply unlocked the car door and opened it, gesturing me away impatiently.

I straightened myself up in the car park, snapped the elastic tops of my hold-ups back in place, pulled my skirt down and re-buttoned my blouse. I would have to sort out my face and hair in the toilets.

Before leaving, I threw the money back inside the car. Much as I could have used a hundred quid, it seemed important that I did not accept it. To do so would have been to concede control of the encounter to him, and I did not want that. If I behave like a trollop, it's because I want to; the pretence is an essential part of the excitement.

Of course, I missed the train.

The memory of my soliciting solicitor sustained me through some long and lonely nights, replaying the scenes on my darkened ceiling while my fingers wandered beneath the sheets.

The hotel was not really on my way anywhere, but sometimes I would take detours just to gaze at its gilded splendour, my eyes moving slowly upwards beyond the striped awning to the windows of the rooms, picturing what might be going on behind those heavy white drapes.

Temptation took a week to lure me back inside.

Another lunch hour, another conference, but this time I was dressed for the occasion in my highest heels, my tightest skirt, my sharpest jacket over a lacy camisole. My eyes cruised the bar while I slunk over to order a drink. Not a coffee this time; they can sour the breath so – this time I would go for a cocktail. Something fruity.

I leant over the counter, wiggling my bum out at the rest of the room. The stuttery waiter was lurking in the background stacking glasses in the washer and he smirked at the barman, a sleazy-looking character, when he swaggered up to ask me if he could help.

'Oh, I'm sure you can,' I said, releasing the inner vixen in full effect. 'What I really fancy just now is a Sloe Comfortable Screw.'

The barman double-took; I had to have a stern word with myself to stifle the unvampish giggle struggling to escape my Bitch Red lips. Then his lip flipped up at an Elvis-like angle, his eyes glazed over slightly and he leant right down.

'I'm sure that can be arranged,' he smarmed. Creepy as he was, there was something primitively attractive about him, though he severely overestimated his own charms. 'Or maybe a Screaming Orgasm?'

Much as I enjoy repetition of this beach-holiday-classic conversation, I was not after shagging the man, so I toned down my performance for his benefit.

'Oh no, I don't think so,' I said primly. 'But I do want an umbrella and a sparkler. The full tarty works, if you can manage that.'

His eyes narrowed and he began shaking ice with venomous purpose. I took advantage of his preoccupation to scope out the room again. Knots of business people in twos and threes were drifting in, beginning to line the counter. Some of them tried to catch my eye; even more so when I took a seat on a high bar stool and sipped at my glass of neon-orange slapper juice. Stocking tops in sight, I unbuttoned and removed my jacket, leaving my shoulders bare and my bra visible beneath the fluttery scrap of camisole. I took a straw from a dispenser on the counter top and began to suck the drink up, pouting my lips.

The barman was barely able to serve the other customers, such was his distraction. I was watching him fumble with a bowl of complimentary olives when a voice behind me caused me to spin around.

'How much for half an hour?'

He was not my type. Shortish, balding, the beginnings of a paunch. But, perversely, the idea of being available to the first bidder was exciting enough to overcome my personal tastes.

I looked him up and down and smiled. 'I don't charge,' I said.

He raised his eyebrows. 'I'm sorry, I got the wrong idea,' he said apologetically, holding up his hands and backing away.

'No, no,' I whispered, beckoning him back. 'I mean, if you can persuade me it will be worth my while, I'll give you a freebie.'

He was motionless for a while, staring at my cleavage consideringly.

'I'm not sure I understand,' he said at last. 'Come and sit with me and tell me what you mean.'

I followed him to an alcove and plonked myself on the cream leather banquette beside him.

'So you aren't a working girl?' he opened, taking a draught of his lager and regarding me enquiringly.

'Oh, I am a working girl,' I contradicted him, deciding to get into character. 'But I'm off-duty at the moment. It was a long night.'

'Oh.' The man chuckled with relief. 'I thought I might have offended you there. So . . . you aren't available then?'

'I'm available to the right client,' I told him. 'Although I had a few earlier on, none of them were up to much. Definitely a case of business rather than pleasure.'

'Really?' The man puffed up his chest a little, clearly preparing to convince me of his Real Man status. 'So you ... you enjoy your work?'

'Oh, yes, I love it,' I told him, sucking on my straw again. 'Do you? Are you here for the conference?'

'Yes.' He shook his head. 'I like my work, but I hate these dos. Bloody icebreakers, meetings about meetings and all that. I'm dreading this afternoon – role-playing, would you believe?'

'Oh, I like role-playing,' I protested. 'How about we do a little one now, just to get you in the mood?'

'You're quite something, you know,' he said, almost nervously. The power of knowing that this man wanted me, feared rejection from me, would probably go to some lengths to have me, was intoxicating. I felt like Cleopatra.

'Thank you. So are you up for it?'

'Depends what "it" is. What's my brief?'

'You're a wealthy businessman. I'm a prostitute.'

'Well, that's not far from the truth,' he said, brow furrowed.

'Good. It'll be all the more convincing then. Come on, let's play.'

I sat back and waited for him to make the opening gambit, wondering if I would actually go through with it. Sex with a man I didn't really fancy, just for the sake of satisfying my newly discovered kink. It was my fantasy, but would it crumble in the face of reality? I had to know. I decided then and there that I would have one rule in my game, and the rule was that I could not say no. Obviously I *could*, in the face of danger or serious illegality – but up to that point, I would say yes to everything and everyone.

'OK then,' he said, sitting back and determinedly getting into role. 'How much for half an hour?'

'Two hundred,' I said.

'Two hundred? For half an hour? You must be good.'

'I am. Do you want to find out how good?'

'I think I do. Hold on a minute though ... I thought you said this would be a freebie?'

'Yes, yes,' I said impatiently. 'It will be. But in the game, I cost two hundred.' I lowered my voice, looked him straight in the eye. 'In real life, I'm a no-strings free fuck.'

'Christ knows you don't get many of them,' said the man, his voice a little uneven. 'Right then. Let's go to my room, shall we?'

'Yes.'

In the lift on the way up, I stared at the pair of us in the mirror. He looked a little crumpled and slightly sweaty. I looked like a tart. It would have been pretty obvious to all in the bar and lobby what our relationship was.

Now we were out of the public areas of the hotel, he seemed to gain an assertiveness that had been only half-present in the bar.

'So you had a long night,' he said, his tone rather severe.

'Yes.' I blushed. 'I didn't get much sleep.'

'Time for bed then, eh?'

He took my arm as the lift door slid open and escorted me along the corridor, our feet sinking in the deep pile of the carpet as if we were walking through snow.

It was only when he slipped his key card into the slot that I began to have misgivings. The solicitor was one thing – carried along on a wave of lust that knocked doubts for six – but this was another. A strange man's hotel room.

Could I really go through with this?

My escort answered the question for me. He strode straight over to the bed, sat down on the edge and unzipped his fly.

'Right, if I'm paying two hundred for this, I want my money's worth. Let's see you with your clothes off.'

14

His sudden switch to 'in charge' mode awakened my wilder streak. I straightened my spine, did a little twirl and threw the jacket I was carrying on to a chair. Never having done a striptease before, I was unsure of the ritual, but once I had unbuttoned and shimmied out of my skirt, everything seemed to flow naturally. Down to the lacy camisole, silk French knickers and lace hold-ups, I slowed the action, teasingly pretending to drop something and bending over to pick it up, or standing with one foot on the dresser while I ran my hands up my leg. I could see myself, at a peculiar angle, in the wardrobe mirror and I was impressed by the figure I cut. I momentarily considered a career in burlesque. If only I had a feathery fan and a Venetian mask.

Indeed, I was loving my work so much that I almost forgot my 'client' was waiting until I was forced by his impatient cough to look back at him. His fist was closed around his erect cock, his face quite red and collar loosened.

'We've only got half an hour,' he reminded me brusquely. 'I'm not paying you to dance. Get the rest of your kit off then get down on your knees over here.'

'OK, just one more move,' I promised him, hip-swaying over to the fruit bowl and taking the banana from the top. I peeled it slowly, ran my tongue up the exposed pale yellow flesh and swirled its tip around the top of the fruit.

'On your knees, now!' entreated the client, groaning when I simultaneously put one hand down the front of my knickers and the banana in my mouth, swishing it around in there, sucking on it for all I was worth. 'Sod the banana, wrap your lips around this!'

He leant back, presenting his cock to me in all its fat purple-crowned glory. Giggling, I tossed the banana aside and fell to my knees in mock-worship of his manhood, ogling and caressing it as if it were made of gold. Slowly and deliberately I ran my tongue around my lips, staring boldly up at him, before taking the plunge, closing my mouth over the considerable girth, forming a seal and sucking for all I was worth.

My fingers played with his balls, squeezing gently and sometimes creeping back to push against his perineum, which tightened the sac all the more. Even when my mouth began to ache, I revelled in the effect I was having on him, his helpless little yaps of pleasure spurring me on to greater efforts. He was going to remember this as the blow job of his life; if I was going to play the part of the expensive hooker, I was going to do it properly.

My tongue played lightly against his steely erection, flicking up and down the shaft and around the frenulum. One of my hands closed tightly around his base while I worked at fitting more and more of him into my mouth; the other continued its foray around his testicles. He was shaking now, making strangled utterances, his hands clenching and unclenching in my hair; the end could not be far off.

'Lap it up, slut,' he panted, before roaring and thrusting into my face. A burst of liquid saltiness filled my mouth, pumping in and down my throat for what seemed like a long time. Even when I thought I had swallowed the lot and slid off his cock, an extra jet squirted on to my breasts, staining the lace border of my camisole.

I sat back on my heels and he lay down on the bed, spent.

'You can go now,' he murmured.

'You still have ten minutes,' I pointed out. 'And besides, I want my turn. I'm going to sit in that chair and sort myself out.'

He propped himself up, squinting. 'You aren't a real whore,' he said. 'A real whore would have been off with the money.'

'Like I said, I'm off-duty,' I told him. I sat back in the plush boudoir armchair, slung one leg over an arm, pushed aside the gusset of my knickers and began to delve into the slippery recesses, throwing my head back and shutting my eyes, imagining an audience crowded round me, brandishing twenty-pound notes. I squirmed on the velvet, flicking and plucking and plunging my fingers, pinching and squeezing my tits until I came hard, imagining applause, whistles, a shower of notes.

Then there was real applause; the clapping of my very own audience, now sitting up again with a noticeable erection threatening to poke him in the eye.

I glanced at the clock. Time was up.

'You'd better go down,' I told him, yawning and rising reluctantly from the chair.

'Hang on, though – for two hundred I should get another go, shouldn't I? I haven't even touched your pussy yet.'

'Time's up,' I said briskly, stepping into my skirt. 'And you have a role-play to perform. Not such an interesting one as this, though.'

'But I want to fuck you now,' he moaned.

'Thanks, but no thanks,' I told him, buttoning my jacket. 'You know where to find me if you fancy another go. And you know what it will cost.'

'How can I go downstairs with this?' he beseeched me, staring disconsolately at his treacherous stiffness.

'Good afternoon.' I smiled, opened the door and sailed off down the corridor, surging with wicked glee.

The lift door opened and I crossed the lobby, feeling every eye upon me, X-raying through to the semen stain on my camisole, the wet spot on my silky knickers, the traces of salty spunk on my tongue. *They all know I'm a whore*, I thought, swinging my hips and letting my heels click on the polished floor.

When I got home, I had to bring myself off again.

* * *

After that, the hunger was upon me. It became a game as addictive as any of those online fantasies; truly a second life.

At least once a week I strutted my stuff, maximally tarty and overdone amid the minimalist décor of the bar, lacking only a flashing beacon on my head to proclaim my shamelessness.

The men came in all shapes, sizes, ages, degrees of attractiveness and intelligence; the rule was, I could only say no in the most extreme of situations.

My juices stained dozens of pristine bedsheets; I took it lying down, standing up, on all fours, on chairs and desks and over windowsills; between my tits, in my mouth, cunt, arse; three ways, four ways, six ways till Sunday; with women, with an audience, with a camera, with a blindfold, with a webcam, with a whip, with a will.

There came a time when I could rely on three or four regular 'clients' being in the bar at any one session; sometimes I would only take up the first to offer; on other occasions, I would treat them all, one at a time or as a group. About six weeks into my new 'career', logistics were careering out of hand. The number of men waiting for their free ride every time I entered the bar was becoming unmanageable.

I pitched up one day at a new and unpopular time – half past three in the afternoon – and was relieved to find just me, the waiter and the barman in attendance.

I ordered a strawberry daiquiri and gave my creepy friend a dazzling smile. Perhaps today his luck could be in after all. For once, he smiled back instead of tossing his fringe sulkily.

'Have you heard? We've got a new manager. He wants a word with you.'

My fingers tensed around the stem of my glass. 'Why? How would he know me? What have you said?'

The barman simply shrugged and leered at me. 'His office is behind Reception. Go on and find out what he wants.'

I cannot say no. So I went.

I noticed that the severe-looking middle-aged woman I was used to had been replaced by a young girl with a pierced nose and an antipodean accent; a temp, I guessed. She smiled brightly at me and pointed to the door at the back of the area when I told her the manager wanted to see me.

I had no idea what to expect, but obeyed the terse instruction from the other side of the door to enter, and pushed my way into a huge windowless office. The manager sat behind a massive desk, about half a mile away, or so it seemed.

'Ah,' he said, and crooked a long finger. I made the epic journey across the carpet, my knees already weak, concentrating on keeping atop my heels and avoiding any humiliating wobbling. He did not stand or attempt to shake my hand, but simply looked me up and down through gold-framed spectacles, neither approvingly nor disapprovingly. Eventually he sat back and said, 'I'm new here.'

'So I've heard,' I replied, hoping for a swift cut to the chase.

'But you aren't. Are you?'

'I'm ... a fairly frequent patron ... of the bar.'

'You've been inside a few of the bedrooms too, I gather.'

So what? It's not a crime. But I bit my tongue.

'Anyway, that's by the by,' he said, waving a hand. 'I've been studying the books. Bar takings have taken quite a turn for the better in the past six weeks. We have many rebookings for rooms, especially in the traditionally unpopular midweek slots. A little business-minded bird told me you might have something to do with that.'

He really had the gimlet-stare off pat. It was quite

disconcerting, but I faced down the blue-grey gleam and shrugged. 'Not for me to say.'

Finally his lips twisted from rigid to relaxed and a half-chuckle leaked out. 'You needn't be defensive. I'm not about to ban you from the premises. The hooker in the bar is a fact of luxury hotel life; I'm inclined to turn a blind eye.'

'I'm not a hooker,' I blurted.

He frowned. 'It's all right; I've told you where I stand. There's no need to deny it ...'

'Really. I'm not a hooker. I just ... it's ... kind of like ... a hobby ...' I broke off, realising that there was nowhere to go with this statement. He would probably prefer a prostitute; somebody with a sharp business mind. A slut, on the other hand ...

'Now that's very interesting,' he remarked, leaning forward. 'That would explain why these men are spending so much in the bar and on room service, as well as going for the more expensive suites. They aren't paying for ... anything extra.'

I scowled at him, then looked away.

'Look at me,' he said, and his tone woke me up; a visceral lurch in my stomach. I had never heard anything so commanding. 'I have a proposition for you.'

'Oh?'

He picked up a pen and wrote something with a flourish on some documents ranged on his blotter. He was signing his name, I thought.

'I'm offering you a job, if you're interested. I need a receptionist – somebody like you: smart, sexy, dressed to kill, with a bit of a come-hither behind the professional veneer. Take a look at the details and tell me what you think.'

I skim-read the contract; the terms and conditions seemed fair, the work easy and the money good. I needed good money.

'I . . . think it looks like something I might consider,' I said cautiously.

'And for how long might you consider it?' he asked sternly, his brows creasing at me. He was, I realised in that moment, exceptionally attractive.

Caution scattered into the four winds. 'For a few seconds,' I said, breathing hard and flushing. 'OK. I'll take it. Thanks.'

It was only then that he stood to shake my hand. He had a firm grip, his skin warm and smooth, his hand comfortingly large.

'Good,' he said. 'I'm Christopher Chase; Mr Chase to you. Or Sir.'

'Yes, Sir,' I breathed, feeling funny in a squirmy sort of way at the use of the honorific. 'Oh, yeah, I'm Sophie Martin.'

'I'm very glad to have you on board, Sophie,' he said, and for a millisecond an image of him lying on top of me on the deck of a ship, thrusting manfully, distracted me from the matter at hand.

'You will be friendly but professional behind the desk,' he reminded me. 'What you get up to when you're off-duty, however, is entirely your own . . . affair.'

He perched on the edge of his desk, curling a flirtatious lip at me. Basically, he was encouraging me to carry on my bar-based shaggery for as long as I liked.

I could not say no.

Conference Facilities

Flipcharts. Water jugs. Overhead projectors. Name tags.

None of these are sexy in themselves, and yet there seems to be something about a conference in a hotel that unleashes the sexual beings behind the drab grey flannel. My friend Maddie, herself a wonderful photographer, has paid the rent since graduation by working in sales for a large software company. Her peers from all points of the region convene annually in our largest conference suite and spend four days being hectored by people with the demeanour of hellfire preachers. One can almost hear the hallelujahs filtering out from the double doors and into Reception. Sales is a scary world, it seems.

Despite, or perhaps because of, the fervour and fever in the air, Maddie always looks forward to these extravaganzas. Partly for the hotel room and free food, partly for the sex. Soberly single for the rest of the year, Maddie treats the conference as her annual binge; a chance for some string-free exploration of her sexuality. She does not really care about the career consequences, because it isn't the job she wants to be doing for life anyway – and so far, I gather, it has worked out as a brilliant networking scheme.

Last year was her fifth and wildest conference. With her permission, I shall relate the tale.

She knew that Phil was going to be there, and she was looking out for him from the moment they were all herded together in the meeting room. He had been last year's memorable conquest; Salesman of the Year for the Thames Valley region, all charm and sincerity and Hugo Boss. Maddie was not surprised he sold so much software – it was him that the punters bought, not his product. He was expert at the art of drawing you in, making you feel important and special, crinkling those spaniel-brown eyes in sympathy and understanding, then, wham, sucker punch, you had signed up for twenty thousand grand's worth of indifferently coded programs. Or sex, in Maddie's case. Great sex, new sex, sexy things she had never done before – in the shower, and over the windowsill with the window open. He had let her photograph him naked and she in return had made him the gift of her virgin backside. It had been amazing, like a full relationship in frantic fast-forward mode, but without the dilemma of whether to keep it going at the end.

He had given her his phone number, but she had not called him. Phil, for her, existed in this hotel, along with her sexual self. Outside in the streets, in their homes and offices, they greyed into ghostlike versions of those Technicolor lovers. Reality would spoil it, thought Maddie. But the conference was not reality, and Phil's name had been on the mailing list.

Waiting for his grand entrance, she amused herself by casting her eye over the male delegates as they trickled in, consigning them to the categories of *Definitely*, *Possibly* and *Not*.

Novelty tie: Not. Nice suit but badly trimmed moustache: Possibly. Horrible shiny suit, ferret eyes: Not. Lanky, square-framed spectacles, beautiful olive skin: Definitely. Barking into a mobile phone and glaring round the room to make sure everybody understands how important he is: Not. *Phil*: oh God, definitely, definitely.

He was even more handsome than she remembered, with his sweep of honey-blond hair, his warm melty eyes and his broad white smile. His lightweight jacket was slung across a shoulder, his crisp white shirt open at the neck, inviting foraging female hands. He cast his eyes around the room and Maddie almost jumped up from her seat to signal herself, but before he saw her he lit on the good-looking olive-skinned man, gave him a thumbs-up and went to sit beside him.

Maddie ignored the way her ribcage seemed to drop; there was plenty of time, and besides, he had probably arranged to meet up with his friend. They might work together as a sales team, though she did not recognise the other man, a new recruit perhaps. Sitting side by side they made a stunning contrast; fair and dark, lighthearted and intense, frothy mousse and bitter chocolate. She thought she would like to photograph them together.

At length they were called into the conference hall for the first session. Maddie managed to swarm up behind Phil, bumping shoulders with him as they squeezed through the doors.

'Hello,' he said effusively, that wide, bright smile dazzling down. 'It's great to see you.'

'Likewise. You're looking well,' said Maddie, then they moved to different parts of the room. Maddie always preferred to lurk on the fringes while Phil favoured high visibility. Not so high that he couldn't indulge in a bit of text-flirting, though, Maddie decided. Putting her mobile on vibrate, she began to key a message as discreetly as she could, hoping that Phil was the kind of man who could never quite bring himself to disconnect from his cellular lifeline. Most salesmen were like that, she had found.

'This brings back memories,' she jabbed.

The phone came to life under the desk within half a minute. Maddie bit her lip to avoid giggling with delight. 'Gd ones, I hope?' read the message.

'The best. Who's ur m8?'

'Meet us in the bar l8r & Ill introduce u.'

'Sounds gr8.'

Maddie, buoyed by the prospect of taking up her fling with Phil where she had left off, decided to switch off the flirtation and concentrate on the session: 'Closing the Deal: Inspirational Techniques from the US'. She tried to skim-read the densely printed handout she had been given, but her phone vibrated once more and she had to look.

'R u wearing those red knickers?'

Maddie blushed and switched off the phone. She was going to have to put Phil out of her mind for the next two hours. But judging by the slight dampness in those notorious red knickers she wore, this would not be easy.

Such was Phil's general popularity that it took him a long time to negotiate the crowded bar to the corner where Maddie sat, pretending to read over her notes. She looked up to see his pale-blue silk tie hanging in front of her as he leant over the table, grinning into her face.

'You didn't call me. You met someone else?'

Maddie coughed, intent on playing it cool but finding that the heat in her groin obstructed her purpose. 'No,' she said. 'Nobody else. I've just been busy.'

'With your camera?'

She smiled, feeling that a joke was being shared.

'Not sharing a room, are you?' asked Phil, sitting down in the bucket chair across from her.

'No, I'm in a single, though. One of the pokier rooms at the back of the building.' *We'll have to use yours*, she managed to avoid saying.

'Ah, really?' Phil frowned, then waved over at his tall friend, whose head was visible above the mass of unwinding sales reps. 'Thing is, Maddie, I've been put in a twin room. With Damo there.'

Maddie tried to keep her cheekbones still and her lips curved upwards. 'Oh?'

'Yeah. He's new in the team and I'm his mentor. There weren't enough singles to go round ... so I said we could share ...'

'Share,' echoed Maddie stupidly. 'You like to share.'

'Are you OK?' asked Phil. 'You seem a bit put out. There's no funny business going on, if that's what you think. We can still go to your room ... it'll just be a bit friendlier than we might have expected.'

He smiled at Maddie and tried to take her hand, but she moved it swiftly down to her drink.

'Than *you* might have expected,' she said pointedly.

'Sorry, am I presuming too much? I'll leave you to it then ...'

'No, look, don't go. I'm sorry. I'm just a little bit disappointed, I suppose.'

'No need to be.' And now Phil's attractive friend was at the table, saying something about the minibar in the bedroom.

'Yeah, you can't deny, this is a classy place. Damian Landers, this is Maddie Crooke from the Capital office.'

'Pleased to meet you,' said Damian formally, shaking her hand.

'Likewise. Have you ever thought of modelling?' The words were out before Maddie could process the thought; everything about Damian screamed 'Photograph me!' to her.

He laughed abruptly, startled at her opening salvo.

'Er ... no, not really,' he said, looking over to Phil for support.

'Maddie's a photographer,' he confirmed. 'She notices people. She must think you've got what it takes. Hey, Damo, this time next year you could be in one of those aftershave ads, strutting about in a pair of Y-fronts.'

They laughed, and Maddie joined in, but somehow the air felt dry, crackling static around them. There was a tension and an expectation now.

Phil wanted Maddie; Maddie wanted Phil; Maddie found Damian attractive; Damian knew it. Was this complex or was it simple? Could it be acted on, or should it remain unacknowledged?

They finished their drinks and left the bar separately, Damian for the twin room, Phil and Maddie for her humble single crib.

Scarcely ten minutes had passed before Maddie found herself straddling Phil's lean pubis, grinding her needful pussy over and on to his vertical shaft, while he gripped her hips, keeping her upright. Maddie's wrists were tied behind her back with his silk scarf, so his steadying hands were welcome, rocking her forwards and backwards, rotating and posing her while she tried to lean down, desperate to align her G-spot with his questing cock.

'That's good; bring those tits down to me,' growled Phil. Maddie's balance wavered and she plunged down, her breasts pressing into her lover's clavicle, their mouths meeting passionately. His hands moved blindly behind her, pushing her bottom hard into his mashing length as he slammed his pelvis up to meet her. They twitched and jerked like that, lips and teeth clashing in mimicry of their conjoined sexes, until Maddie began to spasm, her moans pouring into Phil's receptive throat while her legs weakened and her body collapsed on to his. He gave one last almighty piercing thrust and joined her in her moment of ecstasy, his back arched until she almost slid off him.

'Wow,' she said sleepily, tumbling down on to her side while Phil untied the silken knot. 'It was interesting, not being able to use my hands. I had to trust you.'

Phil gave a low chuckle. 'Everyone trusts me. That's how I sell so much.'

Maddie sat up, disarrayed. 'Do you often use your sales techniques? To get women into bed?'

Phil looked shiftily over at the minibar. 'Do they really have Japanese beers in there?'

'No dodging the question!' Maddie laughed. 'I'm not after your hand in marriage, Phil. You don't have to bullshit me.'

Phil flicked the puppydog eyes up to full-beam. 'Maybe sometimes,' he confessed.

'Do you and ... whatshisname ... Damian ... ever go out on the pull together?' asked Maddie, trying to sound casual.

'It's been known.'

'Wow. That's a dynamite combination. The dark brooder and the charmer – singly they are devastating; together, an unstoppable force.' Maddie mimicked the voiceover for a cinema trailer. Phil flipped his tie at her nose playfully.

'You fancy him, don't you?'

'Why not? He's stunning. I could really do things to him – photographically, I mean.'

Phil pondered for a while, smirking, then went to the minibar and cracked open two of the Japanese beers.

'Here.' He slid back down beside her, snaking an arm around her shoulder and leaning back against the head-board. 'Why don't I talk to him? I'm sure he'd be happy to give you a ... private shoot.'

'Oh, Phil, I don't know ... he's your work partner and all that. I don't want to make things awkward between you.'

Phil paused for a throaty chuckle. 'Maddie, believe me, things would already be awkward between us if we weren't ... comfortable around each other.'

'What do you mean?' Maddie splashed an accidental drip of beer froth out of the neck of the bottle, tutting as it landed between her breasts and slid downwards to her navel.

'I mean ... we've seen each other ... in action. We know what's what and where. No surprises to be had.'

'You ... what? You're lovers?'

'No, no, not lovers. But we went out one night after scoring a massive sale and ... picked up a girl. Took her back to my room. I was the senior salesman, so I went first while he watched, then we swapped places.'

'Really?' croaked Maddie, whose breathing had shortened at the mental image, and whose speech was correspondingly limited. 'She ... had you both?'

'Mmm. Lucky girl, eh?'

'Yes,' whispered Maddie.

'So what do you think? Shall I line him up for a shoot? You could snap us both – two for the price of one.'

'You can but ask,' said Maddie with a nervous laugh. 'Anyway, Philip Ellward, isn't it my turn to tie you up? Put that bottle down and get your hands above your head.'

Maddie came to chat to me at Reception the next morning after breakfast.

'Soph, do you mind if I ask you something?'

Her face was shifty and flushed; I put it down to tending to Phil's morning glory. I stopped arranging leaflets into a fan shape and gave her my full attention.

'Don't tell me you're in love with him.'

'No, no, not that. Just ...' She lowered her voice, leaning way over the desk. 'Have you ever had a threesome?'

I paused, smiling.

'Yes. More than once. What do you want to know?'

'Did you regret it? I suppose not, if you've done it more than once.'

'No, I didn't regret it. I enjoyed it. Are you asking me if you should do it? Well, as long as you're safe, sane and consensual and all that jazz, I'd say go for it. You know Phil

30

well enough, and neither of you are going to get jealous and insecure if a third party joins the, er, party. Is it a man or a woman?'

'A man,' she confessed. 'Friend of Phil's. Gorgeous.'

'Gorgeous, eh? Is a foursome out of the question?' I winked and she giggled.

'Maybe next year.'

Crowds of muttering grey people drifted towards the doors to the Conference Suite. Maddie flitted off to join them, sticking a thumb up at me on the way. I returned to my leaflet fan, deep in pleasant reminiscence.

'As long as they don't end up on YouTube or something,' Damian said with a shrug, 'I suppose it's all right.'

'They'll be tasteful, not tacky,' Phil reassured. 'Maddie's into the artistic stuff.'

'They're just for my personal collection,' she said. 'Nobody else will ever see them.'

Maddie finished setting up her equipment and stepped out from behind the tripod.

'OK, I'd like some shots of Damian first, then it would make my life complete if I could take a few of the pair of you together.'

The men both laughed. 'Ah, well, we wouldn't want to ruin your whole life,' said Phil. 'I suppose we'll humour you.'

Damian stood and stripped down to his boxers, striking numerous poses for Maddie while she clicked and flashed away. Maddie was exhilarated by his naturally photogenic quality and she began to lose herself in her work, ordering him to smoulder, to be sexy, to thrust out his hips, to push back his shoulders, to lie full-length on the bed, to look at the camera as if he wanted to fuck it or fight it or kiss it tenderly.

'God, you're good, Damian,' she praised. 'I knew I was

right about you having modelling potential. Listen, would you mind if I asked you to take off your boxers?'

'Thought you'd never ask,' said Damian, smouldering for her benefit rather than the camera's this time. 'No kinky stuff, though.'

'Kinky? I don't know what you mean,' said Maddie innocently, causing Phil to guffaw from the bed. 'I think I'd like to start with a back view, maybe at an angle so we can see your face in profile. Yes.' Maddie stood transfixed by his perfectly curved arse for a few seconds before remembering to adjust the depth of field. She used an entire roll of film capturing his lean, hard frame in every possible configuration. She did not want to miss a single muscular ripple, shady hollow or flat plane of his body.

Eventually, he began to grumble, tiring of the endless click-flash and running an irritated hand through his dark hair. Maddie realised it was time to move things on.

'Sorry, Damian, I was getting carried away. Call it a compliment. Seriously, I'll be finished soon. I just want a few shots of you and Phil together.'

'What for?' Damian was suspicious.

'My personal satisfaction,' she said, smiling sweetly. 'Just maybe the two of you sitting back to back ... that's it.'

Phil had stripped naked in advance of her request and was happy to comply. Damian huffed a little, bored with modelling now.

'She'll make it worth your while,' said Phil, trying to fit his spine somewhere that did not clash with Damian's.

'Oh yeah? How?'

'Name your price,' said Maddie, thrilling at the thought of what he might demand, pressing the button over and over again in a photographic rapture. 'Could you just sort of recline a bit ... facing each other ... Phil in front a little bit ... yeah. Oh! I know! Damian, why don't you get some grapes from the fruit basket and pretend to be feeding Phil.'

'You're bonkers,' griped Damian, trudging over to fetch a handful of black grapes, as requested.

'OK,' he said, once he was seated a little behind Phil, dropping the purple-black ovoids into his friend's mouth. 'Here's my price. We've sacrificed our dignity for you. You have to do the same.'

'Meaning?' Maddie frowned, not sure this was what she had had in mind.

'You get to see us in the buff. It doesn't seem fair that you're the only one allowed to keep your clothes on. I want some nudie pictures of you.'

'Oh, I never pose for photographs – I just take them,' objected Maddie. 'Besides, you wouldn't know how to . . .'

'I'm not a photographer, no. I'll just use my camera phone.'

'And send them to all your mates?'

'No. Just for my personal collection.' He grinned at the repetition of Maddie's own phrase. 'I promise. Nobody will see them but you, me and Phil.'

'It's only fair,' contributed Phil, his mouth full of fruit.

Maddie took a deep breath and replaced the lens cap on her camera.

'All right,' she said. 'Shoot me.'

Damian leapt gleefully to his feet and went over to his jacket to fish out his mobile phone.

'Right then!' he said. 'Scene one, take one, action!'

'You're not making a film, you dweeb,' said Phil, laughing, as he settled down on one of the twin beds to watch the show.

'OK, Maddie, I want you to take off that top.'

Maddie was wearing a short-sleeved ribbed top in olive green; she began to pull it over her head. Damian took the first photograph while her face was concealed by the material, her raised arms tangled, so that the expanse of her midriff and her burgundy satin Wonderbra were the stars of the shot.

'What a weird choice of pose,' she said crossly, her hair sticking out where the acrylic polo-neck had crackled it into static life. Damian photographed her pouting face.

'Skirt next,' he said. 'I want to know if your knickers match your bra.'

Maddie unzipped the dull beige work skirt and began to crumple it down over her hips. Once it reached her bent knees, Damian took a picture of her, leaning down to push it to her feet, first from the side, then from the back, enjoying the view of her satin-clad bottom.

'Might need a wide angle for that!' he teased. 'Very nice. Ooh, suspenders too! Ooh, matron!'

'I asked her to wear those,' said Phil matter-of-factly. 'She knows I like 'em.'

Maddie straightened, attempting to retain a little pride while she was clad only in her underwear. 'Look, I'm happy to pose for you, but can you stop being so ... laddish? This isn't a shoot for bloody *Nuts* magazine – it's a favour.'

'No, it's not a favour, it's a payment,' Damian pointed out. 'But I'm sorry. I'll try to stick with the tasteful theme from now on.'

'How about if I take over?' suggested Phil. 'I apologise on Damo's behalf – he's young and doesn't always understand the ... social niceties. I'm trying to knock him into shape, believe me.'

Damian made a playful swipe at his mentor, but handed him the phone nonetheless. Phil, businesslike from the start, strode over to Maddie and took a few quick shots of her standing upright with her arms folded beneath her breasts and her face betraying remnants of the storm.

'Now then, Maddie, let's have your arms ... out ... one hand on a hip. I want to see that sexy underwear. Strike a pose.'

Maddie relaxed, breaking into a smile 'Come on, *Vogue*,' she sang, shifting into role. She pirouetted and leant over, arched her arms and parted her legs for all she was worth, until Phil asked her to remove her bra. She reached around to the back, fumbling for the clips, then Phil held up a hand.

'Stop,' he said. 'Damian, could you give her a hand?'

Damian moved up behind Maddie and unfastened the garment, throwing it over on to the bed.

'Great, now stay there, Damian, and put one hand on her shoulder and one on her stomach ... ah yes. That's sexy!'

Maddie gasped at the feel of his unfamiliar hand on her bare flesh, as well as the consciousness of being exposed to him. What did he think of her breasts? Would he like to touch them? The top of her head fitted in snugly beneath his chin and his body felt stable and supportive behind her, something she could fall into.

'Maddie,' said Phil, his voice a little lower, a little gentler. 'What would you say to Damian touching your breasts? Say no if you like, but it would look so ...'

'It's OK,' said Maddie quietly. 'He can touch them.'

Damian's large hands moved to cover them, weighing them up from beneath first, then encompassing the full mounds, treating them tenderly and with respect. Phil photographed the pair, Maddie with half-closed eyes, her head rolling back into Damian's neck while he moved his head down to bring his chin to her shoulder, clearly tempted to taste her skin. 'I want to kiss you,' he said hoarsely. 'Would you mind?'

Her reply to this was to turn her head, catching his lips and welcoming him into a long and sensual kiss.

'Oh God, that's beautiful,' whispered Phil, capturing the

moment, the lips fixed together, the hands flicking at Maddie's stiffening nipples, her legs weakening so that Damian hooked one of his in front to keep her upright. The eroticism of it made Phil wonder how long he could continue as mere onlooker. Perhaps he should speed the action up somewhat. 'What if he puts one hand in your knickers, Maddie?'

'Mmm hmmm,' she consented, pushing her bum back against Damian's hard crotch. One large hand travelled slowly down her stomach and into the waistband of the burgundy satin French knickers. Maddie had to part her thighs a little, wobbling on unsteady legs, to provide unhindered access for the wandering fingers. Damian groaned as they slid between her lips, finding them wet and ready for some serious attention. His wide palm rested against her mons while the fingers rubbed and probed. Phil's photographs depicted the large bumps of his knuckles straining against the satin while Maddie rotated her hips, her mouth still caught against his, her sighs absorbed by his tongue in her throat.

'OK,' said Phil unsteadily. 'Turn her around to face you and take down her knickers now.'

Maddie let out a meek 'oh!' at the withdrawal of Damian's fingers from her secret spots, or was it the return of his tongue to his own mouth? Nonetheless she allowed herself to be moved around, her stomach up against the hot bulge of his cock, while her recent model peeled the knickers and stockings down slowly, revealing her smooth tan bottom to Phil inch by inch as he snapped hungrily. The silky material dropped to the floor, looking eerily like a pool of blood in colour and dispersal. Damian, it seemed, no longer needed to take direction, and he lowered an unprompted hand to knead her buttocks, re-establishing their kiss while the other hand resumed its work between her legs.

'Fuck, I can't do this any more,' said Phil, tossing the mobile phone on to a bed. 'Make room for me.' He nudged up against Maddie's back and began to nip the back of her neck, one hand joining Damian's in the steamy damp while the other reached around to claim a breast. The addition of the extra hand prompted Maddie to lift a leg and wrap it around Damian's thigh, inviting the different sets of fingers to keep up their double pressure. There was a pinch of a nipple, a bite of a lip, a forefinger sliding easily into her willing opening, and Maddie no longer knew whose; Damian and Phil were no longer divided in her mind but were a conjoined many-tentacled being, drawing her down into inner space. The light from the surface was fading; the place where she was Maddie Crooke from the Capital City office was far above her, indistinct and fragmenting. She had fingers everywhere, inside her and outside, on her nipples and in her hair, and now there was one gliding along the crack of her bum cheeks, which were being prised apart, extending the accessibility of her sex as well as revealing the little private part of her that only Phil had ever known.

A voice rasped at her ear. 'Remember last year, Maddie? Remember what went up here?' A thumb pushed gently at the ring, not forcefully enough to penetrate, just enough to make Maddie squirm. She could hardly believe in retrospect that she had let Phil do that. That it had gone in. That it had not been . . . unpleasant, although she had decided after the event that it would probably never be repeated. But now, with Phil's thumb planted at her back door and Damian's fingers plugging her pussy, she began to recall its illicit appeal, the tricks he had used to dissolve her resistance, and she began to push back, moaning uncontrollably.

'Oh, Maddie, you're on fire tonight,' crooned Phil. 'So hot. Isn't she, Damo?'

Damian, freeing Maddie's lips, put his own to her other ear. 'Hot as,' he said reverently. 'So fucking wet.'

'How hard is he, Mads?' asked Phil, resting his upright cock between the bottom cheeks he was still holding open. 'As hard as this?'

Maddie grasped Damian's shaft and gasped, 'Yes, hard.'

'Well, seeing as you're dripping on to the carpet, it's probably time we stepped up a gear then, Maddie, hmm?'

No reply was necessary, Maddie having crumpled backwards into Phil's arms. Damian went to sit on one of the beds, his legs splayed diagonally, providing a haven for Maddie to kneel in.

'Would you like to taste him?' Phil asked her.

'Yes,' said Maddie, hypnotised at the sight. She crept forward and approached the object of her appetites on her knees, guiding herself into the harbour of Damian's thighs and looking up at him shyly. 'Would that be OK?'

'I should think so,' Damian managed to say, and before the words were even out, Maddie was doubled over, licking the tip of his cock, which was long like its owner, swirling her tongue around its circumference, preparing to ease it into her warm, dark mouth. Her mouth slipped over the bulbous head and glided down his length; she pressed her fingers into the root and began to suck.

Phil took advantage of her absorption in Damian to swarm up behind her, lift her by the hips and plunge, suddenly and without warning, into her slippery sheath. She emitted a garbled yelp and almost bit Damian's precious manhood, but he clutched at her hair, urging her to continue, and she settled into a rhythm, plunging down with each thrust of Phil inside her and sucking up with each jerk back. She felt like a piston or some piece of machinery from a film about the Industrial Revolution, and the efficiency of their interaction pleased her unaccountably. A well-oiled machine, pushing back, lunging forward, hissing, sucking, her body the vital component connecting the powerhouses at each end. She maintained the pressure as tightly as she could, feeling Damian bump and thump at the roof of her mouth while Phil widened her narrow tunnel relentlessly, digging his trench further and further, filling her, drilling her until she felt the stirrings of her end. She began to pump frantically at Damian, sucking demoniacally until she wrung victory from him, swallowing and lapping at his seed before allowing herself to give way to her own climax. Phil came last, snorting and trumpeting, toppling his conference conquest over into Damian's lap, where she lay, her cheek nestling against his softening cock, waiting for Phil to pull out of her.

'Bloody hell,' said Phil, unsnapping his condom and aiming it accurately at the wastepaper basket. 'We've never gone that far before.' He grinned at Damian. 'Taking turns was one thing, but this was a whole new world. What did you think, Maddie?'

Maddie smiled gently, enjoying Damian's lazy fidgeting with her hair. 'Mmm,' she said.

That night they pushed the single beds together and shared the makeshift double, Maddie sleeping between her two beautiful boys while the camera, still on its tripod, watched over them till morning.

Damian was first to wake the next day; finding himself unexpectedly beside an attractive woman, he did what came naturally and leant over to lick a nipple while one hand wandered down beneath the sheets. Maddie stirred, turning her warm body towards his and muttered something incoherent before her lashes fluttered open. It took a few seconds for her sleepy eyes to focus on the head of thick black hair bobbing beneath her chin, but she registered the coiling wetness around her nipple and a gentle pressure on her clitoris. If this was a dream, she thought, it was a good one . . . and then last night came back to her. She glanced over at Phil, who slept on, then rooted one hand in Damian's hair, wrapped the other around his rampant cock and whispered, 'Good morning.'

Damian gave her nipple a final delicate lick then looked up at her, grinning lazily. 'It is now,' he whispered back. 'Waking up to a gorgeous body like yours. Makes me want to do bad things to you.'

'Go on and do them then,' said Maddie with a lascivious wink. 'The badder the better.'

Damian chuckled softly, keeping his fingers firm against Maddie's clit. 'How do you get this wet in your sleep?' he asked. 'Were you dreaming about me?'

'Mmm,' yawned Maddie. 'I prefer the reality though.'

Damian reached over to the bedside table for the condom packet. 'You asked for it,' he said, tearing off a foil corner with his teeth. 'You're going to get it. Lie flat and spread those legs, woman.'

Maddie was happy to comply, wriggling joyously into position, watching Damian sheathe his lengthy cock in rubber and thinking what an interesting photograph *that* would make. Then he plunged down on to knees and elbows and crawled over her, dropping savage little kisses at random intervals, on her knees, her hip, her ribcage, until he was lined up, lip to lip, shoulder to shoulder, his hands braced beneath her thigh tops so that the tip of the shaft nudged her opening. Maddie took two handfuls of buttock, urging him forward, needing her intimate space filled quickly. She tingled with pleasure as he broke through, burrowing into her darkness, enjoying the feeling of fullness, even the mild chafing that reminded her of last night's excesses. This was no hammer-and-tongs pounding though;

Damian was considerate of his sleeping friend and he screwed Maddie slowly and teasingly, edging up to the hilt then keeping himself there, rocking a little so as to keep Maddie's nerve endings interested, using every ounce of self-discipline in his reserve to control the pace. She began to knead impatiently at his tight arse, trying to speed his rhythm, but he would not be moved. Gradually he pulled back, a tiny jerking motion at a time, laughing quietly at her little yelps of encouragement, before gliding back down the passage. He repeated this move for long, languid minutes, varying the action above the waist with smoochy kisses on Maddie's lips, neck, breasts, behind her ears. His fingers drifted to and fro around her clitoris and lower lips, never quite lingering long enough to let her find satisfaction so that she had to try and suck his cock up inside her as hard as she could.

It was about fifteen minutes into this slow and stately sarabande that Phil woke up. Maddie, who had been concentrating on lifting her hips high enough to wrap her legs around Damian's upper back so that she could thrust herself upwards on to his cock, did not realise she had an audience until he coughed and said, 'Thought you'd start without me, did you?'

'Uh . . . sorry,' she gasped.

'Don't mind me. I'll just lie here and enjoy the view.'

Maddie, highly conscious of being watched, pushed once more against Damian's bottom cheeks. In this position, Phil would be able to see Damian's root sawing back and forth, in and out; he could see how full and wet her pussy was, and her enlarged clitoris begging for touch.

'No need to keep the noise down now,' grunted Damian, and he began to speed up, plunging down with increasing force while Maddie rocked upwards to meet his thrust.

'Nothing like a good hard fuck to start the day, is there?'

said Phil conversationally, propped up on an elbow. 'Or so I'm told.'

'You'll ... get ... your ... turn,' Damian ground out between hard strokes, his face contorting with the nearness of climax.

'You bet I will,' said Phil. 'One way or another. What do you say, Maddie? Once Damian has had you, will you be able to take another hard cock up there? I reckon yes.'

'Yes!' exclaimed Maddie, turned on beyond endurance, wanting at that wild moment to have the pair of them take turns on her until sunset, or her body melted, whichever might transpire first. Phil began to stroke his erection in preparation, sensing that his chance might come quite soon, if Damian's increasingly unhinged muttering and Maddie's frantic head-tossing were any indication.

Seconds later, the pair were thrashing around and howling fit to wake the entire landing. Damian held himself still, panting loudly for a minute or so, then he rolled off, kissed Maddie hard on the lips and began to unravel his rubber.

Maddie lay, a little spent but still ready for more, smiling lopsidedly at Phil, who had reached out an arm and was tugging her towards him.

'Damian did all the work there,' he said, manipulating her up and over his hips so that she straddled him. 'I'm feeling lazy though. Take me for a ride, love.'

Smiling wickedly, Maddie leant down and lightly bit one of his nipples.

'My little pony,' she whispered, taking hold of his cock and using its tip to circle her slightly sore quim. The red rush of pain she experienced on pushing herself on to it soon abated and she sat down, all the way down, and sighed with satisfaction, crushing her knees into his side as if he really were a horse, bobbing up and down in the saddle until she found her seat. She sat proud, spine straight, chin up, experimenting with all the different ways she could make Phil's cock point and stretch her before beginning the ride at a slow trot. By the time she hit cantering pace, now arched down over Phil, hands on his shoulders, while he fondled her bum cheeks, she had forgotten that Damian even existed. She was near that spot, that angle she needed; she only needed to go a little further, a little faster and then she would be there. She spurred herself on, working hard, using her abdominal muscles to their fullest extent. Now they were headed to the final furlong; she was sweating and so was he; her pussy was beginning to sting and feel raw but the fierce heat that had built up alongside made it more than bearable. She was going to have him, going to take him, going to milk him for all he was worth, oh yes, she put her head down and charged for the finish line and Phil got there with her, exultant in victory, galloping into the breach with yells and screams and a strange clicking sound and a flash of light. Maddie, flattened and exhausted, gathered her breath and peered foggily behind her, where Damian stood proudly beside her camera and tripod.

'I think I've worked it out!' he said in triumph. 'It's good kit, this, isn't it?'

The last two days of the conference are all one merged memory for Maddie now. A memory of heat and steam and dark hair and blond and four arms around her and two cocks inside her. It would seem too insubstantial to be real, if only she didn't have the photographs to prove it.

The Manager #1

In four years, he has looked at me – *really* looked at me, I mean – about half a dozen times. His attention is as rarely captured as a butterfly in winter, and accordingly highly prized, and it is impossible to predict just what will lure his eye in your direction. Short skirts don't do the trick, and neither do high heels or anything conventionally regarded as sexy. I have pouted my lipglossed smackers a million times, batted my spider lashes, leant forward so the cleavage hits him at optimum angle – all to a reception of bland indifference.

In my first year of working here, I tried to use my body to reel him in. I was looking as streamlined as I ever will, thanks to free membership of the basement gym and health club, and it pleased me to flaunt my newly discovered curves and planes at every opportunity.

My crush on Christopher Chase aka Mr Chase aka Sir had gripped me around the throat very quickly and was still squeezing the breath out of my body three months later. I could not spend longer than a minute in his office without thinking how very *large* his desk was – the perfect size to lie on top of – and yet also the perfect height to bend over. How clever. Surely he must have chosen it intentionally? Or was it even designed to his specifications? Then his voice would break into the musings:

'Did you even process that, Sophie? The Emir of Oriental Araby? And the Oscar-nominated actress? Expected this afternoon?'

'Oh ... yes, Sir. It's all in hand.' *Just like I wish I was. In your pale and elegant hand.* And so my reverie would continue until he dismissed me with a tight lip and creased brow.

Soon enough my infatuation started to interfere with my extracurricular amusements in the bar. There I would be, whispering wanton words into some suit's ear, when Chase would cross the floor and I would forget what I'd been saying and stare after him, stunned, chest burning as if I'd just run a cross-country race.

'Go on. You were saying? You're going to lick my balls until the skin is tight enough to burst ... then what?'

'Oh ...' I'd say, abruptly disconnected. 'I dunno. Can't remember. Listen, can you get me another drink?'

Then I would either make an excuse and go home to think about Chase, with the aid of various battery-operated mental aids, or, if Suit of the Day was fanciable enough, I would take him upstairs and use him as a stand-in. Poor chaps – they never realised that it was Chase's mouth on my neck, Chase's hand slipping inside my knickers, Chase's cock pounding me into the headboard. They were usually amused by my orgasmic gasps of 'Oh, Sir, yes, Sir, please, Sir' though. It gave them some food for future fantasy, at least, so I don't feel too guilty about it.

At work, my outfits became progressively less professional. As my body tautened, the clothes tightened, the skirts shortened, the heels heightened, until one day, as I bent over the Reception desk in a black scrap that was little more than a bandeau, Chase passed behind me and snapped, 'Do you think that suitable workwear, Sophie? Cover up.'

Oh, the mortification. Then again, perhaps it was grounds for hope. After all, he noticed me, did he not? Even if the attention was negative, it was attention. Perhaps if I wore the skirt again, he would call me in for an oral warning. Mmm, I could give him an oral warning . . . But on balance, it did not seem worth the risk. Nobody had deliberately flouted one of Chase's orders and got away with it so far; in fact, there had been a veritable bloodbath in the kitchens, with most of the staff replaced in his second week of office.

So I sobered up, threw out my hookerwear and tried to slay him with my understated style, but he remained impervious, in a sexy kind of way, until I formulated my desperate Christmas plan.

I had signed up to work Christmas Day – triple time and I've never liked turkey anyway – knowing that Chase was going to host an evening drinks party for those of us who made it through the festivities intact. This was exciting on a number of levels: it provided further evidence that Chase was a single man, to go with the lack of wedding ring and desk photographs; it furnished my first opportunity to socialise with him; and there was even an outside chance that I might be able to herd him under some mistletoe and share a seasonal snog.

So when eleven o'clock came, after a long day of watching people in paper hats make merry while I brooded behind the desk, I gathered up my bag of tricks and prepared for an appointment with the full-length mirror in the staff toilets.

My hair was still looking good after a session with Suze, the hotel hairdresser, but the rest of me needed rejuvenation. The unforgiving glare of the bathroom lighting showed every blemish and enlarged pore; my eyes were tired and my skirt suit crumpled. I required nothing less than transformation, caterpillar to butterfly style.

Skin primed, brows plucked, hair sprayed, eyebags concealed, lashes lengthened, lips lushened, cheekbones highlighted, I was ready to prepare for my secret weapon; the biggest gun in the night's seduction arsenal. Off came the low-heeled courts, the flesh-tone stockings, the sensible beige skirt and the cream angora sweater until I stood, made-up to kill, in just my bra and knickers.

I glanced at the door. I did not think it likely that anybody else would use this particular loo; it was too out of the way for the kitchen staff and the maids in the basement. I was probably safe.

I unhooked my nude lace bra, admiring the way my breasts now bounced above my ribcage after four months of gym membership. I held my arms out, smiling wolfishly at myself, imagining myself to be a hungry man confronted with this bounty for the first time. It was no wonder they pounced in the way that they did. How could they help themselves?

I chuckled and slipped out of my matching knickers. Yes. No underwear for me tonight. Nothing to ruin the line of my new dress.

I took out a bottle of scented body lotion and applied it generously, over my shoulders, collarbone and breasts, down to my stomach and thighs, bending to reach my lower legs then reaching around behind to slather it over my bottom. I could have done with somebody to sort out my back; where was a predatory male when you needed one?

Once the reachable parts of my body were soft and delicately fragranced, the lotion having thoroughly sunk in, I took out a pot of powder and a puff and began to dab it gently from my knees to my throat, front and back as far as possible. It was important that the dress should glide on with minimal effort; I needed to be faultlessly prepared.

I took one last lingering look at my powdered and painted nakedness, striking a few poses for confidence-building purposes, then I returned to the bag and uncoiled my shiny serpentine secret. How it transformed the light as I held it up, its extraordinary ultra-violetish hue sucking out the harshness and consuming it, making it stronger than ever. If Chase could resist this, then I faced a more serious challenge than I had anticipated.

First of all, I had to relax the lacing that crossed the plunging back of the garment. Somebody would have to tie that back up for me. I had an idea who I might ask. Then I had to step into it and pull, pull, pull for all I was worth while the sheeny cold rubber inched up my slippery thighs. The moment my arms slipped through the holes was one of triumph; a mountain climbed, flag planted in the snow. I was wearing a dress and yet I was wearing nothing. Feeling the sexiest commingling of bare flesh and constricting rubber, I was both held in check and liberated by its tight cling.

I pushed back my shoulders and drank myself in; I was all rises and falls, swelling and nipping, a fascinating glossy terrain that invited exploration and conquest. The shape of my breasts was unmistakable, and should anything ... exciting ... happen, it was pretty clear that the outline of my nipples would be clearly visible. From the back, the globes of my rear were pertly delineated; any tighter and the dress would mould itself to my crevices. It would be obvious that I was naked underneath; short of lacquering myself, there was not much more I could do to mimic full nudity.

Two steps to achievement of my goal remained. One – the slipping on of a pair of four-inch black patent heels – was easily done. The second was less so.

The purple laces hung down my back and swished across my bottom as I made an arduous way out of the toilets to Chase's office, which was mercifully close.

I tried to make my knock on the door as assertive as I could, but there was still that moment of hiatus between the rap and the intoned 'Enter' during which the stoutest heart can weaken. I opened the door a cautious crack and poked my head around.

'Sorry to bother you, Sir . . .'

'Not at all. Merry Christmas, Sophie.' He looked up and smiled – a rare event.

'Thank you, Sir. Merry Christmas. Have you been in all day?'

He shook his head and then just looked at me, expecting something . . . what?

'Are you going to come in?'

'Oh! Sorry!' Now was my moment. Best not to scupper it by gazing mooningly into his eyes. I slid into the room and made a slow, swaying approach to the desk of doom, keeping my eyes on his as I prowled. He did not so much as jerk a brow or twitch a corner of a lip. Was I having any effect on him at all? Suddenly the rubber seemed to be clamping down on more than my skin, pressing into my diaphragm, cutting off my air supply.

'I was just wondering, Sir,' I said, and my voice really was husky because I was struggling to breathe, 'if you could help me with my laces.'

He put his head on one side. 'Laces?' His hands were steepled; he looked calmly contemplative. This was not the effect I had striven for.

'Yes.' I stopped, one hand on a slippery hip, aiming for the killerest of silhouettes.

'At the back, I presume?'

'Yes. At the back.'

'I see. Over here then.' He lifted one forefinger and beckoned. Clever man. My all-time favourite come-hither. As if his crooking finger tugged me with an invisible thread, I hastened forward to the dangerous side of the desk, although hastening was difficult with my knees all but clamped together by the rubber hem of the dress.

He stood up, put one hand on a shoulder and gently steered me around so that my back was to him.

'This is a very interesting dress,' he said, his voice drifting down from behind me, his hand still large and warm on my shoulder. Intuition told me that his eyes were wandering down my outline and I imagined his gaze as a line of flame melting the rubber until it was ragged and blistered. His breath was close, catching a little. I could have tilted my head back and caught his nose and lips in my hair.

'It's one of my favourites,' I said hoarsely. What was that aftershave? I wanted to soak my bedding in it. I twisted my head to the side, willing him to take me up on the offer of the back of my neck. He did not.

His hand left my shoulder and joined the other one, tugging at my loose strings.

'How tight do you want it?'

'Usually, the tighter the better,' I said, 'but I'll trust your judgement. Whatever you think shows off my back best.'

'Tighter the better, eh?' he mused, jerking on the laces as if they were reins. 'You like the feeling of restraint?'

I smiled joyously; this was sounding a lot like flirtation.

'When it's done properly,' I replied, purring a little. 'By experienced hands.'

'I see,' was his disappointing rejoinder. He pulled the laces taut, tied the bow, then his fingers ran down the criss-crossing, checking it for symmetry. 'There. All tethered and tied.' My limbs did that turning to jelly thing. How I stopped myself grinding my shiny tight rubber bottom into his crotch I shall never know.

He stood there for a moment that seemed to drag on into the New Year, but was probably only half a minute, then he moved around to my side and offered me his elbow.

'They'll be waiting in the bar. Shall we?'

I almost felt like crying; I had been so sure that he was

going to run his hands the length and breadth of my rubberclad body from behind. I smiled uncertainly, linked my arm with his and tottered out of the office.

The rest of the evening was a torment of unsatisfied longing. He gave both me and the mistletoe a wide berth after fobbing me off with a cocktail, leaving me to languish and fume at the bar. How dare he resist my rubber charms? Every other man in the room was eyeing me up, assessing his chances, sliding drinks down the bar to me, and yet the only one I wanted would not even look at me.

I was used to controlling men and their desires; I played them like voluptuous violins and discarded them when I tired of their attentions. Christopher Chase was not following the pattern; he was zigzagging all over my chequer-board. I suppose this made him a deviant, which might be some consolation in the long term, but for now his stubborn refusal to live up to his promising surname was the occasion of severe chagrin.

I sat on a high stool, beginning to loathe my rubber prison, which now felt hot in quite the wrong way, clinging sweatily to every crease. It was going to be murder to get the perishing thing off. Ha. Perishing. Rubber. I remembered my fantasy about a ray of fire from Chase's eyes burning the dress off me and ordered another drink.

'Cheer up, Soph, it's Christmas.'

My favourite pool lifeguard, Jake, stood beside me, bowl of mixed nuts in hand, hair as endearingly shaggy as ever. I barely recognised him without his pecs on display, but his top was figure-hugging enough to please the eye regardless. A little younger than I, working his way through an MSc in Rescuing from Drowning Studies or some such, he made up for lack of experience with bags of enthusiasm. And stamina. Oh yes, such stamina. Perhaps he was not the Christmas gift I had had in mind for myself, but he was a nice stocking-filler treat. Really, didn't I deserve a little something?

'Yes, you're right,' I said, popping a cashew into my wildly lipglossed mouth. 'Season of mistletoe and mellow drunkenness.'

'Oh, well, if it's mistletoe you're after,' he whispered into my ear, then he whipped a sprig out from the belt of his jeans and held it aloft.

'Oh, you naughty boy!' I murmured, shimmying off my barstool and pressing the length of my body to his, proffering my lips while my eyes skittered off to the side, looking for Chase, not sure whether I wanted him to be watching or not. He was.

See what you're missing, I said in my head, then I fastened my mouth to Jake's, allowing his big rough hand to land on my cross-lacing, then to wander slowly down to the dip of my back, finally resting just above the crest of my buttocks. Something was hard and swollen against my stomach, easily tangible through the thin stretched layer of my dress. I let him maul my mouth until, from the corner of a half-closed eye, I noticed Chase leaving the room, then I pulled my face back.

'That dress is hot,' croaked Jake.

'Yes, it is. Very hot. Too hot. Let's go somewhere.'

'Follow me.'

There was nothing comfortable in the lifeguards' station; just a slatted wooden bench running the length of three of the walls, some pegs and a pile of lifejackets. Jake pushed me down to sit on the bench, then knelt in front of me, prising my knees as far apart as he could and peering up the dark mysterious cavern they revealed.

'No knickers,' he ascertained. 'Thought not.' He tried to fit a hand into the gap, but it was a struggle. 'How the fook do you get this thing off?'

'You don't,' I told him. 'But if we get to work now, we might be able to get the skirt up before midnight.'

'Right you are. On your feet and turn around then.' I was happy to obey, leaning over the wooden bench with my palms flat to the wall while he inched the rubber painstakingly up my thighs, dry humping my bottom as he toiled. When he finally managed to uncover my willing snatch, he abandoned the rest of the task, leaving much of my bum to strain against the shiny sheath while he found a home for his cock, clad in its own rubber garment.

I revelled in the ability to spread my legs wide after their incarceration, pushing back on his slamming weapon, needing the supportive clamp of his forearm around my midriff to stop me keeling over sideways. The coupling was fast and rude and exactly what I needed, pounding my residual angst over Chase from my head and bringing me back to my self, Sophie, the sex seeker, Selfie, the soak sexer, Sexie the Smoke Sizzler, bleurgh, no more thoughts just slam, slam, slam, steam, scream, cream, done.

'I'll never get this dress off now,' I panted, on my knees on a lifejacket, my head braced in my arms. It was stuck fast, my perspiration acting like glue.

'Let me untie you,' offered Jake. 'I'll go up and get your work clothes from Reception if you want.'

'Uh huh,' I agreed. But I don't want that knot undone. Chase tied it, and I want to be bound by it for as long as I can.

Room Service

I know what she is here for.

She doesn't know I know, but after four years behind this desk, I can read the signs.

She has signed her name in the register as 'Mrs Barker', and her low-key outfit tries too hard to blend in.

She is here to meet a man. A man who is not her husband.

Why though? What will this man give her that her spouse does not? Allow me a moment of speculation. The name Barker makes me think of barking, of dogs, of doggy-style sex that perhaps the husband will not provide. But I think it goes a little bit further than that. I think it goes like this.

Mrs Ross would consider herself happily married in all respects but one.

It isn't even the classic story of a couple growing apart, sex becoming routine, and then surplus to the routine. Mr Ross was a considerate lover who made it his business to provide his wife with a minimum of three orgasms weekly. His own tastes were conservative but not particularly repressed; if the overwhelming majority of his encounters with his wife took place in the missionary position after the required ten-to-fifteen minutes of foreplay, it was because this was the way he liked it. He had no desire to try anything more outré than the odd spot of *soixante-neuf*. If he had known the term 'vanilla' to apply to anything other than ice-cream, he would have applied it to himself.

For a long time, this was fine by Mrs Ross. She did not consider herself sexually deviant; indeed, they had been married three years before she felt emboldened to nudge him into their first attempt at cunnilingus. Whips, rubber and anything of that sort were certainly not her thing. Heaven knows, that Ann Summers party her sister-in-law had dragged her to had been bad enough. Huge plastic phalluses, shrieking women, too many Bacardi Breezers. And all that *nylon*.

But then, quite unexpectedly, once the children were at school and life had settled into a form of equilibrium, a buried memory of her younger years began prodding its way through the layers of denial.

Sipping her mid-morning coffee at the breakfast bar, Mrs Ross would travel back in time to the estate agency where she had filed and faxed for a year after completing her NVQ. She had attracted the attention of Mr Gregg, of Gregg and Saunders, on her first day, kneeling on the sill of the shop window making up a display of properties for sale.

'That's a nice ... skirt,' he had said, creeping up behind her as she bent over, stapling photographs to cards.

'Thanks.' She had giggled and blushed, thinking no more of it.

As the weeks went by, his comments continued, always complimentary, sometimes tending a little towards the creepy, but the young Mrs Ross – who was known back then as Lynnie – found that oddly compelling. It didn't hurt that he looked a little, a very little, bit like Sean Connery; well, all right, he didn't have the accent or the smile, but his eyes were nice and he had the kind of hair that looked quite good with silver threads in it. And he was the boss. Drove a nice car, lived in a big house. Was he married? It wasn't clear – he didn't wear a ring, but men didn't so much back then.

'What *is* that perfume you're wearing?' he asked one morning in November. Then, 'I'm going to measure up at a new property coming on to the market. Fancy a ride out to Cranford Heath? See how estate agents work in the field?'

She certainly did get to see an estate agent working in the field that day. He took her to an empty show home, where they performed a thorough inspection of the fixtures and fittings, concentrating especially on the bed.

'So that wasn't your first time,' noted Mr Gregg, coming up for air after round one.

'No; I broke up with my school boyfriend over the summer.'

'Was he heartbroken?'

'For a little while. I think I just outgrew him though. I was ready for a man instead of a boy.'

Mr Gregg grinned. 'You certainly were.'

They used the state-of-the-art kitchen facilities to make coffee, lounging around in their underwear on the expensive leather sofas.

'We're doing the builders a favour, making coffee,' explained Mr Gregg roguishly. 'It's one of the best smells for selling a house.'

'Really?' Lynnie gazed adoringly at her sophisticated chevalier.

'Yes. Not sure about the smell of fresh fucked pussy though. Perhaps I should spray a bit of air freshener around the bedroom.'

Really! How rude! Lynnie was shocked, but not repelled, by her seducer's coarse remark.

He laughed at her saucer eyes, moving closer up the pristine leather. 'We can tick the box for the bed being in working order, can't we, but what about this sofa?'

His coffee-hot mouth was upon hers again; his hands worked at removing her underwear while the sofa creaked soft protests at their grappling. Soon enough, Mr Gregg had his trainee on her stomach, hanging on to the arm, while he clasped her under her ribcage, pulled her up to her knees and entered her from behind.

This position was quite new to Lynnie, who was used to doing it as quietly and quickly as possible in the upstairs bedrooms of family homes, but even the novelty of this paled beside Mr Gregg's next move.

He pulled apart the cheeks of her bottom and plunged a thumb directly into her unsuspecting anus.

Lynnie screamed and wiggled her hips furiously, desperate to dislodge him from his unwelcome excavations. 'What are you DOING?' she yelled, close to tears, when he didn't immediately desist.

'Don't you like it, Lynnie? Lots of girls do.'

'It's ... ugh ... it's WRONG! Stop it!'

Mr Gregg sighed and popped his thumb out of the tight little hole. 'I'm disappointed in you. I thought you were more open-minded than that,' he said, still pumping away at her more conventional orifice.

'I am open-minded!' protested Lynnie, mortified and on the verge of crying, wanting nothing more than to run and hide in the state-of-the-art shower cubicle. 'I just don't see why any woman would want to do ... THAT.'

Mr Gregg moved his fingers down to Lynnie's clitoris, giving it a desultory flick. 'Sadly, neither does my wife.'

For the second time, Lynnie screamed. 'Your *what*? You BASTARD! Get OFF me!'

Mr Gregg tried to persuade her that she was his wife in name only, that he was preparing to leave as soon as the children were in college, that she was a cold fish who resented him, but Lynnie stood firm and he reluctantly withdrew.

As did she. From Mr Gregg and his estate agency.

Then she had met Mr Ross, fallen in love, got married, had children, and the whole débâcle had been forgotten. Until now.

The cream in her coffee swirled like a flashback sequence in an old film, taking her back to those elusive seconds on the show-home leather.

Why did he do it? Were there really women who enjoyed it? Was she one? And, most importantly and frustratingly of all, *How had it felt?*

She could not quite remember, and she wanted to. She recalled feeling shock, which had distracted her from the sensation, and then her anger at finding out he was married had superseded the significance of his prying thumb. But the thumb was still there, lurking in the less browsed pages of her mental back-catalogue. And, for good or ill, the page lay open now, demanding detailed perusal.

Had it hurt a little? She cast her net again and again over that fragment of her sexual past, but it would not be captured. Had it not hurt at all? Had it, in fact, felt good? Could it feel good? Why did she want to know?

It was the very shockingness of it that appealed to her now. There was something so elementally rude about the notion of a thumb in one's bum; it was certainly not something she would have told her husband. Or was it?

She wondered if he would like to try it – just to assuage curiosity, of course. It wasn't as if she really *wanted* to. It would just ... scratch that nervous itch. There was no way she was going to broach the subject with him, though, so she tried to shelve it.

She tried very hard to shelve it. She really did.

But that thumb would not stay where it was put; it broke the surface of her consciousness like an obscene jack-in-the-box a dozen times a day. She could be on the phone, or pruning a bush, or brushing her teeth, and the snippet of filled-pussy-and-thumbed-arse would flash into her brain, causing her to gag on the toothpaste or prick her finger or cut off the call accidentally. It was no good. She had to get it out of her system.

On sex nights (Wednesday, Friday, Saturday), Mrs Ross started wearing an abbreviated satin slip, bending over at every opportunity to show off a portion of cheeky cheek beneath the lace before events got into their full swing. She incorporated a heavy sway into her walk up the stairs, making sure she was in front of her husband, who would get an interesting view of her.

When this did not seem to shift his traditional focus, she began positioning herself unusually on the bed – instead of lying down on her back, she took to rolling over, tucking a leg against her stomach so that her posterior was tautened and her lips opened temptingly.

'I can't get at you from there, love,' reproved her husband.

She pouted. 'Of course you can.'

'But I want to see your face.'

'Oh.'

There was the rub. He always wanted that slow, sensual, full-eye-contact type of lovemaking, when what she wanted was something earthy and rough that didn't go with champagne and light soul music on the stereo.

'Wouldn't you like to try something different?' she asked, several weeks into this regime of unsatisfying romance.

'Different? I'm not up for wife-swapping, if that's what you're driving at,' he said jokingly, giving her hair a little stroke. She yanked her head away, uncharacteristically.

'Don't be daft. Just . . . a new position or something.' She hesitated to say anything as coarse as 'doggy-style' and settled on: 'From behind, for instance.'

'Oh, Lynnie, I have too much respect for you. You're my

princess, and princesses don't get treated like that. Princesses deserve lots of spoiling and stroking.'

And he proceeded to spoil and stroke until Mrs Ross had to restrain herself from hitting him.

She found herself straying to the scruffier end of town on her shopping trips, pausing in front of the window of 'Desirez', a place she had signed a petition against eight years ago. Behind the scratched perspex window were mannequins clad in shiny black miniskirts and fishnet vests, one of them dangling a pair of pink feather-lined handcuffs from a wrist.

Could she go in? She looked around nervously. Somebody she knew might be near, though there was little here to interest her fellow PTA members, unless they had secret tastes for pound-shop tat and sordid sex. Which was possible, she supposed. She laughed at herself and made a bolt for the safety of Waitrose.

'Check the booty on that!' crowed her teenage son to his friends one Saturday afternoon in front of MTV. A selection of amply reared young women shook their sheeny cheeks in skimpy thongs and stack heels.

'That girl has got a handful!' One of the group cried out.

'Boys!' remonstrated Mr Ross.

'They have got lovely bottoms,' conceded Mrs Ross, with a meaningful look at her husband. 'You can't expect a boy not to appreciate them. That's what they're *for*.'

Mr Ross coughed and said something about the car engine needing tuning.

Mrs Ross said she'd forgotten the mayonnaise and needed to pop out to Waitrose.

Could she? Would she? No, it was ludicrous. After all, what was actually *in* there? There might be CCTV. She might find her pixellated image all over the local press. But that was silly. 'Respectable Married Woman in Sex Shop Scandal' had never been a headline, as far as she remembered. All the same . . .

Her hand was on the scuffed paintwork of the door, just below the 'Strictly Over 18s Only' sign. She took it away. She put it back. She took it away. She put it back and the door suddenly swung inwards, causing her to stumble against the person behind it.

'I'm so sorry,' they chorused in unison, then they looked up.

'Is it . . . Lynnie?'

'Oh Christ, Mr Gregg!'

'I think you can call me Tony. Well, well. Miss Lynnie Speedwell.'

He took her elbow, ushering her out of the shop to the opening of an adjoining alleyway full of rubbish bins.

'It's Mrs Ross now,' muttered Mrs Ross, flooded with horror as full realisation of the circumstances dawned.

'Mr Ross is a lucky man, then, to have such an open-minded wife.' Mr Gregg raised an eyebrow in the direction of Desirez.

'Oh, I wasn't going in,' rushed Mrs Ross. 'I was just . . . short of breath, so I leaned against the door . . . I was going to Waitrose.'

Mr Gregg laughed out loud. 'Waitrose, eh? I can see how you'd mix the two up.'

'Don't tease,' snapped Mrs Ross, noticing at the same time how well Gregg had aged. Silver hair had been the right look for him, just as she used to think. He must be nearing sixty now, but he had kept the weight off and his blue eyes had attractive crinkles at the sides.

'Not teasing!' he said, holding up his hands. 'Lynnie, seeing you is bringing back all kinds of memories. Fancy a drink, for old time's sake?'

'I'm a married woman!'

'I know. I'm not a married man any more though, and I think I owe you at least an apology for the disgraceful way I behaved back then. Come on. Let me buy you a drink. There's a nice place near here, if you can believe it.'

Mrs Ross crumpled. She had to admit, she felt the need of a strong gin and tonic, and after another two, things began to get interesting.

They had covered the intervening twenty years, their children, their jobs, their hobbies, their tastes. The one thing they hadn't covered . . .

'So what were you doing in that shop then?' asked Mrs Ross, making a playful swipe for the brown paper bag on the table. After swaying back from the Ladies', she had sat herself down beside Mr Gregg instead of opposite, and the warmth and closeness of him were adding to her fuzzy intoxication.

Mr Gregg snatched the bag away. 'Not for a lady's eyes,' he said gallantly.

'What if I'm not a lady?'

'Mrs Ross! Are you telling me that you really did mean to go into that shop? I'm intrigued. Tell me more.'

'Only if you show me what you bought.'

'You'll think badly of me.'

'Can't be worse than what I thought of you for twenty years. You cheating louse.'

'Lynnie!' he remonstrated. 'All right. I'll show you. But it's our secret, all right?'

'Guide's honour,' she said with a clumsy salute.

'It's just a magazine,' said Gregg, sliding it halfway out of the bag. 'For a specialist taste.'

'Oh? Just a porn mag?' Mrs Ross was disappointed, until she saw what came out. A pair of huge pale arse cheeks, held apart by red-nailed hands while the puzzled-looking blonde they belonged to pouted over her shoulder at the camera. The magazine was entitled *Backdoor Love Affair*.

She looked at Mr Gregg, then back at the magazine, then back at Mr Gregg.

'You ... ?'

'I think you always knew I was an arse man,' said Gregg with an embarassed smile, slipping the magazine back into its hiding place.

'Yes. Yes, I remember,' said Mrs Ross huskily. 'And I remember what you said then ... "lots of women like it" ... is that true?'

'You mean you still haven't tried it? After seventeen years of marriage?'

'No. I must admit, I've been curious. Very curious. But Colin just doesn't seem to want to ...'

Mrs Ross looked helplessly at Gregg, suddenly needing a fourth gin very badly.

'Well,' said Gregg neutrally, draining his whisky and soda. 'If you're ever *that* curious, you know where to find me.'

'Are you serious?'

'Here's my card. The agency is still in Pitt Street. It's up to you.'

Mrs Ross stared at the business card in her palm. 'Can I get you another whisky?' she asked tremulously.

'No. You should go home before you do something you regret. You're not sober, Mrs Ross, and I don't take advantage of women these days.' He stood up, took her arm and kissed her on the cheek. 'Another time, though, I'd be more than delighted,' he whispered. 'Don't forget ... if you're still curious when you've sobered up ... call me.'

Mrs Ross weaved out of the bar, wondering how she would explain to Colin that she had to leave the car in town. Bumped into an old friend. Few drinks.

She forgot the mayonnaise.

* * *

She held on to the card for a month before she did anything.

In the cold light of day it seemed impossible and wicked to follow up on Gregg's offer. Colin was a good man and she was a good woman; good women did not do things like this.

But the cover of that magazine was burned into her mind; the secret cleft wantonly exposed, the pinky-brown bud at its centre, tight but apparently not too tight. How would something bigger than a finger get *in* there? Mrs Ross was not clear on the detail. She thought about looking it up on the internet, but then she worried about Colin finding it on the search history, or accidentally downloading something incriminating. Maybe if she went to Desirez again – but how on earth would she hand a copy of that thing over the counter? Impossible.

On the last night of that month, she got Colin drunk with the intention of seducing him into exploring her very limits. She wore her new leopard-print basque with stockings and suspenders and performed a lapdance for him (the children were on sleepovers) in the living room. For the grand finale, she turned backwards on his thighs and waved her bottom in his face before pulling it rudely apart from the base of the cheeks.

'God, Lynnie, what is up with you these days?' he moaned. 'That was very sensual, up to the end. Why don't you light a few candles and I'll give you a foot massage.'

The next day, at around coffee-break time, she found herself holding Gregg's card in trembling fingers, staring at the numbers as if challenging them to disappear.

She began to punch the number in three times, abandoned it three times. Took a swig of coffee. Tried again. It rang.

'Gregg and Saunders, Tony Gregg speaking.'

She was stumped, unable to think of anything to say.

'Hello?'

'Oh ... Mr Gregg ...'

'Lynnie!' She was taken aback at his instant recognition of her voice, and speech temporarily eluded her. 'Great to hear from you! Are you ... is there a reason for this call?'

He sounded so hopeful that her courage returned. 'Hello ... yes. There is.'

'OK, calm down, love. I understand that this isn't easy for you. Do you want to meet for lunch?'

'Yes, please. Somewhere discreet. Obviously.'

'Obviously. How about the Hotel? At one?'

'Oh, yes, good. I'll see you there then.'

I saw them arrive separately and leave together. I recognised Gregg, who had booked rooms and attended meetings here on a number of occasions. He isn't a bad shag, actually. I did not recognise Mrs Ross; she wasn't his usual type. Crossing the lobby she looked ready to collapse with nerves, but when he stood up from one of the couches that line the room and held out his hand to her, she seemed to straighten up, smiling at him and accepting his arm as he led her to the restaurant.

'What you must understand, Lynnie, is that I need some evidence that you are serious about this.'

'You mean ... isn't this enough? I've met you in a hotel and you ... you know what I want, so ...'

'Wham, bam, thank you, Ma'am? No. I don't think that's good enough. I like you, Lynnie, and I want this to be a positive experience for you. In my experience, you need to build up to this kind of sex. You need to get into ... training.'

'Training? I don't understand.'

'What I mean, Lynnie, and pardon my French but there isn't really a delicate way of putting it, is that I can't just ram my cock up there from scratch. You need preparation.'

'What sort of preparation?'

'I have a little task for you to perform. I want you to go to Desirez.'

'Desirez! No!'

'Yes, and this is what I want you to do there . . .'

Mrs Ross loitered in the boutique across the road from Gregg and Saunders for longer than she had planned. For the eighth time, she peered into her handbag to make sure she had not dropped or lost the items that were burning a hole in the leather. Still there. She still could not quite believe she had actually crossed the threshold of Desirez, still less placed these two things on the counter and handed over money for them. She had avoided the cashier's eye quite successfully but he had insisted on asking, 'You're sure this is the size you want?' and she had been able to do no more than nod tightly.

The thought of that anxious exchange was unaccountably erotic now, though; every time she remembered it, an additional peripheral detail slotted into place. How the raincoated man at the magazine stand had looked at her. The bizarre items hanging from the wall. The row of huge dildoes behind the glass counter. It was like a different world, and yet it must be normal to some people. Normal to Mr Gregg. Mr Gregg and Desirez stood on one side of a line dividing her self, while Colin and Waitrose inhabited the other. Talk about a split personality, she thought, disapproving of herself even as she was psyching herself up to cross the road.

Nothing was going to stop her now that the wheels were in motion, least of all her own conscience. That ordeal in the sex shop would have to be redeemed.

'Mrs Ross is here for her appointment, Mr Gregg.'

'Ah, good. Show her in.'

The receptionist replaced the receiver and smiled brightly at Mrs Ross, who was reminded of herself as a young trainee. Was Gregg knocking this one off as well? she wondered. None of her business if he was, of course, though she could not help but twinge at the idea.

'You went to the shop?' were Gregg's first words to her once they were closeted in the office.

'Yes. Somehow. I'm not sure how I got through it.'

'Brave girl.' He smiled. 'Come and show me what you bought.'

Mrs Ross fumbled in her handbag, placing the two purchases side by side on Gregg's desk.

'Ah, yes, this is the right size to start off with,' he said, turning the little pink silicone plug around in his hands. 'And the lube ... yes. That'll do nicely. I must say, Lynnie –' he looked up, grinning '– you have surprised me. I thought you'd take fright when the prospect was real. You're still on board?'

Mrs Ross found the management-speak a little incongruous, but she nodded, transfixed at the sight of the plug, and the man who meant to put it in her, together.

'OK. Then I must ask you to come over here, Miss Lynnie Speedwell, and lift up your skirt.'

The use of her maiden name made Mrs Ross feel like his young employee again, banishing all doubts and thoughts of resistance. She shuffled shyly to his side of the desk and stood in front of him, performing a slow shimmy of the pencil skirt until it bunched around her waist, exposing stocking tops and a pair of high-cut tight-fitting briefs.

'Good; just what I said you should wear,' said Gregg approvingly. 'Now I'd like you to put yourself over my lap, please, young lady.'

'Over your lap?' Mrs Ross baulked slightly.

'Yes, it's easier and more comfortable, the first time. Don't worry, I'm not going to spank you. Unless you'd like me to?'

Mrs Ross giggled hysterically. 'Not right now,' she managed. She bent forward awkwardly, balancing herself with one palm on the floor while her stomach pressed into Mr Gregg's thighs and her legs hung down, not quite finding the ground.

'Get as comfortable as you can,' advised Gregg, moving about in his chair to accommodate her until she was settled. 'A sofa is best for this kind of thing really. Never mind. Now then.'

He peeled the skin-tight knickers down over her backside until it was fully exposed to his view, tugging them down as far as the stocking tops so he had an extra little peek at the lips of her pussy, which seemed temptingly sheeny.

Mrs Ross felt a little awkward, dangling so, with the dry office air circulating around her naked bottom, but the first brush of palm on curvaceous cheek was so much more than she had been hoping for that she let out a little sigh.

'Aren't you ever touched here?' Gregg wanted to know.

'Hardly ever. It seems like some kind of forbidden zone for some reason. I have to make it clear though, that this is the only part of me you get to touch. No straying off the beaten track.'

'Beaten? You really would like a spanking?'

'No! You know what I mean!'

Gregg chuckled and began gliding his palm across the surface of her posterior, brushing in broad circular motions, moving inward and inward until Mrs Ross was a compliant ragdoll oohing and aahing with satisfaction and getting perilously close to staining the dark trousers he was wearing.

'Does that feel good?'

'Oh, it does ... better than I imagined ... it feels so naughty somehow.'

'Well, it's about to get naughtier ... stay nice and relaxed now ...'

Mrs Ross stayed still as glass while Gregg gently opened the furrow and worked skilled fingers down the sheering sides, so slowly that she could not take fright, so effectively that she began to breathe again, properly, heavily, and then she knew she would have to move.

She had ordered herself not to, but she began to gyrate a little, pushing her bottom up further and looking for relief for her very wet and very needy sex. Now that Gregg's fingers were circling the central opening with an inevitability she was finding highly erotic, she could finally understand the lots of women who liked it. She knew where they were coming from ... and why they were coming. On a mental level it felt richly, wildly rude, but on a physical level it was also unexpectedly delicious; she had not realised that attention to her rear could connect up to her clitoris, as if a row of flashing lights lit up in sequence between the erogenous zones.

'So what do you think?' murmured Gregg, his thumb having reached the apex of his intentions. 'You can still say no if you want.'

'No, no. I mean, please. I mean, do it.'

'OK. Hold tight and don't tense those muscles.'

There was a pause, then Mrs Ross squeaked momentarily at the sensation of cold gel against her tightest hole, kicking her legs until Gregg put a steadying hand on one thigh. She could hear sounds from above, very faint liquidy sounds of things being squeezed from tubes. She could also hear tiny squishes from between her legs, every time she made a move. The suspense was almost too much.

And then it wasn't! 'Ah!' she announced when the thumb returned, slipping around the lubricated circle then pushing, slowly but inexorably, against the barricades.

'Don't tense,' advised Gregg, stopping momentarily as the ring of muscle closed around him. Mrs Ross made a herculean effort and unclenched, letting him through, giving him access, squirming and babbling a little, but making no other attempt to halt his excavations. It felt strange but not significantly painful, she thought, even when he twisted the thumb around, prodding and poking at her secret passage.

'How's that, Lynnie?' he asked.

'It's . . . good, I think. Doesn't really hurt.'

'No, this shouldn't. You'll need to work on taking anything bigger though. All right. Now I'm going to insert the plug. Keep still and don't tense.'

His thumb popped out, to be swiftly replaced by the slim length of silicone, feeling a little chill at first, but soon warming up. Its presence was certainly noticeable, but it did not stretch or sting or hurt. Gregg pushed and pulled it back and forth, until Mrs Ross had to bite her tongue to keep from begging him to fuck her. She wanted it badly, madly, cock, fingers, tongue, whatever.

'See, it's good, isn't it?' crooned Gregg, steering the plug with relish, mindful of the juice flow he was precipitating. 'I was right, wasn't I? Aren't you sorry you didn't take the chance before?'

'Oh yes, I am, very sorry,' gasped Mrs Ross. 'Oh God, oh God.'

'Good. Right.' Mr Gregg stopped abruptly and pulled Mrs Ross's knickers back up. 'On your feet, Mrs Ross.'

She almost howled with disappointment, but she did as she was told, feeling her bottom cheeks clamp together and her muscles tighten around her little invader. While she pulled the skirt down, Gregg issued further directives.

'You will keep that in until you get home,' he told her. 'And on the way home, I want you to call in at the town library and look for all the information you can find on anal intercourse. Tomorrow morning, you will re-insert the plug yourself and come back here so I can replace it with a larger one. And so it will go on until you are ready. Yes?'

'Yes,' whispered Mrs Ross.

'Good. You've done very well today. I'm proud of you. I'll see you tomorrow then.'

Mrs Ross dithered for a minute, staring at him pleadingly, then said, 'OK,' and scuttled out.

All the way to the library, she imagined people could see what she was wearing, X-raying beneath her skirt and underwear. Did it affect her walk? It did a little, for she had to keep her muscles taut to stop it from slipping out. By the time she got to the library, she was burning up with the need for an orgasm; she grabbed the first sex-related book she could see, raced to a cubicle and sat down, grinding her bottom against the seat to fully feel the impact of the plug while her hand sped straight down the waistband of her skirt to her knickers. Head down on the open book, legs splayed and bum plugged, Mrs Ross brought herself to a muffled, tearstreaked climax in the Silent Reading area of the Central Library.

Slowly, carefully, Gregg opened Mrs Ross's bottom further and wider, bending her over his desk each day to give her stretching arsehole his tender and thorough attentions, until the day came when he judged her to be sufficiently trained to receive the ultimate plugging.

Not in the office, though, where the staff were beginning to raise eyebrows at the frequent appointments which left Gregg flushed and the air unaccountably perfumed.

No, Gregg was taking Mrs Ross upmarket – to the best hotel in town.

'The name's Barker,' he told me, peeling off notes from a wad into my complicit paw.

'Very good, Mr Barker,' I said, entering him on the database.

'When my wife –' he paused to wink '– turns up, show her straight to the room, please.'

'Mrs Barker? Will do.'

'Thanks. Take a twenty for yourself, Sophie.'

'Thank you, Sir.'

Mrs Ross – or was it Barker? Oh, she hated the subterfuge but she had come too far now – stepped out of the lift, tightening her sphincter subconsciously for her final moments as an anal virgin.

'I feel as if I ought to kiss you. I want to kiss you,' said Gregg, on opening the door.

'No kissing,' said Mrs Ross tightly, taking in a symphony of muted creams and beiges from the full-length curtains to the carpet to the . . .

'It's a nice bed, isn't it?' Now that they were here, Gregg felt a little awkward; this was not the sort of social scenario he often played out. What was the etiquette when you were meeting a happily married woman to give her her inaugural buggering?

'It's enormous,' remarked Mrs Ross nervously.

'So . . . do you want a drink or something first?' Gregg hovered by the minibar, squinting at a packet of dry roasted peanuts.

'Oh, God, no. Let's do the deed and get out of here.' Mrs Ross laughed, a little too shrilly. Gregg saw that somebody needed to take control of the situation and decided that it might as well be him.

'All right,' he said. 'I'll ignore the blow to my pride and self-esteem and cut to the chase. Take off your skirt.'

Mrs Ross caught her breath, obscurely grateful to Gregg for seizing the initiative and taking it out of her hands. *He made me do it.*

She walked to the foot of the bed, slowly unzipped and let her tweed pencil skirt crumple around her ankles.

Gregg was heartened by the sight of her firm flesh framed by white suspender straps and sheer stockings. Mrs Ross had not bothered with knickers today, which was practical in one way, but it would deny him the pleasure of ripping them down.

Ah well, there were other ways to work off frustration.

'Very nice; get on the bed on all fours now. I suppose I can't persuade you to take off your blouse?'

'I'd rather not,' said Mrs Ross, crawling on to the plump duvet and sinking her hands and knees into its soft embrace.

'And as for foreplay?'

'I . . . just do what you would do, as if foreplay was over,' gasped Mrs Ross, starting to wetten at the very thought of what was to come. 'I'll be fine.'

'If you're sure.'

She shuddered a little at the sounds of uncapping, unbuckling, unzipping that ensued, knowing that the next un- might well be her undoing. She bit her lip when the mattress tilted underneath Gregg's weight. *He's behind you*, she thought, wanting to giggle at the pantomime association of the phrase. She listened to the sound of lubricant being squelchily warmed between his palms, letting her mind run on in this vein. *Oh no he isn't!* The mattress sloped ominously lower; a breath of air from his movements wafted over her displayed bottom. *Oh yes he is!*

And now a hand descended, grabbing a plump handful of bum before parting the cheeks, opening her to her fate. She felt the lubricant on the tips of his fingers as they massaged her well-trained bud, prodding and probing, precipitating a wanton need for him to go further, so that she welcomed the eventual blunt pressure of his erection in their place.

Knock knock.

It felt wider than any of the plugs, and the heat of it was unfamiliar after a week of cold smoothness lodged inside.

Mrs Ross was suddenly sure it would never fit, bucking in a moment of panic until Gregg had to clamp an arm beneath her stomach, holding her in place.

'It will be all right,' he reassured.

'It seems so thick,' she whimpered.

'It will hurt a little, but you knew that, Lynnie. You know what to do. Don't tense and it will soon pass.'

He began to push. Mrs Ross tried very hard to keep from clamping him, but the ring of muscle had a treacherous will of its own. All the same, Gregg was patient, holding still until she had controlled it enough to let him continue. Infinitesimally, he glided onward while Mrs Ross's eyes stretched as wide as her rear orifice, astonished that he had even made it this far and disbelieving his clear intention to forge ahead regardless.

'Oh! Oh no!' she cried, stabbing pain shooting through her stomach, but Gregg had come this far and there was no turning back.

'Yes, it will pass,' he repeated through gritted teeth, her hips tightly gripped, his head full of the sight of his glistening shaft disappearing inexorably into the sunless depths of her backside. 'Take it all, Lynnie. God, I wish you could see it. I wish you could see your arse stuffed full of my cock.'

'Aaargh!' she replied, but he was right; the worst of the pain was swiftly over, replaced by the most intense fullness and an inescapable, strangely sexy sense of helplessness. There was a man's cock in her bum, and nothing she could do about it.

He crept up to the hilt and stayed there for long gloating moments, staring at his rooted tool and the stretched sheath in which it reclined.

'How does it feel?' he asked.

'So weird,' she said faintly. 'So full. Stuffed. Full.'

'Good,' he said, and then he began to draw back. Mrs Ross felt as if her entire being and body were concentrated in the nerve endings along her back passage; just to make sure that this wasn't the case, she let her hand flit down between her legs to that other seat of sensation. Oh, it was ready for some stimulation, it seemed.

As Gregg continued to plough his new furrow with diligence, Mrs Ross batted her clitoris between finger and thumb, falling into a new world of sensation, enjoying every element of it, moaning into the duvet with ever-increasing volume as her bottom was comprehensively commandeered.

Mr Gregg felt luxuriously wicked, like a melodrama baronet with a twirly moustache, pounding his cornered lust object into ultimate submission; while Mrs Ross felt wickedly luxurious, like the favoured concubine of a powerful ruler, offering the final bastion of her virtue to her master.

The fantasy saw them fly into an enormous stew of an orgasm: Gregg pumping in a frenzy, Mrs Ross shredded by the combination of climax and filled arse, lifted for a few seconds beyond her body and into an otherworld of pure sensation.

'Take it,' growled Gregg. 'Just . . . take it.'

She took it, and gladly, and she would have taken much more, although it was starting to sting again back there, and besides, time was pressing.

'How was it?' asked Gregg, withdrawing in a way that made her face crumple and reaching for the tissues on the bedside table.

'God. Just. Thank you. It was . . . more than I even thought. You were great.'

'Yes, wasn't I?' he preened. 'So were you. I'm glad you enjoyed it.'

'I did.' Mrs Ross lay down flat, meekly allowing him to dab at her widespread arsehole with the tissue.

'You'll feel that for a while,' he advised. 'But it'll be fine in a day or so. Just don't go ramming any large foreign objects up there. Or if you do, give me a call and I'll come and watch you.'

Mrs Ross snorted. 'Pervert.'

'Yes.' There was a short pause while he zipped himself back up. 'You know, I'd be more than happy to do this again, Lynnie.'

'No,' she said, rolling over and scanning the room for her skirt. 'It can't happen again. It's a one-off; a glorious one-off. I'll never forget it.'

'I understand,' said Gregg with a rueful smile. 'And neither will I.'

Mrs Ross has still not managed to convince her husband of the benefits of backdoor love, but she has some excellent toys, and a very good memory. And a lot of spare time.

On Demand

A smart man with shiny shoes, a briefcase and a golf bag crosses the lobby. A businessman, you might think, staying for a few nights to negotiate a deal. And while he is here, he will relax with a few rounds of golf before breakfast, perhaps, or talk over some of the finer points of the contract while teeing off with his colleagues. Except I know for a fact that there are no golf clubs in that bag.

How do I know?

Dr Lassiter and his golf bag make an appearance here roughly every six weeks. He hires a room for the night, but never stays until morning; he usually checks in at two and leaves around dinnertime. Between two and two thirty, a shy-looking blonde woman comes to Reception and asks for Dr Lassiter; I always ring the room and tell him she is here; he always asks me to send her up.

At first glance, nothing more to it than that most common of scenarios here, an illicit tryst between otherwise attached lovers. But what's with the golf bag?

I found out on the occasion of their fourth liaison.

The hotel was very busy that week; three conferences and an international film festival in town. Dr Lassiter and his friend would have to make do with one of our lowlier rooms at the back of the building, a set of small double suites with (locked, of course) interconnecting doors. I sent the blonde up as usual and settled in to an afternoon of flirting with obscure European actors at the desk. A particularly mouth-

watering Croatian chap was asking me about local restaurants and bars when I was interrupted by a peremptory ring
of the bell.

'Ahem, excuse me, young lady,' said an elderly man in a
safari suit. 'I wonder if you could help me with a delicate
situation.'

I smiled regretfully at Mr TDH and turned to the customer.

'Delicate?'

'Yes. I think so. I'm in Room 209, trying to sleep in advance
of a very important meeting this evening, but there is a
terrible racket coming from the room next door.'

'Next door? To your left or your right?'

'Right.'

So that would be Dr Lassiter and his friend. Interesting.

'What sort of racket is it?' I asked, expecting creaky
bedsprings and shouts of 'Yes! Yes!' as per.

'Well, it's rather a worry. It sounds as if there is some kind
of assault taking place.'

'Assault?' Perhaps they liked it rough.

'Yes, it sounds rather as if a woman is being beaten in
there.'

'Oh.' I dithered for a few seconds. Dr Lassiter did not seem
the violent type, but then, that is not necessarily relevant.
He was probably engaging in some kind of consensual
role-play with his friend. All the same . . .

'Come up and listen for yourself,' invited the elderly
gentleman. 'You can hear it all quite plainly through the
connecting door.'

'All right,' I said, retrieving my set of skeleton keys from
beneath the desk. 'Though you realise I will not be able to
disturb them unless there is a crime taking place. If they are
just . . . noisy people . . . I will have to leave them to it.
Within reason. You will find a set of earplugs in the top
drawer of the bedside table.'

Entering the lift, he told me, 'I can't abide earplugs. I can't sleep with them in at all.'

I shrugged and we remained silent until reaching the obscure back corridor where his room was situated. A low cry travelled along the corridor towards us, eerily disembodied. It sounded like a woman's voice.

'Is that her?' I whispered.

'Yes. Come in.' He ushered me into the room and we made for the interconnecting door, where we crouched down with toothglasses at our ears.

At first all was silent. Then there was the rumble of a man's voice, his words indistinguishable. A short reply from the woman, something like 'Yes', maybe. More silence. Then I staggered back at a sudden cracking sound and a shuddering 'ooh' from the woman.

'What was that?' I whispered to my companion.

'I don't know. It sounds like he's hitting her, don't you think?'

I listened again. It sounded like a cowboy cracking his whip in a Western film, though perhaps a bit less sharp. The cries of the woman increased in volume until it became obvious that she was saying 'No, please, no.'

I stood up, staring at the elderly guest in consternation.

'Oh my God, it does sound as if she wants him to stop whatever he's doing. Damn! What the hell can I do?'

'Can't you go in there on some pretext?'

'I'm afraid to. Perhaps I should get the manager?' But if it should turn out to be innocent fun ... I didn't want to risk incurring Chase's wrath. At least, not in this context. Maybe in the bedroom ... 'OK.' I strengthened my resolve. I would sort this out as quickly and simply as possible.

I marched round to the room next door and rapped at the door. There was a 'Do Not Disturb' sign on the handle but, for once, I ignored it.

The whipcracking and crying stopped dead.

'Who is there?'

'Reception. Could I have a quick word, please?'

'Don't you see the sign on the door?' Lassiter's tone was autocratic, but there was a touch of something nervous behind it.

'Yes, but it's important. Please can I speak to you?'

'I specifically asked for no interruptions. Leave us alone, please, or I shall have to call the manager to complain.'

Fuck! Now what? I made a pained face at my elderly whistleblower, who shook his head. 'What if he is killing her?' he whispered.

He was right. It was a risk I was not prepared to take. I put my bunch of skeleton keys up to my lips for an indecisive moment, then I opened the door. I was confronted by a scream and a pair of rather red thighs leaping away from me out of eyeshot, while Dr Lassiter, wearing a long black cloak and mortarboard, spun round furiously, throwing a leather strappy thing on to the bed in the process.

My eyes popped. Oh no! This was a miscalculation after all! Or was it?

'I'm so sorry,' I squawked, feeling as if there was a hand around my throat. 'But the lady sounded as if ... she was suffering. I just wanted to make sure she was all right.'

The blonde peeped around from the bathroom door. Her hair was in pigtails, I noticed. 'I'm absolutely fine,' she said hysterically. 'Please go away.'

I spun around, noticing an array of fierce-looking implements on the bed, including a whippy item with a number of purple tails. Very striking. Ha.

Anyway. This was a good old-fashioned headmaster/ naughty schoolgirl role-play and there was no way I was sticking around to incur Dr Lassiter's displeasure, judging by the state of that girl's backside. A bit of slap and tickle is one thing, but not being able to sit down for a week is quite another.

I made my excuses and left. And spent the rest of the afternoon pondering.

Although the scene I had found had unsettled me, I was also intrigued. I felt the need to know more. What did the girl get out of it? What was Dr Lassiter's motivation? Were they lovers, or was it Strictly Come Caning? How did that strap feel? What about the cane – was it as painful as I imagined? If so, what was the payoff? I imagined myself, bent at the waist, clutching my ankles while my pale and vulnerable bottom awaited the first cut. I had to admit, my curiosity was piqued, and that was always dangerous. If I was a cat, I'd be dead by now, for sure.

So when Blondie emerged from the lift and glanced over at the desk in a panic, intent on getting out without being seen, I had to stop her. I rushed out across the lobby.

'Madam! Excuse me, Madam!'

She turned and thrust out her lip at me. 'Haven't you done enough damage for one day?' she hissed. 'Dr Lassiter is furious; I don't suppose we'll be able to use this place again.'

'I know. I'm so sorry about that,' I replied quietly. 'I hope you will come back. I'll put you somewhere soundproofed next time. Please accept my apologies!'

She sniffed. 'Well, it isn't up to me. It'll be Dr Lassiter's decision.'

'I suppose it will. I'm going to apologise to him too. Listen, do you have a minute? Can I get you a drink?'

'I have a train to catch. But it's not for half an hour. I suppose so.'

I took her into the bar and ordered us a dry Martini each.

'Take a seat,' I offered, waving my hand at the near-empty expanse of seating.

'Thanks, I'd prefer to stand,' she deadpanned, causing me to put a hand over my mouth and stifle a giggle.

'I suppose so,' I said, grinning at her. She returned my smile, relaxing a little. 'I suppose the train ride home might be a little uncomfortable?'

'It usually is. What did you want to talk about?'

'Just . . . I'm interested. Oh, my name's Sophie, by the way.'

'Rachael.' She put out a hand, its nails square-clipped and unvarnished. I noticed that there was some ink on a couple of fingertips. She caught my frown of enquiry. 'Dr Lassiter is a great one for the little details,' she said. 'You're not shocked? You seem to be taking this in your stride.'

'No, not shocked at all. Horses for courses,' I said with a shrug.

'Mmm, I love a riding crop,' she said, looking at me archly for a reaction.

'Why?' I asked her.

'Why?'

'Yes, why do you like it? What's the draw?'

'Oh, Sophie, if you don't understand, you never will. It's something you get or you don't. I can't explain it. It's hardwired into me.'

'I'm not sure I don't understand it,' I told her. 'When I caught you . . . there was something in me that couldn't look away. I felt as if I should run, but I didn't want to. I wanted to see more.'

'Well, perhaps you're a latent submissive,' said Rachael ruminatively. 'Sometimes it can manifest a little later. Personally, I've always known I was this way.'

'Really?'

'Yes. All my fantasies were of being dominated, tied up, disciplined. Never anything soft-focus or romantic for me. For me, the big strong arms of a protective man can't compare with the cane in the hand of an authoritarian.'

'Wow. But what is it that appeals to you? Is it the pain?'

'No. You're surprised, aren't you? It isn't the pain. I don't even like it that much. To be honest, I long for the caning to stop almost as soon as it starts.'

This was confusing. If she hated the pain, why did she do this?

'So when you called out for him to please stop . . . and he didn't . . . what was going on there?'

'Oh, I wasn't really asking him to stop.' She was enjoying my blank-faced bewilderment, smiling impishly as she bit the cocktail cherry off the stick.

'So . . .?'

'If I'd wanted him to stop, I'd have used my safeword. It's "Basingstoke". That's where I live,' she said.

'Oh, right, you have a safeword. Have you ever used it?'

'So far, no. It's kind of a matter of pride for me. I've surprised myself at how much I can take. I really am much stronger than I thought.'

'Stronger?'

'There is strength in submission,' she said serenely. 'You could try it. You'd see.'

'So it's all about . . . giving yourself up? Putting yourself in somebody else's hands?'

'You're starting to get it,' she said, draining the cocktail.

'You must trust Dr Lassiter very much,' I commented. 'How did you meet him?'

'Oh, on the internet,' she said offhandedly. 'Slaveseeker. com.'

Slaveseeker.com? Now I really had heard it all.

'So you don't even know him?'

'Sophie, sweetie, I know what I need to know. I know he can give me what I need. I don't need to know more than that, do I?'

'You think of yourself as . . . his slave?'

She sighed. 'No, I don't. Some submissives do, some don't. You know, not everyone who practises BDSM is this hogtied girl in PVC crawling around the place on her hands and knees. There are just as many shades of dynamic as there are in vanilla sex. Like I said. You should try it.'

She put down her glass and checked her watch.

'And now I really have to go. But it was nice talking to you. I forgive you for barging in on us. I'll try and persuade Dr Lassiter to give you another chance.'

She winked at me and left the bar.

I mooched after her minutes later, my head full of leather thongs and scarlet flesh, and bumped straight into Dr Lassiter, knocking his golf bag to the highly polished floor.

'You again!' he spluttered. 'Were you put on this earth to plague me?'

'I'm sorry! So sorry!' I reached for the golf bag but he swiped it jealously from the floor before I could touch its hallowed cloth.

'You will be when I've spoken to the manager.'

'Oh, please, don't! I mean . . .' His lips were pinched and white; he seemed hellbent on getting me fired. 'Of course, it's up to you. But if there is any other way I can make it up to you . . .'

'I want a refund for today's fiasco,' he said.

'No problem; I'll organise it straight away.' I hopped over to the desk and began the complicated refund process while he glowered beardily down. He would make a good head-master in real life, I thought, at least as far as intimidating the malcontents was concerned.

Tapping in codes, I wondered how to approach the situation. I wanted to make him an offer. An offer of reparation. Rachael seemed to think he was good at what he did, and if I was going to perform this experiment, I wanted to be in the hands of an expert.

'Do you mind my asking ...' I opened cautiously.

'Yes, I do,' he snapped.

The door behind me opened and Mr Chase looked out, frowning at my efforts on the computer.

'Everything all right here?' he asked, lowering his spectacles in Dr Lassiter's direction.

'Fine!' I said hastily.

Dr Lassiter looked as if he was on the verge of dobbing me in, but unexpectedly he nodded instead and made a non-committal gesture. Chase returned to his lair.

'Thanks!' I said. 'I owe you one.'

'You do,' agreed Lassiter tightly.

'I'd like to ... pay you back. However you like.' I swallowed, holding his eye, which widened.

'I'm not sure I understand.'

'I, um, well, if Rachael isn't available any time ... I mean, I don't know how exclusive you are, but if you aren't ... I mean ...' Good Lord, this was turning into the worst bout of verbal diarrhoea of my life. How the hell does one ask a man for a good thrashing?

Dr Lassiter leant forward so his elbows were on the desk and his flinty eyes connected to mine. I tried to look submissive. How do you look submissive? I went for a sexually available, startled-fawn type of thing.

'Are you saying, young lady, that you share certain of Rachael's tastes?'

The 'young lady' made me feel a certain squirminess in the pit of my stomach. Suddenly I was very small and very helpless. Was this normal? I didn't know, but I rather liked it. An acquired taste, perhaps, but then most of the finer pleasures in life are.

'I don't know, but I'd like to find out. If you don't mind, I'd be very grateful if you could ... test me.'

'Test you?'

'Try me out.'

His voice was very low and his face very close to mine.

'It would be a pleasure,' he said. I drew in a deep breath. 'You strike me as a young lady in dire need of discipline.'

'Yes, I think you could be right.'

'Yes, I think you could be right, *Sir.*'

'Yes, I think you could be right, Sir.'

The tiny barrier of air between us quivered. 'Very well,' he said briskly, straightening up with the first recorded Lassiter smile. 'Rachael is regrettably unavailable most of the time, due to her personal commitments. Would next Thursday suit?'

I checked my rota. 'I get off at six, Sir,' I told him, very much hoping that this would turn out to be true in every sense

'Six it is. No later.' He stepped back again, took me in long and expansively from my head to my midriff, where the desk curtailed me, then hoisted up the golf bag and strode off.

I was unreasonably excited by the prospect of this new direction in my boudoir life. The anticipation took me through the eight celibate days and nights leading up to my initiation. I lay in bed imagining the sting and the throb and the shame and the voice lecturing over my head as the lashes fell. Except the voice was not Lassiter's, it was Chase's, chiding me for some future piece of misbehaviour that threatened to derail our delirious happiness together. Lassiter would be another substitute for the man I really craved, and I wondered if it would gall him to know that. One imagines that these dominant chaps don't take kindly to unfavourable comparison with others. Perhaps he'd whip me all the more soundly if he knew. The thought made me come, hard, flooding my busy hand with my deviant juices.

You're a bad girl, Sophie. You're a very bad girl. Ooh, I know.

I was antsy all of Thursday afternoon, my eyes flicking over to the revolving doors every few minutes. Dr Lassiter had called the day before to stipulate my dress code – no trousers, plain white cotton knickers, over-the-knee socks or hold-up stockings, nothing patterned or colourful. Minimal make-up and any mascara should be waterproof. Rachael had not been wrong about Lassiter being one for the details.

I had opted for over-the-knee socks, to make the occasion stand out, since I wore stockings or hold-ups most of the time anyway, on the offchance that Chase might unexpectedly fling me on to his desk and give me one while the guests were at breakfast or cocktails. Without hope, what have I, eh? They should probably have been white, but mine striped black and red all the way up to my lower thighs, making me look like Minnie the Minx. I wondered if Dr Lassiter was a *Beano* man; probably was, with all the whacking and thwacking that went on in those cartoons.

At ten to six, my putative punisher walked through the door, golf bag ominously slung over his shoulder. He did not wave, or smile, or acknowledge me in any way, but simply strode up to the desk, purposeful as the Terminator.

'Good afternoon, Sir,' I quavered, my fingers slipping on the keycard as I fished it off its hook.

'Young lady,' he said formally.

'You're in room 137,' I told him. 'It's pretty soundproof.'

'I should certainly hope so,' he said, then he lowered his voice. 'I will expect you in ten minutes. Don't be late.'

He swivelled on his heel and headed for the lift, the golf bag rattling behind him.

* * *

Ten minutes later, in the first-floor corridor, fear and excitement were gummed together, all twisted up and inseparable in my stomach. Lower down in the crotch area, excitement was winning the day, though, routing fear up into the far reaches of my brain, where it had run up against the forces of rationalisation.

It will be fun, they said. He is experienced. He will know how far is too far, and will stop well before that point. I will know how it feels, so I don't have to wonder any more. I might like it. I probably will like it, if those sticky night-time fantasies of merciless taskmasters are anything to go by. Merciless taskmasters. Chase. Oh, if only Dr Lassiter could be him.

I knocked on the door.

He opened it slowly and stood at the crack, ushering me in with a look so genuinely terrifying that I reconsidered my plan for a second.

'So you are here. I applaud your courage,' he said, directing me to the centre of the room where I was to stand, feeling spotlit, while he ran through the drill.

'Sophie, I gather that this is entirely new to you. You have never practised submission?'

'No, nothing like it, really. Maybe in a very playful form, but ... you know ... that's all.'

'I see. And which aspects of this practice do you most wish to try out? I can accommodate most tastes. What would you like to gain from today's session?'

Lassiter was circling me, not in an intentionally intimidating way, but I felt intimidated all the same. And I quite liked it. It reminded me of being in Chase's office.

'What you were doing with Rachael,' I began haltingly. 'That's what I want to try. It doesn't have to be a scene or anything. You don't have to role-play. I just want to know what it feels like.'

'Corporal punishment?'

The words gave me a frisson. 'Yes.'

He smiled, not reassuringly. 'Well, given the circumstances that led you here, that would be entirely appropriate. I was tempted to bend you over the chair with Rachael and stripe the pair of you last week, I must admit.'

'I'm sorry about that,' I repeated. 'It was a difficult call.'

'Well, you called wrong, didn't you? But never mind. You will pay for it.'

Something in his sinister tone was causing patches of wet warmth to seep into my knickers. I almost felt like kneeling and begging for mercy, and yet I didn't want mercy. I wanted punishment.

'Before we proceed,' said Dr Lassiter, 'I need to make a couple of things clear. First of all, do you have a safeword?'

'Oh . . . I suppose I should . . .'

'I see you haven't thought of this. We shall use the traffic light system then. You may call "amber" if you want me to ease up or slow down or you need to tell me something. If you call "red" you want me to stop, unequivocally. Does that make sense to you?'

'Yes,' I said gratefully. 'Red to stop altogether, amber to change or slow down. Green if it's good, yes?'

'Yes. Perhaps "bearable" rather than "good".' There was a hint of ghoulish humour behind his clipped phrasing. 'Secondly, do you expect any sexual element to the experience? It's entirely up to you.'

'Ah.' I had been unsure of this, but was glad he was asking the question rather than making an assumption. Dr Lassiter was not what you might call a handsome man, and he was older than my usual type, but his dry verbiage and his absolute poker-straightness were strangely compelling. I would only have to go and masturbate afterwards anyway. 'Well, I think I would like you to be in charge, completely.

Consider my body yours to use however you want. You know, as part of ... the price I have to pay. That seems to be the way the dynamic should be, if it's going to be hot instead of just painful.'

'Mine to use however I want?' His eyebrows jumped; he was taken aback. 'That is a reckless invitation, Sophie. It's lucky for you that I am a gentleman, isn't it?'

That frisson again. 'I don't know,' I said saucily, biting my lip. 'Is it?'

There was a moment laden with significance, then he turned to the bed and emptied the contents of his golf bag. A thing that looked like a table-tennis bat, a leather strap, a crook-handled cane. A bottle of lotion and another of lubricant. A pack of condoms. The cloak and mortarboard, which he put back in the bag. We will not be role-playing, the action told me. This will be 'real'.

He turned back to me, clasping his hands together against his chest and looking me up and down. I shuffled diffidently on my Mary-Janed feet, feeling the hem of my kilt brush against my sock-clad knees.

'Your manners last week, young lady, left a lot to be desired, didn't they?'

'Uh ... did they?'

'Yes, they did. And you will address me as "Sir" when you speak to me. You acted in haste and your impetuosity led to considerable embarrassment.'

'I know. I'm sorry, Sir.' I stared at the ground, just as if I was back at school, being berated for late homework. I would find it hard to take this seriously from most men, but somehow Dr Lassiter had that knack of unlocking your shame and playing with it. Was it something he had learned to do, or did it come naturally?

'I daresay you are, but that does not preclude you from suffering the consequences of your actions. You and I both know that you need a sharp reminder of what constitutes acceptable behaviour. Ask me for it, please, Sophie.'

My head shot up. *Ask* him? In words? From my own lips? I could tell that he was suppressing some satisfied amusement behind his mask of severity; he knew I had not been expecting this.

'I cannot proceed unless you have spoken the words,' he said softly. I supposed it made sense that he needed my explicit and unambiguous consent. Perhaps, then, it was only fair.

'Oh ... right. Please will you ...' I hesitated, not sure I could say the 'p' word, so weighted did it seem with mortifying sexual connotations.

'Please will I?' he prompted, gently but firmly.

My volume dropped to a whisper. 'Please will you punish me, Sir?' I looked past the side of his head, not wanting to see how his face reacted to my words. The wall mirror needed polishing, I noticed. This was Jade and Maria's floor; no doubt the lazy bitches had been slacking off again. I would have to have a word with Elaine, the head of Hospitality Services. I was jolted out of my dissociation by Lassiter's voice, strong and confident now.

'Indeed I will.' He beckoned me towards him, seating himself on the edge of the bed. 'Place yourself over my lap, young lady.'

Now was the time to giggle and make jokey remarks, but somehow I could not. Something inside me did not want this to be simple light-hearted fun. Something inside me really wanted to submit, to gain his approval, to be a good girl. It was all wrapped up in my feelings for Chase in one way or another. Perhaps I wanted it whipped out of me.

I lowered myself tentatively on to the sharply creased trouser legs of Dr Lassiter, hoping I wouldn't flatten them. Still, at least there was a trouser press in the room. My

elbows sank into the duvet beyond him, while my legs
rested in the featherdown at his opposite side. My lower
torso was elevated, presenting my bottom as the target; he
tucked my knees up against his thigh so that I was
half-kneeling, raising my arse higher.

'Good, Sophie. Now, while you are under my authority,
you will abide by my rules. You may cry and squeal as much
as you like, but you may not try to shield yourself from your
punishment, nor may you break position. If you do either of
these things, I will bring a stronger implement to bear on
your rebellious bottom. Do you understand me?'

'Yes, Sir.'

The words, the way they were spoken, the significance of
them, were making me shiver. I shivered even more when
he took the hem of my kilt and raised it to my waist, leaving
my white cotton knickers and stripy socks on display.

'Are these regulation socks, Miss?' he demanded ominously.

'I'm . . . not sure.'

'I do not think they are. There will be an additional
penalty to pay for those.'

Woe is me. His hand descended to the top of the socks, a
finger running beneath the turn-ups, then it ran up my bare
thighs and came to rest on the twin cotton-covered crests of
my bum. He moved the hand around as if taking measure-
ments, up the hill and down the dale and even swooping a
finger along the valley, which made me jiggle my hips.

'Such pale skin you have, Sophie. Let's see if we can't put
a bit of colour in these cheeks.' The first smack rang out,
sudden and shocking enough to make me gasp, although
not in itself terribly painful. The succeeding volley lulled
me, made me think that this was, after all, a pleasure game,
a bedroom folly. They were not hard nor fast, just little
warming slaps that made me want to moan and push my

bum out for more. His hand was firm but considerate, covering the entire area of my big school-issue knickers and sometimes straying over the elasticated border to my unprotected thighs, which stung, but in a good way.

He was lecturing me as he spanked away, but I was not catching much of it, though the steady rumble of his voice added to my enjoyment, enabling me to lose myself in the punishment fantasy. The sense of being at his mercy intensified the sensations, making much more of it than the usual bedroom rough and tumble. The warmth became heat, and the heat was not only on my rear cheeks. It had spread and was now oozing between the lips of my sex, a liquid fire that interfered with my ability to keep still beneath Dr Lassiter's hand. I began to grind myself against his thighs, wiggling my bottom and gasping.

He stopped abruptly and said my name in a warning tone. His fingers plunged between my legs, pushing the cotton up inside my streaming lips so that a damp stain spread across the whiteness.

'You are making a mess of these knickers,' he said, tutting. 'I think it's time they came down, don't you?'

'Oh!' I snuffled my protest, trying to trap his fingers between my thighs, but he escaped and wrenched the knickers down to my knees, keeping them there.

The air circulated around my wet pussy and warm bottom. He put his hand back down on my rear. 'Well, Sophie, your bottom is pink, but what colour are you? Still green?'

I nodded vigorously. *Don't you dare stop*, I said in my head.

'Good. I think we can take things up a level, then. See if we can get you properly hot.'

I was not sure it was possible to get much hotter, but I supposed he meant my skin rather than my libido.

His hand began to fall faster, stingier, peppering my cheeks with shot. Instinctively I tried to put a hand back to shield my bum from this new campaign, but he pre-empted me, twisting my wrists up into the small of my back while the smacks continued in a random unpattern, sometimes down as far as my knees. Now I was writhing with discomfort, considering calling 'amber' but knowing that I would despise myself if I did. This was nothing, surely. But, oh, it really didn't feel like nothing. It felt like searing vengeance on my poor bottom, and the worst of it was that I had no idea when it would end. I compromised with myself, moaning, 'Pleeease stop, it huuuurts,' instead of mentioning a colour. Somehow, though, I knew that this would inspire his arm to swing higher and his hand to slap harder, which it did.

'Now you're getting what you deserve, Sophie,' he said. 'You're beginning to glow.' I could vouch for that. His hot rain stopped abruptly; I sighed and pushed my bottom up, wanting his fingers to slip down into my burning crevasse. To my infinite joy, he took me up on the offer.

'Hmm, dripping wet,' he observed, skating around my eager spread, pushing in and pressing down. 'Perhaps this is not punishment for you, Sophie? You seem to be finding some pleasure in it? Is that so?'

'No, Sir, no, I don't,' I lied, backing shamelessly into his touch. 'It's awful, Sir. It's too painful for me.'

'Ten strokes of the hairbrush for your dishonesty,' he decreed, withdrawing his fingers with a squelch and reaching for a large wooden-backed number from the bedspread selection.

I flopped back on to his lap, defeated and doomed. The brush cracked down and it really, really hurt. Only ten of these, I told myself, I could handle ten. *Mamma mia*, but I had no idea wood was so hard! I would have congratulated myself at this point for my choice of soundproofed room, if only I could have thought of anything beyond the sizzling heat and swingeing impact of the oval terror at my rear. What made it more difficult still was that he seemed to be concentrating on just one area – the crease between buttock and thigh, sensitive flesh stretched taut in my bent position. I howled through the remaining nine strokes, then fought to regain my breath.

'Good girl, Sophie; you took that well,' he praised, putting the brush aside.

'More than ten of those would definitely have been amber,' I gasped, and then I lost the words again because his hands were returning to soak in my juices a second time.

'Do you like to hand control over?' he asked me, working busily on my tenderised clit.

'I think so,' I wibbled. Two fingers slipped inside, possessing me.

'Good. I am responsible for you today, Sophie. I am responsible for your punishment, but also for your pleasure. What I want you to do now, Sophie, is tell me when your climax is close. Can you do that?'

'Yes, Sir,' I wailed stickily, riding his hand, luring it up inside, knowing it would take very little. I felt on fire inside and out, tensed as a bowstring. When I snapped there would be a white-out of sensation.

I rocked up and down, sucking him in. I could feel the pressure rising, a counterpoint to the fading sting of my bottom; it would not be long, it was close, I was close. 'I am close, Sir,' I confessed unevenly.

He took his hand away and smacked my bottom hard.

'NO!' I cried.

'Dirty girl,' he gloated. 'Come and look at yourself.'

He stood, toppling me to my feet, then turned me away from him and tucked my skirt into my waistband. I had to keep the knickers at my knees while I waddled over to the full-length mirror on the wardrobe.

I looked over my shoulder, transfixed by the scarlet skin which faded to pink further down my thighs before graduating to its normal whiteness. I looked well tended to and thoroughly chastised.

'I haven't finished with you yet,' Lassiter murmured into my neck, his hands at my hips. 'But you need a break. Rachael's rear end is hardened and can take a lot more in one session. You need a little more TLC.' TLC. Tender loving care. Even as my bottom throbbed, I felt undone by the phrase. He was in control, he was hurting me, and yet he was caring for me. It was a dizzying thought.

I allowed the thought to dizzy me for the entire half-hour I spent in the corner with my hands on my head, waiting for Dr Lassiter to finish drinking a mineral water and do some kind of techy thing with his PDA, all the while taking in an eyeful of my exhibited bottom. I was conscious of its diminishing heat as much as of my slicked thighs, growing colder while my clitoris cried for attention. If Lassiter would only go to the bathroom, I could touch it. Oh, how I needed to touch it.

But he remained obstinately present until he called me back over, gave me a draught of water and then ordered me to bend over the bedside chair.

'You're cooling, girl – we need to heat you back up again, don't we?'

'Erm, yes, Sir,' I replied uncertainly. Still unused on the bed lay a supple-looking strap and a whippy-looking cane, by far the two most villainous characters of the bunch. I had a feeling I was going to want to remember my safe-words.

'Now then, Sophie, for your curious choice of hosiery, I intend to lay this strap across every part of your skin, from the tops of your socks to the centre of your bottom, until it is quite, quite hot. I estimate that I will need to place twenty strokes to achieve this end. I am going to make you count each one. Do you understand?'

'Yes, Sir.' Twenty sounded like a lot. But it was better than an undetermined number. I gritted my teeth, flexed my toes and gripped the side of the chair hard. I did not want to fail myself, or him.

The first crack of the strap was breathtaking; my teeth clenched so hard I thought they would break as I hissed through them. But through the fire I managed, 'One, Sir,' and braced myself for the next. Dr Lassiter took it slowly, magisterially, laying each scorching line with deadly accuracy, one above the other. A couple of times I let go of the seat and leapt up, clutching at my bum, but he merely waited patiently for me to resume my position and then the next whistled down.

At ten, I had to invoke amber. He knelt beside me, rubbing my tight skin, speaking words of reassurance, telling me we could stop here and now if I wanted and I had done so well already, remarkably well for a novice, and should be proud of myself. The whisperings nerved me; I told him I could take the rest, and I did.

Twenty solid strokes until my arse was lit up like Blackpool illuminations and hot enough to cook a fry on. 'Twenty, Sir,' I mewed in jubilation, my legs like jelly, my forehead dripping, my knuckles white, but my sex aflame and needier than I had ever known it.

'Well done, Sophie; you deserved that,' said Dr Lassiter. 'Stay there, part your thighs a little more.'

His hands were upon the inside of each leg, swooping upwards, gathering the juices, marinating in them, and then he granted me the orgasm I had been craving, crooning into my ear while the bubble burst and my legs buckled beneath me. He caught me, wrapping an arm around my waist, bringing me safely to my knees.

I felt an urge to worship him, a peculiar gratitude. Gratitude for giving me a bottom sorer than sunburn – what was I thinking? Perhaps I really was a closet submissive. He sat himself down in the bedside chair and patted my head.

'I like my submissives to thank me for their punishment,' he said, half-smiling. 'I go to a lot of trouble to keep you girls on the straight and narrow, after all.'

His hand was on the buckle of his belt. I knew exactly what he meant.

My mouth full of rigid prick, I glanced sideways at the bed, noticing that the cane remained untested, wondering if this really was it, or whether there was more. My bum, transferring warmth to the heels it sat gingerly upon, was probably not capable of taking any more. All the same, I could not help but wonder. Was it that much worse than the strap? Was it really the instrument to fear above all others? I licked lavishly up Lassiter's shaft, squeezing the base until he spurted in my mouth, pulling at my hair and thrusting fast so that no drop of seed escaped my throat.

I ran my tongue around my lips and smiled coyly up at him. A certain lassitude had overtaken Lassiter and he even returned my smile, hazily, his fingers fumbling to replace the detumescing cock in its hiding place.

I looked back at the bed, and his eyes followed mine.

'I don't think you're ready for the cane yet, Sophie,' he said wearily. 'Perhaps another time.'

'Oh, I don't want a proper caning,' I assured him. 'But . . . couldn't you give me one stroke? I just want to know what it feels like.'

He mopped his brow, exhaled hard. 'You're an interesting girl, Sophie.' He paused, wiping at his face with a handkerchief, crisp and smart as the rest of him. 'Go on, then, get up,' he said with a show of reluctance.

I took my final position, hands on the bedframe, legs spread, arse up, while he whipped the cane through the air, practising angles. The sound it made was frightening enough that I thought of abandoning the plan, falling forward on to my stomach and sleeping off my post-thrashing enervation, but I had asked for it, and I was going to go through with it.

He tapped it gently against my reddened flesh. 'This will hurt, I can guarantee it,' he said sharply. 'Last chance to back out.'

'No, give it to me,' I insisted, my own worst enemy as usual.

He drew back, the air sang, the cane fell, absurdly quiet in its impact, and for a second I just thought, 'Oh! Is that it?' Then white stars of torment sparked in a line; I jumped up and palmed the welting stripe, trying to push it back inwards.

'Red!' I exclaimed, turning around to Lassiter with popping eyes and a near-dislocated jaw.

'Yes,' he conceded, nodding sagely. 'So you'll believe me next time, won't you?'

'Yes, Sir,' I said contritely.

'Good. Now if you lie down on your stomach, Sophie, I have a lotion that can ease the effects. And I'll ring down to room service while I'm at it. I think you deserve a little treat now.'

Lotion notwithstanding, I had to watch how I was sitting for a few days afterwards. But it didn't put me off. I still call on his services from time to time when my itch for Chase is driving me insane. Six of the best take the edge off quite nicely, I find.

The Manager #2

My lunatic infatuation with Chase led me down some strange avenues. If most of them were dead ends, at least I gained a little better understanding of my psychogeography on the way.

A few months after my disastrous Christmas campaign, I began to worry that my promiscuity was what held him back. After all, we had a good working relationship, there was a definite spark between us and he often expressed concern for me in small ways – a cup of tea, an extra break, a more comfortable chair, insistence that I take all my annual leave. If we were friends, what stopped us being lovers? My reputation, that was what. It must be.

I began to avoid the bar after working hours, spending my evenings out in the city taking photographs of its desolate corners. That summer, you were more likely to find me beneath the dripping archway of a 1930s council block than in a luxury hotel bed. Kebab shops with missing neon letters in the signage replaced the Michelin-starred restaurant. I lurked in hidden places, wanting to obscure myself, wanting to be taken seriously.

At work, my hemlines dropped and necklines rose. I kept my hair scraped back and replaced my contacts with square-framed spectacles – smaller, feminised versions of Chase's own. I kept my nose to the grindstone, my make-up neutral and my presence minimally noticeable. I was discreet, understated and sober. I was not a slut.

God, it was boring.

Chase gave me some curious glances in the first few weeks, but refrained from comment. I took to working late when he did. When the restaurant was dark and the lobby empty but for the stragglers on their way back from shows and clubs I would rearrange the Reception desk yet again, singing under my breath, 'There are worse things I could do/Than go with a boy or two . . .'

Sometimes my gentleman friends would pitch up at the desk, ask when they could see me, what was I doing, was I OK. I fobbed them all off with a tight smile, until I became bored with the rigmarole and told them I had genital warts. Only a couple continued to bother me after that.

One night in late July, I was filing and singing again. 'But to cry in front of you/That's the worst thing I could do.' I finished crooning and looked up at the door of Chase's office. He was standing there, peering into the lowlit Reception area, frowning at me.

'Sophie, it's past midnight. Why are you still here?'

His jacket was off, collar undone; he looked tired and drawn and yet still incandescently sexy.

I did not know how to answer the question. 'Just wanted to tidy up,' I mumbled, continuing to arrange a selection of tourist guides into height order.

'Go home,' he said tersely.

'You're still here,' I pointed out, my heart beating a little faster at my own temerity. 'I can make you coffee, if you want.'

His fingers tightened on the door handle. 'Go home,' he repeated.

I went and took a series of pictures of a deserted greyhound stadium. By four o'clock I was naked in my bed, and the night had turned out differently. Chase was with me. He was on me. He was in me. He gave himself to me, and took me for his own. My legs were open for his cock, my mouth for his tongue, his hands pinned my wrists above my head and he ravished me, insatiable thrust by thrust, until I was screaming, and even then he didn't stop but just flipped me over on to all fours and pushed back in for another turn. Spent and dazed, I watched the ceiling circle above, my hand still grasping his fat cock. Except it wasn't his fat cock. It was my fat vibrator. And now some DJ was wittering from my alarm clock, telling me that the Talgarth Road was already jammed and there were delays on the Northern Line.

I was dead on my feet, but I splashed cold water on my face, ran a bath and fell asleep in it. When I woke up, it was to my mobile phone playing a tortured version of the March of the Toreadors. I shook my head, took in the midmorning sunshine streaming through the louvred glass. I had to be late for work.

Running wetfooted into the bedroom with a towel pressed to my front, I discovered that my surmise was correct. It was ten to eleven; I should have been at the front desk by nine. Fucking fuckity fuck, Chase was going to be furious. I dragged on a demure linen shirt dress and a light blazer, low-heeled sandals and massive sunglasses and ran out to the station with my hair still wet.

On the train I tried to calm my nerves by imagining the scene the way I wanted it. I would be called into his office. He would tell me he was disappointed in me; he knew I was capable of a better performance. He did not want to blemish my record with a written warning, but there was no question that discipline was called for. He would bend me over the desk ... yes, then he would lift my dress ... then he would spank me, not too hard, just enough to make me wet ... then he would pull down the knickers and fuck me hard from behind, reminding me throughout that he insisted on punctuality and professionalism from his staff. Once he had filled me with his spunk, I would have to pull up my knickers and keep it there for the rest of the day. Or . . . no, that would not happen. Once he had ejaculated, he would draw me into his arms and kiss me passionately, telling me that he had resisted me for so long his strength was sapped and he must now have me for ever. Or perhaps he would do that before spanking me? Or would he just smile and say we both needed a day off and take me out for a picnic in the park first, where we would lie in the shade of a spreading oak and . . .

My station.

'Christ, Sophie, where have you been?' squeaked Jade, one of the chambermaids, who had been filling in for me on the front desk.

'Sorry, sorry, how mad is Chase, scale of one to ten?'

'Oh, not really,' said Jade in her airy New Zealand twang. 'He seemed OK. Mind you, I can never tell with him. He's a funny kind of guy, don't you think?'

Hmm, well, Jade prefers girls, so I suppose I can forgive her lack of judgement. 'Funny kind of guy' indeed.

'Funny ha ha or funny peculiar?' I mused, frowning at my computer screen. No major meltdown was in evidence, which was pretty good going for Jade.

'Oh, you know, he's kind of aloof, isn't he? Nobody knows much about him.'

'I know what I need to know. Which is that he pays my wages,' I lied. There wasn't room in the British Library for the volume of information I wanted on Christopher Chase Esq.

'I guess,' said Jade doubtfully. Our speculations were cut short by the man himself, emerging from his office. Speak of the devil, as they say. Is he devil? Or is he angel? I think a blend of both. Oh, please, Lord, let me find out one day.

'Ah, Sophie. A word please,' he said. I could not deduce much from the tone. It was mild, but was it deceptively mild? Could I expect a tongue-lashing to rival anything Lassiter's canes could deal, or would he be sympathetic? I was a bit too spaced out to feel the fear as I stepped across his threshold.

'Thank you, Jade, just another ten minutes or so and then you can go home. I do appreciate this,' he said from the doorway. This sounded like a blatant attempt to guilt-trip me, so as soon as we were alone I began to blurt apologies.

'Hush.' He dismissed my outpourings with a wave of his hand, coming across to sit opposite me at his desk. 'Coffee?'

I nodded dumbly and watched him pour me a cup from the cafetière on the shelf behind him.

'Strong, I should think,' he said, hitching his eyebrows at me as he looked down his nose. I smiled nervously.

He pushed the cup and saucer across the desk and watched me sip for a minute or two, arms folded, before sitting back down.

'Sophie, is there something I should know about?' he asked at last.

I swallowed nervously, the coffee scalding my throat.

'I don't think so.' Except that I am being eaten alive by my maddening love for you, of course.

'Everything all right at home?'

'Fine.'

'Are you happy here?'

'Oh, completely.'

'Sure?'

'Positive. Why?'

'You aren't the woman I hired. You don't act like her or dress like her. You seem to have . . . lost yourself.'

'Oh, do I? I am the same person, I promise you.'

'You're exhausted. You haven't taken any leave since

Easter. Take a week off, Sophie. Go to the coast, or the countryside, or just spend the week in bed if that's what it will take. I need you refreshed.'

'I'm fine,' I floundered, though I really wasn't. He wanted me to be a slut again? For ... oh, I got it! The bar takings must have been down. That was all I was to him – a pound sign. A prostitute.

'You're not fine,' he insisted. 'I don't want to see you here after you finish this shift until next week.'

'Fine!' I said venomously. He gave me a startled and curious look. 'Whatever you say. You're the boss, after all.'

I set down my cup with a violent china clash and flounced out of the room.

'Jeez, Sophie, are you OK? Did he give you a hard time?'

'Go! Go home!' I said.

'Oh, right. See ya.' She left, with an uncertain backward glance at me. The words, 'Wouldn't wanna be ya' reached my acute ears despite the low muttering. Once she was through the door, I dropped to my knees behind the desk and began to cry all over the piles of leaflets underneath.

I took Chase's advice and got out of the city. Instead of photographing derelict factories and windswept under-passes, I captured bucolic scenes of sheep and cottage gardens. I ate cream teas in places with doilies on the tables and bought a National Trust season ticket. I wondered if I might be cut out for country living, imagining myself married to some rough-hewn son of the soil, frying freshly laid eggs on top of my Aga, wearing a Cath Kidston apron.

Chase would not be up for that, I was sure. Perhaps I just needed to adjust my fantasies, to let some other men into them. But the other men would not come. Chase blocked the way. I could keep him away during the day, warding him off with herbaceous borders and duckponds and elderflower cordial. But at night he seeped through the casement windows like toxic erotic fog, curling into my brain through my ears and nostrils.

'This isn't you, Sophie,' he would say in his rich, distinctive voice. 'Clean country air is for wholesome girls. You belong to the exhaust fumes and the roadside pizza stands and the cigarette smoke. You belong to the dark. You belong with me.'

He would lift my skirt and brace me against an alley wall or a railway bridge and have me in the street, his belt buckle jingling with each forward stroke, careless of the crowd of voyeurs that would build up around us. He had a lesson for me, and the lesson was that I was his.

It was no use. The longest holiday in the furthest-flung resort on Earth could not prise Chase off my consciousness. I might as well just get back to work. And order a new vibrator. Clearly I was going to need one.

A month later, I was grabbing a post-shift lunch in the bar. I was actually wearing a trouser suit for the first time in two years; if anything was symbolic of my new rule of chastity, that was it. Never more would I be felt up in the lift or bent over a washroom sink. One of my former 'client'/lovers was in the room, but he had learned not to approach me now. He peered moodily over his pint at me from time to time, but I ignored him and pretended extreme interest in the rocket salad on my plate.

So successful was my pretence that I did not even notice Chase crossing the room towards me until he had slipped into the seat opposite and adjusted his glasses for maximum staring-down-nose impact.

'Who are you?' he opened, somewhat confusingly.

'Um, Sophie Martin, your receptionist, last time I checked.' I hoped he wasn't having some form of brain seizure.

'Are you though?' No, it wasn't a brain seizure. He was making a point. He wanted to talk about me! I wanted to talk about us, but this was a start.

'What is the point you are making?' I asked, as politely neutral as I could be. 'Have I done something wrong?'

'No, no, nothing wrong as such. But when I hire a person, it's because they have particular and special qualities. I want those qualities to be sustained throughout their employment.'

'And ... what were those qualities then?' I asked, holding my breath for his reply.

'Don't you remember?' He gazed at me wistfully; my heart began to pound. 'It was nothing to do with your telephone manner or your filing skills, was it?'

An ugly obstruction in my chest made my voice come out wrong. 'You hired me because I was good for business. You hired me to whore for you.'

'Sophie, no!' he said, obviously alarmed that I might burst into tears. Not without foundation – I was even more alarmed than he was at the prospect.

'What then?' I managed to blurt.

'Sophie, listen to me. There aren't many people in this organisation I would retain after they had accused me of being a pimp.' He smiled self-deprecatingly. 'But you are one of them, and I want to tell you why. Now, I don't know what has happened to change you. I don't know and I don't want to know.' He gave me a very significant look. He *did* know. 'The quality I hired you for, and which seems to have fled lately, is *joie de vivre*. A certain sparkle. A swing in your walk. A sense that you would be fun to spend time with. The customers relate to that. The ladies want to share cocktails and dirty stories with you; the gentlemen want to take you to bed. It works.'

'What if I don't want the gentlemen to take me to bed?' I

felt stubborn. I did not want to hear this, unless he was about to declare himself as one of those gentlemen.

'What if you do?'

He had steepled his fingers and laid his head on one side. 'What if I do? I don't understand.'

'You used to,' he said bluntly. 'And now you don't. Have you, if I might ask a personal question, Got Religion?'

I snorted. 'I think not.'

'Right. So why the Born-Again Virginity? You seemed a woman who was at one with her sexual appetites, Sophie. And now you don't. It saddens me to see it.'

'Perhaps I'm looking to direct my sexual appetites towards just one person,' I said pointedly.

'Well, perhaps you are,' said Chase without missing a beat. 'But what if that one person never materialises? Will you, as the girl in your current favourite song says, throw your life away on a dream that can't come true?'

I had to take a deep breath. This was all a little too close to the bone.

'Who says he'll never materialise?'

'Oh, nobody is saying that, Sophie. But sometimes people are prevented from following the path they really want to take. Sometimes there is too much standing in the way.'

He looked, for a moment, achingly sad. I thought about asking him if he was married after all, then thought better of it. Keep things cryptic, make no personal admissions, and perhaps we can maintain our fragile fantasies.

'Yes,' I said softly. 'I see what you mean. But some people want their future partners to wait for them. Or at least to be a little less . . . excessive . . . than I have been. Some people think an interesting sexual history devalues a woman.'

'A person like that would be wrong for you, Sophie,' he said. 'Some people love a confident, adventurous, experienced woman. Given half a chance.'

'Given half a chance,' I whispered an echo. Oh, Chase. Whoever she was, I hoped she was worth it.

He sat back, unclasping his hands, raising his voice a little. 'I suppose what I'm saying, Sophie, is that you should do what you like. Enjoy yourself. Get that twinkle back in your eye. I won't think any less of you, and neither will this shadowy future lover of yours.'

He stood abruptly and stalked away to his office. The rocket salad was getting limp, the small appeal it had had to begin with rapidly diminishing. I twisted the weedy strands with my fork, thinking over what Chase had said. It made sense.

Whether there was any prospect of ending up with him or not, it was likely I had a long wait ahead of me. Maybe an eternal one. What kind of waiting room would I most want to kick my heels in? An austere bunker full of copies of didactic texts? Or a pleasure garden designed to my own specifications?

I went home and put the trouser suit on eBay.

My next shift started at two the next day, but I had an hour or so to kill beforehand. I leant against the arched entrance to the bar and looked over the heads of the drinkers, searching for familiar faces. If I smoothed a hand across the front of my pencil skirt I could feel the telltale bump of a suspender snap. My ankles thought they had come home at last, back in heels that made them work their little tendons and sinews. A red-haired banker I had given head to a few times looked over and caught my eye. I fluttered my fingers in a flirtatious little wave and winked. Maybe it was his lucky day. Maybe it wasn't. I hadn't decided yet. But whatever I decided was fine. My pleasure was my business, just as it should be.

Taking Dictation

I have become quite friendly with Rachael over the months since my first taste of the tender mercies of Dr Lassiter. She has taken to catching a later train home and joining me for a drink in the bar, or a coffee behind the Reception desk if I can't get away. She revels in showing me her marks, and gives me a wince-inducing blow-by-blow account of proceedings before we move on to more general chit-chat, or sometimes more specific discussion of the fascinations of Dominance and Submission.

'How did you know?' I asked her one rainy Monday afternoon, watching the streaming smoked glass from a corner booth in the bar.

'How?'

'Yeah, how. And when? When did you know?'

'I always knew,' she said laconically. 'Well, deep down, at least. Maybe not on the surface.'

'So what brought it to the surface?'

'Ah, it's a long story.'

'My shift finished ten minutes ago. I have all evening.'

'Oh, so do I. OK then. You sure you want the full story?'

'I always want the full story.'

'OK. Two more vodkatinis and then I'll begin.'

Rachael took a year out after graduating and decided to earn a bit of Interail cash by temping at the tax office. It was the most boring job imaginable – tons of photocopying on an ancient machine that didn't even have a collate facility, so she had to put the hundreds of twenty-page booklets together by hand, day in day out, week in week out. On the plus side, this was highly conducive to daydreaming, so while the copier flashed and hummed she was on the battlements of a Castilian castle, or eating *moules marinière* on the Breton seafront. Usually in these daydreams she had wandered off without the gaggle of girlfriends she was planning the trip with. She would find herself lost and alone in the streets of a medieval walled city, or on an isolated beach, or a terraced vineyard that stretched for miles beneath a mellow sun. And this was where He would turn up. He might be a Carlos or a Jean-Pierre or a Giovanni, but he would always have a Southern European goldenness about him; he would taste of sunshine and olive oil. Dark curls, broad shoulders, strong features, passion, seduction . . . and, most importantly, a cute accent. She longed to be called 'Cherie' or 'Bella' or 'Guapa'. 'Luv' was just not doing it for her.

At lunchtime she would bolt from the office as quickly as possible and eat her sandwich on a bench overlooking a war memorial. Anything so as not to have to associate with the dreary drone-boys of the Inland Revenue, in their cheap suits and stinking aftershave, with their dull chatter about Beckham and Oasis in their horrible accents. Why did English boys have to be so unappealing? She was born in the wrong country, she mused, biting into her tomato and basil focaccia. The two boyfriends she had had at university had been nice enough, but without the rudiments of finesse. One of them had bought her flowers, once, but the most romantic gesture she could usually expect was a portion of chips in curry sauce after the clubs kicked out. The men around here would have to raise their game, she decided grimly, or she was going to marry an Italian man and leave them to their football and beer. (She conveniently airbrushed the Italian passion for soccer out of her fantasy.)

Then it would be two o'clock, and time for more copying and collating, over and over, hour in hour out, until doomsday. Except for that one day, a Thursday, when everything changed.

Paul Everett was the Senior Executive Officer, the final destination for the buck in this neck of the tax woods. Rachael had no opinion of him really, except that he was too boring to even look at, but luckily seemed to like her. He had given her the job, at least, so he must do. His fond indulgence seemed to have left him today, however, for he was looking distinctly rumpled.

'Rachael, did you make up these booklets?'

She squinted at them: *Distraint Procedures 32a(1987)*.

'Er, yeah, I think so.'

'There's a problem with them.'

'No, there isn't.'

For the first time, Rachael noticed the power of his eyes, which seemed to turn her to stone with the intensity of their glare.

'Come with me,' he said finally, once his astonishment at being defied by a temporary Admin Assistant had abated. She shrugged and followed him past the rows of dusty desks and plastic trays to his office door. Why did offices have to be so drab? She thought continental European offices would be different; full of greenery with light tiling and a smell of freshly ground coffee.

Everett's office was a little better, she supposed, but still everything was that muted grey-brown except for the hospital-green walls. These places were designed to strip the colour from your soul, she thought. What she didn't realise was that she had thought it out loud.

'I beg your pardon?' Paul Everett was discomposed, frowning at her.

'Oh!' Her hand slapped her mouth. 'I didn't ... sorry.'

'Perhaps you'd be happier working somewhere more ... vibrant.'

'No, honestly!' she gabbled. The civil service might not pay very well, but it was easy work that made no mental or physical demands on her. If she left she'd have to get bar work or waitressing – all that running around. So stressful.

'I know you don't intend to make a career in taxation,' he said drily, 'but there is no need to sneer at those of us who do. Now, about these booklets.'

He put one into her hand. 'Page five,' he said, one eyebrow witheringly raised.

Rachael riffled through, then dropped the booklet with an appalled cry of 'Oh my God!' on finding the terrible evidence of her mistake.

'Pick it up!' Everett had gone from ignorable nonentity to person of interest in one stentorian phrase. The tips of Rachael's every fibre stood to attention; the command entered her via her ears and seemed to stir strange untended areas within. Including her groin.

She dropped to a crouch, seeing that the open booklet lay across the toe of Everett's lace-up brogue. He stabbed his foot towards her unexpectedly; she fell off-balance, grasping the shoe in both hands, bent over it with her lips inches above. Oh God. She had the wildest urge to kiss it! As if burnt, she leapt back and picked up the booklet, shooting to her feet again, wanting to look at anything but Everett's face. The face she had thought of as Bland British. Pale, slightly freckled, a little sun-damaged but with eyes whose sea-blueness she had not previously picked up on. Sandy hair that had once been ginger, receding now. And hands. Nice hands. Wedding ring! Stop!

'I'm sorry,' she whispered. 'I'll do them all again.'

Paul Everett did a strange thing. He put two fingers beneath her chin and lifted it. He kept them there long enough for her feet to start rocking and the rest of the office to blur away.

'Your travel plans are interesting,' he said, 'even if they aren't strictly relevant to the Distraint Act of 1987.'

Rachael laughed uncertainly.

'I wish I could come with you.'

'With your . . . wife . . .?'

He took his fingers away. 'We're separated,' he said. 'Last year. She's suing for divorce. Unreasonable behaviour, she says.'

'Oh.' Rachael blinked. There had been rumours. It was said that Everett was a much too frequent visitor to the Grapes next door as well. 'Are you? Unreasonable?'

He sighed, gave her a searching, hooded look. 'Probably. I probably am.'

'Oh,' she said again, feeling as if she had just been flung out of a plane with a parachute bag and no instructions. Which cord was the right one? Would she float or would she crash? 'You don't seem that bad to me . . . I mean . . . you know . . .'

'I don't know, Rachael, and I don't think you do either. Anyway. Enough of this. Administrative duties don't seem to suit you. You're overqualified for them, and yet you still manage to mess them up. I need a new PA. Why don't you do it?'

'What? Shouldn't you advertise?'

'It's just temporary. She's gone to visit relatives in Canada for three months. I believe that takes us up to the start of your World Tour, doesn't it, Rachael?'

The way he said it, and his accompanying flash of teeth, made her stomach flip-flop. It was playful and yet steely. It said, 'Don't mess with me, unless I give you permission.'

She would not have believed it, but it took just those few minutes in Everett's office for Rachael to decide that she wanted him, but only in a very particular way. Only if he took her.

He took his time with the taking. For the first four weeks, their working relationship was close, cordial, but professional. She performed all her duties well, even taking calls from the soon-to-be-ex Mrs Everett, who often made dark and cryptic remarks while leaving messages about solicitor's fees and decree nisis.

'Make sure you don't get on his wrong side, dear.'

'I bet he's got you taking dictation.'

'Just obey orders and I'm sure he'll give you a leg over, oops, I mean up.'

In the fifth week, there was a three-day taxation conference. Everett and Rachael had interconnecting rooms at the Luxe Noir. For Rachael, a luxury hotel was a new experience. Sitting opposite Everett at dinner, she was so self-conscious about using the right cutlery and not calling the napkin a serviette that she knocked back her first glass of wine a little too quickly.

'This place is amazing,' she said, staring up at the ceiling, spotlit to look like a night sky. 'Do you come here every year?'

'I spent my honeymoon here,' Everett revealed. 'Before the refurbishment, that was. There were crystal chandeliers on the ceiling back then.'

'Oh. Wow.' Rachael very much wanted to ask him about his wife, about what sort of behaviour she considered 'unreasonable'. Did she dare? She reached for the wine bottle to pour another glass, but Everett got there first and moved it beyond her reach.

'Slow down,' he said warningly. 'The starter hasn't even arrived yet.'

'Is that what your wife didn't like? Did she think you were too controlling?' Rachael kicked herself violently on the ankle at the way it had come out, but it was too late to unsay it.

'I'm surprised you'd take an interest in my marriage, Rachael, but if you must know, there was an element of that, I suppose. Just probably not in the way you mean . . .'

'In . . . what way . . . then?'

'I am quite controlling, but not as part of day-to-day life. Our marriage was an equal partnership in every area except one.'

'Except . . . one . . .'

He looked down and smiled into his wine. 'There's no reason why you'd want to know, Rachael, so perhaps we should leave it at that.'

'I do want to know,' she said. Where were all these mad words coming from? What was she trying to do?

'I'm not sure you'd be comfortable with it,' chided Everett.

'I think I would,' she countered. It was happening. Eye contact. Momentous silence. His hand, twisting the stem of the glass this way and that. It was happening.

'Two lobster bisques.'

Two plates of soup the size of dustbin lids landed in front of them. The waiter bowed his head, picking up on the atmosphere straight away, and made himself scarce.

Suddenly Rachael did not think she could eat her soup, or at least not in front of Everett. The idea of plunging the spoon into that velvety broth, the rich seafood smell of which might well remind him of . . . something else . . . and sipping it up between her lips seemed much too suggestive for polite company.

Everett seemed to feel the same, for he spent far too long fussing with the napkin and the salt cellar, looking over his shoulder as if hoping for an escape route to materialise.

It didn't. He turned back to Rachael, took a deep spoonful of the bisque and asked, 'Do you have a boyfriend?'

Rachael shook her head. 'Not at the moment.'

'Not worth it, I suppose. With your travels in the offing.'

'I can't make a commitment.'

'No, of course. You don't want to be tied down.'

Tied down. He was trying to look casual, but his spoon hovered above the soup bowl, expectant of her reply.

'Oh, I wouldn't say that,' she said, trying a mischievous glint. She wasn't sure if it came off or not.

'You don't know what you're saying,' said Everett gruffly, turning away to wipe his lips with the napkin.

'No, I suppose I don't.' Rachael gave up, threw the spoon down in the dish and stood up. 'I'm not hungry. Think I'll get an early night. See you tomorrow.'

She heard his voice calling, 'Rachael!' rather indignantly, but decided to leave him to it. She was not going to put it on a plate for him. That was not the way her fantasy worked.

Up in her room, she undressed grumpily, pulled on a robe, poured herself a glass of minibar wine and began flicking through the cable channels. She settled on an undemanding detective drama, lay back, ripped open a packet of peanuts in lieu of supper and tried to banish the frustrations of the evening from her head.

They were not easy to banish though. That phrase 'tied down' kept floating in and out and she continually found that she had missed crucial plot points in the drama whilst imagining her wrists lashed to a headboard, her legs forcibly spread for the benefit of Paul Everett, who prowled at the foot of the bed, explaining exactly what he meant to do with her helpless body.

She sighed heavily, popped the last handful of peanuts into her mouth and muted the TV. After licking the salt from her fingertips, she pulled down the top of her robe and frowned at the state of her nipples, which were definitely ready for something. Could she tie herself up? Just to see how it felt? She unlooped her dressing gown cord and wrapped it experimentally around her wrists. The soft towelling material rubbed kindly against her skin, but how would leather or metal or tape feel? Cautiously she tied one wrist to a bedpost, tugging hard to get the necessary tension. Her blood seemed to sing, the vessels fit to burst. She moved her other hand down between her legs, finding it wet and tender there. She bunched the fingers up against her clitoris and began to stroke, pulling at the cord all the while, whispering to herself the phrases a man might use to a naked bound woman.

'I'm going to use you every way I want ... oh shit!' Rachael's bedside phone began to shrill. She grappled frantically with her bonds, managing to free herself just in time to snatch the receiver from its cradle.

'Yes?'

'Rachael? It's Paul here. I need you to take dictation.'

Rachael held the phone away from her ear, trying to decipher the message, not sure she was understanding its import. His voice sounded brusque and businesslike enough. But what did he mean, 'take dictation'? It was night time. She was in bed, for all he knew.

'I'm sorry?' she said.

'I mean you are to present yourself at my door in the next sixty seconds, or there will be trouble.'

Rachael held her breath. Unless she was wildly mistaken, this was it – Taking Time.

'But I'm not dressed ...'

'Never mind that. Come as you are. Now.'

'Yes, Sir,' she whispered.

Hastily looping the cord back around her waist and

pulling the gown tightly shut over her spilling breasts and dewy thighs, Rachael did not even think to squirt a bit of liquid soap over her fingers, such was her fluster. She bolted from her room and knocked on the one next door, thinking only of meeting her minute deadline and pleasing her boss.

He opened the door, his mouth flickering a little when he saw what she was wearing despite his best efforts at keeping a stony face.

'Good,' he said, putting a hand on her shoulder and steering her to the foot of the bed, where he sat down, ready to instruct her. 'Rachael, I've decided to assume that you were not teasing me at dinner, but that my interpretation of your hints was accurate. If at any time it turns out that I have misjudged the situation, just let me know and I'll release you from this ... overtime. Clear?'

She nodded, enthralled.

'Right, take these.' He produced a notebook and pen from his breast pocket and handed them solemnly to her. When her hand came up to take them, he sniffed the air. 'What's that?' He took her fingers and pressed them to his nose, then smiled broadly, shaking his head.

'Oh, Rachael,' he admonished, his sorrowful tone patently false. 'What have you been up to in there on your own?'

Rachael's pained expression was her only reply.

'I see you can't be left alone without falling into wicked ways. It's just as well I've called you in here. It seems you need to be kept busy.'

Rachael had never stopped to consider the erotic potential of embarrassment, but now, caught out and laid bare, she felt utterly, wantonly vulnerable. Stripped of her everyday layers and veneers, she was goosepimply and yet not at all cold. Rather the opposite, if truth be told. She was thankful only that her robe still preserved a tiny bit of her modesty, because she would not have been at all surprised if the area between her legs was glowing neon-red, screaming 'Look at me! Touch me!'

But Everett was looking elsewhere, at Rachael's opposite wrist, which was braceleted with redness. 'What caused that?' he asked.

'My … er … my dressing gown. The towelling … chafes a bit.'

He narrowed his eyes, pondering this, then shook his head, apparently saving the snippet of information for later.

'Never mind. Take the pad and pen and get down on your knees, please.'

Rachael, rather relieved to have an instruction to follow which put her out of the line of Everett's scrutiny, dropped down immediately, her knees sinking into the soft deep pile of the carpet. She wondered how easy it would be to write in this position, but Everett had further instructions.

'Put the pad and pen on the carpet in front of you and lean forward on to your elbows. That's it.'

Rachael complied almost unconsciously, though once she was in position, she was strongly tempted to peer over her shoulder, aware that her robe must have ridden up near the top of her thighs now.

'Good. Now I want you to maintain that position while you copy down this contract. Are you ready?'

Rachael clicked the pen nervously, made sure her legs were clamped tightly together, and nodded.

'I didn't hear you, Rachael.'

'Yes, Sir.'

'Good. Take, as they say, a letter. "Dear Rachael."'

She coughed in surprise and craned her neck up at him, but he nodded swiftly down, returning her attention to the notepad.

'Yes, "Dear Rachael. In view of recent revelations

regarding your personal interest in my bedroom tastes" – are you getting this?'

Rachael was scribbling furiously. '"Recent ... revelations,"' she muttered.

'Ready? "I have decided to offer you the position of my submissive for the period of two calendar months." A position you are demonstrating very adequately just now.' He stood and moved behind his dedicated assistant, prodding her bare soles with the toe of his shoe.

'"I offer the following terms and conditions. You may terminate the contract at any time without notice. Your additional duties will not prejudice your principal employment nor any future references. Although I will want to tie you up and spank you, I will not seriously hurt or harm you in any way. Any and all sexual scenarios proceeding from acceptance of this contract may be halted by the utterance of the word ..." Well, what do you think?'

'A word?' asked Rachael blankly.

'A safeword. You say it when you don't want to play any more and I stop. Any ideas?'

Ideas were a long way back in Rachael's racing mind at this point, so intoxicated was she by the swirl of words she was painstakingly copying, and the enormous import behind the looping script.

'Basingstoke,' she hazarded.

He laughed. 'Why not? OK, "... the utterance of the word 'Basingstoke'. On expiry of the two-month period, I undertake to never contact Miss Rachael Bates again unless she instigates such an activity." What do you say?'

Everett had moved in front of the prostrate Rachael now, and when she looked up she saw a tall, slender column of navy pinstripe, stretching way up to the ceiling, topped off by a pale face that looked, in that moment, reassuringly anxious and vaguely kind. Not the stereotypical whipcracking man in leather at all, she thought, bemused. But a man she could probably trust. And, furthermore, a man she had grown to like, respect and even find attractive.

'I accept the terms,' she said.

He broke into a smile and dropped to his haunches in front of her.

'I'm very pleased to hear it.' His hand reached out to trace a path through her hair, moving down her cheeks until he held her chin, leant in and kissed her gently on the lips. 'Let's put our names to it, shall we?'

He picked up the notepad and signed his name in a sharp cursive hand beneath Rachael's loops and scrawls. She looped and scrawled in turn.

'We have an agreement, then,' he said briskly, rising once more to his feet. 'No, stay there. I haven't given you permission to stand. Reach down to unfasten and remove your robe, please.'

Rachael balked, but the cleft between her thighs lit up as if electrified, knowing what she wanted before her head caught up. She untied the knot, leaning awkwardly on one elbow and thanking her stars that the carpet was expensive, then slipped the towelling robe off, unsure whether she should keep down or kneel up to do it. She took the less dangerous but more clumsy route of keeping down, which earned her the praise of her new extracurricular boss. She was pleased with herself; perhaps she would turn out to be good at submitting. It was funny how easily it seemed to come to her. Even naked on all fours, being inspected by her manager, she felt that her desire for his approval overrode any discomfort at her predicament.

'Sit up for me, please, Rachael,' he ordered, and she crouched back on her heels. 'Spine nice and straight.' She threw back her shoulders, aware of the inevitable out-thrusting effect this had on her breasts. They were small, but the nipples were twice their usual size, joyous crimson attention-seekers. 'Pretty,' crooned Everett, running a finger-tip around them before pinching them slightly, causing Rachael to mew. 'Sensitive too. Now sit at the foot of the bed and spread your legs as wide as you can.'

Rachael, ever eager to please, sat her bottom gingerly on the tip of the mattress and splayed her thighs so wide that she risked straining a muscle. If they ached tomorrow, then so much the better, she thought, having always enjoyed a little bit of bodily fatigue the day after sex. She flushed and rolled her head back when Everett knelt down between her knees and moved in close to the exposed spread.

'You feel lovely,' he complimented, kneading at her lips with his thumbs and breathing warm air over her clitoris. A finger poked rudely up inside her; she squirmed upon it and he added another. 'So tight and hot. This turns you on, doesn't it? Have you done anything like it before?'

'No,' she moaned, riveted by the slow in and out of his fingers and his tormenting hot breath against her most sensitive spot.

'You must be a natural, then. Oh yes, you do feel wonderful.' He chuckled, astounded by his good fortune. 'But how do you taste, Rachael?'

She almost screamed when the tip of his tongue darted out to scoop up her juices, circling her clitoris like a hungry predator while his fingers continued to pump. Oh, this was too good, so good it was cruel, if he kept it up for much longer, she was going to . . .

He stopped, pulled out, kissed her clit then sat back, grinning.

'Not yet you don't,' he said. Rachael made a face, a red one, and stared down at her recently bereft sex, which was a similar shade, as well as shiny wet. Everett took her wrist, from which the cord marks were now fading, and examined it closely, running his fingers along the sensitive underside in a way that did not help Rachael calm down after her near-orgasm.

'How did you get this?' he asked, his eyebrow supplying the question mark. 'The truth this time, please.'

Rachael could not answer. Not from fear of disapproval, or even ridicule, but because it seemed too personal an admission.

'How do you think?' she said eventually, slightly sulkily.

'Don't answer my questions with a question, Rachael, unless you want to see how I enforce discipline. I was planning to save that for a little later on, once the dynamic was properly established.'

Rachael flushed even darker, the word 'discipline' sending fresh rushes of wetness to her core, feeling sure that Everett could see her excitement.

'Sorry, Sir,' she improvised. 'I . . . it was my dressing gown. It chafed my wrist . . . somehow.'

'Not "somehow", Rachael.' She gasped as Everett dealt a slap to her thigh, not a hard one, but it shocked her enough to bring the truth out in a tumble.

'I tied myself to the bedpost.'

'Good. There. That wasn't so hard, was it? So you really are a kinky little thing, aren't you? Have you ever been tied before?'

She shook her head.

'But you've thought about it? And you'd like to try it?'

Rachael nodded.

'Well, the dressing gown cords might not be ideal.' Everett loosened and whipped off his tie, then retrieved another from his bedside drawer. 'Silk, on the other hand, is always nice. Lie down. Arms above your head.'

Rachael found that the businesslike enunciation helped her to comply. In an essential sense, this was no different from being in the office, being told to make a call or collect a file. The relationship remained the same; it was only the nature of the tasks that varied. Rachael had always been an approval-seeker and her wired-in eagerness to please would make this easy on her.

She stared up at the ceiling, which had discreet spotlights dotted across it, imagining herself in a painting or a photograph, hanging in a gallery. What kind of comments would people make? Would they be able to guess from her stance that she was about to be tied up? Did she look like a woman embarking on a thrilling new journey into her sexuality? Or did she look like a slag? Oh dear, no, hush that nasty little voice, the voice that tells you to wall yourself up until a husband comes knocking on the door of your tower. Why is it so insistent?

She dismissed it, stretched her fingers up towards the bedpost, then gasped when the mattress sloped downwards either side of her, Everett's knees straddling her hips. Even in his suit, he looked shockingly primitive, bearing down on her to bind each wrist with a tasteful paisley-patterned tether. She almost expected him to lunge down and take a chunk from her neck. If he wanted to, he could. There would be no way of stopping him. Perhaps she ought to feel afraid – properly afraid, rather than this pleasurable tension. Everett was all right, wasn't he? His ex-wife was alive, not hacked into several pieces under the patio. It would be fine.

He crouched low over her, his hands around her bound wrists, his pale pointy nose touching hers. 'I can do anything I want to you,' he said, putting a voice to her greatest fear and greatest desire. 'But since you're a novice to this, I'm going to play fair. I'm going to ask you what you'd like me to do.'

'Oh.' Rachael had not expected this. She was calling the shots? Was that allowed? And what shots should she call?

'Well . . .' She hesitated. He moved his face to the side and murmured into her ear.

'Any ideas? Anything you like.'

He sat back on his haunches, looking down at her, smiling like the cat who got an entire dairy full of cream. It was a stirring look, a look that banished Rachael's fears and made her feel as powerful as a woman tied to a bed can possibly feel.

She smiled back. 'What you were doing before . . . that was good.'

'Making you write out a contract?'

'No! With your fingers . . . and your tongue.'

'My fingers and my tongue? Where, Rachael? Here?' He bent back down, slipping the tip of his tongue between her lips, prising open her jaw while his fingers made pleasurable ripples along her scalp and down her neck.

This was what they meant by plundering lips, she thought, opening up without complaint to the thorough probing of her mouth and throat.

He sat up again abruptly, leaving her lips stinging and raw, and began to take off his shirt. 'Was that what you meant?' he asked, unbuttoning his cuffs before flinging the garment, toreador-style, to the corner of the room.

'Not quite,' she admitted shyly, casting an eye over his lightly freckled chest. It was not exactly beefcake, but she didn't like beefcake anyway. In fact, what the heck was beefcake? Some kind of burger? No, this would do fine; the beginnings of a paunch might not get him on to the cover of *GQ* but it would feel enjoyably heavy on top of her. She had always liked to feel weighed down, almost crushed, by her lovers.

'Maybe this then?' His hands drifted down to her modest breasts, playing with them as if they were an arcade game, flicking and twisting the switches that made her light up. He dabbed his tongue across a nipple and hit the jackpot.

'Oh, not there! That's good but … lower …' pleaded Rachael.

'Lower, eh?' Everett grinned demonically. 'I'm not a toesucker, if that's what you're after.' He unbuckled his belt and swished it from its loops, doubling it over and cracking it into his palm for effect. 'Do you like a bit of pain, Rachael?' he asked, running the cold leather across her nipples and down her stomach. 'I hope you do, because soon enough I'm going to want to warm your arse with this.'

She squealed a little and bit her lip. Her heart was pounding, and her clit echoing the rhythm. To her partial relief, Everett dropped the belt to the floor with a jingling clink, then began to undo his trousers. He shifted, parting her thighs and kneeling between them, to remove them completely, getting rid of his boxers at the same time. The erect cock that sprang up from its nest of pale gold was decently proportioned and ready for action. All at once Rachael changed her mind, wanting to feel this inside her. Fingers and tongues could wait for another day.

But there were certain proprieties to attend to first.

'Oh, you're still wearing your shoes and socks,' she pointed out. Strange that a mature man would make this schoolboy error, but somehow touching.

'So I am. Getting carried away,' he muttered, pulling them off. 'You'll have to pay for that.'

'Me?'

'Oh, yes. You'll find that the fault is never mine.' He smiled again, recovering from his temporary embarrassment, and made a dive between her knees.

'I want you to fuck me!' blurted Rachael, before Everett's tongue took its chance to addle her brain.

He leant up on his elbows, perfectly triumphant, the naked civil servant.

'I'm happy to oblige,' he said. 'We ought to use protection, I suppose.'

'Yes, we ought,' said Rachael, amused by the glumness this seemed to produce.

'Some submissives don't like it,' he said, fumbling in his trouser pocket.

'Some submissives.' Rachael shrugged, finding it odd to hear herself referred to as an adjective. Everett pushed his moment of pique aside, rubbered up and returned to his predatory position, shinning up Rachael's body, lifting each thigh in his hands and sucking hard on their insides before covering her upper half, braced as if about to perform a set of athletic press-ups over her. She pushed her bottom up off the covers, digging her heels in, welcoming the new visitor to her doors, straining against the silken ties that were so much better than the dressing gown cord.

Almost abruptly, Everett surged up inside Rachael, impaling her at a stroke. He formed a cradle with his hands under her bottom, keeping it raised at the angle he needed to perform the fastest and most blistering fuck he could manage. This was going to be a statement of intent, a promise of things to come. Rachael crossed her ankles behind his back, hanging on for dear life as he began to stamp his ownership at a pounding pace, angling diagonally down so that he crossed her clitoris with each stroke.

'I could do this all night,' he growled. 'You couldn't do anything about it.'

'No, I couldn't,' she agreed happily, her words jolting out. His hands gripped her arse cheeks, pulling them apart, opening her wider to the punishing thrusts. She flexed her thighs and knees, pushing herself aggressively into his crotch, egging him on to take it harder and faster and higher.

'You do like it rough, don't you, you little trollop,' muttered Everett. 'Well, you'll get it. Hard and fast and often. Whenever and wherever. Whether you're sore or not. And you will be.'

Rachael's wrists were beginning to numb but she could not have said so, she could not have felt it, because all her blood was down between her legs. She began to keen, began to cry, began to come and Everett crashed into it with her, pushing and pulling her, marking her, taking her. Rachael yanked hard at her bonds and, with a tearing sound, one of the ties ripped in half.

Everett untied the half that was still attached to Rachael's wrist.

'Present from my wife,' he said, checking the label. 'Tested to destruction.' He aimed it at the bin and smiled tenderly down. 'I hope that was good for you.'

'Yeah,' said Rachael, still dazed. 'Good.'

'I can't quite believe my luck,' said Everett, and he untied her other wrist, kissing it back to life.

'So did you see him again?' I asked her. 'After you came back from your trip?'

Rachael smiled inscrutably into her drink.

'Only by accident. At a couple of parties. He said he wouldn't bother me once the contract was up, and he kept his word.'

'You didn't want to take it up with him again?'

'No, it wasn't that. He met somebody else while I was in Europe. They're married now, I think.'

'Oh, right. But he'd given you the taste?'

'God, yes. He'd given me the taste. I went to Europe and suddenly romantic olive-skinned guys in vineyards weren't doing it for me. It was older men in suits all the way. Would you believe, in Paris, instead of sitting at pavement cafés in Montmartre, I took to hanging around the Bourse.'

I laughed. 'Did you pull *un stockbrokeur*?'

'Nope. Most sexually frustrating year of my life. Surrounded by beautiful boys, but not remotely interested in any of them.' She sighed. 'Life has a sick sense of humour sometimes.'

'I suppose.' I sucked my orange juice through a straw. Chase passed through en route to harangue the Head Barman about something.

'Now he'd make a good dom, I bet,' said Rachael, following him with her eyes.

'No, he wouldn't,' I said hastily. 'He's gay anyway.'

'Gay? Are you sure?' She squinted at him, sizing him up.

'Might as well be,' I muttered. 'So these parties that you bumped into Everett at. Tell me about them.'

She ordered another drink.

Health and Fitness

He's at it again.

The banks of static cycles, treadmills and stepping machines might as well not exist. The non-stop VH1 on the big screen should just switch itself off, for all the attention it's going to get. Weight benches and pull-up bars are just part of the seduction furniture in this gym. For the poor sap undergoing Lincoln's Special Induction, there is nothing but Lincoln and her. I allow myself a nostalgic smile and walk away from the gym window, thinking back to the time I underwent Lincoln's Special Induction. We've all been through it, some of us more than once, and for a time it was a legend of the hospitality industry. It went a little like this.

New girl shows up at gym, asking for an induction session.

New girl is instantly floored by honed masculine perfection of Lincoln.

She turns up for induction in newly purchased most-flattering-possible Lycra outfit.

Forty sweaty minutes later, Lycra lies on the shower-room floor while Lincoln shows New Girl a whole new world of aerobic moves.

That's the bullet-point version, of course. There is more to it than that. There is the way he stands four-square, arms folded, a Mount Everest of man in a tight vest and trackpants watching you emerge from the changing rooms in your suddenly too-revealing leotard and joggers. There is his unexpectedly boyish smile coupled with his predictably velvet voice – sophistication and mischief blended inside the body of a god. Well, who could resist that? Even before he puts his wooing wheels in motion, most women are lost.

As the settings on the rowing machine ratchet up and up, so does his flirtation. There are the low-spoken compliments and the almost-but-not-quite jokey remarks. There is the encouragement, the 'believe in yourself, baby, believe you're the best' that makes every new inductee wonder if he thinks she is Special. And yes, she is always Special, for that one day.

He moves to the next stage, the touches, the hands on her calf, the massage of her shoulders, the tactile demonstration of the workings of her muscles. She feels his rock-solidity, begins to wonder if such steely flesh can ever yield or melt in the blast furnace of passion. She realises that she would very much like to know the answer to this question. She holds his gold-flecked chocolate eyes a little too long, and then he knows he has won.

'There's another kind of workout I'd like to give you, baby,' he might say. Depending on the quarry, there will be giggles, or coquettish looks, or a straightforward acquiescence. He will fetch his master key and lead her towards the sauna and shower room, which will remain locked for the next half-hour.

The shower is the wet-room sort, large and tiled in black. He will put two exercise mats down on the rubberised floor, then he will hook one enormous forearm around the small of her back and curve her against his chest. He will wait for her gasp of realisation that the swollen mound pressing into her stomach is not a skittle. Then he will capitalise on her wide eyes and gaping mouth, lifting her into his arms and kissing her into submission en route to the exercise mats.

There will be an agonisingly slow peeling off of Lycra and cotton. There will be awestruck tracing of the ridges and inlets of Lincoln's physique, which he will respond to by finding her corresponding softnesses. There will be marvelling at the satin smoothness of his shaved head and the iron rigidity of his biceps and triceps.

Now the two sets of limbs will entangle, legs within legs, arms over arms, more often than not a colour contrast of skins. Her streamlines will mould sweetly against his bulk; together they will work through a series of poses that would inspire any sculptor. Large hands over firm breasts, faces merging at the lips, manicured nails pressing into taut dark buttocks. The scanty underwear, now salty with their excitement, is finally discarded. She might find herself on her back, flexing her toes over the broadest shoulders they will ever encounter, showing off her Brazilian, or American, or French waxed mons to his single-eyed conqueror. She might find herself straddling his pelvis, hovering above that thick, straight stalk, summoning the nerve to lower herself on to its prodigious girth. Or she might be sandwiched between the shiny black tiles and his shiny black six-foot frame, drilled to the wall like a soapdish by his hardworking tool. There are many variations on this picture, enough to fill a catalogue, but they always end the same way. Whether it's hard and fast or slow and sensual, she is brought to the screaming bucking orgasm of her life while he congratulates himself on another job well done before filling the rubber sheath within the heated flesh.

'Babe,' he'll say, every single time. 'Oh, babe.' And then he'll turn on the jets and they will lie there on the drenched exercise mats, panting and moaning while the pearly droplets cleanse their steaming bodies.

They have both had what they wanted, but woe betide the woman who wants more. Lincoln has only that much to give. It is good, oh yes, is it good, but it is all you can ever expect. Or at least, it was.

Mostly, we would shake ourselves off, dust ourselves down and accept that the Special Induction was our last taste of Lincoln. Sooner or later, the women moved on. It took some of them a long time, but eventually, after fruitless months on the treadmill or the rower, they would see him work his magic on the next new girl and realise how the land lay. The thing about Lincoln was that he was always travelling towards the next peak on the horizon, always passing through and never staying. There would be a girl with bigger tits, or longer legs, or – most importantly – a more famous name along soon, and he had to be ready for her. Lincoln did not have emotions so much as an endless bedpost, incompletely notched, stretching away to infinity, representing his ego and his self-worth. Poor vulnerable Lincoln. In the end, you had to feel a little sorry for him.

I was not feeling particularly sorry for him, though, on the day his nemesis checked in.

'Hey, Sophie,' he hailed me, jogging over the lobby to the jingle of gold jewellery. 'You heard who's signed up for Inductions?'

'The Queen?' I hazarded, scarcely bothering to veil my indifference.

He unleashed that rich chuckle, the one that made every female nipple within a half-mile radius tingle.

'No, baby, you know who I mean. Our famous friends.'

'Uh huh. Kitty and Kat. I know. Did they sign up separately, or do you get them as a tag team?'

So successful had Kitty and Kat's TV sketch show proved that they were now filming a movie in the city. The plot was basically the same as all of their sketches – Kitty is beautiful but dim; Kat is frumpy but saves her friend's bacon time after time. Startlingly original premise, no? I was not a fan, I had to admit, but the girls had been friendly enough at the Reception desk and had made no ridiculous diva-ish demands of the staff, so I was prepared to accept that they weren't as annoying as their show might lead one to suspect.

'Well, I've got one after the other. Kitty at ten, Kat at eleven. I might not have time for Kat though.'

'And she doesn't have the model looks,' I pointed out sourly.

'Hey, she's a name, baby. A name doesn't need the looks. Besides, the homely girls have compensations to offer.' Lincoln winked, flashed his teeth and bounded off towards the basement health complex.

'Arrogant twat,' I mouthed in his wake, and thought no more of it.

The following day, Kat – real name Karen – rolled up at the desk to ask whether she could have another newspaper delivered to her door.

'Sure,' I said with my professional smile (which is slightly wider than my ordinary one and comes with an incline of the neck). 'Is there anything else you need?'

'No,' she said lightly, then she frowned. 'Well . . . actually . . . Kitty has been asking whether there's a decent gym in the area.'

'Oh? I thought you did the Induction at our health complex yesterday?'

Kat sucked in her cheeks and made a number of her trademark comedy faces, although there didn't seem to be a punchline at the end this time.

'Yeah,' she said at last. 'That's the problem.'

I regarded her from lowered brows, hoping my silence would tease a confidence from her. It didn't.

'Problem?' I finally said. 'Lincoln will be mortified. He prides himself on his . . . track record.'

Kat barked with laughter. 'So I see. He's quite impressive

in action, isn't he? Look, it's not a complaint as such, so please don't treat it as one, but he's a bit . . . predatory, isn't he?'

'Many bear the scars of his cross-training techniques,' I told her. She smiled. She was warming to me. Now I needed the dirt.

'I mean, I expected him to come on to Kitty. Everybody does. She takes offence if they don't, frankly. And if the guy is good-looking enough, she'll usually grant her favours. Lincoln is good-looking enough. And that's all I'm going to say.'

'Message received and understood,' I told her. 'But if Kitty likes him . . . why does she want another gym?'

'Oh, that's not her – it's me. He came on to *me*, straight after. I mean, what is that about? I don't care if he's Adonis himself, I don't want to shag him.'

'You don't? Well, that's fair enough. I think he can take no for an answer.'

But then I had to rethink. Actually, *can* he? Has he ever? Has anyone ever rejected his advances?

'I'm not sure he can,' Kat echoed my inner voice. 'He seems like a guy who has never had to work for it in his life. And I can see why – he has the six-pack and the lunchbox; he only needs a tartan groundsheet to be the perfect picnic set.'

Ah, a meadow of wildflowers, a bottle of champagne and Lincoln . . . I drifted off for a moment, brought back by Kat's clicking fingers.

'Tell you what,' she said. 'Could you have a word with him? Tell him he's welcome to Kitty, as long as she can still totter on to the set, but he can lay off me. I'm not interested and I'm not worth it. Would you do that for me? And then I can go back to the gym.'

'OK,' I said. 'I'll try.'

And I did. I did try. But Lincoln did not believe me. He accused me of jealousy in the first instance and then he decided to see it as a challenge.

'Link, she doesn't want you,' I said, gesturing wildly in my frustration. 'Move on. She isn't even your type.'

'She is my type,' he insisted bullishly. 'And if she wants to play hard-to-get, I can do that.'

I shook my head. 'I don't fancy your chances,' I said frankly. 'Sexual harassment isn't attractive.'

'That's pretty funny coming from you,' he said rudely, leaving me to gasp and slam my clipboard on the desk as he strutted off. I shrugged. He would learn, one way or the other. Either that he was truly irresistible, or that he wasn't. I was rather hoping for the latter.

Kitty and Kat were booked in for six weeks, and over the course of that time, something happened to Lincoln. He de-swaggered, unpreened, lost a few peacock feathers. Everybody noticed it, but nobody knew what was causing this decline. Nobody except Kat, who told me the whole story later.

On the day after their Induction, Kitty and Kat visited the gym together before breakfast. Lincoln well understood the maxim that the early bird catches the worm, so even at six thirty he was presiding magnificently over his domain.

Kat made an unobtrusive start on a treadmill, while Kitty fussed and flustered over the settings on her static cycle. 'Oh, Lincoln,' she cooed helplessly. 'I don't understand the digital thingy. Can you help me?'

Kitty's firm thighs and calves still ached from the wheelbarrow-style banging Lincoln had given her the day before. The cycle saddle was unforgiving on her sore quim, but there was no way she was equal to running or stepping, so it seemed the lesser evil. When Lincoln bent to adjust the setting, Kitty's trainer toe glided up the back of his track-suited calf, coming to rest in the crease at the back of his knee.

'Thanks, big boy,' she simpered. Kat looked on in mild disgust. 'Big boy' indeed. Who did Kitty think she was, Marilyn Monroe? Actually, she probably did. Her blondeness might not be real, but her dizziness certainly was.

Lincoln, far from joining in with Kitty's flirtatious game, stood up stiffly and said, 'No problem,' before retiring into his office. Kat watched her comedy partner's face drop and felt a stab of sympathy. Lincoln was a louse, perhaps even a louse with a spouse. Shame Kitty hadn't managed to squeeze a diamond or two from him before finding out.

'Are you OK, Kit?' she asked, a touch puffily, from the treadmill.

'Fine,' said Kitty, the untruth of it almost tangible.

'We can use another gym if you like.'

'Don't fuss! It's nothing!' Kitty began to pedal maniacally. Kat sighed and returned to her pounding rhythm. Lincoln, she perceived after a minute or two, was watching her from the doorway. Watching *her*. Not watching Kitty's tight glutes as they strained on the exercycle, but her strapping thighs as they wobbled in a smart run. Not watching Kitty's becoming flush, but her patchy sweaty cheeks. Not admiring Kitty's second Lycra skin, but her baggy Editors tour T-shirt and fading trackie bottoms. What would a man like Lincoln want with a girl like Kat?

Kat was no idiot, and she worked out somewhere between his hint of a smile and his almost-wink that what he wanted was the conquest – it was nothing to do with her at all.

Well, he would not have it, she vowed. No amount of cheeky glints or sly touches or insincere flattery was going to land her on Lincoln's exercise mats.

'Let me help you with those weights, baby,' he rumbled.

'Your leg needs to be a bit further back, baby, let me show you,' he advised, closing his grip on Kat's thigh.

'Boy, your shoulders need unknotting,' he opined, placing heavy hands at the back of her neck.

She wriggled away. 'I'm fine. I'll book a massage if I need one.'

This dance of mock-courtship continued all week long. Kitty forgot about him and threw herself into a romance with the third assistant director instead, getting enough exercise in bed to allow a little slacking on the gym front. But Kat was enjoying the chase and continued to frequent Lincoln's kingdom, deflecting his attentions with skill and ingenuity.

'Are you married?' he finally asked bluntly at the start of the second week of filming.

'No, Lincoln, I'm single. Are you?'

Lincoln filled two paper cups with water from the cooler and handed her one.

'I sure am, baby. Until you say the word.'

'Lincoln, you can stop bullshitting me. I know what you're about. You just want to be able to say you've shagged Kitty *and* Kat. You're not the first and you won't be the last. But I'm not a trophy, so give it up.'

She looked at him expectantly, a little regretful to be ending the game. She could not deny that she had enjoyed his onslaught of attention, and his touch did bring the prickles up on the back of her neck. All good things had to end though.

Lincoln made a face of disbelief, shaking his head. 'Kat, baby, you know that's not true! I'm no kiss and tell merchant, I've got more class than that.'

'No, Lincoln, I don't think you'd kiss and tell. You'd just know. It would make you happy, for about ten seconds, until the next challenge came along.'

'I'd be lying if I told you I couldn't make your nastiest dreams come true, baby,' drawled Lincoln, inflaming Kat's senses despite herself. 'But I like you as a person, Kat. I'd like to get to know you ... really get to know you. And I'd like you to get to know me.'

'Would I be the first?' asked Kat drily, trying not to feel too flattered. She had to keep her head around this man.

'You know, you just might be,' said Lincoln thoughtfully. Then, after a pause, he said emphatically. 'Hey, lady, you think you've got me pegged, but I am going to prove you wrong! Let me take you out. A date, no strings. You think I'm a gigolo but I want to show you who Lincoln Van Demeter III really is!'

'The third?' said Kat, cocking her head to one side. 'You mean there are two more of you?'

Lincoln chuckled. 'The world couldn't take more than one Lincoln Van Demeter III,' he said.

'You know, I think you're right. Let me get back to you about the date. I'd better change and get on set. See ya.'

Kat hopped off with a cheery little wave, considering Lincoln's proposition. A date. Dinner and conversation. Would he settle for that? If he would, then perhaps she might be tempted ... No. She really shouldn't. He was so very arrogant, it would simply fuel his monstrous ego. But then again ... he was so handsome. And he was fun. He would be good company. And Kitty was never off her back since taking up with that director boy.

Thus it was that Kat found herself staring into Lincoln's eyes across a circle of white linen interrupted by a slim vase containing a single rose stem.

'Do you come here often?' she asked politely, one eye on her escort, the other on the menu.

'Not really.' He sat back expansively, creasing the sharp white suit he had worn for the occasion.

'The women fall into bed with you that quickly?'

'Hey. I just don't usually do restaurants, OK?'

'I'm not letting you pay. We split the bill. No obligations, no guilt-tripping.'

'You ever heard of romance?'

'You ever heard of feminism?'

'Damn, I was hoping that was just a rumour.'

They smirked at each other, the awkwardness passing, and ordered the food.

'So what was wrong with Kitty?' asked Kat pointedly, her mouth set in a straight line.

'Man, she's beautiful,' sighed Lincoln, 'but I just didn't feel her. Do you know what I mean?'

'Not really. It seems to me that you felt her pretty comprehensively. And she certainly felt you.'

'I'm upfront, Kat. I'm not dishonest. I don't offer anything I can't deliver. I could offer Kitty a real good time, but I couldn't deliver any more than that. Besides, she's happy with that skinny dude from the movie set, isn't she?'

'What are you offering me then? An upfront good time, wham, bam, thank you ma'am?'

'If that's what you want. But if you want more . . .'

'Yes, I do want more. Don't look so spooked. Not a big white wedding or a pack of kids with your looks and my brains. Nothing like that.'

'What then?'

'As Aretha would say, R.E.S.P.E.C.T., find out what it means to me.'

'Hey, I do respect you, babe.'

'Well, I dispute that, *babe*. Although you might have just a shred or two more of it for me than you do for women in general. And that's only because I've thwarted your . . . juggernaut of seduction.'

'My what?'

'You find 'em, fuck 'em and forget 'em, Lincoln. You can't relate to a woman beyond what it takes to get her joggers off. You need to understand that we aren't fucktoys. We are people.'

'Sheesh.' Lincoln toyed with his chicken salad, reminding Kat of nothing more than a sulky nine-year-old who'd had his favourite action figures confiscated. 'You are harsh, Kat. You don't know me. You don't know how that hurts me.'

'The truth does, or so I'm told. But, hey. Cheer up. I've got something planned for later. Something that will help you with your little problem.'

Lincoln perked up, holding his fork close to his gleaming teeth. 'Tell me.'

'I don't want to spoil the surprise. Let's just say that ... nudity is involved.'

'For real?' Lincoln's favourite toys were back in his hot little hand. He grinned and made short work of the salad. 'Do you want a dessert? Shall we just pay now?'

'Sure. Halves, remember,' Kat reminded him sternly.

'You're the boss,' teased Lincoln.

'How very true.'

They took a sharp right through the glass doors of the restaurant and headed for the basement stairs.

'Aren't we going to your room?' asked Lincoln.

'Not yet.' Kat winked. 'I have a different kind of workout in mind first. You'll need to empty the gym, though I don't suppose it'll be busy at this time of night.'

'You'd be surprised,' muttered Lincoln, but when they arrived at the state-of-the-art health suite, only Kitty was present, rowing fiercely against an imaginary tide.

'Sorry, sweetie, time's up,' drawled the gym trainer, but Kat held up a hand.

'Actually, I'd like Kitty to stay.'

'Why?'

Kat moved to the door, turned the key, which was still in the lock, and pocketed it.

'Because we'd like you to let us entertain you, Lincoln,' she said quietly.

Lincoln was still gawping at Kat when Kitty arose from her rowing machine, redirecting the focus of his gawp to her. She was wearing the briefest and tightest of leotards; the high cut made her legs appear to start at her hips and carry on and on and on, while her breasts fought to escape from the inaccurately titled neckline. More like a titline, thought Lincoln salaciously. He was sure that this leotard would have a thong back, and he was tempted to ask Kitty for a twirl so he could find out. Would that be disrespectful? Probably.

The gods appeared to be smiling on him, though, for she walked over to a mat and sweetly asked, 'Mind if I do a few stretches?'

She turned and bent, touching each of her toes in rapid sequence. Oh Lord. Oh yes. A thong back. See those glutes strain and tense and then go back to perfect peachiness. Surely that must be uncomfortable up the crack of her ass, though?

'Earth to Lincoln,' said Kat drily. 'Look what you kicked out of bed. You silly, silly boy. I see you regret it now.'

Almost casually, Kat brushed the back of her hand against the crotch of Lincoln's only pair of non-gym smart trousers. It was misshapen and hard, the placket stretched to busting point.

Kitty straightened up and sauntered over. 'My, I'm hot after all that stretching,' she remarked, fanning herself. 'I need to catch a breath.' She lowered the shoulder straps of her leotard, setting her imprisoned bounty free. 'Ah, yes, much better. Would you like to touch them, Lincoln?'

147

'I . . .' Lincoln's Adam's apple jerked in his big neck as he turned to Kat, bewildered but horny. 'Kat, I thought that we . . .'

'This is what you wanted, isn't it, Lincoln? The pair of us. The double act. Go for it, babe. Enjoy.'

'OK, if you're sure . . .' He put out a meaty hand towards Kitty's famous tits, but she stepped back, tutting and wagging a finger.

'You have to earn it first,' she said. 'Kat will tell you how.'

'What the fuck is this shit?' asked Lincoln, starting to feel uneasy.

'Just a bit of fun, Link!' Kat assured him. 'What I want you to do is this. Strip naked, then go and get comfortable on the weight bench. We want to put you through your paces. See if you're man enough to take us both on.'

Lincoln could not resist a physical challenge. He chuckled and began shedding clothes. 'OK, ladies. I'll play it your way.'

'Damn right you will,' said Kat, smiling pleasantly.

When Lincoln was down to his boxers, Kat made him stand still for a moment, so that she and Kitty could drink in the glory of his body prior to the big reveal. It was impressive, even Kat had to admit. The biceps, the triceps, the abs, the chest tapering down to the narrower hips, the solid thighs, the powerful shoulders, the glutes, the pecs, the sex. But that was all it was. A body. A functional thing made beautiful, but only on the outside. Kat regarded it as she would a work of art. It was an object, but Lincoln had confused it with his self. He needed to be disabused of his delusion – you could call it an act of charity.

'OK, sock it to us,' requested Kat, and Lincoln slowly, oh so slowly, steered the elastic waistband of his boxers over the gigantic mound that blocked their easy slippage. 'Oh, that's nice. I bet it feels nice. Does it feel nice, Kitty?'

Kitty shrugged. 'It does the job,' she said.

'Hey, c'mon, Kitty, it does a bit more than that!' exclaimed Lincoln, stepping out of the star-spangled pants.

'We'll be the judge of that, shall we?' said Kat, still with her disorientatingly friendly smile. 'Now get on that bench, babe, and lift some weights.'

Lincoln lay back on the narrow padded bench and gripped the bar of the dumbell that lay over his head.

'Girls, this is too easy,' he professed, lifting the weights as if they were marshmallows.

'Let's give you a bit of a handicap, then, shall we? What do you think, Kitty? Any ideas?'

'Oh, I have an idea,' she said. 'But why don't you go first?'

'OK.' Kat stepped up beside Lincoln and waited until his arms were straining vertically to hold up the weights before reaching out and encompassing his fat cock with her fist.

'Hey!' he cried, his voice an octave higher than usual. 'Mind the family jewels, girl!'

'Relax, Lincoln. I'll be gentle.' Kat was as good as her word, running her fingers around Lincoln's semi-erect prick with curiosity and wonder. 'It feels good,' she remarked, moving up to its circumcised head and exploring it with her thumb. 'It's so well proportioned. Not vast but you'd definitely feel it up there. Could you feel it up there, Kitty?'

'Oh yes. That full feeling. I love that.'

'It's completely hard now. Good boy, Link. I wonder if you can train cocks?' Kat began stroking her hand up and down the rod, such yielding skin outside such inflexible muscle. 'You know, make them obey instructions. I mean, if I said "Down, boy" now, nothing would happen. Poor Linky Link here is too excited now. But I wonder if you can condition a cock to rise and fall at your will. I kind of like that idea. I think it would be tricky, but you could do it. What do you think, Lincoln?'

'Guhhh, don't stop, baby,' entreated Lincoln, his gargantuan arms now floppy and relaxed, his fingers clinging tightly to the dumbell.

'You've stopped lifting,' accused Kat sharply. 'Lift that weight and keep it in the air until I tell you.'

Lincoln wanted to protest, but there seemed to be a loose connection between his head and his mouth. He pushed with all his strength, although his arms seemed pumped full of a weakening liquid now and all he could feel was his eager cock reacting to Kat's clenched hand. Most girls did that too gently, but not Kat. She gripped it for dear life, milking it, just the way he liked it.

'Yes,' whispered Kat, 'I'd love to train you. You'd be such an eager little puppy. You'd sit up and beg. You'd roll over for a little taste of this.'

Kitty placed extra weights on each end of the dumbell. Lincoln began to perspire, a vein throbbing at his temple. Kitty stroked his forehead considerately then moved down opposite Kat, leant over his groin and breathed warm air over his balls before poking out the tip of her tongue and licking them.

The dumbells came crashing down again.

Kat immediately removed her hand. 'No, no, Lincoln. You have to work for it. You've never worked for it, have you? You have to know how it feels to work for it.'

'Just . . . do me . . . baby,' he puffed, then he gritted his teeth and, with an almighty roar, lifted the weights once more.

'Kitty, would you like to do the honours?' Kat stepped back and watched while Kitty lowered her gorgeous plump red lips down over Lincoln's bulbous head and steely shaft.

'Ohhhhh, yes, yes,' groaned Lincoln, his arms shaking, but still finding the strength to thrust his pelvis into Kitty's face.

'Bad manners, Lincoln,' tutted Kat, then she left Kitty to suck and nuzzle while she went into the office to look for some resistance bands. Finding them, she came back out and proceeded to bind Lincoln's ankles to the footrests, leaving him helpless on his back with his arms shuddering under the weights and his cock swelling and urging in Kitty's soft, wet mouth. God, it was torture, but it was exquisite. Lincoln was sure he could not last much longer. What a story this would make for the red tops.

As if she had read his treacherous thoughts, Kitty popped off the end of his tool and shook her head. Lincoln dropped the weights again and let out a long bellow of frustration. Kat swooped forward and attached his wrists to the dumbell shaft, leaving him entirely at her mercy.

'Please, girls,' he whined.

'How much do you want it?' asked Kat.

'A lot. Go on. Just do me. Do what you want.'

'I want to tease you.'

He yelped incoherently, realising now that this might not be his night after all. He had been judged and found wanting, and now justice was to be meted out.

Kitty stepped carefully over his tied legs until she straddled his thighs, then she bent over and began rubbing her dangling breasts against Lincoln's needy length, squeezing it, teasing it, brushing it with her nipples. Desperate to move his hands down and take a handful of the soft flesh for himself, he found himself struggling in his bonds and cursing his two captors. Kitty took the sweatband from around her forehead and handed it to Kat, who stuffed it into Lincoln's mouth.

'You can't say you're not enjoying this, Link,' admonished Kat. 'Your cock says otherwise. But why should he have all the fun? I want some fun too.'

Kat, still fully clothed in a light cotton shirt-dress, suddenly gripped the dumbell bar and swung herself over Lincoln's shoulders until her knees rested on the padded leather, either side of his neck. She slowly lifted the hem of her skirt up and up in front of his popping eyes until her sheeny satin knickers were exposed.

'Watching you like this is getting me wet, Lincoln,' she said huskily. 'If you're a very, very good boy, I might take that gag out of your mouth and let you lick my snatch. Would you like that?'

Lincoln nodded frantically. He would never have imagined that being tied to a bench, weighed down in place by two vengeful women, having his cock teased by a pair of breasts, could feel this hot. Kat reached down and took the sweatband from his mouth, replacing it immediately with the stretched sateen of her knickers. Lincoln laid his tongue flat against the material, which was already a little damp and smelling strongly of her arousal. He pushed upwards with the broad base of his tongue, soaking and covering the material with his saliva until she caught her breath and ground herself down on him.

'Lick me, Lincoln! Do it properly,' she commanded.

His tongue snaked underneath the elastic, and he pushed it aside with his teeth so that her cunt lips and clit were open and exposed to him. She rotated them over his mouth and nose, pushing down so that he had to open wide to accommodate them. His tongue began to slide and slip all over her sensitive nerve endings, sucking at her engorged clitoris, gliding around it and zigzagging backwards to take a cheeky poke into the entrance of her sleeve. He crammed her all in, soaking up her juices, giving her the licking of her lifetime. Kat jammed her knees against his ears and clung on to the dumbell bar for purchase, rocking back and forth on his hot wet muscle until she began to quiver like a jelly, drenching his face with her orgasm.

'Oh God, Kitty,' Kat gasped, lifting herself up on trembling knees. 'You need to feel that. He even works out with his tongue.'

'It's a muscle,' said Lincoln smugly. 'I've never had a complaint about a muscle of mine.'

Kitty pulled herself upright, her tits tugging at Lincoln's cock on the way.

'He never gave me head,' she complained.

'Well, now's your chance,' said Kat, hopping off the bench and removing her tongue-wettened knickers. 'As for you, Lincoln, I mean to make use of that lovely fat cock of yours. That's what this is about, you know. Using you. Taking your body and using it for our pleasure. How does it feel to be used?'

'Pretty darn good,' said Lincoln, a note of surprise in his voice.

Kat barked out a laugh. 'Just our luck, eh, Kitty? We try to teach a guy a lesson, and he turns out to be a closet submissive. Hey ho.'

'Hey, I am not submissive!' asserted Lincoln. 'I just like a good threesome!'

'Whatever you say, Link, whatever you say.' Kat patted his bald pate indulgently. She waited for Kitty to slink out of her leotard and station herself with her crotch hovering inches above Lincoln's shiny sex-slicked chin, then she hauled herself over his hips.

'Right, then, are we ready? Three ... two ... one ...' At one, the two women lowered themselves on to their respective targets. Kitty whinnied in delight to find that Lincoln's tongue still had plenty of life in it, while Kat edged herself carefully on to his prick. Realising from his high sigh of bliss that he probably would not last very long, she slowed even further, using his tip to rub shallowly against her front wall until finally it hit her g-spot. She kept him in that penitential limbo, just beyond the hell of neglect but nowhere near the heaven of good, hard fucking, for as long as she could get away with. He tried and tried to thrust deeper, but she was able to hold him off, pinching his base firmly between finger and thumb when he threatened to unseat her with his bucking. If only his vocalisations didn't pour directly into Kitty's muffling quim, he would have begged and pleaded, but he could make no sense, and if he tried to rest his tongue, Kitty tweaked his ear painfully, so that was no good.

He had underestimated Kat, he realised now. This was, just as she had said, the simple use of his body for their pleasure. He was their fucktoy, nothing more than that. His needs came a very poor third in the pecking order.

Kat continued to manipulate the head of his cock until she climaxed again, rubbing the purple tip against her clit to prolong the sensation. Kitty came moments later, bouncing up and down on his aching, overworked jaw, smearing her essences all over his face.

'Mmm, thanks very much, Lincoln,' purred Kitty and Kat, taking a breather on the exercise mats, sated and satisfied in every possible way.

'Please!' he wailed, trying to direct their eyes to his poor untended cock while he lay in bondage on the weight bench. 'You can't leave me like this. I need to come so bad, babes.'

'Put him out of his misery, Kitty,' said Kat. Kitty looked a little stunned for a second, then she giggled when Kat handed her the crumpled sweatband. She hopped up and stuffed it back in Lincoln's dry, pussy-flavoured mouth. 'Shower?'

The two women headed for Lincoln's former favourite seduction bunker, laughing all the way.

Apparently, it was Chase who found him there. Kat messaged him, so Lincoln faced the unutterable nightmare of being found, ankles and wrists bound, mouth gagged and redolent of cunnilingus, cock at full mast, by the hotel manager. I thought Kat went a little too far there, but it certainly seemed to have an effect. For about half a day, he raged about going to the tabloids, but they made it up to him that evening with champagne, muffins and the kind of threesome he had had in mind, and eventually he conceded that he ought to start treating women with a bit more respect.

So it's a new improved Lincoln we lust after in the gym these days. A humble and mannerly Lincoln, a considerate and gracious Lincoln. He still seduces girls, but he's nice to them the next day too. And until he settles down – which is more of a possibility than it ever was before – he has a guaranteed *ménage-à-trois* every time Kitty and Kat are in town.

The Manager #3 (Chasing Chase)

There are no photographs on his desk.

I never have to transfer non-business calls to him.

He has never asked me to pop out in my lunch hour and buy flowers or chocolates. He has never asked me to cover for him in any way.

To all intents and purposes, Chase appears to be a man with no private life. His public persona is who he is – the urbane, efficient, diplomatic and charismatic manager of the Hotel Luxe Noir. Sometimes I try a bit of fishing. I might ask him about his annual week of holiday – the only leave he takes. He will tell me where he is going, but never with whom, if anyone. I offer to book flights, but he always has everything in hand. He is a man who has everything in hand; that is who he is. That is what I like about him.

When he works late, late hours, I sometimes wonder aloud if his dinner will be burnt. He smiles politely and doubts it.

Further canvassing of staff opinion confirms that not one of us knows a thing about him beyond his managerial capabilities. We know he has rooms in the hotel, but we don't know where they are – any crisis is referred to him via the Reception Desk, and he arrives at the scene minutes later, as elegantly groomed as ever regardless of the hour. I have tried to locate his suite, but it is difficult to follow Chase without him realising it. He has a sixth sense and eyes in the back of his head. He is a phenomenon. He is the sexiest phenomenon in the world.

I wrestle with his utter enigma until I can no longer stand it. I have to know something about this man who pays me and directs me and engages me and obsesses me, beyond what brand of suit he favours and whether he prefers sushi to sashimi for a working lunch. I decide that a touch of espionage is in order. And when better to start than the mysterious monthly Wednesday assignation he never fails to attend.

Is it a dangerous liaison? A twelve-step programme of some kind? Access visits to a child? My brain works double-overtime; it is clear that, unless I find out, I will end up in some obscure retreat for the terminally lovelorn. Half of me is hoping I will uncover something that will prove his inaccessibility to me – a gay lover, a crack habit, membership of a terrorist cell. The other half rather fervently hopes not. I want it to end, but I never want it to end. Oh, my head hurts.

Jade is already at my station behind the desk when he leaves the building. He gives us a glance of reproof, assuming that we are wasting time with idle gossip, then his tall, impeccably dressed frame disappears through the revolving glass.

'OK then,' whispers Jade complicitly. I have told her that I am going to a secret audition for *The X Factor*. That girl will believe any old rhubarb. I wink at her and race across the shining tiles in my only pair of flat-soled shoes, primed for pursuit. Through the glass I can see him on the pavement, frowning at an iron-grey sky before putting up an umbrella. Oh! He means to walk. I banish exciting 'follow that cab' scenarios from my disappointed imagination and wait until he has set off towards the park gates at the end of the street before slipping out in his wake.

The pavement is helpfully crowded, although it is still easy to make out the back of Chase's perfectly groomed head as he cuts a swathe through the masses. His stride is swift and long-legged, and I have to half-jog to keep him in sight, weaving between charity muggers and school groups until I make it to the park.

Will he meet someone here? Is it that simple? Will he take a girl out on the lake in a pedalo? Or is it more of a behind-the-bushes affair?

Neither, it seems, for he skirts the neat flowerbeds and fountains until he has reached the opposite side, whose exit feeds directly into the seedy fleshpots of town.

It is raining steadily by the time I leave the innocent freshness of the park and head into the narrow neon-lit streets. The lowering sky makes the green and red fluoresce all the brighter, reflected in the puddles on the uneven tarmac. I splash a foot in a backwards-flickering 'GIRLS! GIRLS! GIRLS!', wishing I had a little leisure time to inspect more thoroughly the dark doorways and blanked-out shop windows of this district.

Chase seems, for a panicky moment, to have disappeared, before I too happen on the tiny alleyway he has turned into. On the corner, a loud and bustling café in the style of a 1950s American diner stands invitingly, but beyond it things get substantially murkier. The first doorway leads into a tiny, cobwebby shop packed with dog-eared paperbacks. The display in the grimy window is of titles like *Lord Fotherington's Folly* and *Lashes for Lucinda*. The kind of thing I would read myself, lent a sinister air by the setting. The second doorway frames a surly-looking girl in fishnets and some kind of dress made from shiny plasticky stuff. She snaps her chewing gum as I go past and prods the door jamb with one enormous platform sole. The buzzing sign above the third doorway promises a burlesque show. Or rather, a buleque shw, since three of the letters fail to light.

None of these doorways are Chase's final destination. No, he leaves the alleyway, passes the back of a terrace of buildings, finally finding the one he wants, and ascends a rickety fire escape to the top floor. I stand in the shadows, watch him knock, watch him being admitted – without seeing who did it – and watch the door close behind him. The prospect of climbing the fire escape myself and possibly being caught peeking on it and thence tossed to my death does not really appeal. Instead, I try to find a way to the front of the building, to see if there is an alternative entrance.

It takes a while, but I soon find myself staring up at the façades of the line of long, lean five-storey buildings. A hostel, a sex shop, a jazz bar, another hostel and ... this was the one. A peep show. Oh, God, I can't go in there. Can I?

Presumably Chase is not actually here for the peep show, but it seems a fairly safe bet that the rest of the building is in use as a brothel. I feel a little sick. My antics in the hotel bar are one thing, but who knows whether the girls walled up inside this gloomy tenement have any say in who they fuck or how they do it. Do they cater to a specialist taste? I do not want to even think about this.

Can I just turn and leave and never know? Can I sit at the Reception Desk every fourth Wednesday afternoon for evermore, wondering where he is, what or whom he is doing? No. I can't. There is nothing for it.

A narrow corridor, fustily decorated in ancient textured wallpaper, leads to a blank-eyed tattooed man, sitting at a table with a cash register on it.

'You here about the job, love?' he asks, obviously thinking I'm a little smartly dressed for a peep show.

That's an in. I'm here about the job. Presumably I'll be taken somewhere, to talk to somebody. Maybe I can ask to use the loo and find a way to sneak upstairs to the top floor. Maybe I'll find out that Chase is into dungeon sex. Maybe I'll be knifed by a gang boss. What the fuck am I doing?

'Yes,' I say. 'I am.'

The man shifts himself reluctantly, leading me around a corner, where a row of booths are found. The pungent smell of stale semen and sweat hangs over the place. Three of the five booths are occupied and we walk past the overcoated backs of the peepers, most of whom seem rather elderly. I suppose this might be a dying 'art form' – the young men all go to Spearmint Rhino now.

'We'll wait until Sonia there has finished her set, and then you can show us what you can do,' the man tells me, to my barely concealed horror. 'What? Did you think you were going to have a formal interview?' He laughs. 'This is an audition, love. Under Job Description, it says, "Being sexy, so that the punters jack off and come back for more". You don't need no business qualifications for this game, sweetheart.' He laughs again, uproariously, and I pretend to join in.

'I know that!' I lie.

'Good. Get your kit off then, and put this on instead.'

He flings a hideous skimpy gold lamé minidress with matching thong at me and shuts me in a cupboard to change. It occurs to me that I may well not be the first girl to wear the knickers, and I decide against putting them on. Am I really going to go through with this? Can't I tell the man it's a mistake, that I got the wrong address? I work at calming down and gathering my thoughts. It's not that bad. Dancing around in next to nothing for five or ten minutes. I've done it for lovers; why not for strangers? Anyway, I can ask to use the loo before I go on and escape upstairs. Or should I wait until after the show? I probably should wait; he won't care what I'm doing or how long I take once I've performed.

OK. Deep breath. I unbutton my blouse, unzip my skirt, unfasten my suspender clips and get naked in the cupboard, which has a bare light bulb, a flyblown mirror and a faded pink velvet vanity stool in the way of furnishings. I fold my clothes neatly on the stool and struggle into the ugly gold dress. It has a halter neck and the top half barely covers my tits – just two diagonal lengths of fabric that skim my nipples and then meet around a large metal ring which is all my midriff gets in the way of cladding. A tiny stretchy skirt, skimming the cheeks of my bottom, makes up the rest of the outfit. Just as well I had a wax this morning; a less than impeccable bikini-line would be blatantly evident in this outfit. I frown at my legs – summer's tan is long gone and I could use a can of spray-on, but I will have to do. A horrid pair of knackered gold high heels, like something you'd find in a child's dressing-up box, completes the outfit. One of the heels needs mending, so I have to practise walking around the cramped space before I emerge.

'Very nice.' The tattooed man leers, his eyes zeroing in on my breasts. I would disagree, but there seems little point. 'Give us a twirl then.'

I rotate a slow three-sixty, worrying that the hemline will give him a flash of my snatch, but I'm not sure why that would worry me. Where has that shred of modesty come from? I have to abandon it in the next few seconds when he says, 'Bend over.' There is no way I can do that without exposing my privates. I lean forwards, my arms hanging down to my ankles, feeling the skirt ride up the cheeks of my bum, above the point where my shaved lips and vulva will be visible. He takes his time, gets a good long look, then growls, 'Oh yes. That'll do. Stand up then.'

'Do I keep the dress on?' I ask him, trying to be as casual and businesslike as possible.

'Depends. We give each punter a notebook and pen. They get to put their requests up in the booth windows. You just do what they ask.'

'Everything they ask?'

'Yeah, unless it involves something dangerous or illegal. You'll get the odd chancer who will ask if you can let him in the room, or meet him outside for a blow job, but you just ignore those. It's usually standard stuff. Bend over, spread your legs, feel your tits up, type of thing.' He shrugs, as if he has just recited a mundane shopping list. 'Ten minutes, and, if everyone's happy, you get a short break before the next lot. If someone hasn't come yet, he might pay for another five minutes. You'll be told if that happens.'

I swallow. 'Right.' Suddenly, I am weirdly turned on by the whole idea. I've decided to ignore their faces and pretend they are all hot men. Chase and a group of his friends. That's the way to get through this.

The door to the peep show room clicks open and a girl wearing nipple tassels, chain-mail bikini briefs and a fuchsia feather boa ambles out, yawning.

'All right, Sonia? This is Sophie. We're trying her out. You can take a half-hour break if you want.'

'Good, these tassels pinch like bastards,' she remarks, sidling into the cupboard-room without so much as a glance in my direction.

'Right, you'd better get in there. I'll go and take the money. You start when you hear the music. Yeah?'

'Fine,' I say briskly, then I totter into the peep show room. It is a long rectangular box, wallpapered in black, with black rubber tiles on the floor. Along one wall are five perspex letterbox windows, narrow enough that I won't have to see the punters' faces, but wide enough to place a readable message against. One armless chair rests in a corner, but other than that, there is no furniture. I go and sit on the chair until it is time to do my 'act', staring up at the spotlights on the ceiling, which are red.

I'm a sex worker, I think to myself. After years of being a sex player, now I'm finally a sex worker. I'm getting paid to be lewd. He hasn't told me what the remuneration is, I realise. What is the going rate for this kind of thing? And where is Chase? What is he doing right now? Is he buggering some young man, dressed in a corset and high heels? Is a tweedy lady whipping his bum with a riding crop?

My speculation is interrupted by some saxophony elevator music crackling through the ancient wall-mounted speakers. Five sets of eyes gleam at me from the wall. I rise to my wobbly feet and begin to gyrate slowly, wiggling my hips, rubbing a hand up and down one thigh, licking my lips. That's sexy, isn't it? I'm not sure. Within a couple of minutes, I spot a message, in fluorescent felt tip, at window number three. 'I want to see your nips,' it says.

It is almost a pleasure to push aside the scratchy gold cloth and expose the throbbing nubs. I take my spindly heels over to window three and thrust my nipples towards him, holding my heavy tits upright with my hands. It is Chase, and when I finish dancing, he will lick them and suck them until they are like shiny wet cherries. But first there is a request in window number four to attend to.

'BEND OVER AND WIGGLE YOUR ARSE.' Capital letters, so he must be serious. Picturing Chase's pupils in a state of dilation behind his desk, I turn my back to the window and reach down again for my ankles, feeling the rough hemline move up above the spot where bottom meets thigh. I shake my hips, feeling my rear cheeks jiggle, then I stroke my hands up from the backs of my knees to my lower bottom, rubbing the rotating globes provocatively. Is that enough? I straighten up again and see two more messages at each side of the booth.

'Pinch your nipples,' says the first, while the other reads, 'Lift up your skirt.' I can do these simultaneously, I decide, so one hand hikes the cheap rag up, up to the top of my thighs so that my smooth mons peeks out while the other pinches and tweaks my nipples.

Three out of five windows now carry variations on the instruction 'Frig yourself.' One of the others goes for the more controversial 'Fuck yourself with a shoe.' I go with the popular vote and fetch the chair from the corner before sitting widely astride it, skirt around my waist and thighs splayed. I pretend to ride it like a horse along to the rhythm for a while, then I press my fingertips into the soft pink flesh. I am playing with myself at Chase's suggestion; he wants to watch me make myself come so that he knows the way I like it. As I push a finger into the yielding slot, he is crouching between my legs, watching with a frown of concentration.

Are you tight there, Sophie? Do you ever use a vibrator? Should I touch your clit while I'm fucking you?

His ghost questions urge me on so that I begin to buck hard on the chair, its front legs lifting every now and then. The paper messages have ceased; all five of my voyeurs appear to be transfixed by my performance, until window number two warns me 'U'd better not be fakin it girl.' I shut my eyes, shut them out, lock Chase in. It is his fingers now, not mine, probing singly and then doubly and then triply in my warm slickness. His thumbs keep my lips well spread and his tongue bathes my clitoris.

'Oh, oh, oh.' I lean forward, doubling over, brushing my knees with my hard nipples, bunching my fist against my clit, spearing my cunt, biting my lip, screwing my face, which is Chase's face, above me now while he swarms over my body and only when I start to come do I remember . . . where I am.

I tip my head down and rest it on my thighs, not daring to look up, wanting to just sit here until they go away. Eventually the music clicks off and the door opens. I look up sharply to see tattooed man grinning at me.

'You nearly caused a riot, love,' he says. 'Sensational. Job's yours. In fact, if you want to earn a bit extra, I could set you up upstairs as a cam girl.'

Blearily, I remember what I am here for.

'You keep cam girls upstairs?' Is this what Chase is here for? Somehow I can't make that connection.

'Yeah, a few. They work shifts, four hours at a stretch. It's easy work – just sit on a bed feeling yourself up with a few toys. What do you reckon?'

I shake my head weakly. 'Can I use the lav?'

'Course. You aren't up for it then? Cos you seemed really . . . you know, to really get into your work there.' He leers. 'I thought you'd jump at the chance to show yourself off to thousands of men at a time. That seems to be up your street, love. Isn't it?'

I look at him through tired eyes, tits out, legs still spread, thighs sticky. It's hardly surprising he would make that assumption, and on another day he'd probably be right. But I need to poke around upstairs, now, quickly, before Chase leaves.

'Can I get back to you? And seriously, I need to clean myself up. Please?'

'Sorry. Course you do. It's up the back stairs, first door on the landing.'

I dash up to the loo, readjusting the horrible dress quickly and giving myself a splash of water over my face and between my legs, then I tiptoe up the rest of the staircase. At the fourth floor, something captures my attention through the grimy sash window. It is Chase, clattering down the fire escape. Damn, he is leaving already. I press myself to the wall, wondering if it is worth knocking on any of these blank white doors to investigate. Suddenly one of them opens. A very large, very burly man with a moustache looks me up and down in my gold frock from hell.

'Hey. You come about the job?' he says, but this time I have no desire to broaden my experience of what goes on behind the closed doors of the red-light district. I shake my head. 'Sorry, got lost,' I mumble, and hare back down the stairs to the cupboard where my work clothes are stashed.

'Thanks, I've changed my mind,' I shout hurriedly at the tattooed man, loping through the narrow corridor to daylight, or what passes for it around here.

He half-stands, makes to give chase, then grunts and has sat back down by the time I emerge into the dirty grey streets of the rainy city.

'You're wet, Sophie,' notes Chase, coming out of his office half an hour later. 'Why is that?'

'Had to dash out ... guest wanted ... something.' My fabrication skills need honing.

He looms over me from behind and with an impatient hand brushes some of the water that has dripped from the ends of my hair on to the Visitors Book. I watch the blue ink blur. It looks like tears.

'Go to the Ladies' and dry yourself off,' he says, one hand on my damp shoulder, which twitches under his palm. 'And next time you take a prolonged unscheduled desk break, it will be going on your record. Do you understand me?'

Oh, how I wish I did. I look up at him, meaning to apologise, but the combination of wrath and wistful regret in his face silences me.

He lifts his hand and I find the nearest drier. I will pin him down yet.

Staff Training

'Yes, yes, yes!' I put down the phone and tap in the booking with a celebratory flourish. My favourite trade fair of the year, back again for its annual jamboree.

Pleasurama. The name says it all.

For three days, representatives of every flavour of sex shop and erotic outlet, from dingy downtown dives with blacked-out windows to the new breed of female-friendly upmarket fuck boutiques, will descend on the Luxe Noir, with their briefcases full of crotchless lace and silk-lined leather, poppers and crops, collars and cuffs, tethers and feathers.

I have made some splendid purchases at discount prices in the past. The lubricant that smells uncannily like Old Spice. The brown leather arm cuffs linked by a brass chain. The cupless corset, bejewelled and constricting. The vibrator in the shape of a reverse S. The tickly pink feather thing. The satin blindfold. I could go on ...

I have saved a bit of money this year and I intend to treat myself to something from the top of the range. But how shall I choose? I shall employ the same shopping methods as I always do, of course. I shall try before I buy.

From Reception I can hear a hum of activity in the Exhibition Hall. The fair has been open for an hour, and I have been measurelessly entertained by the constant stream of interesting characters to-ing and fro-ing through the lobby. Alien-looking models in glitter body paint, leopard bikinis and not much else stroll over to the trestle table by the door and pin on their admission badges, followed by a bona fide member of the Dirty Mac Brigade and a chubby lass in head-to-toe black PVC.

Chase materialises at the back of Reception. 'You can go now, Sophie,' he tells me, looking over at the Hall. 'Don't let anyone buy you.'

I turn around and grin from ear to ear. 'They couldn't afford me; don't worry.'

I get the ghost of a flicker of a twitch of a lip in return – a major concession from Chase. It is enough to warm my cockles on the way over to the Exhibition Hall.

'Name?' asks the clipboard-wielder.

'Sophie Martin.' I look over his shoulder at the list. 'Look, there I am. Demonstration model for the Sweet As Sin boutique.'

'Right you are.' He pins the badge to my lapel, hands me a map of the stall layout and waves me through.

Sweet As Sin occupies a corner plot, in keeping with its high-tone luxury brand identity. Chintzy Victorian curtains swathe the stall; on closer inspection it becomes clear that the swirly patterns are actually tiny pornographic images gleaned from ye olde smut such as *The Pearl*. Inside, old-fashioned mannequin busts sport corsets and basques, while sex toys that could double as exotic ornaments, formed of crystal, jade and obsidian, line the shelves.

I am inspecting a range of clear glass dildoes when Lura appears from the back of the shop, dressed in an antique black velvet riding habit, complete with veiled titfer.

'Sophie,' she exclaims in that cracked voice, so suggestive of perfumed cigarettes smoked in ornamental holders. She kisses both my cheeks and stands back, her sharp black eyes assessing how best she can use me in her display. 'You're looking stunning as ever, darling,' she says theatrically.

'I'm just admiring some of your new products,' I tell her. 'There's an awful lot for my wish list here.'

'Oh, yes, we have some fabulous new designers this year. You are in for a treat. Now, I think I have the very thing to dress you up in, to begin with. Come backstage and I'll prepare you.'

Behind the stall, away from the prying eyes to which I will soon be exposed, lies a mountain of frills, ribbons and laces. Lura begins picking up and discarding items, explaining her vision for me as she sifts. 'I am going to turn you into a present. An exquisite gift, to be unwrapped and unpackaged. At three, I have scheduled an auction. The highest bidder in each round gets to unwrap a layer. Each of the winners will be invited to a private demonstration of some of our newer models. We earn a little revenue and hopefully make some sales. I know you are not shy, Sophie – do you think you can help me with this?'

'Do you think it'll draw a crowd?' I ask, thrilling at the idea of performing such an intimate show for a throng of avid strangers. It will be like a safe, regulated, classier version of my peep show experience.

'I hope so.' Lura smiles coldly. 'But why are you still dressed, Sophie? Off with your clothes, dear.'

The skirt, shirt, jacket and pedestrian underwear are soon neatly folded on a chair, while I stand naked in front of my doyenne of the lascivious. She trails a burgundy nail down my torso, weighs my breasts and checks that I am fully waxed, even spreading my buttocks in her exploratory zeal.

'You are always so well groomed, Sophie,' she approves, turning me back round to face her. She takes a pot of some heavenly perfumed unguent and begins to smear it indiscriminately and heavily until my entire body shimmers with a pearlescent sheen, missing no crevice or crease, from the hollows behind my ears to the arches of my feet. I am placed on a chair, legs akimbo, to have rouge rubbed into my nipples and labia, then the same rouge is applied to my lips and cheeks, part of a whorish mask of maquillage.

Coverage achieved, I twirl for Lura's verdict in my lewd base coat.

'I wish you were mine,' she says.

Twenty minutes later I am standing on the small stage at the front of Sweet As Sin, strapped into high heels and wrapped in a floor-length diaphanous black robe. Over the PA system, Lura announces the imminent start of the auction and the trickle of passers-by is augmented, minute by minute, until it reaches flood proportions. A sea of faces, eager, upturned, bearded, lipsticked, pink-haired, peroxided, and all with their eyes pointing at me. Amongst the crowd I spot a friendly face – Neil, the chief buyer for the Desirez chain. Not my sex emporium of choice, being a bit on the utilitarian side, but Neil is always happy to throw a free demonstration model my way in return for a ... free demonstration.

He winks at me and I crack my kabuki mask of foundation in return, and then Lura is up in front of the crowd, slashing her antique riding crop through the air to establish order.

'Ladies and gentlemen,' she opens. 'Welcome to Sweet As Sin.' She yarns on for a while about their market positioning and appeal to the connoisseur before explaining the way the auction will work. All at once, those eyes grow greedy; tongues emerge and lick nervous lips; some of the men finger their collars, unbuttoning, while the women frown at their handbills. Many of the mouths broaden into salacious grins and a few fingers from the front brush against the hem of my robe.

I give them a twirl, leaving them to imagine what might lie beneath, and then the bidding begins. At first it is desultory, the audience still a little bemused by Lura's plan, but then Neil and another gentleman enter into a bidding competition, which Neil eventually wins. He steps forward, grins down at me, and pulls the ribbon tie of my robe, which whispers down to my stilettoed feet.

There are gasps from the crowd, who take in my jet-beaded corset and tiny frilled skirt, under which my knickers are tantalisingly almost visible. The suspender straps emerge beneath the pleats, snapped on to the sheerest of silken stockings. From my wrists to my elbows run gauntlets of exquisitely tooled soft black leather, cut out to form lattice-work patterns. A single silver ring glints from the wrist of each, hinting at possibilities of erotic restraint. Around my neck is a matching collar.

Neil whistles and takes a seat at the end of a line beside the stage – winners' row, as Lura calls it. He will be the first member of the audience for my private show.

The auction continues apace. The next winner removes my skirt, revealing sheer black knickers with an extravagant ribbon bow at the back. Now my thighs are bare and Lura makes me stand with one foot on a stepstool so that prying eyes can zoom into the region between my legs, X-raying through the black mesh to glimpse the outline of my pussy lips. A woman is next, very tall, one of the other models, and she relieves me of my corset with relish, whipping it away so that I am left in a quarter-cup bra with sparkling pastes on my nipples. The model seems fascinated by my fuller breasts and she reaches to touch them, but Lura almost slaps her hand away. 'Look,' she admonishes, 'but don't touch. Not yet.' She smiles complicitly; the model under-stands and retires to winners' row. The bidding is rapid and frantic now, handbills waving in the air, the shouts almost drowning out Lura's commentary on the underwear.

My bra is removed and then it is time for the *coup de grâce* – the shedding of the knickers. I am made to turn my back for this last round, so I do not see who wins. I can only wait for them to mount the stage and then pull, gently but firmly, on the ribbon that furls and flounces over the curves of my bottom. Once undone, the fabric slips away, falling over my nude rear cheeks and floating slowly down to the floor. Now I am naked but for the collar, gauntlets, stockings, suspenders and heels. All my hidden parts are on display, while the clothing that remains accentuates my nudity, reminding me that I am simply female livestock, to be gawped and leered at, to be desired and lusted after.

'Bend over, Sophie,' orders Lura. The crowd clap and cheer when I grab my ankles; I can see them, upside-down but quite distinctly, swarming closer to get a really good look at my open lips and spread buttocks. 'Is she wet?' one of them asks another. 'Can you see?'

'I think so. Damn, I wish I'd brought more cash now. Ah well. It was a good show.'

I straighten again and present my front perspective to their view; they nod and grin at my Brazilian, while a few girls begin to argue over their preferred intimate topiary styles. Lura thanks them all for their interest and hands out catalogues, which is their signal to drift away. The five denizens of winners' row – four men and a woman – are shepherded backstage, to the same black-draped corner I used for my transformation from desk girl to fucktoy.

Lura seats me on a red-plush armchair while the winners sit in a semicircle facing me.

'I have some lovely new toys to demonstrate today, and I hope my lucky winners will be able to help me with the show,' she says, smiling. She lays a large case out on a low table between me and the audience and opens it up. 'Take a good look at what is inside,' she invites. 'Choose your favourites and then, when we are ready, you can try them out on Sophie here. Please don't be shy to do whatever you wish to her. I am paying Sophie to do as she is told, and she will get to choose and keep her own favourites after the show. For the next hour, no part of Sophie is off-limits – you may use her tits, her pussy, her arse, exactly as you please.' They look sidelong at me, curious and ravenous at once. Furiously flushed, I stare down at the lacy tops of my stockings, drinking in the shame and transfiguring it to a strong gush of need between my thighs. 'But of course,' Lura finishes, wagging a bony finger, 'you may only use the products. No flesh is to meet flesh, please. This is a high-class establishment, not a brothel, and Sophie is here to demonstrate, not to service you.'

'Not yet,' mutters Neil and I aim a killer glare at him. He winks back at me, then the group bow their heads over the suitcase, picking things up and inspecting them, sometimes looking over at me as if speculating on the effect they might have on me.

I see long columns of smooth metal, precious mineral rings, acres of discreetly hued silicone, pots and bottles and horsehair and silk.

'Has everybody chosen?' asks Lura. 'Who would like to begin?'

The female model steps forward, holding up a glass vial. 'I'd like to try some of this on her,' she says. 'I've heard good things about it.'

'Be my guest.' Lura nods and the model smiles widely at me, opens her vial and dabs the stopper on my temples, then she peels off the sparkling pastes and treats my nipples. There is a moment of sting and a dizzying aphrodisiac aroma once my skin absorbs the contents. I take a deep breath, noticing how my nipples are an even darker red now, throbbing lightly and begging to be touched.

'How does that feel, Sophie?' asks the model.

'It's . . . heightening my senses . . . and it smells gorgeous,' I say, gasping as she grabs hold of a calf, hoiks it over the velvet arm of the chair and then glides the stopper along my labia majora, once, twice, three times, until the potency and intensity of it have caused my clit to expand and emerge from its hood. I see all eyes upon it, eyebrows raised, chins stroked. I think some sales may have been made, but I am too unfocused and needful of more touch to think of much else. I wriggle my bare bottom against the plushy pile and bring my hands up to my nipples, which seem to explode into spangles, oh, God, it's almost enough to make me come already. How long have I been here? Five minutes? I signed up for an hour.

'Sophie,' says Lura sternly. 'Hands off your nipples. I'm not paying you to touch yourself.' I moan and grip the arms of the chair, gazing longingly at some of the dildoes and vibrators the men have chosen. One of those is just what I need now. But Lura is busy hyping up her new concoction. 'Imagine the possibilities. A few dabs on your lover's skin and he or she is helplessly aroused, beyond reason. You can use it during normal sex, as a stimulant, or those with wickeder imaginations can devise schemes for pleasurable torment. Leave them tied up and burning for you. Make them wear it in a public place, underneath their clothes. And I'm led to understand that it can add a whole new dimension to a spanking. I will leave your admirably filthy minds to come up with your own scenarios.'

'It certainly seems to be working a treat,' comments Neil, frowning. 'I could be persuaded to carry this.' To my horror, he involves Lura in a long and involved conversation about costings, mark-ups and the like, while my inflamed pussy rages and melts on the velvet.

'Neil!' I eventually have to plead. 'Please!'

He laughs. 'OK, we'll talk about it later. Is it my turn yet? I think Sophie might need something a little stronger.'

I lift my bottom off the seat, offering him my spread as he approaches.

'She is hot,' remarks one of the strange men. 'She wants it so badly.'

'Have you ever seen one as wet as that? I am buying a bottle of that stuff before I leave here tonight.'

Neil leans over and takes a good look at what I have to give him.

'You want that stuffed, don't you, Sophie?' he asks lightly. I screw my eyes tight and nod vigorously. 'Bad luck, love,' he sympathises. 'I've got something else in mind. Turn around and bend over now.' He brandishes an implement that I can't quite identify for a few seconds, before I realise what it must be. As I wriggle around and kneel on the velvet seat, elbows down and bottom in the perfect presentation position I was taught by Dr Lassiter, I hear Lura's voice, once again giving the hard sell.

'This is a dual-purpose toy, lady and gentlemen, which can give pleasure in different ways. Is it a flogger that doubles as a butt plug, or vice versa? You can use it for one thing, or the other, or both. If Neil here would be so kind as to give us an idea ...'

The horsehair falls stingily on my bare behind, but the sting is faint and sweet, erotic rather than punishing. It both relieves and accentuates the longing in my sex – at first it seems to dissipate some of the unbearable greed of my clit, but then the warmth spreads and returns there, to redouble the delicious torment. Neil flogs me evenly across both buttocks and the part of my thighs above my stocking tops, drawing it back and swishing it down until I am groaning with lewd want, pushing my bum back for each stroke, widening my legs until the lash falls on my lips and clit, hoping that pain might lessen my ungovernable desire. It does not.

'She's loving this. Watch her push out her arse for more.'

'I'd give her more. She's bright red and she still wants him to carry on.'

'Look at her pussy lips, all puffed up and shiny.'

'Look at her clit. Ouch, that has to hurt.'

Neil finally finishes when I am hot and tingling from tailbone to lace-top and all points in between. I am still tortured by the empty state of my soaked entrance, but Neil has no intention of assuaging my need.

Instead, I feel his finger, cold with lubricant, prodding rudely between my reddened cheeks, preparing my ring to receive the instrument of recent chastisement. 'You're going to wear this whip in your naughty little arse now, Sophie,' he tells me. 'What a fitting punishment for such a rude girl.' He chuckles. 'I love this. Might have to get a few of these in too. Let's finish here first, though.'

The cold rounded end of the whip handle, slippery with lubricant, is swivelled between my bottom cheeks, right, left, right, left, inexorably forward with each half-rotation. I feel my pucker twitch and expand, slowly stretched. Neil performs the task carefully, pushing in an inch, then pulling it out again, pushing back in a little further, then pulling out again. I gasp and my ring spasms in confusion.

'Come closer,' Neil invites the audience. 'Watch it going in. It's going in all the way.'

There is an eye-watering split second while the widest point of the plug stretches my ring almost beyond endurance. Neil holds it there, resisting my efforts to either suck it in or expel it, making sure the crowd gets a good eyeful.

'That's really stretching her,' gasps the model in wonder. 'She must be used to this.'

'She is,' chuckles Lura.

Neil takes pity on me and shoves it all the way up so that only the horsehair tail protrudes from my cheeks. I gurgle with pleasure at the invasive sensation, drawing it into me, keeping it close, shedding my self-conscious skin so that the animal slut underneath is revealed. I wiggle my hips enticingly, inviting further usage. Neil tugs on the horsehair tail, jerking me backwards. 'Here, little pony,' he says. 'Are you ready to be saddled?'

The velvet chair is adjustable and Lura lowers its back while Neil turns me round so I am lying with my spine against the gentle incline, my legs spread and bent at the knees, the horsetail whip-plug held firmly inside my bottom by the seat.

'Which one of you has the bondage kit?' he asks politely.

An unfamiliar gentleman steps forward, bikerish-looking with massive ginger sideburns and a slew of fierce tattoos. His fists are full of chain links and leather straps and his mouth crowded with gold teeth. He clips the rings on my gauntlets together, joining my wrists, then attaches them to the collar ring, so I have no choice but to hold my hands around my neck. He arranges my arms and elbows so that they angle outwards at either side of my breasts, keeping them exposed and ready for anyone who wants to touch them. My body has only one line of defence left to it – my legs and feet. But not, it seems, for long. The man, with a metallic grin, lifts my legs, one at a time, and secures a soft leather strap above each knee. A length of stretchy rubber with clips at each end is passed through the ring at the back of my collar, then clipped to each of the leg straps. The result is that my legs are lifted high and pulled back over my body until my knees hover above my breasts. I am spread and split, on inescapable display, my horsetail drifting down the front of the chair.

'Nothing to hide, eh, Sophie?' Lura revels in my trussed-up

state, walking around the chair and trailing the tip of her crop over my nipples, belly and the underhang of my still-red bottom. She flicks it carelessly on my sore cheeks a couple of times, so I kick and try to move, but I cannot. 'Are you happy down there?'

My answer is a sigh. Ambiguous, I know, but all I can muster.

'Shall we take that as a yes, Sophie?'

'Ahhh.'

She strikes the crop a little harder. 'I need your answer, Sophie, or I will have to unlock your tethers. Are you quite happy?'

'Yes.' A tiny leak of speech.

'That's good. My dear, I didn't catch your name.' She is not speaking to me now, but to the model, who is looming over me, staring in fascination at my plight.

'Jacqueline,' she says.

'Jacqueline, I think the effects of our marvellous medicine might be receding. Would you care to touch it up a little?'

Jacqueline's beringed fingers uncap the bottle once more.

'Oh no,' I moan, 'not again. Please won't somebody just . . .'

She brushes my nipples again until they glare and pulse like two panic buttons, then she moves back down to the lips, and this time she dabs a tiny smear on to my clitoris. My teeth clench and I thrash in my bonds, setting them clinking. My arse contracts madly around the horsetail plug and I try to grind against it, to find a speck of relief, but it is not to be. I teeter on the edge of madness, twisting this way and that, hearing voices amid the crackling of my body's flames.

'My God. I'm recording this. Have you got one of these phones, Neil? This is the latest model.'

Driven to florid distraction by the men discussing gadgets while I suffer and burn, I begin to yelp. I am begging for mercy as coherently as I can, but nobody seems to want to grant it.

'Oh, poor Sophie,' clucks Lura, stroking my hair. 'Poor little pony. All tailed and saddled and groomed, but with no stud to mount her. Look at that gaping hole. What would make it feel better?'

'Cock!' I gasp, beside myself. 'Give me cock, please, please, I need to be fucked, please, please.'

'Well, we have some toys still to show our customers. We have a lovely vibrator here that looks just like a lipstick. Perfect for a lady's handbag.'

Another man comes forward, holding the dinky miniature shaft up for my perusal. I groan; it is far too small to satisfy. The most it can do is give my clit a bit of a buzz – but I want much more than that now.

He flicks it on and begins to run it around my sex, sloshing it through my juices. The pulse is weak and about as effective as somebody urinating on a forest fire.

'No, I want it in me!' I complain. He gallantly begins to circle my cunt with it, even pushing it a little way in, but it is hopelessly inadequate to assuage this conflagration.

'You want to come, do you?' asks the man, who is smartly dressed and rather handsome. I nod and he tuts, shaking his head. 'You want to come in front of all these people who have watched you being tied up and whipped and plugged. You don't have much shame, do you, Sophie? May I call you Sophie?' The mild buzzing continues to tantalise my nerve endings, while I push up from my spine, hoping to swallow the vibrator and all of his fingers into my quim.

'Call me what you like – just make it bigger and harder,' I whisper.

'I'd love to put my fingers in there,' he murmurs, with a questioning glance at Lura, who shakes her head firmly.

'No.'

'Yes!' I yell in contradiction.

'This is my show, Sophie, not yours. I suppose we'd better put you out of your misery though. Sir?' She nods at the final witness, who approaches bearing a dildo whose size holds no fears for me now in my extremity of need. Unusually, it is made of glass, a pellucid crystal through which the man's face is virtually undistorted. His avid lust beams through the dildo and tears into me; I know he is going to give it to me just the way I want.

'All the way in?' he asks softly, teasing my hole with the cold glass bulb. It is both shocking and heavenly, the chill smoothness of it; I wrench at my tethers even as I beg for him to fill me.

He puts a hand on my belly, keeping me immobile, and begins to slide the dildo smoothly in. My tension unravels, quickly, too quickly, spinning me round and out of control. I can hear myself gibbering but I have no idea what fragments of words are coming from my mouth; I have collapsed inwards so that my whole body now resides between my glass-brimming thighs. The plug in my bottom has narrowed my channel so that the dildo feels burstingly, lusciously tight as it glides up to meet and greet its anal neighbour. I am left there for a moment or two, to get used to the wonderful front and rear occupation, and for my audience to admire the state of me, naked and tied with my holes packed tight.

'Please,' I whimper, so close to satisfaction, yet so far away.

'Is there something I can do for you?' laughs the man, grinding the heel of his hand into the end of the dildo, forcing it even further in.

'Please fuck me with it, please.'

'Of course! You only had to ask!' He begins a leisurely manipulation of the tool, sometimes twisting it this way and that, sometimes bringing it slowly down and back, sometimes ramming it back and forth. His lack of predictable rhythm makes it difficult for me to attain the release I am striving for, but there is no way I can moderate his movements in my powerless position, so I just have to take it and hope he will find some pity for me eventually.

'Why don't you put the vibe on her clit?' he suggests to the previous man, who steps up and begins treating my outsized bud to some much-needed stimulation, while his companion continues to thrust the dildo in and out of me. I come, immediately and hugely, vast tremors laying me waste, while the audience clucks and coos, staring down at me. The men continue, though, until I am wrung out and running with sweat, holes distended, cunt raw, clit numbed after three, or is it four, high-voltage orgasms.

Then there is applause and praise that I barely take in. I lie there, feeling filleted, still full of dildo and plug, still in bondage, while Lura makes a number of lucrative business deals with her audience. Some of them bid me a cheery goodbye as they filter out back to the fair proper; Neil bends to my ear and says, 'My room tonight, sexy?' but I can't answer. The way I feel right now, it's probably a no.

'Oh, Sophie,' sighs Lura, removing the crystal dildo and plunging it into a basin of hot soapy water. 'That was superb.' She begins to wipe the lipstick vibrator with a cloth, clearly in no hurry to unleash me. 'Did you enjoy it?'

I exhale deeply. 'I nearly went mad. I think the memory is going to see me through a lot of sleepless nights though.'

'Well, you know,' says Lura, leaning over me and unclipping my restraints, 'if you have that many sleepless nights, you need more sex.'

'More? More sex?' I shake out my limbs, which are painfully stiff now. 'Does not compute.'

'Perhaps those boys aren't satisfying you.' She pouts at me, flirtatious in her uniquely intimidating way. 'Perhaps you need something more.'

'I don't need a mistress, Lura. Besides, don't you have enough members of your harem now?'

'I'll always have a vacancy for you, Sophie.' She removes my suspender belt and stockings, my collar and gauntlets, and sponges me down. She takes such care of me, dabbing my nipples so gently, wiping delicately between my lips, mopping my brow and removing the excess make-up with cold cream and tissues. Then she has me turn over on all fours, and performs the part of the operation I always dread – the removal of the butt plug.

'You know you should push, Sophie,' she scolds, slapping my bum when my treacherous muscles contract around the whip handle for a fourth time. 'It isn't as if this is new to you.'

'I know,' I mutter, shamed and subdued, but I cannot seem to stop myself until she finally wrenches it out with a flourish and gives me a few extra expiational swats of the horsehair. Then she bathes my sore arse with balm, rubbing it in long and tenderly before laying me down on my stomach and covering me with a satin throw.

'Rest for a while, Sophie,' she advises. 'I'll fetch coffee. You've another three hours behind the till to do yet. And wait till I show you what you're going to wear for that.'

She winks and pats my satiny bum with her riding crop.

I shut my eyes and drift off, making the most of the break. Everyone knows that Lura never leaves with less than her full money's worth.

Pool and Jacuzzi

One of the best things about working here is free or subsidised use of the many hotel facilities. I am coiffed and buffed by the salon, trimmed by the gym and fashionably fed in the restaurant. For a small fee, I can have my body covered in mud and pummelled into submission, though I'm pretty sure I could get something similar free of charge from my gentleman friends in the bar.

My favourite perk of all, though, is use of the pool. The pool is where all the tangled threads of the day are unknotted; my burning for Chase is extinguished by the lapping waters while any petty affronts or annoyances are diluted to insignificance as I float beneath the flickering tips of light on the ceiling.

And then, if I still need additional stress relief, there is always Jake.

Jake is still my favourite lifeguard, still here even though he no longer has to support himself through academic study, still my shaggy-haired, broad-chested, cheeky young chopper of choice. He is temporarily constant, erratically reliable. If I need an uncomplicated bit of in-out with a man who knows my erogenous zones, Jake is always on call. Not that I'm using him for my own sordid ends, you understand. Oh no, it works both ways. We are mutually safe harbours from the dark waters of passion and romance. We like it like that.

On one particular Thursday in December, the pool was quiet save for a pair of middle-aged German men in the jacuzzi discussing the banking crisis. I did my little mermaid impression for half an hour, diving and swirling in the blue-green depths, until I was suddenly seized around the waist. The suddenness of it caused me to scissorkick but the weightlessness of my legs sent them off in completely the wrong direction and I was easily overpowered by my subaqueous attacker.

'Jake!' I protested, once my head broke the surface. I was clamped with my back to his chest, his arms wrapped tight around my ribcage. I continued to kick my legs, but more for aerobic exercise than in a serious escape attempt.

'What's the matter? I thought you were drowning!'

'Oh, yeah, right, of course you did,' I scoffed. Jake used this excuse for a watery grope roughly once a month.

'Just doing my job, ma'am,' he said in a cheesy Dudley Do-right accent, shuffling backwards through the water until he was leaning against the pool wall. The depth here was mid-chest for him, while the surface of the water played about my shoulders and collarbone. He relaxed one arm and sent a hand down to my bikini briefs, breaching the elastic. His palm lay flat against my mons while his fingers curled underneath, pushing between my sex lips.

'Not now!' I whispered urgently. 'Those German guys!'

'Don't tell me you don't like an audience,' chuckled Jake into my ear, his fingertips dancing a teasing jig on my clit. 'You've done it in front of people before, haven't you?'

'Yes, but only people who wanted to watch! These guys might be here for a conference of the Virtuously Pure League of Berlin or something.' Tiny exhalations of mirth tickled my earlobe. One of Jake's fingers found my vagina. My bikini bottoms now had water seeping into them and it felt strange and cold between Jake's hand and the bare skin of my groin.

'They're fat-cat bankers, Soph, not priests. I bet they'll finish up in here and go and wank over porn flicks on cable all evening. I bet they'd love to see a flash of your arse or a nipple or something. It'd make their day.'

Jake's hand, like a firm, muscular fish, flipped this way and that, back and forth in my gushing channel. He began using the other to rub my nipples over my bandeau top. My wet hair was plastered to my neck and it was beginning to feel decidedly tropical in there. He nuzzled my neck with his lips and nose.

'Look over at them.' I did. They were pretending not to look, but every so often a guilty eye slid in our direction. 'They're voyeurs. Give them something to . . .'

'Voy?' I suggested.

'Yeah. Listen, I dare you to go and sit in the jacuzzi with them and take off your bikini.'

'What? No!' I squirmed and squished against Jake's unyielding fingers.

'They won't see anything. The bubbles will cover you. But you'll know. And I'll know. Don't you think it would be mindblowing to be sitting in the jacuzzi, naked and getting fingered by me, right in front of them, not knowing whether they knew what was going on or not? Don't tell me that doesn't turn you on, Soph.'

It did. The idea of it. The reality though . . .

'What if they complain? Isn't it sexual harrassment or something? We could lose our jobs.'

'They won't complain. They might want to join in though.'

'Shut up!'

'Are you losing your nerve? Have you lost your edge?'

'Shut up! Oooh!' Three of his fingers were widening my passage now, but the water had an oddly anti-lubricating effect and their manoeuvres were beginning to chafe. 'All right then. I'll give it a go.'

Jake kissed my neck in triumph. 'That's my Sophie,' he said approvingly. 'I really fancy a jacuzzi as well. I'm going to turn up the bubbles to full whack, OK? I'll see you in there.'

He let me go and quickly hoisted himself up to the poolside, racing over to the jacuzzi in the hope that speed would blur the huge bulge in his trunks. I decided to help him out with a little distraction, fixing my eye on the jacuzzi men and emerging slowly up the pool steps, trying to channel Ursula Andress in *Dr No*. I enjoyed the feeling of the rivulets running down my body, soaking into my bikini, and I shook my wet hair back, half-closing my eyes. I made sure they were not fully closed though. Didn't want a stubbed toe ruining the effect.

Then I was padding along the blue and green tiles with their inlaid scenes from Greek mythology, my feet shaking droplets all over the nymphs and satyrs as I approached. The German men's faces grew comically larger and more expectant with each step I took until I could see them scrambling to make room for me.

Jake looked slyly up from the setting switches, grinning at me. I climbed the steps to the lip of the spa bath, then descended into its foaming welcome, sitting myself down on the lower ledge, so that only my shoulders crested the bubbles. I smiled politely at my fellow occupants, who nodded back, one of them baring white teeth below his moustache. They lolled opposite me, taking every opportunity to show off their gold signet rings and impressively tanned chests, exchanging the odd remark in German whilst keeping their eyes trained on my neck.

Finally, one of them spoke to me. 'You work here?' he opened.

I smiled and nodded, then I asked them how long they were staying for. Their self-glorifying exposition was all I needed to refocus their attention away from my body; as they spoke, I reached behind and unclipped my top. The bubbles fizzed and popped pleasingly against my bare breasts, hidden from plain sight by the endless vortex on the surface. Jake came to sit next to me and I discreetly passed him the balled-up bandeau, which he stuffed inside his trunks for safe keeping. He slid an arm around me, so that the men understood I was not to be courted. One hand covered my right breast, squeezing and kneading.

'Are you seeing each other?' The Germans were now addressing their questions to Jake, as if asking his permission to lech over me.

'Yeah.' Jake smiled smugly. He knew I hated it when he got all boyfriendy, not that he did it often. 'We're getting married next year.' I pinched his hip, but he barely seemed to register it.

'Congratulations,' the men chorused. 'We should buy you a bottle of champagne,' one of them continued. 'Champagne goes so nicely with a jacuzzi.'

'It's the bubbles, I suppose,' I said vaguely.

Jake lowered his mouth to my ear. 'Where are your knickers?' he growled. 'Get them off.'

He headed the Germans off by describing the sumptuous reception party the hotel was going to host for us, while I wriggled about on the ledge seat, pushing the elastic down over my bottom until it was bare. Slowly and painstakingly they traversed the length of my legs until they arrived at my feet. I gripped them between my toes and plunged an arm down to retrieve them. Now I was fully nude in the jacuzzi and the feeling of powerful bubbling between my thighs was as exquisite as ever. Jake and I had often shared a naked jacuzzi, but never before while it was open to the public.

Covertly, I passed the scrap of material to Jake – another item for his crotch stash.

'Do you miss your wives while you're away?' Jake was asking politely, the conversation still on the subject of love and marriage.

The Germans laughed, a little uncomfortably, and assured us that they did.

'Our wives are not like yours,' one of them said dreamily, looking as if he wanted to pierce the opaque water with his eyes. A shiver ran down my back as I became flooded with the certain knowledge that he knew I was naked down there. Jake's hand clamped hard against my sex; this was turning him on too.

'What, not to look at?' he asked, massaging my labia and clit with firm, sure motions. The combination of his fingers and the bubbles fizzing up and down my bum crack was difficult to bear with a straight face. My wits were losing control of the situation, handing it over to my senses. *Let them watch*, whispered a wanton inner voice. *You came in front of an audience of total strangers before . . . what makes you too modest to do the same thing again?*

'No, not to look at,' answered the man. 'Also, your girlfriend seems to . . . enjoy life. She seems to like a bit of fun.'

'Oh, yes,' Jake agreed, moving one thigh around the back of me until I sat between his legs, clamped in position while he played with my tits and pussy, his hard cock parked between my arse cheeks. The bubbles bounced off me and my blood felt hotter than fire. 'She's always liked a bit of fun.'

'Maybe you would show us? What sort of fun?' The Germans were leaning forward, their hands fishing towards me, their feet pushing against my calves. Oh, what was happening?

But Jake shook his head. 'No, sorry, gents. She's all mine. You'll just have to invest in a spa bath for your own homes and persuade your wives to jump in with you.'

'I've tried it, believe me,' muttered one. 'OK, no problem.'

The two men stood, revealing tightly tented Speedos, picked up their towels and bade us a formal good evening.

'I thought you were going to offer me to them then,' I whispered breathily to Jake, the idea thrilling me now that it was not likely to be realised.

'I wanted to,' Jake admitted. 'But you aren't mine to offer, so I had to leave it.'

'Never mind,' I said, spreading my legs wider and laying my head back, ready for an electric whirlpool of an orgasm.

'Would you have let them?' Jake asked, pinching my nipples and biting my shoulder, taking his fingers away from my alarmed sex and flinging my bikini into the centre of the jacuzzi. 'I bet you would. You would have loved it. Sitting between two strange men while they fingered you and fondled you. One thigh over each of their laps, spread wide for them.' He turned me around so I was kneeling on the ledge, my pussy pressing into the hard swell of his crotch. The bubbles caught me on my perineum, feeling as if they were going to penetrate me in each orifice above and below. Jake began to stroke my bottom, then he dipped his head and sucked at a nipple, lifting it out of the water to face this new version of wettening. Our crotches ground against each other, bubbles bursting between them, trapped between the pressure of the water and the thrust of competing groins.

'God, these bubbles feel good,' I moaned at Jake, who swiftly spread my rear cheeks and let my sensitive pucker feel the full force.

'Just think, Sophie,' he said, his tongue gliding around the nooks and hollows of my ear, 'You could be sitting on one cock, while another pushes into you up here.'

'And where would you be?' I grunted, pondering this thought as I bounced around, buffeted this way and that in the maelstrom of lust and water jets.

'I'd be watching. But not just watching. I'd be standing at the side, just over the ledge here, and you'd be sucking me. Just think of it, Sophie, three cocks, one girl. And when it was all over, you could just sink back into the bubbles and let them wash you off.'

'Mmm.' I voiced my appreciation roughly in synchronisation with my orgasm. A jacuzzi orgasm, bubbling up and frothing, bursting past every barrier.

Later on, while Jake sat on the ledge with his cock in my mouth, he made a suggestion.

'Could you really do it though?' he wondered aloud. He tasted of chlorine and salt. 'Would you really enjoy that?'

I half-nodded, as much as I could without grazing him with my teeth.

'Yeah. I think I would too. Especially if there were more girls involved too. Kind of like an orgy. Have you ever been to an orgy?'

I shook my head gingerly. I'd had threesomes, I'd taken up to five men in one session, but I'd never had three cocks all at once. And there had never been another woman present either.

'Why don't we have one? Here in the pool. A pool party. A Christmas pool party.' These little bursts of inspiration hit Jake one at a time, his final thought coinciding with the spurting of his citrus-tasting semen into my mouth. Jake always had this hint of lime with his spunk, which I rather appreciated.

I popped off, licking my lips, and looked up at him. 'Might that not be a little risky?'

'Not if we pick the right time.' Jake winked and pulled his shorts back up. 'Leave it with me.'

I left it with him. Two days before Christmas, once I had decided that it was just a silly fantasy and he had abandoned the idea, he cornered me in the cocktail bar and told me gleefully that it was all on for tomorrow night.

'Christmas Eve?'

'Yeah.'

'But there are hundreds of bookings and the staff Christmas drinks.'

'I know. They'll all be safely in the ballroom though. The pool is closed from nine o'clock in the evening until Boxing Day. Nobody will come down.'

'What if we're needed? What if our absence is noted?'

'Nobody on the list will be needed. Reception will be covered. Nobody can use the gym or pool, so Lincoln and I are fine. Jade and Maria have the week off.'

'So that's five? You, me, Lincoln, Jade and Maria? You realise that Jade is gay, don't you?'

'Yeah, but Maria is bi. So that could work. I'm happy to watch them anyway.'

'Ah well, my triple-cock dream may come true another time.'

'No, I forgot to mention. I invited Lloyd too.'

'Oh, you DIDN'T!'

Lloyd the creepy head barman had spent three years in unsuccessful attempts to remove my knickers. It isn't that I'm fussy – really, I'm not – but there is something about him that makes me think that he would be secretly filming us for some pervy website. I just do not trust him.

'What's wrong with Lloydy? He's a good bloke!'

'Only a man would think that. I don't think he's a good bloke at all. I think he's spent so long trying to fuck me that now he just wants me fired. I think this might be his opportunity.'

'Oh, no way, Sophie, no way. He wouldn't. He'll be as guilty in this as the rest of us anyway. How can he grass us up for something he's done himself?'

'Can't you ask someone else instead?'

'I've asked him now. He's well up for it.'

'No kidding?' I pushed my dish of rice crackers away. 'Well, I don't think I am now.'

'Sophie, Sophie, don't let me down.' Jake ran a hand through his shagpile so that it hung alluringly in his eyes – his default gesture when he wants something. But it's so cute. 'Three cocks, remember – and Lloyd's is championship material. I've seen it in the shower.'

I gurgled into my wine. 'Right. Look. You have to make it clear to him that this is just sex, just once, and will never, ever happen again.'

'He's cool with that. He has a girlfriend anyway.'

'The dirty dog.'

'I reckon he is. I reckon he'll have a few tricks up his sleeve.' Jake raised a saucy eyebrow, setting me off on an optimistic train of thought. Yes, Lloyd would probably be filthy. And that's how I wanted to feel. Full-on down-and-dirty used-in-every-orifice slut. I thought Lloyd could do that. I liked Jake too much, and couldn't take Lincoln seriously enough, but Lloyd was a bit villainous and a bit dangerous.

Yes. Now I came to think it through, Lloyd was practically the perfect man for the job.

I suppose all of us were a bit on edge during those festive cocktails. While the rest of the staff were knocking back the Baileys until the paper crowns slipped over their eyes, six of us were keeping our heads clear.

Jade and Maria, canoodling in a corner, smiled their twin smile at me every time I passed them, while Lincoln seemed unable to switch himself out of pulling mode even with the promise of guaranteed group sex in the very near future. An overexcited Swedish lady almost succeeded in luring him to her room until Jake intervened.

But the person I really had my eye on was Lloyd. And I have to say, the reverse was also true. He was working until twelve, shaking and pouring and crushing ice. I had never really bothered to watch him before, but he was quite graceful in his way. He had strong wrists, though his fingers were still fat. His sleek hair, flopping over his collar, might just counterbalance the shifty little eyes. He didn't have much in the way of angles, but his lips were suggestively plump.

He came on to every female customer. I had never found this irritating before – had always considered it part of his job description, just as part of mine was to flirt with the men and compliment the women. But now an obscure threadworm of resentment burrowed beneath my skin. It's *me* you should be looking at, *me* whose pants you should be trying to charm off, *me* who is letting you win a final victory in your three-year campaign. Look at *me*.

I tapped the foot of my glass smartly against the counter top.

'Is a bit of service here out of the question?'

Lloyd smiled a tender apology at the woman he had been chatting up, removed his odious eyes from her cleavage and directed them at me. You could have sewn a patchwork quilt of emotions from the look he shot across my bows. One square of challenge, one square of annoyance, one square of knowing smugness, one square of menace, and one gigantic huge fuck-off square of lust dead centre.

'Madam?' he drawled, sliding down the bar as if on castors.

'Don't madam me,' I snipped. 'If I'm going to go through with this I need another Whisky Sour. A large one.'

'A Whisky Sour? Sure I can't tempt you with . . .'

'If you say Sloe Comfortable Screw, I will deck you,' I warned him.

'No, I was going to say a gangbang,' hissed Lloyd, grinning. I swear there were fangs in there somewhere. 'Except we've got that to come, haven't we? So to speak. And I'm very much looking forward to it. Aren't you?'

'I'll be straight with you, Lloyd. You weren't my first choice of orgy partner. You weren't even my thousand-and-first choice. But I suppose we should just try to ... pretend we aren't each other. Pretend we're complete strangers.'

'Well, that is what you go for, after all, isn't it, Sophie?'

'Shut the fuck up. I mean, you won't be having me. You won't be having Sophie the person. It'll be pure, neat sex. No mixers, no fizz, no olive on a stick. You are cock and I am cunt. That's all.'

'You put it so nicely.' He bared his teeth, but you couldn't have called it a smile. 'Don't worry, sweetheart, I know I'll never be good enough for you. Unlike every other man in town. It's strictly a pole in a hole for me too. Whisky Sour, you said? The sourer the better.'

I drained my glass recklessly, wanting to get into the mood, but my encounter with Lloyd had sent my libido wildly out of kilter. I would have been happy just to leave with Jake and have a little friendly festivity of our own, just me and him and a gallon of Baileys. Or Chase ... where was Chase? With family, he said. Surrey, he said. I wasn't so sure.

But the clock struck twelve and Jake gave the signal, watching as first Jade and Maria, then Lincoln, then Lloyd made discreet exits.

'Are you ready for this?' Jake asked me, taking my hand and drawing me out of the messy revel.

'I don't know how to be ready for it,' I confessed. 'But ... it'll be all right, won't it?'

'Still worried about Lloyd?'

'Let's say there's no love lost. But we're going to try and put that to one side.'

Jake kissed my brow.

'It'll be amazing, you'll see,' he told me.

Our four co-conspirators milled by the pool entrance, waiting for Jake to unlock the promised land.

'Just a sec,' he said, organising lights and the switching on of filters and jacuzzis and the like. The rest of us looked sideways at each other, smirking, sheepish, fidgety.

'How are we going to do this?' Lincoln opened. 'I mean, you know. There's logistics to consider. Three straight guys, one straight girl, one bi girl, one dyke. Should we do a rota or something?'

The girls snorted and I rolled my eyes. 'A rota?'

'OK. Not a rota. What then?'

'Lincoln, I believe you're meant to just ... go with the flow.' I put a hand on his chest in its expensive black mesh vest. Some luxury sports brand or other. A flicker-flutter, like what you might feel in the breast of a captured bird, against my palm. I melted. Lincoln, of all people, was nervous.

'The flow?' he said.

'Yeah. Shall we get into the water? Just you and me?'

'The water, yeah. The water's good.' Lincoln brightened and began stripping off. It occurred to me that it was the presence of other men that was bothering him – being watched and assessed and judged. The pool was a hiding place.

'Last one in gets a spanking!' I challenged, kicking off my high heels and knowing perfectly well that Lincoln would beat me to it, unless he had stockings and suspenders on underneath those baggy trousers.

'Bad idea, babe,' he chuckled, already down to his jock-strap while I was still fumbling with my skirt zipper. He ridded himself of the surplus covering and stood, a magnificent block of man, with his arms folded, obstructing my path to the pool steps. 'I'm ready to slap some ass.'

Rolling down my stockings, I noticed that the others had drifted off to the jacuzzi. Maria and Jade were sitting in it, kissing, while Jake stood behind them, his hands cupping Maria's breasts, nibbling at her neck. Lloyd, still clothed, simply watched them, his eyes slipping between the snogging sapphists and my striptease. I kept my eyes on Lloyd, grinning and giggling with pleasurable fear, until the knickers were off. Lincoln made a lunge for me and I skipped sideways and threw myself into the pool, as always relishing the moment that its perfect static calm ruptures into froth and wavelets.

He roared and dived after me. I plunged beneath the surface, zigzagging and doubling back, enjoying the feeling of the water rushing up around every part of me without the barrier of Lycra. I lasted mere seconds before King Triton captured his absconding mermaid, our two heads cresting the wave together. We spluttered and coughed and laughed and squealed, then he hauled me over the edge of the pool and gave me three hard smacks to my wet behind before pulling me back in against his chest and starting a game of octopus-hands.

I was so busy twisting and slapping and splashing that I did not see Lloyd break away from the jacuzzi group until he was sitting on the poolside, dipping his bare feet in the water, still wearing his white shirt and boxers.

'Lincoln!' he called. 'Oi, Lincoln!' Lincoln tucked me under one arm and looked up in annoyance.

'What, man? I'm getting down to business here.'

'She can wait. Jade's got a challenge for you.'

'Jade?'

'She wants to know if a man can hit the same spots with his tongue as a woman. She thinks not.'

'Can't you do the honours?'

'She's asking for you. Besides, I've got other things on my mind.'

We looked over at the jacuzzi. I could see the back of Maria's dark head, bobbing up and down Jake's abdomen in an unmistakable way. Jade lay back, looking bored, soaking up the froth. Lincoln looked at me, then over at Jade.

'Think I could turn her?' he asked with a low chuckle.

'No chance,' I said. He dropped me like a stone and I fell briefly underneath the water's surface, seeing his blurred legs striding off out of the pool and knowing that now I would be alone at the tender mercies of Lloyd. I resurfaced, shaking my head until my ears were clear. Lloyd was still sitting there, watching me, leaning back on the palms of his hands.

'Come here,' he said. 'There's something I want to do to you.'

'Just one thing?' I asked, swimming over but keeping my distance, beyond range of his hands or feet.

'No,' he admitted. 'Not just one thing. But this is the thing I want to do right now.'

'Tell me.'

'Come here and I'll show you.'

'You'll have to catch me first.' I pushed off with my feet against the side of the pool, swinging on to my back and waving at him while my legs kicked up mountains of foam.

'You bitch! I've chased you long enough. You're not getting away this time.'

Without removing his clothes, Lloyd launched himself off the edge and into the water. His build was bulky, so I did not expect him to catch up with my streamlined stroke too quickly, but it seemed there was a shade more muscle than fat on those bones, because he gained pace alarmingly once he embarked on his pursuit. I did not know which way to turn, and it was looking less and less likely that I would make it to the steps to effect a dripping escape across the tiles. Less than a foot from the poolside, he make a lunge for me and grabbed an ankle. Kick and scream as I might, I could not shake him off; he reeled me in and flipped me around so that I faced him, holding me to his heaving wet shirt by my hips. The water lapped over my breasts and the soaked cloth of his boxers covered my pubic triangle. I tried to push against him with my legs, but he stood firm, grinning victoriously before switching into a more sinister gear.

'I've got you at last,' he said, reminding me of Snidely Whiplash. I had the strongest presentiment that I was about to be tied to a metaphorical railway track. 'I've waited so long for this.'

'Make the most of it,' I advised him. 'It won't be happening again.'

'We'll see,' he rasped, and then he bent and put his lips to the side of my neck, kissing the droplets at first, then licking up and down a little, then suddenly clamping down fiercely, sucking and nipping with full force.

'What are you doing? Don't make a mark!' I fretted, but he continued his vampiric claiming of my skin, pulling me tighter against him, encircling me with steel. His erection unfurled between my thighs, the cloth of his boxers pushing between my lower lips, while the upper part of me withdrew into glorious reminiscence. Oh yes. This was why we did this as teenagers. Because it feels good, it feels so good, so primal, so vicious and yet so delicate. I was being marked, in a place I would not be able to hide it, and I should have been angry, but it felt so good, it drained the anger out of me. There was something behind it, something I had not felt in so long, in all those years of seeking my pleasure and taking it where I found it ... a feeling of being ravished. Ravishment, delirium, captivation, possession. I gave myself up to it, yielded to its seduction and strength, bowed my head and laid it against his shoulder, giving up my neck for more.

He gave me a final leeching suck, then surveyed his work with satisfaction, pressing against it with a wet finger.

'I'm going to tell everyone in the hotel I did that to you,' he whispered. 'Including Chase.'

'Don't you fucking dare!' I exclaimed, tumbling immediately back into struggle and rebellion. He laughed, hanging on to my upper arms while I tried to trip him up.

'Have I said something I shouldn't? You seemed to be having fun before.'

I sank my teeth into his shoulder. He cried out, let go of me for an instant. I lashed towards his face but he caught my wrist and twisted it. We fought like that, in a kind of slow-motion forced by the water's weight, until he succeeded in getting me to the side of the pool, where he jammed me up against the side, snatched my wrists in one hand and the back of my head with the other and proceeded to kiss me to death.

The kissing was harder and more bruising than the fighting, a conflict of tongues and teeth, a war of lips. My initial impulse to knee him in the groin, blocked by his solid bulk, gave way to pinching and hair-pulling and then eventually surrender, once he had kissed every martial spark out of me. He tongued and probed me into a final accord. Lloyd had won the battle. I would reconsider my war strategy once I had had a chance to estimate casualties.

'You're a bastard,' I whispered, once he was sure enough of his conquest to release my lips, but there was no fire in the words.

'Yes,' he acknowledged. 'I'm just what you need.'

I didn't want to want him, but I did. I had exposed a vulnerable corner and he had swarmed into it, enforced an occupation and would be the devil himself to shift now. I broke our eye contact and glanced briefly over to the jacuzzi. Maria appeared to be straddling Lincoln on the ledge, but

Jake and Jade were both staring over at us, jaws on the floor. Jake, naked, dishevelled and semi-erect again after Maria's oral ministrations, strolled over.

'Room for one more?' he asked hoarsely.

Lloyd looked him up and down with a measure of contempt. He wanted it to be clear that he was the alpha alpha in this scenario.

'Give me a few minutes, Jakey,' he requested. 'I'll let you know when we're ready for you.'

'Sure. I'll just ... watch for a minute, then?'

Lloyd shrugged. 'Unless you want to give Maria one.'

'No, I'll watch. Thanks.'

I sensed a competitive edge, a locking of antlers. I would never have put money on Lloyd against Jake or Lincoln, but now it seemed all bets were off.

Lloyd returned his full attention to me, taking my breasts in reverent hands and swishing the water over and around them. His tongue returned to my overwhelmed mouth and his rampant cock – championship material indeed – continued a bruising assault on my pubic bone. Once he was sure that no atom of my oral cavity remained unexamined, he turned to the spot behind my ear, then began sucking at my neck again until my eyes rolled backwards, moving ravenously down until his chin met the water. He lifted me a little, keeping me steady against the cold tiles at my back, so that my breasts were above the licking waters, which he replaced with his licking tongue. He nipped the nipples until they bulged and throbbed, then sucked at the surrounding flesh, leaving dusky red patches on its whiteness.

Then he lifted me higher, until I sat on the edge of the pool, spread my knees and pounced. He gorged on my slippery wet core, burying himself nose-deep, and his tongue was everywhere at once – circling my lips, pressing my clit, poking my opening urgently and hungrily. He feasted on me until I could bear no more and I kicked up a lather, trying to hoist myself back from the brink of an orgasm I didn't want from him. But he was not having it, and he held fast to my thighs, retreating a fraction to bite and suck and leave marks on their soft insides before returning to his cruel pleasuring of me. We both knew that if he made me come, he had won, won, won and he kept up the pressure until I had nowhere to go but orgasm. I came, I swore, he conquered.

He laughed up at me, his whiskers flattened down by damp, his face shiny slick.

'Jakey,' he called over to our avid voyeur, 'fetch us a couple of those floats, would you?'

'What for?' I gasped, still recovering from his oral onslaught.

'Shuffle back, lie down and you'll see,' he said, finally removing his trunks, inside the pouch of which he had cunningly hidden a condom wrapper. He levered himself out of the water and stood at the poolside, dripping down all over my supine body, eating it up with his eyes while his teeth tore a corner in the foil package.

I strained my neck to look over at the jacuzzi again. Maria was fucking Jade from behind with a strap-on dildo, while Lincoln seemed to have persuaded the lesbian member of the party that she really ought to at least taste a man's cock before she rejected the idea outright.

Jake returned with the oval polystyrene floats. Lloyd skinned on the condom, crouched down and parted my legs, placing the floats between my thighs.

'These tiles are hard on the knees,' he explained, kneeling down and spreading my lips with a finger and thumb. 'I don't want to be thinking about my knees while I'm giving you the fucking of your life, Soph, do I?'

'Don't set your bar too high,' I cautioned him sulkily. I

still could not quite find it in myself to give in to him gracefully.

'Never mind all of the others who were here before me,' he said, dipping his tip into my juices and swirling them around. 'If this is going to be my first and last time with you, I'm going to see that you remember it.'

'I think I probably will,' I squeaked, raising my bottom from the tiles when I felt his crown begin to open and spread me.

'But the thing is,' he said, his voice strained as he pushed and stretched, easing in and up, 'I don't think it will be the last time.'

'Don't fucking count on it,' I snapped. 'Ohhh.' God, it felt good. I was filled to the brim, pinned beneath him. I could see now that much of his stockiness was down to muscle, though there was some evidence of a love of the other sensual pleasures of life around his middle and hips. I like substantial weight on top of me, though, and he fitted me better than those gangling angular boys I so often went for. I lifted my thighs and rubbed them up and down his sides, my feet occasionally tapdancing on his bottom.

'Keep still,' he growled, and then he held me down, his hands on my shoulders, and I almost came then and there, while he pulled very slowly back out, very, very slowly, setting every single nerve ending inside me jangling.

'Oh, don't!' The words tumbled out quick and sharp. 'Don't!'

'Don't what? Don't pull out? Do you want this, Sophie?'

'Yes, please, keep going.'

He grinned. 'Beg me.'

'You fucker!'

'No, that's not begging, is it, Sophie? Beg me nicely.'

'I want your cock. Give it to me.'

'Mmm.' He savoured the words for a second, shutting his eyes raptly. 'But what's the magic word?'

'Please,' I snarled, shaking my head from side to side so he wouldn't see my expression. 'Please fuck me now, properly, hard.'

'Properly, hard,' he echoed, slamming his full length back up to the hilt. 'I can do that for you, Sophie.'

And he could. Properly, thoroughly, lengthily, widely, the pool floated away, the mingling moans and expletives of my fellow fuckers drifting on the humid air until they were far, far away from my world. My world, which consisted of my cunt, and the hammering it was taking, and the man who was responsible for the sparks and stars that streamed through my blood. And *there* was the difference. The man who was responsible. The cock-owner rarely figured in that heated mental world of sex; for the most part, the men in my encounters were simple conduits of sensation. I used them and they were happy to be used. But Lloyd would not put up with that. For Lloyd it was crucial that I was constantly aware of him, of the himness of him, of the cock being his, of his ownership of my orgasm.

I was going to come again, and he knew it. 'Say my name,' he rasped.

I never say a man's name when I come. I've usually forgotten it by then. But I did it for Lloyd. I don't know why I did it, but I did.

'Lloyd, Lloyd, Lloyd,' I chanted brokenly.

'Sophie,' he crooned, taking one hand from my shoulder and stroking a thumb across my brow before dropping down to kiss it. He began to pull out. I sat up, confused. Surely he hadn't . . . ? He was still as stiff as a flagpole. 'So about that orgy?' he said to me, raising an eyebrow.

God, I'd forgotten all about it. I looked around, seeing Jake loitering above us like a third wheel, hand clasped around his erection, face vaguely disappointed. The other three were still hammer-and-tongs in one configuration or another.

'Is it what you want, Sophie? Do you still want to have three cocks?'

I was unsure of myself suddenly. The one I hadn't wanted ... the one I had hoped to avoid ... that was the one I wanted now.

'Do you think ... ?' I had no idea what I was saying.

'I know you'd love it, Sophie. I know you'd like to feel it. I want you to feel it too.'

'Have you ... done this before?'

'Group sex? Yeah.' He smiled louchely, took my hand and led me to the graduated pool steps. 'Ready for it, Jake?' he asked over his shoulder.

Jake coughed and loped over to us, watching helplessly again when Lloyd took over my lips for yet more kissing. 'Come on then,' he broke off to harangue the hapless lifeguard. 'Touch her. Do something.' Back into the kiss, but this time Jake stood behind me, fingering my pussy and squeezing my nipples. The water tickled my ankles; I was beaded with steamy sweat, and both their bodies stuck to me.

'Sit on the step,' Lloyd told Jake, who did as he was told dumbly, his prick pointing at the ceiling from its damp nest. Lloyd kissed me one last time, then turned me towards Jake, put his hands on my shoulders and lowered me down until I straddled the long, lean erection. My knees plashed down into the shallows; I put my hands on Jake's tight biceps and wrapped his rubbered cock up in my sleeve. Jake sighed and threw his head back, grinding his hips into me. I began a slow ride, stroking up and down, rotating my pelvis until he had touched my walls at every angle. I kept it loose and languid, enjoying Lloyd's burning eyes on us, enjoying how very wicked he made me feel. Then Lloyd moved around behind me, and the next thing I was aware of was my rear cheeks being spread and a wetted finger probing my back passage. I breathed in sharply and contracted the muscles, but he continued to circle it, running his other hand up from my occupied slot, across my perineum to where that one stubby finger was doing its damnable work. Shivers and goosebumps took hold of me; I loved any attention to that area, especially when I was also otherwise engaged.

'How's that, Sophie?' breathed Lloyd, dabbing his fingers in the pool again before setting back to work. 'Does this feel good?'

'Mm hmm,' I confirmed, rocking on Jake while Lloyd's thick finger crossed the ring, giving me my first hint of double penetration.

'Do you like to be buggered, Sophie?' he asked, pulling and pushing the finger quite roughly, preparing the tight channel.

'Yes,' I mewed, biting my lip, blushing across my body.

'She does,' Jake seconded.

'I knew you would. I knew you'd like it. And I'm glad, because I've been thinking about taking your arse ever since Jake invited me to this. Well, I'll be honest, I've been thinking about it for three years. And tonight, I'm having it. Do you have any objection to that?'

'None,' I whimpered as a second finger speared inside.

'Good.' His fingers popped out and then his tongue was there, drawing a wavy line around the expanding ring that almost drove me out of my mind with exquisite intensity. I squirmed violently, trying to elude his warm breath, but I was trapped on Jake's pole. His hands were on my hips, while Lloyd wrapped an arm around my waist and there was that blunt knock at the door, that impossibly round and wide visitor to my secret sanctum.

'Oh, it'll hurt!' I yelped.

'Just for a second,' he reassured, his voice all treacly warm now. 'Then it'll be sooo nice, Sophie, so very nice.' He continued this stream of comforting nonsense-talk until his tip had widened my hole enough to push through. 'You're doing so well, Sophie, you're doing so well. That's it, don't panic, keep still.' He was boring ahead, gently but relentlessly, the thickness beginning to stretch and sting. I screwed up my face and puffed. Jake played with my clit, distracting me through the dreaded few seconds of stabbing pain, then Lloyd was in, halfway, three-quarters, all the way. I was impossibly full, laid waste by cock, pussy stretched and bum stuffed to bursting. How would I move?

As it happened, I did not need to move. They did that for me. Jake and Lloyd seemed to reach a tacit agreement, a rhythmic alliance, one thrusting while the other pulled back. Streams of painful pleasure poured up and down both recesses, up, down, back, forth until I thought I would soon be nothing but pulpy mush inside. Throughout, Lloyd kept up his sin-soaked commentary, making me mutter yes and no answers amidst the blinding sensation. Did I know that my arse was his now? Had I ever been taken so hard or so well? Did I realise I'd met my match? Did I realise my arse was so very, very tight and so very hot and so very sweet? Did I realise that I would be bending over for him many more times? Did I have any idea what I did to him? Jake kept up a yowling counterpoint of 'Oh God, yes, oh God, oh that feels good' until he came, digging his fingers into my hips, and I came too, wildly and violently, banging my knees on the floor, sinking my fingers into Jake's scalp, even screaming, while Lloyd reamed me through it, finally releasing his load when the tears started leaking out of me and on to Jake's chest.

'Shhh.' Lloyd, still inside me, pulled me up against his chest and kissed my tears. 'Wasn't that bad, was it?' He chuckled, but there was a nervous catch to it.

'No ... it was ... intense,' I sobbed. What the hell was all this about? Crying after sex?

'I thought you were an old hand at all this,' he murmured.

'I thought so,' I said. I looked around. At some point during our bout, Jade and Maria had entered the pool and were swimming and smooching at the far end. Lincoln stood on the side, glowering down at us.

'Hey!' he said. 'I thought Sophie was going for three cocks. I thought she was going to suck me while you two fucked her.'

'Might have to . . . rain check,' I said faintly.

'Haven't you had it all sucked out of you yet?' asked Lloyd drily. 'Maria and Jade seemed to be doing a good job of it.'

'Sophie gives the best head,' said a querulous Lincoln.

'That's experience,' said Lloyd. 'Maria is keen though, isn't she? And she looks as if she could take a bit more. Go on. Show her how it's done.' He waved Lincoln away and laughed as his godlike physique descended into the depths, seeking yet another willing mouth.

My limbs regained a semblance of functionality and I began to unwind myself from Jake's softened cock, climbing over his thighs, still in Lloyd's tight embrace.

'Why don't you join them?' Lloyd suggested to his rival, pointing an elbow in the direction of the frolicking trio. 'I'll take care of Sophie. She's a bit shell-shocked but she'll be OK.'

'I . . . don't know.' Jake frowned between the two of us. 'Sophie?'

'Yeah, you go and play. I'll be fine.'

Lloyd picked me up, carried me to the jacuzzi and plonked me down on his lap. We sat like that for a while, letting the insistent bubbles cleanse and heal us, watching the riot in the pool. Jake had got some inflatables out and the four-some were demonstrating the impossibility of having sex on a lilo.

Lloyd laughed when Jake and Maria were plunged

sideways into the water for a fourth time. He kissed the top of my head. 'Do you still hate me?' he asked.

I could not answer for a while. I felt skinless, endangered, laid bare. And I wanted Lloyd to kiss me again. For a long time.

'Of course I hate you,' I answered dreamily. 'Hate is not hate which alters when it alteration finds.'

'So I'm not what you thought? Better or worse?'

'Both.' I gave him a weak smile, feeling those treacherous tears at the back of my eyes.

He kissed me again. For a long time.

Maids on Call

If you called Maria a starfucker she wouldn't be offended; she takes pride in this little sideline of hers. She would never stoop so low as to sell to a tabloid, but I've heard some juicy titbits or two. Did you know that that long-haired international footballer loves nothing more than to wear your stilettos during sex? Or that a certain well-known balladeer hits notes higher than he ever can on stage if you offer to massage his prostate with a dildo?

I thought of it as harmless enough – nobody was hurt, and I had no interest in the celeb guests, finding their vanity tiresome. Any man whose ego is bigger than his cock can get them both stroked elsewhere; Hotel Sophie has no vacancies for him.

But Maria derives a spinetingling thrill from watching the latest famous man or men as they stride up the steps with eyes shaded to deflect the popping flashbulbs, and storm through the lobby with a backwash of publicists and stylists and documentary film-makers in their wake, and thinking *You're next*. It is a personal challenge that she rarely fails to meet. She turns up with a chocolate for the pillow or fresh flowers for the vases, does a lot of unnecessary bending over in her short, tight skirt and before you can say Room Service she is on her back on the Egyptian cotton with her knickers around her ankles.

Of course, there is the odd failure. The ones who have spent their careers crouched beneath the media gaydar. The ones who are too drugged or drunk to want an honest-to-goodness no-strings shag. The ones who are faithful to their wives or girlfriends. Maria shrugs and moves on to the next, like a contented bee who knows that the pollen is never going to run out.

She had joy, she had fun, she had seasons in the sun, but the sex and the snogs, like the seasons, are all gone. Or so it seems today, at least.

In the no man's land between Christmas and New Year, the hotel is usually low on celebrities, but this year a very famous and fancied rocker had flown to town to appear on a New Year's Eve music special and was living it up in the penthouse suite. So far so good. No televisions on the pavement. No orgiastic coke-snorting. No demands for hedgehog and spacedust sandwiches.

So I was optimistic as I breezed into the lobby on the last day of the year, expecting a quiet day and an early escape to toast the chimes of Big Ben alone in my flat. If I didn't decide to watch a dodgy horror movie, that is. I could do whatever I defiantly jolly-well chose. And no man was going to change that. No man at all, whatsoever, not even Chase and especially not some jumped-up ice-shaker.

And then Jade hobbled over, hands in the air, rivers of mascara on her cheeks, and my cosy plans were ruined indefinitely.

'Christ, Sophie, you have to help. Something awful's happened.'

'What? What's the matter? Where's Chase?'

'I can't tell him!' Her eyes were discs of blue fear.

'OK, tell me then.'

'It's ... oh, shit, I can't even ... could you come into the cocktail bar? Maria's in there, and she's in a state. Lloyd's trying to calm her down.'

My heart thumped down to my feet and I felt slightly sick. The cocktail bar was the one place I definitively did not want to enter. In fact, since Christmas Eve, the red neon message flashing on and off in my brain at all hours had been 'AVOID LLOYD'. Mere mention of his name made the backs of my hands prickle as if I were about to grow hair and turn into a werewolf.

'Isn't Lloyd busy?' I asked primly.

'Well, yeah. He's supposed to be inventing a New Year champagne cocktail. C'mon, Sophie, please.'

'Can't the housekeeper help?'

'NO! Come ON!'

I didn't want to see him, but I supposed I couldn't spend the rest of my life ducking behind the desk every time he crossed the lobby. I followed Jade, cursing my jelly legs, trying not to think about that night, and failing.

'Get dressed,' he said. 'I'll take you home.'

'There's no need!'

'Yes, there is.'

I wanted to argue but I was too limp, inside and out.

In the back seat of the cab, we sat in silence, watching the coloured lights go by. Crossing the bridge, he took my hand and turned it over and over, examining it like a palmist. He put my life line to his lips and breathed in my scent, some of which was still his scent. I couldn't look at him.

We left the cab together, which made me wonder if he lived nearby. He walked me to the entry of my block of flats, holding me by the elbow as if he thought I'd fall on the floor unsupported. He might have been right.

I fished for my keys. 'Thanks,' I said. 'Goodnight.'

When he didn't reply, I had to look at him. I saw his intent, or I thought I did. I've seen enough come-to-bed eyes in my time. But these were different in a subtle way; these seemed

to search me. Come-to-bed-and-stay-there. I hadn't seen that
for years.

In a panic, I snapped, 'You're not coming in.'

He moved my hand from the lock it was scrabbling with,
hooked his arm behind me, pulled me into him.

'I'll have to do it here then,' he said, and set to seducing me
with his kiss all over again. I had thought all the kissing must
have been drained from us by now, but no, there was more,
much more. Once I was warm and melting into him, once his
hands had burrowed inside my coat, once his cologne was in
my hair and on my face and all over my scarf and I was lost
at kissing sea, he let my lips go.

'Let me in, Sophie,' he said.

I unlocked the door and took him upstairs.

In the stock room, Maria was sniffing noisily on a keg,
half-dressed, while Lloyd stood beside her, massaging her
shoulders and making soothing noises.

'What's happened?' I asked, the sight of Lloyd's fingers on
Maria lending an irritable note to my query. Maria simply
burst into fresh tears of lamentation.

'What is it? Were you raped? Attacked? Tell me!'

'Go easy on her,' Lloyd said, a curious look in his eye. 'She's
upset.'

'No fucking kidding? And you don't need to be here now.
The bar's unmanned, so I suggest you hop to it.'

Lloyd's hands flew from Maria's shoulders; he looked
furious and for a second I thought he might slap me. I
wanted him to slap me. I wanted to fight him. *Bring it on,*
sang my blood.

Instead, he made as dignified an exit as he could muster,
stopping briefly beside me and waiting until I deigned to
look him in the eye. 'We're having words later, Sophie,' he
claimed. Hah. Not if I can help it.

I snorted and flapped him away. Phew. He was gone. There is only so much of Lloyd's presence I can handle without going terribly wrong. Wrong. It was so wrong. I should never have done it.

I led him up the stairs to the first-floor flat, wondering vaguely what Mrs Treadway opposite might say if she saw us. Unbelievably, I had never brought a man here before. Mrs Treadway would sometimes ask me if I had a 'someone special' and I would laugh and shake my head, making noises about my busy work schedule and my photography. She would sigh and advise me not to leave it too late. I think she worried that I was lonely.

But Mrs Treadway's door didn't open; she was celebrating Christmas with her loved ones, like everyone else except for me and Lloyd.

I thought about changing my mind even as I turned the key in the lock, but he kept a hand in the small of my back and gently nudged me across the threshold, and then it was too late. He was in.

'Do you want a drink or something?' I asked, feeling stupidly shy and inarticulate.

'No,' he said, his hand at the back of my neck now, fingers combing the roots of my hair. 'I want to see your bedroom.'

'I don't have one,' I confessed with a nervous half-laugh. 'I use it as my darkroom. I have a sofabed in the living room.'

'Then lead on, Macduff,' he said, the silly phrase revealing his own nervousness. He kissed one of the lovebites on my neck. His palpable desire weakened me. He was expecting to stay the night.

'I didn't say you could stay,' I told him, even as I was throwing cushions off the sofa and watching him wrestle with the iron bedframe.

'I can, though.' He said it calmly, looking up through his floppy curtains of hair. I always thought his eyes were shifty but now they looked dark, the irises a tiny ring around gigantic black pupils. 'You don't want me to go, do you?'

The lifeline. I could grab it or toss it away. I hesitated, which was the equivalent of flinging it to the seagulls. He broke into my moment of vacillation with a smile.

'Ah, I see I was right. You want me to stay.'

'I don't,' I said obstinately. It galled me to the core to have to admit that I did want him here.

'I don't believe you,' he said lightly. He threw the cushions back on to the bed and knelt on the mattress, holding out an arm. 'Come here.'

What was it about him? Was it a pheremonal thing? Was there a secret compartment in my soul that only opened for him? Against my better judgement, I joined him on the bed.

And then there was such kissing, such licking, such laying on of hands, such sighing into mouths, such pinching and stroking that my dark inhibitions evanesced and I found myself for the first time following instincts rather than internal scripts. Liberated and terrified, I let Lloyd do this thing to me. I let him be tender and slow and steady and all those other qualities I had derided and avoided. 'Making love', such a sappy phrase, but I could not think of a satisfying alternative. He watched my face throughout, and he made me watch his, and I had never been so afraid, so fragile, so giving of myself. When it was done and we were spent and I lay in his arms, seeing swirly patterns in the dark, he said, 'I can't let you go now. You do realise that, don't you?'

Maria allowed Jade to comfort and calm her down while I paced between armies of champagne bottles, pleading for enlightenment.

'Can somebody please tell me what all the fuss is about?'

'I got papped,' said Maria suddenly.

'What? Photographed? With one of your famous shags? So?'

'It was a telephoto lens,' said Jade significantly. 'Somebody was out on the balcony. I saw him there!'

'What? You were there too? So what were you doing? Please, my head hurts!'

Jade, more coherent than Maria at this stage, filled me in.

The famous rocker had been watching MTV on a black leather sofa, swigging from a beer bottle, when Maria knocked and came in, wiggling her bottom all the way over to the drinks cabinet, which she replenished on her knees, making sure her hold-up stockings were visible beneath her skirt hem.

'Hey, baby,' drawled the rocker. 'That's a fine booty you got there. Why don't you shake it over here?'

Maria grinned. She liked the direct approach. She shook her fine booty all the way over to the rocker and giggled when he tipped her up and pulled her into his lap.

'You're pretty,' he said, looking directly into her cleavage, which she helpfully exposed a little more, undoing two buttons. 'Are you dirty too?'

'Oh yes,' said Maria eagerly. 'I'm such a slut!'

'Wow, that's good to hear. You got any sisters?'

Maria's eyes opened wide and she playacted shock and disgust. 'Sisters! No! I do have a girlfriend though.'

'A girlfriend?' The rocker looked intrigued, though whether this was because of Maria's words, or the way she had just tugged his hand inside her already damp knickers, was not clear. 'You mean just a friend, or . . .?'

'No, not just a friend,' said Maria throatily, grinding her clitoris down on his knuckles while his fingertips sought her open sex. 'A lover. We like to lick and suck each other's tits and pussies, and sometimes we give each other a good seeing-to with my strap-on dildo. What do you think of that?'

It was pretty obvious from the straining leather crotch Maria's bottom rested on what the Rocker thought of that.

'No fuckin way,' he breathed. 'I'd love to watch. Then I'd fuck the pair of you.'

'No, you can't fuck Jade. She is gay. She doesn't mind putting on a show though. She is open-minded. Ooh, yes, that's nice. More of that.'

The Rocker removed his fingers squelchily. 'Call her. Get her over. Then you can have more.'

'You're serious?' Maria bit her lip. 'I don't have much time . . . I'm working . . .'

'Fuck that. I'll sort out any problems. Call her. Now.'

'You're sure you don't just want a blow job?' asked Maria doubtfully, reaching out a hand towards the leather bulge.

He slapped it away. 'Sure I'm sure. Call your dyke friend. I'll pay.'

'You'll pay?'

'Yes.' His terseness prompted Maria to pick up the phone and dial down.

'Hello, Sophie! Can you tell Jade to come to the penthouse suite, please? I have a job for her.'

Jade showed up less than five minutes later, which impressed the Rocker, who had not realised she was a fellow chambermaid.

'She's more properly dressed than you,' he remarked to Maria, slapping her bottom. 'Longer skirt, not so much tit showing.'

Jade stared, wondering what was going on.

'What did you want me for?' she asked.

'How does a thousand pounds sound to you?' asked Maria excitedly. 'Dr Rock says he'll give us that, just for showing him what we get up to in bed. What do you think?'

'A thousand? OK. That seems fair,' said Jade level-headedly. 'What do you want us to do?'

'I love you British girls!' exclaimed Dr Rock, clapping his hands.

'Actually I'm from New Zealand,' said an offended Jade.

'Oh, sorry. I'm not good with the accents. OK, why don't you get naked and get on the rug. We'll take it from there.'

The black-and-whites came off rapidly until the girls were down to their underwear – Maria's skimpy red thong and Ultrabra; Jade's sturdy white Marks & Spencer cotton.

'So . . . how about a little kiss?'

Jade puckered up, took Maria round the waist and began to kiss and nip, enjoying as ever the cushiony softness of her lover's lips. Jade was about six inches taller than the diminutive Maria, and of an athletic build where Maria was all curvy softness. Jade's pink and white flesh contrasted with Maria's olive tones in a way that pleased Dr Rock, who had unzipped his fly and was delving down into the leather to take a firm grip on his cock. He watched, glassy-eyed, as Jade took control of the kiss, pushing her tongue deep into Maria's throat, lowering the cups of her frilly bra to palm her nipples. Maria's fingers twisted and twirled around Jade's neck as she hung on for dear life, moaning and gasping almost theatrically. She was a hot little bitch, thought Dr Rock, and he would enjoy giving her the one thing Jade there couldn't.

'Mmm, good girls,' he applauded. 'I can see who's in charge here.' The maids broke apart and looked over at him, still fondling and straining against each other. 'Maria, you're Jade's bitch. Right?'

'Sometimes,' said Maria. 'But I can take control too. It depends what mood we are in. For instance, right now, I want to push Jade on to the floor and lick her pussy until she begs me to stop.'

'Yeah!' Dr Rock was impressed. 'Don't let me stop you.'

Maria began to ease Jade's white knickers down, pausing to give her backside a little slap. Jade protested and wrestled Maria to the floor, where the pair of them shrieked and giggled and struggled for an arousing few minutes, limbs meshed, hair flying, breasts swinging this way and that, until a feral-looking Maria had her lover exactly where she wanted her.

'Great! Now eat that pussy, baby!' cried Dr Rock hoarsely.

Maria did not need telling. She hoisted Jade's knees over her shoulders and dived down, gobbling greedily, licking and sucking and flicking and slurping for dear life. Dr Rock was living up to his name now, hard and throbbing at the sight, panting as he stroked but conscious of not wanting to peak too quickly. This was one of the sexiest sights of his life, and he did not want it to end any time soon. Maria's pink tongue probing and circling Jade's ruby treasure beat any porn film on the hotel channels into a cocked hat. Jade's hands began to grab at the long pile of the rug, then her legs kicked up in the air, and she was coming, wailing and arching her back, crying out Maria's name.

'Fuck, that was hot,' sighed Dr Rock. 'Was that hot, Jade?'

'It was,' admitted Jade dreamily, lying back on the shagpile and gazing at the miniature chandeliers on the ceiling.

'Time for Maria to get hers, though, isn't it? What about this strap-on I've been hearing about?'

'Oh, jeez, I'm sorry. It isn't at the hotel. It's at my flat,' apologised Jade, coming to and sitting up again.

'OK, well, I can improvise. I do it onstage, after all.' Dr Rock chuckled to himself, then he handed his empty beer bottle to Jade. 'See what she thinks of that.'

'Oh my God!' squealed Maria. 'Our dildo is not that wide!'

'I think you can take it. Suck it and see.'

'I'll give it a go,' said Jade. 'Get down on the rug, Maria, and get your legs really as wide as you can.'

Maria pouted a little, but did as she was told eventually, spreading her short legs and holding them in the air with hands around her thighs.

'Hey, that's a nice view,' contributed Dr Rock, then he nodded at Jade that she could start. Jade prepared Maria diligently, fingering her to maximum lubrication before she made any attempt to insert the glass neck of the bottle.

Maria, grunting, began to beg for penetration, jerking her hips upward to emphasise the point. Jade slowly and carefully slid the bottle into the slot, having no difficulty with the narrow top section. Maria began to whimper and wriggle a bit once the bottle's shape began to gradually widen; both spectators could see how her little circle of muscle grew and broadened to accommodate it until it was bigger and rounder than it usually managed. All the same, it seemed capable of accommodating its cold and smooth intruder. 'Is this OK?' asked Jade. 'Am I hurting you?'

'No, it's fine,' puffed Maria. 'Oh, I feel so full though!'

Jade had only to rock the bottle gently backwards and forwards for a few minutes before Maria came crazily, banging her head on the thankfully luxurious carpet.

'Amazing!' enthused Dr Rock. 'My turn now. I'd better get down to it before I shoot. Stay there, Maria. Hey, Jade, how about you sit on her face?'

Maria, weak and faint from her bottle-fed orgasm, could only lie compliant while Dr Rock inserted his cock into the gaping void that was left. As Jade's blonde snatch descended towards her open mouth, she could hear a distant clicking noise. Without properly registering it, she put it down to the TV and set to an enthusiastic bout of cunnilingus while Dr Rock banged away at her lower half.

'Here, honey,' she heard the estimable doctor – surely he wasn't really a doctor? – say to Jade. There was a crackling sound and Maria thought it must be the money. Looking sideways, she saw a number of pinkish banknotes crammed into Jade's hot little hand. This coincided with such a loud frenzy of clicking and popping that she tried to lift her head. Despite the solid obstruction of Jade's groin, she managed to raise it enough to look towards the source of the noise – the French door that led out to the balcony. There were flashes of light – flashes of light that happened at the same time as each click. There was an outline. A shadow. A person!

'STOP!' shrieked Maria, directly into Jade's clitoris. She kicked her legs in a frenzy, unseating the disgruntled rock legend.

'Hey, what's going on here?' he raged.

'Look! At the window! Someone there!'

Dr Rock, wearing only a ripped T-shirt, shades and an erection, made a break for the balcony, roaring furiously.

'Oh my God, be careful!' entreated Jade, leaping up to follow him and smashing her ankle against a coffee table on the way.

Maria simply shrieked hysterically until Dr Rock returned. 'I didn't catch him. He shinned up to the roof. I saw the camera, though – and he dropped this.' He held out a Press ID card.

'No! Not *Sauce on Sunday*,' wailed Maria. 'It'll be all over the front page!'

Dr Rock shrugged. 'Well, y'know, I'm kinda used to it. It's expected of me.'

'But we'll lose our jobs!' appealed Maria. 'Can't you do something?'

'What can I do?' Dr Rock lay back down on the sofa, his erection now just a memory. 'Thanks for the ride, girls.'

'Get your people to call his people!' suggested Jade desperately.

'Nah. It's no big deal. You girls can sell your stories, right? You'll make enough to live on while you look for another job. You might get lucky, get some offers. Way I see it, I've just done you a favour.'

This was not the way Maria and Jade were seeing it, though.

Still beached on her beer keg, Maria speculated on the effect the Sunday splash might have on her poor old Colombian mother, while Jade worried that she might never get to realise her dream of working with children.

'We really have to tell Chase,' I decided.

'He'll kill us!'

'He'll kill you anyway, once the story breaks. And if I've kept it from him, he'll kill me too. Two deaths are better than three.'

'Fuck you, Sophie!' exclaimed Jade.

'Yeah, well, a little less fucking and we wouldn't be in this mess. I really don't see another way. At least Chase might know some people; perhaps he can do something to stop the story coming out. Don't you think he's a man with connections?'

'I suppose,' said Maria doubtfully.

'It won't save your jobs, but he'll do whatever it takes to avoid bad publicity for the hotel. At least your mother might avoid a heart attack.'

'Yeah. I guess you're right,' sighed Jade.

'You know it,' I soothed. 'Come on. Let's break the news.'

I led the disgraced maids out through the bar, avoiding Lloyd's eye. His voice arrested our progress.

'Are you going to talk to Dr Rock?'

'No, we're going to talk to Chase.'

'Seriously?' I looked at him. He was wiping a glass with a tea-towel. He managed to make wiping a glass with a tea-towel look sexy. In a hateful way.

'No, I'm joking. This is all just a massive piss-take, after all.'

'I mean, Chase will sack the lot of you. I really do advise you to try and get Dr Rock's people to lean on the papers first.'

'Chase,' I said glacially, pushing my shoulders back, 'would never sack me.'

Lloyd didn't move a muscle, the tea-towel and glass held in suspended animation for the longest seconds on record. 'Oh, Sophie,' was all he said, and the affectionate sorrow of it almost made me leap over the bar and push him over.

'Merry Christmas.'

The words came from the region of my thighs, and in my half-awakened state I wondered if I was still dreaming. But when I looked down, there was a messed-up head beneath the sheet, tired eyes still capable of mischief. He smiled, then I felt a whiskery prickle on the lips of my sex, and then I had the longest, lushest morning licking of my life. He was note-perfect, seeming to know my secret buttons as well as I did myself, pushing every one in series, at just the right moment.

Once my orgasm had washed over me, he flipped me over on to my stomach and pushed at me from behind. I was quite chafed from my previous exertions, but he was careful, keeping the movements small, harvesting my juices with fingers and cockhead and using them to lubricate my well-used opening.

'Mmm, I bet this is sore,' he said, gaining an inch of ground, his bulbous head now through the portal.

'A bit,' I hissed, screwing up my eyes. But once he was a little further down, the sting became sweet and I opened for him despite myself.

'How about here?' His thumb against my puckered anus; I whimpered as he broke the ring.

'Yes, that's sore,' I confirmed.

'You can't say you haven't been thoroughly seen to, can you, Sophie?'

'No. Oh.'

'And who made you this way, hmm? Who filled your poor little pussy and arse so full that you can still feel it today? Who did that to you?'

'You ... did ...' My breath shortening, agony and ecstasy.

'I did. And I'll do it again and again and again until you get the message.'

'The message?' He was thrusting hard now, the headboard slamming the wall. Poor Mrs Treadway.

'That you ... should be ... with me ... Sophie.'

His hand was on my neck, the other fishing at my clit. The space in front of my eyes looked blue, then purple.

'Do you understand me?'

'Dunno, just keep going!' I screamed. He was pulling my hair. Fuck! I love having my hair pulled when I'm being pounded from behind. How does he know? How does he know me?

He even seemed to know the tiny throaty sound that is the prelude to my climax. His fingers swished across every possible bundle of nerves and I felt the power of his thrust hit hard, hit home, and he held back no longer, clenching momentarily then releasing inside me with a feral cry.

I let him kiss me and coo into my ear ('You see, we're good, aren't we?') before I collapsed back into sleep.

When I woke up, an hour or so later, I was alone beneath the sheets.

I raised my head groggily; had he gone already? In a way, that would make things easier, but there was definitely a pang in there somewhere. Regret? Loss? Well, it didn't matter. I had to be at my grandmother's by midday. I should make a move.

Before I could swing my leg, rather wincingly, over the side of the frame, I heard a noise. Two noises, actually. One was the gurgle of my coffee percolator. The other was ... coming from my darkroom.

I leapt up, not even stopping to grab a robe, and blundered into the blacked-out room. He was in there. Lloyd was in my darkroom.

'How fucking dare you?' I yelled. 'Get out! Get out now!'

Unfazed, he took a long, slow look at the walls. Papered with photographs of Chase – different versions of the one he let me take for the hotel brochure. A veritable Warhol tribute, made of nobody else but Chase, Chase, Chase. Yes, it made me look obsessed. It made me look like a crazed stalker. But I was not so much embarrassed as enraged at being found out in my pathetic infatuation this way.

'Why are you still here?' I fumed, picking up a tray of developing fluid, preparing to fling it in Lloyd's face.

'Don't waste your time on Chase,' he said, ducking as a wall of red and black Chases were drenched in the liquid. 'He isn't right for you.'

'What are you, match dot com? Fuck off! I never want to see you again. Get back to your poor bitch of a girlfriend and leave me alone.'

I ran to the door and flung it open, then gathered up his coat and boots and hurled them on to the landing. I stood naked in the doorway, ranting and raving, until Lloyd, shaking his head and fixing me with a piercing eye, left the flat. Just as Mrs Treadway's friends-and-relations appeared on the stairwell bearing gifts.

'Merry fucking Christmas!' I shrieked at their stunned faces before slamming the door shut and sobbing on the floor until it was time to leave.

We marched past Lloyd and his odious I-know-better-than-thou smug mug, onward to the lair of Chase.

'Why are you so horrible to him?' Jade asked, despite her imminent unemployed status. 'He really likes you, you know.'

'He does not.'

'How can you say that after that pool party? That was the most chemistry I ever saw since ... a chemistry lesson,' she finished lamely.

'Never mind chemistry, prepare for an explosion,' I said grimly, knocking on the door of the inner sanctum.

'Enter.' His voice still gave me the shivers. As did his steely under-the-spectacles stare. 'Is this important, Sophie? I'm very busy.'

'I'm afraid so,' I said apologetically. 'Something potentially embarassing to the brand has happened.'

'Really? Come in.' Chase was fixated on 'the brand' and its image, to the point of issuing long directives concerning what we were and were not allowed to tell outsiders.

The three of us made a sheepish journey over to the desk, where two of us stood wringing our hands.

'It's unfortunate,' I opened, keeping my tone bright and breezy, 'but probably salvageable. A press photographer has managed to get some shots of Jade and Maria here, in the company of Dr Rock.'

Chase put down his pen and leant forward. 'In the company? By which you mean ...?'

It was pretty obvious from the rich scarlet of the maids' complexions what I meant. I smiled wanly. He did not smile back.

'Were you in uniform?'

'Partly.'

'Not completely undressed?'

'No.'

He drew in a sharp breath. 'And the photos depict what, exactly?'

Jade spoke up. 'Well, um, Dr Rock is, uh, having sex with Maria. And I'm ... sitting on her face.'

Chase's eyebrows. Gawd.

'Compromising, then,' he said with the kind of heavy sarcasm you could not contemplate laughing at.

'And ... oh, you forgot to say, Jade,' said Maria, almost inaudibly, 'about the money. You were holding money, that he'd given you. I think the photographer might have caught it.'

Chase could do nothing but stare for upwards of a vomit-inducing minute.

'You prostitute yourselves to the clients?' he said at last.

'Not usually for money!' I defended them.

He turned to me, freezing me to ice. 'You mean ... it's a regular occurrence? And you know about it?'

'I ... know they sometimes pull one or two of the famous names. I ... thought you would have turned a blind eye. So I did too.'

'You thought wrong, Sophie. I see I have some calls to make. Where was the photographer from?'

'*Sauce on Sunday*,' we all muttered.

'Perfect. Jade. Maria. Collect your things and leave.'

'Yes, Sir,' they whispered, clutching each other's hands as they turned to leave.

'They didn't mean to ...' I started, but he cut in, his voice a blade.

'You too. Get your things and get out.'

I literally staggered forward, my mouth agape, no words forming for what seemed like aeons.

'You can't mean it?'

'I can. Go, before I call Security.'

'But I thought! We were! You know! That you!' Somehow everything was coming out in exclamatory jerks.

'I know what you thought.' One long finger hovered over the intercom button. 'Shall I call them? Or can you go quietly?'

It seemed I could not, because without thinking or feeling or knowing anything of what I was doing, I collapsed in a heap on the carpet and began keening like a banshee.

When a hand fell on my shoulder, I expected roughness and pushing and shoving, but the hand stayed there while its owner began talking to Chase. I was not even listening at first, too wrapped up in hysterical woe, but my ears began to prick up when the voice appeared to belong to Lloyd.

'... your famous last stand? Because it isn't a very glorious one, if it is.'

'Get out, Ellison. I have no intention of discussing personnel issues with my cocktail waiter.'

'Enjoy your final few moments as manager, Chase. Sophie will be a fixture here for a lot longer than you will.'

'Get out! Get out!' I had never heard shrillness from Chase before; even in the throes of my darkest hour, I had to satisfy my curiosity and look up. His usually impassive face was transformed into a mask of rabid panic. There was even spittle in the corner of his mouth. It wasn't a good look. He was jabbing the button for Security so hard I thought it might break.

Lloyd pulled me up by the shoulder and began to escort me from the room, turning at the door to deliver a parting shot.

'I might call the papers myself. I know a story they might find interesting.'

Chase threw a paperweight with some force, narrowly missing Lloyd's head as we bolted through the door and towards the bar. My cocktail champion steered me past the leather banquettes and the marble-topped counter, past the gleaming mirrors and the tasteful Christmas decorations into the stock room again. We slid down on to the floor together, backs to a tower of wine boxes, and he held me while I choked and spluttered on his shoulder.

Once his shirtsleeve was completely drenched and my tear ducts drier than the Sahara, I raised my puffy face to his.

'What was all that about?'

Lloyd kissed the tip of my nose. 'Chase won't be here much longer,' he said.

'Why not?'

'He has debts. Enormous debts, to the wrong kind of people. At first they were personal debts, but he's been dipping into the hotel takings as well.'

'What? How on earth do you know this?'

'I needed a second income, so I have a sideline working in a casino. Not a legit casino, though. A private gambling club on the other side of the park. Chase is a member.'

'Oh! Is it above a peep show?'

Lloyd widened his eyes questioningly, but I was not about to give away the secrets of my stalker past.

'Yes, as a matter of fact, it is. Let's just say that Chase's luck has not been in lately. He is way down. Too far down. The owners want their money back. And the hotel shareholders don't know what's been going on. At least, not yet.'

'Shit. How . . . is he going to pay them? What if he can't?'

Lloyd mimed a throat-cutting slash. 'I've a feeling he might have a flight booked for later on,' he said. 'To somewhere very, very far away.'

'Blimey.' We sat in sombre silence, ignoring the pleas of the junior barman for some help out there. 'I think I need a cigarette.'

'You don't smoke.'

'No, but let's get out of here anyway. Let's go outside.'

Behind the kitchens there was a yard cowering in the shadow of the multi-storey hugeness of the Luxe Noir. It housed bins and laundry hampers, but beyond a wicket gate was a small herb garden with a stone fountain at the centre.

We went to sit on its plinth. Lloyd offered me a cigarette, but I didn't really want one. He lit one for himself, breathing in deeply and exhaling a wavy blue column of unspoken tension.

'Filthy habit,' I remarked.

'Not that you'd know about those,' he parried, flicking ash on to the hard, cold earth. 'You won't lose your job,' he said ruminatively. 'I'm pretty sure the new manager would want to keep you on.'

'I just can't believe it. I can't take it in. Chase. I thought he had some kind of pervy secret sex life. Nothing like this.'

'You would think that,' said Lloyd, ruefully affectionate. 'Sex-mad Sophie.'

'Lewd Lloyd.' Comparisons with the driven snow were rarely drawn when Lloyd was the topic of discussion.

'I'd say we were pretty well suited, wouldn't you?'

'Oh, don't start.'

'Don't start? I've started already. We've started already. And now I can't stop.'

I shut my eyes and breathed in the smoke, wincing when its harshness hit the back of my throat. Tar and nicotine, a source of strength and comfort to millions. Perhaps I should try it.

'What do you mean, you can't stop? If I say you have to, you have to.'

'Why? Why do I have to? What are you afraid of?'

'Afraid? I'm afraid of his 'n' hers bathrobes. They terrify me.'

Lloyd chuckled and dragged deep on his cigarette. He looked sexy and rumpled and a bit dangerous. I could feel victory slipping away from me.

'Well, I share your horror of all that. I promise I'd never make you wear a matching bathrobe.'

'No, but maybe you'd spend all night watching *Match of the Day* while I manicure my nails and read *Take a Break*.'

'Nope. Not a big football fan, to be honest. Too much commitment required. And if I caught you reading *Take a Break* I'd spank you.'

Laughter bubbled inside me; the kind of ridiculous, frothy laughter you get when you realise you might be unexpectedly in love with somebody. He stubbed out the fag with the sole of his boot, turned to me and grabbed my wrist.

'Well, perhaps ...' I was clutching at straws now. 'You would expect things of me! Things I can't give you!'

'What can't you give me, Sophie?' He kissed the underside of my wrist. 'I don't ask for much. Just you.'

'I'm not girlfriend material,' I blurted.

'I know. It's why I like you. Listen.' His eyes were glittering with grave intent now, and he had gathered up my other wrist, imprisoning me with the twin forces of his physical strength and his will.

'I understand you, Sophie. We like the same games. Why don't we play them together? As a team. Not as a boyfriend/girlfriend couple. A team. We play together until it stops being fun. That is all I'm asking for.'

'So ... other men?'

'Not out of the question. Not at all. In fact, I'd encourage it. I'm not jealous or possessive. I want you, and I want you to be you. If you ever decide that you want to be exclusive, then I'd be happy with that too. It's in your court, Sophie. But if you lob it out, I'll get a hundred more balls and keep on firing them at you until you return one.' He grinned sharkily.

'Persistent bastard, aren't you?'

'Yes, I am.'

'You seriously wouldn't stop me seeing other men?'

'As long as I can watch. Or join in.' He shrugged.

'You're very strange.'

'I know. That's why you like me.'

'Must be.' And then we kissed until our blue lips and fingers finally convinced us that it was too cold to continue.

Luxury Bedding

I never thought I'd make it to the Honeymoon Suite.

It has always been a loosely held principle of mine not to bother with men who are obviously married, and they don't come much more obviously married than a bridegroom. So the petal-strewn four-poster bedroom with its champagne bucket and Himalayan fruit basket was off-limits to me.

Until today.

No, reader, I did not marry him. No sparklers have been exchanged, let alone vows of lifelong fidelity. But a certain proposal has been made, and I have accepted it. So today, we seal our compact in the Honeymoon Suite.

It is so beautifully pristine that I am almost loth to blemish it with our coarse intentions, but it seems that my partner does not share my qualms, for the moment we are over the threshold he picks me up and flings me on to the plump pillows, diving down next to me while I breathe in the rose-scented spritz that permeates the cotton.

'Wow,' I purr, stretching out on the crisp linen, picking up some of the petals and scattering them like confetti into his hair. 'This is worth the money. Almost worth getting married for. Perhaps I'll change my ways and become one of those serial brides. I think I need to line up a few sugar daddies.'

'Oh, really,' he says, walking warning fingers up between the valley of my breasts and turning on to his side to look down on me. 'You would, as well. I can just see you, in a St

Trinian's uniform, sitting on some elder statesman's lap, twirling your hair and pouting.'

'Oh, yes, so can I. I hope he'd be wearing some sort of starched blazer and an old school tie. Not too old though. Silver hair rather than white.'

'Hmm, yes, maybe a member of the House of Lords.' His fingertips graze my collarbone, hovering around the neckline of my silk dress. 'He'd spend all day arguing political points and drinking sherry in his club, then he'd come home to you and give you a good spanking and send you to bed.'

'You don't need to be a Lord to do that,' I point out.

'Not the last part, no.' His lips are on my neck, now there is hot breath in my ear. 'And besides, you can have your sugar daddies as long as you come back to me. And I'll do the spanking and sending to bed.'

'You already do.'

'I'm not planning to stop.' The hem of my skirt is travelling slowly, ticklishly, up my thigh. He halts at my suspender snap and lays a heavy hand on my lace stocking top. 'Do you think any of the brides that spend their wedding night here are virgins?'

'No more than the grooms, I should think.'

'Mmm, I think you're my blushing virgin bride,' he says, glinting filthily. 'And I'm the wicked man who has snared you into my clutches. It's your fortune I'm after, my dear, though your ripe little body is a substantial bonus. And you have absolutely no idea what you have let yourself in for.'

I squirm against the coverlet, enjoying the fantasy. 'Oh my,' I gasp in a hokey cartoon-heroine accent. 'Is this really what a bride has to do?'

'This is just the start, my dear,' he croons, nipping at my earlobe. 'You don't think I'm going to let you wear that hideous nightgown your mother packed, do you?'

'That's antique lace! It's a family heirloom!' His finger slips beneath the lace stocking top and strokes my thigh, a nail sometimes snagging against the mesh. 'You can't mean I have to be . . . naked!'

'That's exactly what I mean, my dear. I've bought these goods and now I intend to examine them.'

'Goods! Bought! Oh my, what a thing to say!'

'Stop your lamenting and strip, my dear, or I shall do it for you.'

I try to push him off, but he puts a hand on my ribcage and begins to unfasten the buttons that run from the neck to the hem of my shirt dress. I picture it as a wedding gown, with an ivory bodice and a blossoming of tulle and net, unlaced, ripped from me, revealing my pure white foundation garments.

In fact, I have worn white underwear today – a choice made by my subconscious when it found out it was visiting the Honeymoon Suite, perhaps. A sheer white bra and matching briefs, with tiny pink hearts embroidered into the material; rather less whorish than my usual boudoir costume, though the inevitable suspender belt sexes it up. His lupine grin when he parts the two sides of the silk to reveal it indicates his approval. He brushes a hand down the centre of my torso, places it firmly on my bare stomach and bends down to ravage my lips and mouth in a seal of possession that masquerades as a kiss.

My Sophie self sinks greedily into the embrace, even as my reluctant bride self pants and gasps and pushes at him in vain. He makes it clear that every spot, however remote, between my lips and my tonsils will be visited by his rampaging tongue, and I welcome it, my mock struggles weak and unconvincing, my cunt beginning to throb at the sense of being thoroughly taken and overpowered.

Sometimes our fucking is like this, and sometimes it isn't.

Sometimes I seduce him over dinner, running my foot up his trouser leg beneath the table; sometimes I join him unexpectedly in the shower and demand soapy satisfaction; sometimes I bundle him into an alleyway, fish out his cock and give him impromptu head, ruining the knees of my stockings in the process. Sometimes our moods coincide and sometimes they don't, but one or other of us can always be persuaded to compromise.

But today, we are kicking and restraining and smacking and biting our way into the role of evil groom and virgin bride. Not too far into the role though – or I would be kneeing him sharply in the groin and putting paid to any chance of the good firm shag I am fantasising about.

He has one wrist pinned down at my side and is lowering the cups of my bra with his teeth. I pull his hair; he growls and wolfs down a breast, sucking and gnawing at it, flicking his tongue over and over the nipple until my sheer white panties are soaked and my squirming owes more to pleasure than pretence.

'Oh, oh, mama never told me about this!' I squeal, for now there is scrabbling at my knicker elastic and a fist bunched inside, knuckles bearing down between my slippery lips. He jams a knee between the softness of my inner thighs, crouched over me like a predator on the verge of tearing my flesh.

'Mama never met Sir Jasper Baddun,' he snarls, making me giggle for a second before he distracts me by whipping the knickers down to my knees. One finger explores the seat of my non-virginity while he pins my upper body to the bed with his chest. 'Oh yes, nice and tight. Nice little maidenhead for Sir Jasper.'

'You are a scoundrel, Sir!'

He chuckles, lifting his pelvis slightly so he can release his cock from the jeans he irreverently chose to wear for our rendezvous.

'I know,' he says simply, then I scream for real at a sudden penetration that knocks the wind out of my fighting sails. I thank my stars that there is no actual defloration going on – Sir Jasper's technique is not the gentlest, but the game demands a forceful, pitiless sheathing, and that is what he is giving me. He keeps my wrist down and thrusts so hard that even these well-oiled bedsprings creak, shoving it up so far and so hard that I have to stop struggling or my hips and pubis will be bruised.

'I-will-take-what's-mine,' he grunts through gritted teeth. 'And-I'll-see-that-you-remember-it.' The depth of his reach, the profundity of the friction and the fingertips jamming my clit all combine to send me soaring out of my body so that only sensation remains.

'I'm yours, make me yours,' I wheeze, my head banging against the soft padded headboard, my legs slicing the air, and then I come hard, very hard, so that the phrase 'like a steam train' rushes to mind, all steaming and whistling and roaring into the tunnel.

He throws back his head and shouts, 'Oh, yes, that's it,' and pulls out, but I don't think he has come yet, and one glimpse of his resolutely erect prick proves me right.

'We need virgin blood,' he says, somewhat alarmingly, but instead of ripping my flesh, he reaches over to the fruit bowl, picks out a handful of strawberries and proceeds to mash them into my well-used pussy. Their coldness makes me try to shimmy up the bed, but I am at the top already, and he steadies me with a hand on my stomach, continuing to pulp the juicy fruit against my clitoris and up into the stretched hole behind.

'Oh, that feels ... kind of ... nice,' I say, fearing all the same for the bright white sheets. We'll have to bung something to the laundry people.

'Your virginal bleeding feels nice? That's novel. That's not what most of the wenches say,' he tells me, still in character. 'Look how you're staining the sheets. Did that hurt, little bride? Was I too rough? Did I stretch you too far?'

He is smearing the strawberry mess all over, inside and out, using his fingers as fruit paintbrushes.

'You have ruined me,' I reply, jittering when he puts his mouth to my succulent core and begins to lick.

'I like you like this,' he murmurs. 'Fruity.'

Again he reaches for the basket, plucks some black grapes, bites into them and places the halves on my nipples. Pretty soon my abdomen is purple with blueberry stains, my thighs sticky with peach juice. Strawberry and raspberry mash is on both sets of lips and a banana sticks rudely out of my cunt. He eats the banana, as far as he can get, lapping up juices on the way, then his tongue and teeth work at getting inside to consume the remaining half. Once he has retrieved it, he gives it to me to eat – it has a unique flavour – and kneels up between my legs, looking me over.

'That's what I call a fruit salad,' he says with relish. 'Just needs a bit of cream.'

Although my mouth is crammed with banana à la jus de Sophie, he manages to stuff his cock in there as well, mixing and coating it with the munched-up pulp, pumping with his fist at the root. When I swallow the banana, he pulls out with a moan, points at my grapey, berry-smeared tits and shoots, topping them with his own brand of creamy drizzle, which he then rubs in with the palms of his hands, mingling fruit and semen until my breasts and stomach and most of my mound are covered with the mess.

'God, we need your camera,' he pants. 'You are the most obscene thing I've ever seen. I want to fuck you all over again.'

'Mmm, maybe later.' I yawn. 'How about a bath? A hot tub. I know how much you like those.'

'OK. Shall we take the champagne in with us?'

'I think it's practically compulsory to.'

He frowns down at his shirt, once white, now blue, purple, red and pink in an interesting tie-dye effect.

'I'll just go and get it running.'

The bath is enormous, a luxurious corner spa with shelving and bubbles. He has emptied all the creams and unguents and emollients in at the same time, so it brims with scented foam, not so much cleansing us as sheening our skin with the veneer of luxury.

I rest back against his chest, sipping at champagne, occasionally clinking his glass. 'I could get used to this.' I stretch like a cat, feeling the bubbles burst off my out-stretched legs.

'You could,' he says. 'But I don't think this suite is often empty. It's booked up most of the year.'

'I'm not surprised. It's heavenly.'

Framed sketches on the walls, the towels and flannels folded into origami shapes, tiles that glitter with tiny jewel pinpoints. Mirrors so shiny that you can imagine stepping into their reverse-world with a shiver-shimmer. And every-where the smell of money, that expensive aromatic fusion that convinces you you are cocooned from the dirt and danger of life.

He takes the champagne flute from me, places them both on the shelf behind us. 'I don't want you drinking it all now,' he says. 'There are all sorts of interesting things you can do with champagne.'

'Well, I know that. I've used more complimentary hotel champagne in non-traditional ways than you could even imagine.'

'You are underestimating my imagination. You need to stop doing that.'

We are still chuckling at each other when our lips bump together and our mouths open greedily. We slide down the seat, scrabbling and slithering all over each other until we slip off into the whirling vortex, drowning in our mutual absorption.

Our heads, conjoined, break the surface of the water from time to time while our limbs thrash and splash like half an octopus.

'Look, you're going to wear me out and I'm not even started yet,' he protests, shaking out his sleek wet hair so that droplets shower me. 'I'm going to get you clean before you start getting dirty again.'

He scoots over to the edge of the tub with me under one arm and retrieves a small bottle of luxe brand shampoo, which soon enough is lathered into my hair by his strong fingers. My scalp and my neck and shoulders are given a workout that leaves them free and floaty, ready to lie down and let the bubbles take me to sleep.

'No, no,' he reproves when I lay my soapy head back against his chest and shut my eyes. 'Get that backscrubber off the side.'

I heft it in my palm; it is solid varnished wood with decent bristles, not the unforgiving plasticky variety. 'Go on then, you scratch my back and I'll scratch yours,' I offer, handing it over to him.

He makes me bend with my palms flat on the shelf-seat while he runs the tickly bristles along my spine and then in circles from my shoulders downwards, sending vibrations through my pores. The pattern of soapy waves and circles gradually covers my back until it drifts over my coccyx and meets the crack of my bottom. The bristles cover the shiny wet globes, gently at first then more firmly, brushing with serious intent. I am grateful for the moisturising property of the soap, without which the sensation might become unpleasantly raw. As it is, I am on a tantalising precipice: pleasure if I step back, pain if I jump.

He scrapes along the underside of my buttocks, an exquisitely tender spot, and I moan and bend at the knees, but my attempt to elude the brush results only in a sudden and almost overwhelming crack of the wooden side against the rounds of my bottom. Not only is the bathbrush heavy and wooden, but my wetness accentuates the sharp pain of its contact.

'Ouch! What was that for?'

'Don't move.'

My thighs, back and inner, are scrubbed pink before his job is done, then he turns me round and puts two blobs of foamy bubble on each side of my collarbone, watching as they ski down the slopes of my breasts, blowing at them to increase their velocity. Once they settle on my nipples, he massages them in, then lathers my stomach, then the suds drift lower until I have a mock-pubic triangle of frothy whiteness which is used to clean and refresh the unclean parts of me.

His attentions end with his mouth on my fresh and fragrant nether regions. He breathes in long and deep, his nose buried down there, then he tastes the difference, running his tongue slowly between my lips, sucking at my clit, then kissing it and standing back up.

'My turn then,' he reminds me, and I wash him from head to toe, missing out nothing, not a crease, not a hidden hollow, even introducing a soapy finger to his arse, which makes him yell and buck off me as quickly as he can.

'That stings, you bitch!' he gasps, looking around for the retributive bathbrush, but I have put it beyond his reach and he has no recourse but to trust me to complete the task.

'This won't,' I promise, and my creamy hands soap his perineum, moving forwards, lathering up his scrotum, then manipulating his cock into life with a slippery hand job. I soap it then rinse it, then pull back the foreskin and clean the tip with my tongue.

'The champagne!' he suggests eagerly, so I take a mouthful then lower myself again over the sweet-smelling head of his prick, swirling the drink around it.

'Ooooh, that's nice,' he confirms, leaning back to grip the side of the bath with both hands. I bend lower, swallow more, breathe him in and try to place the scent. Almond blossom? Japonica? Sandalwood? All three? The steely apple tang of the champagne mixes with the slight bitterness of the cleansers, all heated up by his wanton animal warmth. Hot champagne, soap and erect cock. I wonder what name he'd give that on his cocktail menu.

When I begin to speed up a little, he slows me down, then stops me with a hand at the top of my head.

'Not yet. Don't want to peak too soon,' he says. 'Let's get out. I haven't finished with you yet.'

The towels are three times as fluffy as anything you might own yourself, huge and fat and yet also absorbent so that we are dry again in a jiffy.

He finds a scented body oil somewhere amongst the gigantic hamper of products and covers me in it, starting with my toes and ending with my neck, calling at all points north, south, east and west, so that my body has a slippery veneer by the time he has finished. He holds me against him and dabs two oily fingers between the cheeks of my bum, slipping them swiftly and shockingly into my ring before I can stop him.

'Revenge,' he breathes darkly in my ear, and I have to submit to having my arse fingered until he is satisfied I have paid the price of my folly. 'Right then,' he says, once my passage is fully oiled, 'Let's get some air.'

He pulls on the complimentary bathrobe, but when I reach for mine he shakes his head and takes my wrist, pulling me out through the suite to the balcony doors.

'I'm naked!' I object. Luckily it is a sunny day, but it's still January and the temperature is not far above freezing.

'I won't let you die of exposure,' he promises, pulling open the doors and standing with me in the frame, looking out over the city from the twenty-first floor. Only this floor and the penthouse above have balconies, and there are few other buildings in the vicinity high enough for us to be seen from. All the same, someone in the financial district a mile across town might have an interesting floorshow for his lunch break. Hopefully none of the traffic report 'copters or planes heading for the docklands airport will pass this way. Or would that be so bad? Would that, actually, be a little bit thrilling?

I allow his knee to nudge me out on to the freezing tiles. Instantly, my nipples are stiff and painful and I cross my arms over them, hugging them warm.

'Go and lean over the balcony,' he says.

'It's cold.'

'You'll soon warm up. Go and lean over.'

My breasts are pushed up against the cold chrome handrail; I crane my neck and look over and down at the tiny insect people dotting around far below. I wonder if any of them will look up and notice my bare shoulders and wet, icy hair.

'Baby, it's cold outside,' says Lloyd, and he isn't exaggerating. He stands behind me, pressing me into the fine metallic mesh, causing indented patterns to begin forming on my knees and stomach. I am grateful for the warmth of his bulk at my rear and the scant coverage of his robe. He braces his arms around my waist and claims me in a fierce bear hug that squeezes the breath from me.

'Need warming up?' he whispers into my numbing ear.

'Just a bit,' is my testy reply.

'Hold tight; might be a bumpy ride.' He lifts me a little, so I have to grab on to the lower rail of the balcony with my feet, slipping my toes between it and the embossed metal rectangle that preserves my fictitious modesty. Now if I stand straight the mob below can theoretically see my tits waving cheerfully down at them, though I crouch enough to hide them. The crouching bends me at the waist, so my bottom rubs against my lover's crotch. I am dangling my arms over the balcony, hanging on tight, my chin level with the handrail, waiting for Lloyd to start giving me the public fucking I expect, when he completely unbalances me by taking one arm away from my waist, parting my rear cheeks swiftly and efficiently and commencing a firm annexation of my bum.

'Hey ... what?' I exclaim, feeling him glide in easily, thanks to the oil he liberally applied earlier on, quarter way, half way, all the way up. Oh glory. I am standing outside, naked on a hotel balcony in January with a man's cock buried deep in my arse. Of all the things I've done ... this might be my favourite. Maybe not the January part.

'Don't you like?' he croons, his breath steaming in my ear. He jiggles his cock a little, making sure I don't forget it's there. 'Are you worried the people in the penthouse might be able to see you being buggered on a balcony?'

'No,' I moan. 'I like it. Oh God. I really like it.'

'I knew you would.' He begins to unsheath, slowly and effortfully, almost all the way down, then he jolts back up, banging me into the balcony with a metallic clang. 'You don't care where, do you? Just as long as you get your arse filled. Could be over my bar or in the middle of the road down there. Anytime, anyplace, anywhere, as the advert used to say.'

'Though,' I grunt through the rattling and the forceful in-and-out, 'anyplace and anywhere are the same, surely.'

'Stop deconstructing, Sophie, and open that arse as wide as you can for me. That's it.'

I need one arm to attach myself to the bar, the other to somehow wedge between the balcony and my body so I can bring my clit to the party too. It is sweaty and bangy and rattly and achy but so seething with filthy goodness that I do not notice the minor inconveniences, the bruises forming, the diamond shapes on my knees, the straining of my muscles. I only know what is happening behind me, and in the unlikely event that I should forget, Lloyd is keeping up a running commentary.

'Oh, yes, that's it, Sophie, take it all, all the way, keep it spread, keep it stretched wide ...' His words become indistinct, disappearing below a rude whirring from the sky, then we are buffeted by an unforecasted high wind and I remember how cold I am before I realise that we are directly in the sights of ...

'The eye in the sky! Stop, Lloyd!'

'Nothing it ain't seen before,' yells Lloyd, who is beyond the point of no return, continuing to slam while the gigantic metal bird hovers above us, close enough to see the reporter with his earpiece.

He is looking at us. He is speaking into a microphone and I imagine him telling the entire city that a traffic jam by the park is caused by Sophie Martin having her arse fucked by Lloyd Ellison on the twenty-first floor of the Hotel Luxe Noir – come along if you want to watch, but don't expect to find a parking spot. And then I come, deliriously, imagining my howls speeding down the radio waves to half the households in town. 'Dirty mare,' clucks a woman, while her husband wanks furtively behind his evening paper.

The helicopter wheels to the right and flees towards the financial district, leaving Lloyd and me to pull apart and stare at each other, hands on mouths, scarlet with exhilarated shame.

'Can you believe that?'

'I don't know – I found it added something to the experience,' says Lloyd, insouciant as ever in the face of adversity. 'I'd like to know what he was saying though.'

'Do you think he mentioned it?'

I am at the French doors now, in a race against hypothermia. Somehow I win.

'I need another drink.' I pour us both another glass of champagne and slide under the marshmallow duvet, hugging it around my bitter body. Lloyd joins me a few minutes later and suggests ringing down for room service.

'Let's eat,' he says. 'I'm in the mood for one of those triple-decker sandwiches held together by a cocktail stick. Or maybe a big plate of steak and chips. How about you?'

'Hmm. Maybe a turkey dinner. Seeing as you ruined my Christmas lunch this year.'

'Did I really?'

'The whole day was a farce. I could barely walk. I had to wear a scarf around my neck to hide all those bloody love bites. I nearly fell asleep face first in the sprouts and gravy.'

Lloyd chuckles. 'Mine wasn't the best. Had to finish with the girlfriend, for one thing. Not that it was ever serious. She was seeing two other men anyway.'

'You didn't have to finish with her.'

He leans over and robs my lips. 'I did,' he says.

We drink our champagne in companionable silence, which he breaks with a soft chuckle.

'We should have a toast. To the new managers of the Hotel Luxe Royale. Sophie Martin and Lloyd Ellison. Bottoms up!'

We clink our glasses and drain them, fizzing with more than the sparkling wine.

'So can I make you a cocktail, Sophie? Anything you'd like?'

I nestle into the crook of his arm and rub the top of my head against his chin.

'I never thought I'd ask you this, but how about a Sloe Comfortable Screw?'

Please turn the page for

The Number

A short story
by Justine Elyot

The Number

Justine Elyot

'9.45 a.m. from Colliton South.' That had been the text message in its entirety.

Anyone scrolling through Charlotte's inbox would infer that this bald line of digital information had come from a timetabling service or similar; its true provenance was known only to Charlotte herself. And even she only knew that it had come from The Number. Identities of the sender or senders could not be revealed.

She screwed in her iPod headphones and looked again at the message – so perfectly straightforward and yet so unutterably cryptic. Arrowing down to The Number provoked a shiver of delicious nervousness. How many people had The Number? How many people were involved in this game? And how would it play out? She did not even know where she would be this time tomorrow.

All the same, she supposed she had better prepare to play, and she took one of her college texts, *Social Psychology of the Workplace*, from her tote bag. Within a few minutes, her absorption was such that she huffed under her breath at the click of the compartment door before she remembered what she was actually doing here and looked up.

'Mind if we join you?'

She looked swiftly away again, the paragraphs swimming under her eyes. *Them!*

The men from the station; pinstriped professionals, both in their forties, both carrying large briefcases, one bespectacled, one silvering at the temples. If this was Fantasy #3, as she presumed it was, they fitted the bill perfectly. She had spent the twenty minutes by which the train was delayed sizing them up sideways along the platform, and they certainly seemed to be doing the same, but more openly. If they were simply innocent bystanders, they were not very well-mannered ones.

The train had drawn in just as Charlotte could have sworn they were talking about what she was wearing, causing her to flush hotly and cross her arms over her chest, hiding the swell of her breasts in the light white silk blouse she wore on that May morning. Could they see the outline of her white lace bra underneath? she wondered. Was her mid-thigh plaid skirt too short? Had one of her nude hold-up stockings fallen to her knee without her knowledge? It was a relief, and yet also a disappointment, to hoist herself up in the carriage away from their predatory scrutiny.

When, after fifteen minutes, she still found herself alone in the compartment, she had assumed they were not involved; that the players would embark later on. But it seemed now that she might have been mistaken.

The taller and senior-looking of the two men stood in the doorway, one hand keeping the sliding portal from springing back, staring down his bespectacled nose at her with an expression that owed less to query than coercion.

Charlotte was a courteous, rather shy young woman; a people-pleaser by upbringing, and answering his request in the negative would have been as unthinkable to her as a plain 'fuck off'. Besides, there was something effortlessly intimidating about this man, a sense that, for all his outward civility and charm, you would not want to mess with him. Exactly what she had ordered up. Surely he must be . . .

He smiled, entered the compartment, and his companion followed. He wore a lighter suit, and seemed lighter in almost every other sense, including his manner and the piercing grey blue of his eyes. Charlotte expected them to sit at the far end of the compartment, by the door, and she was instantly disconcerted when they slid their briefcases onto the rack directly above her. The older man – whom she thought of as Alpha Male – sat down by her side, his friend opposite her, smiling ingratiatingly.

Defensively she turned her eyes down to her book and made to switch on her iPod, but before she could drown out the suddenly scary reality of her situation, the man opposite her spoke and she reluctantly halted her fingers in their mission. It would be rude, she supposed, not to engage in conversation if that was what they wanted, even if they were just simple strangers on a train.

'*Social Psychology of the Workplace* – now that sounds like a nice bit of recreational reading.'

'Oh, no, it isn't for pleasure. It's for a course I'm doing.'

'Shouldn't you have read that before setting off to college?' The other man this time, his tone mock-censuring. Or was it mock? Perhaps it was real. 'I hope you're up to date with your assignments.'

'How do you know I'm on the way there? How do you know I haven't just left college and I'm so keen I'm doing the assigned reading already?'

The men raised eyebrows at each other. 'Feisty,' noted Alpha Male.

'Isn't she?' responded his colleague.

Charlotte flicked her eyes nervously out of the window towards the sheep and trees rolling past. If it was nothing to do with the game, this was wrong somehow. This was not normal. But she had the oddest tightness at the base of her belly and her heart was racing. Were they flirting with her or ... what? Perhaps she should not go through with this. Perhaps she should leave now, but something held her back. The same thing that got her into trouble time and again. She loved a story and she always had to know the ending.

'So what do you read for pleasure?' The Alpha Male again, his voice rich and alluring with a flirtatious edge. It was a voice he used, she thought, perhaps professionally. Extremely distinctive, rather wicked, a voice that could seduce without the aid of its corporeal host.

'Oh...' Charlotte was overcome with confusion. She had not signed up to discuss her literary tastes with these men.

'I'm guessing –' the man opposite took up the conversation; his voice higher in register, clipped and well-bred '– you seem like a classics sort of girl to me. Jane Austen? The Brontës? Perhaps a little Thomas Hardy when you're feeling melancholy?'

'Oh, I don't know,' Alpha Male interrupted before Charlotte could confirm or deny. 'I think there's a little undercurrent of darkness there. Something a little bit . . . wanton. Perhaps Henry Miller, or even Anaïs Nin. Hmmm?'

He was looking directly at her, one long finger against his lips. Full lips. Cruel lips. Charlotte felt a creepy-crawly ripple from the base of her spine to the nape of her neck. Was this what they called 'hackles rising'? Or was it something else? She felt caught out, as if he could read her mind. How could he have guessed that? Did she have some kind of aura marking her out as a lover of kink-lit? Perhaps she did. Still, there was only one course a nice girl could take when confronted thus. Resort to outright lying.

'No,' she stammered. 'No, just . . . the ones you said.' She shot a look of appeal to the man opposite, hoping he would pick up on her misgivings.

But if he did, he wasn't going to pay any attention.

'You know, I think you're right,' he said to his friend. 'Judging by the luscious blush that's spreading from her cheeks to her ears . . . you might just have hit on something. Are you a connoisseur of erotica, my dear?'

'You're certainly a transparently bad liar,' Alpha Male averred.

'I'm not! I don't know what all this is about!' But in that moment, Charlotte knew exactly what it was all about. These men had come from The Number. This was what she had ordered. All she had to do now was play the game.

'Oh really?' Alpha stood suddenly, extending his lean frame to its full height, a couple of inches over six foot, and retrieved his briefcase from the rack.

No! Don't go, thought Charlotte in a panic. Things are just starting to happen.

But he seated himself once more and snapped the case open, plucking from its depths ... yes ... Charlotte mock-gasped as he laid his briefcase aside and brandished in front of her nose the notebook she had been instructed to leave in the station phone box.

She made a wild swipe for it. 'What are you doing with that?' she cried, her voice cracking in alarm. 'It's mine; give it back!'

'Oh, you want it now? You need to learn to take care of your property, young lady. We found this on the station forecourt, where you dropped it.'

'Yeah, well, thanks,' said Charlotte, trying to keep the tremble out of her words. 'Thanks for bringing it to me.' She flung out her arm, but her tormentor flipped it out of her reach.

'Patience, Charlotte,' he said. He knew her name. He had opened it. He had read it. No wonder they had been watching her with such avidity on the platform. 'I just wanted to clarify a few things before I return it. This *is* your notebook, isn't it?'

Charlotte bit the inside of her cheek, considering lying just to see where that would take the action, but she knew there was no point. She nodded, caught between the twin beam of her companions' intense attention.

'You've quite a talent, Charlotte,' the man opposite paid tribute. He appeared to be the good cop of the duo.

'A talent for getting yourself into trouble. How much of what you have written about here is based on fact, I wonder?'

Charlotte knew how the script went now. 'I've ... most of it. All of it,' she mumbled.

'Really? You have picked up strangers for money in the bar of the Colliton Grand?'

'Well ... I'm a student. I have to pay my way. I was just doing favours ...'

'Interesting defence,' remarked Alpha Male to his friend. 'Extenuating circumstances; first offence. Though of course she seems to be under the impression that the law recognises gradations of sexual transaction. Of course it does not, as we know.'

'Indeed,' his friend backed him up. 'All instances of giving sexual favours for financial remuneration are illegal.'

'Punishable, according to the judge's discretion, by custodial sentence.'

'Harsh but true, Charlotte.'

'And even if you keep your pretty arse out of prison, the local press will make sure you can never show your face in town again.'

They both watched for her reaction, Alpha Male holding the book very deliberately within her reach if she wanted to snatch it away. Now was the time. Laugh it off or go with it. She could take the book and thank them for their gesture; say it had been a fun idea, but she had had second thoughts. Or . . . *a chance like this might never come again.*

She swiped overdramatically for the notebook. *'Give it back!'* She hoped her manner would make her response to their unphrased question clear.

'I'm not sure I care for your tone.' Alpha Male frowned and replaced the notebook in his briefcase, snapping it shut with near-vindictive finality. Charlotte yelped and lurched forwards, almost launching herself into his lap. 'You certainly don't appear to appreciate the gravity of your situation.' He placed one finger on the bridge of his spectacles, his eyes boring into the helpless young woman before him.

'Please,' she whispered.

'Better.'

'Just be a good girl, Charlotte, and do as you're told,' the man opposite advised, his voice strangely soothing.

'Yes. Can you do that?' The older man's slender fingers reached for her chin, holding it in a firm grip while his eyes roved slowly around her face and body. 'Can you be a good girl and do as you're told?'

An incoherent 'uh' sound was Charlotte's only response. She was committed now to following the story to its end.

'We know what you like, Charlotte,' said the older man. 'We were very interested when we read your story.'

'We like what you like,' contributed his colleague. 'Isn't that a pleasant coincidence?'

'Yes,' said Charlotte dreamily, finding that the way her neighbour stroked her hand, rhythmically, gently but inescapably, was pushing the waves of anxiety far back, back behind their barrier.

'She likes this,' remarked Alpha Male. 'She's like a skittish pony; just needs a firm touch to keep her docile. Take her foot and give it a rub.'

The younger man crouched forwards and did just that, lifting one of Charlotte's legs so that her foot nestled between his thighs. He removed her sandal and began to massage the ball of her foot with both hands, moving slowly around, then dipping into her instep in a feathery-tickly way that made her shiver. Alpha had moved her hand to his lips and was kissing the knuckles, prior to taking her fingers into his mouth and sucking on them. His other hand rested on her skirted thigh, feeling hot and heavy, as if it clamped her in place.

Alpha Male removed her final finger with a popping sound and squeezed her hand tightly within his. 'Now listen carefully, Charlotte. This is what will happen now. You will refer to me as "Master" and my friend as "Sir". You belong to us until we say otherwise, and accordingly you must be obedient and respectful. We do not intend you harm and will endeavour to give you the pleasure you seek, but you must not question our orders or our motives. Is that understood?'

'But where are we going?'

'Is that understood, Charlotte?'

'Oh . . . yes.'

'Yes what?' Master hauled Charlotte to her feet by the elbow and laid two hard smacks on her bottom.

'Yes, Master.'

'I hope you're a fast learner, young lady, or you will find this afternoon both long and painful.'

'Oh, I am.'

'I'm going to advise you not to speak unless explicitly questioned, Charlotte. Do you think you can do that?'

'Yes, Master.'

Charlotte was still standing, facing away from her interlocutor and towards the man she was to refer to as 'Sir'. She felt the indignity of her position, standing up on the grimy carriage floor with only one shoe on, giving her a perilous lopsided feel.

'What a lovely figure you have, Charlotte,' said Sir. 'I'd very much like it if you could give us a little twirl. Nice and slowly. That's the ticket.'

Charlotte pivoted on her one sandalled foot, trying her best not to rush the process and incur either man's displeasure.

'She has an hourglass shape,' said Sir to Master. 'My favourite kind.'

'Yes, and the skirt is tight enough to cling nicely to her hips and backside. We can get a good idea of what might be in store for us.'

'That blouse is perfect; almost transparent. More a promise than a garment, don't you think?'

'I do. Charlotte, stand facing me and unbutton your blouse, please.'

Charlotte's impulse was to stall, to stare, to stammer, but when she caught sight of Master's gimlet eyes and straight-set mouth, she knew that she had no alternative but compliance. Her fingers flew to the little pearly buttons, slipping them carefully out of the slits, mindful that a couple were hanging by loose threads. The thought that she really ought to buy a sewing kit flashed through her head, almost occasioning a giggle in its incongruity.

The blouse hung open, exposing a column of pale skin from navel to throat, interrupted by the white lace of her bra.

'Pull it aside; show us your breasts,' instructed Master. Charlotte draped the edges of her blouse carefully at either side of her bosom so that the frothy twin cups with their spillage of flesh were plainly visible, along with the gently convex expanse of her belly.

'Good girl, turn around and show Sir.'

Sir nodded and gave her a warm smile of encouragement. He was much easier to face than Master, Charlotte thought. He seemed as if he might actually be quite nice, whereas Master was simply cold and terrifying, seductive voice notwithstanding.

'Now raise your skirt to your waist, Charlotte.'

Charlotte continued the languid movements her new owners seemed to favour, edging the rough cloth up her thigh, past the lacy elasticated top of her stockings until nude flesh felt the cool air. She had just hiked it past her white mesh knickers when a click of the door made her jump a foot in the air.

'Tickets, please.'

In a confusion, she bent forwards, desperately fumbling to adjust her clothing, but a cold and irate, 'Hold it there; don't you dare cover up!' caused her to freeze with a bunched-up handful of skirt and an arm across her chest.

From the corner of her eye she could see that the ticket collector was a skinny, acne-scarred youth fresh out of school. Far from looking shocked and appalled, a voyeuristic leer plastered his face. 'Thank you, gents,' he said thickly as Master and Sir flashed season tickets.

'Straighten up,' commanded Master. 'Skirt back up now. Give the man your ticket.'

Charlotte, feeling slightly seasick from the motion of the train and convinced she must be the hue of beetroot all over, reached into her bookbag for the ticket. She handed it to the guard without looking at him.

'Very nice, luv,' he said, clipping it and handing it back. There was a moment that seemed to last an age during which the guard just stood there, lapping her up with his eyes on stalks, holding on in the hope that he might be invited to join in the fun.

'Thank you,' said Master dismissively, and with a shrug and a slump, the ticket collector went on his way. 'As for you, miss, you had better rid yourself of any notions of false modesty. If we want you on display, we will have you on display, no matter if the massed ranks of the Scots Guards pass through this carriage. Bend over and grab your ankles now.'

Charlotte swung over as quickly as she could, hoping the speed of her response might garner her a little of Master's hard-won approval. The tight white mesh of her knickers stretched taut over her straining bum, which was directly in Master's line of sight. She gasped and almost toppled over when a volley of hard, loud smacks lit up her bottom.

'You-will-do-as-you're-told,' Master punctuated the impromptu spanking. 'Do-you-understand-yet?'

'Yes, Master.' Charlotte gulped, swallowing back dry sobs of mortification and shock.

'Good. Turn around and show Sir your bottom now. Any more of this nonsense and you'll be getting off this train and parading through the terminus naked on a leash. Would you like that?'

'Oh. No, Sir,' she said, avoiding his stare from beneath sulky lashes. 'I mean, Master!' she amended, shocked to find that Sir had clearly leaped up behind her and was adding to the spanking tariff. She had thought he was on her side!

'Hmm, I'm not convinced. I think you probably would. Anyway. Pull your knickers down to your ankles.'

Charlotte pouted, biting the inside of her lip, as she eased the thin knickers over her glowing pink bum and down past her knees where they dropped of their own accord to her ankles.

'Quite nice; do you wax, Charlotte?' asked Master conversationally.

'I do, Master.'

'I approve. Now, Charlotte, until we reach Capital City, I would like you to take a seat in that corner and sit there with your legs spread as wide as you can manage. That way, both Sir and I can get a good long look at you whenever we need a break from our work.'

Blinking at this slightly unexpected turn of events, Charlotte backed over to the corner seat indicated, next to the compartment door, diagonally opposite Master and at the far end of the banquette from Sir. She shuffled down, feeling a little sting on her backside, both from the after-effects of the men's hard hands and the stiff fuzziness of the upholstery on her bare bottom. As instructed, she parted her thighs as wide as she could muster, so that her seated lower body described a rough diamond shape, flaring out widely at the knees then tapering back to where her ankles were restricted by the knickers.

'Very nice. Now pull down the cups of your brassiere so that your nipples are visible, please. That's right. And I'd like you to hold the lips of your pussy apart so that nothing is hidden at all. That's it. We need you fully and completely exposed to our view, Charlotte. That's excellent.'

'Exquisite, dear.' Sir smiled, all friendliness and reassurance once more.

And then, as if this were any ordinary commute from a provincial town back to the capital, the two men clicked open their briefcases and took out sheafs of reading material and mobile phones, into which they intermittently barked orders and information.

Charlotte sat in this uncomfortable position for more than half an hour, screwing her face up every time shadows passed beneath the blinds. If she could make out their shapes behind the thin cloth, it stood to reason that they might be able to discern her erect nipples and the awkward sprawl of her legs and put two and two together. Master and Sir did not allow her discomfiture to influence them for one second though, occasionally looking up from their absorption in work to drink in the view or issue a curt, 'Keep those legs spread, Charlotte.'

It was a curious realisation for Charlotte that she would prefer to have her two mysterious 'owners' paying attention to her, even if that attention was humiliating, than all but ignoring her in this way. Even more curious was the way the air at the top of her thighs was cold with that particular chill that affects wet skin. If her skin was wet, did that mean she was . . . turned on? She had to be honest with herself; this scenario was one that had come from her own brain on one of those nights when unfulfilled longing for sensual domination kept her awake. She blushed with recollection of the story she had penned a few days ago, in which she was taken blindfolded to a gentleman's drawing room and violated repeatedly in every orifice by a succession of anonymous men. In front of a roaring fire, of course. Master and Sir had read it, undoubtedly. It was obvious that they would draw certain conclusions from it.

But that story did not form part of Fantasy #3. Surely they

would stick to that particular narrative. Wouldn't they? She shivered, wondering if the rest of the day would really go according to her design. Would it be the only day? Master had said that she belonged to them until they released her. What if they never released her? Indeed, who were these men? An impulse of panic led her to remove her fingers from her prised-apart lower lips and shuffle to her feet, intending to retrieve her mobile phone and send a text update on her whereabouts to her flatmates. The look Master gave her on registering her unbidden movement, however, pinned her back into place, shrinking against the dusty fabric of the seat.

'I don't recall giving you permission to move,' he said icily. 'There will be a punishment for that.'

'Please, Master,' she said, trembling, 'may I send a text message ahead to my flatmates? They will expect me home by a certain time. Perhaps I could tell them ... When *will* I be home?'

He stared at her just long enough to lead her to wonder if the blood had actually frozen in her veins, then said, 'Speaking out of turn too. Well, well, we will have some issues to address later, won't we?'

'It's not a bad thought though,' struck up Sir, and Charlotte mentally cheered him on. 'We don't want anybody making inconvenient waves if they have been expecting Charlotte back. I mean, we have plans for the rest of the day, don't we?'

Phew! Only the day, not her entire life then.

Master contemplated this, then reached into Charlotte's bookbag and retrieved her mobile. But her hopes were dashed when he flipped open the cover and began jabbing at the buttons himself.

'What's her name? Your friend?' he asked. 'Or is it a he? Do you have a client to cancel?'

'No, I don't!' retorted Charlotte, stung. 'I don't have "clients". They're just people who don't mind paying for my company when they're lonely.' *And I'm only an escort in the fantasy*, she held off from saying.

'How touching. You're quite the charitable soul, aren't you, Charlotte? I didn't catch your friend's name.'

'Lynnie,' groused Charlotte, and she watched with her lower lip stuck as far out as she could muster while Master scrolled through her contacts and began composing a message on her behalf. Charlotte was desperate to jump up and read it over his shoulder – he could be saying *anything* – but something kept her glued to the seat in her inglorious position as the buttons bleeped. She shifted uncomfortably, feeling a familiar and inconvenient urge. Would they grant permission for a toilet break? It was worth a try. But she would ask Sir, not that Master bastard. She cleared her throat timidly.

'I beg your pardon, Sir, but could I ask you something?'

He turned to her, smiling gently but reprovingly. 'You know the rule, Charlotte.'

'I'm sorry, I know, but I . . . need the loo. Really urgently.'

'I'm afraid it will have to wait. Only ten minutes to go now.'

'But I can't hold on!'

'Of course you can. Now keep those lips spread good and wide for us, my dear, or there will be serious consequences. You can do it. Good girl.'

Still smiling, he began folding his papers and replacing them in his briefcase. Charlotte noticed that the bucolic landscape outside had been exchanged for brick villas, then tower blocks. The corridor beyond began to bustle with passengers preparing to alight. Any one of them could bend down to push a case along on its casters and peer through the crack of window that was not covered by the flimsy blinds.

Master closed his case and began fiddling with his tie. Glancing over at Charlotte, he said, 'Take off your knickers and give them to me. You won't be needing them today.'

Charlotte swallowed at this blatant statement of intent. She eased the knickers off her feet and handed them meekly to Master, who put them in his breast pocket, leaving a portion visible at the top like a pornographic handkerchief.

'Thank you. Now you may lower your skirt and button up your blouse again just for as long as we are in public. But . . . no! Do not replace the cups of your bra. I want you to be conscious of your nakedness and availability beneath your clothes.'

Charlotte gasped, trying to appeal with her eyes, but it was no use. The blouse was so thin that surely everybody would be treated to the sight of the dimpled silk that outlined her nipples. Still, at least she could be assured that there would be no visible panty line under her tight skirt.

The train lurched to a halt, and Charlotte was escorted out into the corridor in single file, Master ahead and Sir to her rear. Master helped her down off the high step, but his apparently gallant gesture concealed his true intention, which was to see that he had a firm hold of her in the wide open space of the terminus, precluding any chance of escape. Sir took her other elbow and the trio paraded swiftly down the platform, Charlotte's shorter legs struggling to maintain the rapid pace of her two tall companions. To outsiders, many of whom gave the group covert glances, it must have looked exactly like what it was: two professional men with their owned girl, their possession, spiriting her away to be . . . what? Oh God. What?

Charlotte kept her eyes to the ground, beyond mortified. 'Keep up, Charlotte; no dawdling,' chided Sir, and he gave her bottom a resounding smack that rang out like a pistol shot in the echoing space. Several bystanders jumped and all eyes swivelled towards them, but thankfully they were nearly outside now, heading away from the prurient peepers and towards a row of taxis.

Something caught Master's eye though, before they could hail a cab and he doubled back, stopping abruptly before it. It was one of the silver toilet cubicles that had sprung up on the pavements of the capital recently. Charlotte breathed out, wondering if she had misjudged Master, and he possessed a hitherto unrecognised quality of thoughtfulness. She was quickly forced to reassess that idea though, when the door had slid aside and he stepped inside himself, dragging her and Sir after him.

The door shushed shut. Charlotte, squeezed into the tiny space with two men, simply gaped at them. Did they really expect her to relieve herself in their presence?

'I thought you were desperate,' said Master mockingly. 'Come on then. You can't say I'm an unreasonable man.'

'Can't you wait outside?' stammered Charlotte.

'No.'

'Relax, Charlotte,' said Sir, with a reassuring rub of her upper arm. 'It's really nothing we haven't seen before.'

'What a strange time to decide that you are coy, Charlotte,' whispered Master. '*After* you have shown us everything. It's just a bodily function.'

'Like fucking.'

'Exactly. Like fucking. You like to be watched fucking, don't you?'

Charlotte allowed them to push her down, a hand on each shoulder, until she was hovering above the cold steel of the lavatory. She squeezed her eyes shut, unclenched her bladder and let her body follow its course.

'Good. That's very good, Charlotte. You are such a quick learner.'

'A true submissive,' contributed Sir. 'I am so looking forward to our afternoon now.'

They left the cubicle, heedless of some double-takes from onlookers, and marched her along the taxi rank, past the waiting cabs to the back, where a maroon-painted vehicle waited a few spaces behind its more traditional company. They processed into the back, Master leaning forwards to speak to the driver in a low mutter, which Charlotte could not quite make out. She made to sit down, but Sir caught her shoulder and said, 'Lift your skirt first, please.'

Charlotte made a great effort to lift the skirt so that the back rose high enough but the front still covered her with some semblance of modesty. She sat carefully, drawing in a small breath at the cold smooth leather of the seat against her nude bottom.

'Your tie,' said Master blandly to Sir, and he immediately loosened it and handed it to the senior partner. 'Unbutton your blouse, Charlotte, and expose your breasts as before.'

Charlotte gave a meaningful glance towards the cabby, who was sitting at the exit of the station forecourt, indicating steadily. Surely he could see them in the rear-view mirror.

'Don't worry about that. He will have seen it all before. Do as you're told, or he'll be seeing a lot more.'

Charlotte's fingers set to work on the buttons once more, while Master wrapped the tie around her head, blindfolding her against the view of the passing urban streets.

'I feel I should be scared,' she mumbled, feeling the trousered legs of her owners nudging up either thigh above the elasticated lace of her stockings.

Two hands alighted on each expanse of bare flesh, kneading and stroking.

'There is nothing to be afraid of,' said Sir's voice on her right.

'Nothing will happen that you don't want,' confirmed Master in her other ear. 'We are taking you on a journey into your own needs and desires.'

'We are going to pleasure you.'

'And punish you.'

'Punish you with pleasure.'

'Pleasure you with punishment.'

'Because that is what you want.'

'Because that is what you need.'

The words were sufficient to quieten the nagging doubts that had prevented Charlotte's full immersion into the experience. A weight lifted; she rolled her head back on the seat and breathed a heavy sigh.

The hands were moving inexorably higher, underneath her skirt. Another hand cupped her right breast while mouths pressed against her neck on the other side. Fingers arrived at her outer lips, prising them apart then dipping into the waters with a luscious slicking sound.

'Well, well, something tells us our Charlotte is enjoying herself.' It was Sir's voice, just above her shoulder.

'Did you ever doubt it?'

Two sets of fingers delved the velvet depths of Charlotte's most intimate places, while mouths breathed warm air across her swollen nipples, then flicked the tips with their tongues.

'When we get to the hotel, Charlotte, we are going to make you come, over and over and over again,' Master informed her, half-eating her ear as he poured his voice down it.

'Until you can't walk.'

'Or talk.'

'Or think.'

'Or move.'

One finger, two fingers, three fingers, more, scissoring inside her, scattered across her clit, pushing, poking, pressing, arousing every one of her nerve endings all at once. Her thighs spread wider and wider, until they were hooked over forearms, the skirt having now ridden irrevocably around her waist, no further thought given to the cab driver. Every part of her body was under sensual attack, defences stripped down, surrender ignored by the marauding hands and mouths and tongues and teeth. Charlotte felt herself to be no more than one gigantic pulsing organism; every pore in her body shot sparks down to her clitoris, which seemed enormous now, and rapacious in its need.

Twenty fingers worked at her core while two sets of lips caressed her breasts. She was pushed back in the seat with her legs forming a wide V in the air above her; one calf held firm while the triumphant digits invaded further and further across her borders, pillaging her most intimate parts.

When she came, writhing on fingers that thrust down and down while others circled her swollen clitoris, she kicked so hard that a shoe fell off and clattered to the floor of the cab.

One tongue then two plunged into her mouth before it had finished its broken keen of defeat. They drew back, the fingers leaving with them to remove her blindfold with a flourish, so that Charlotte lay, legs limp and loosely spread, skirt around waist, shirt wide open and bra cups down to reveal sorely reddened nipples, hair wild and eyes glazed, in a post-orgasmic slump.

'I think you needed that,' proclaimed Master. 'Don't you think she needed that?'

'She needed that,' confirmed Sir with a nod. 'Do you agree, James?'

'She got what she needed,' said the cab driver in a rough Cockney brogue.

'You did, didn't you, Charlotte? Say it.'

'I needed that,' whispered Charlotte, her tongue rolling around hugely in her parched mouth.

Sir chuckled. 'You need to smarten up your act, Charlotte. Wake up. This is simply an introduction.'

'We have many more plans for the afternoon,' agreed Master. 'We have booked the room overnight. We thought you would probably need a full night's sleep after we leave.'

Charlotte struggled to bring her shattered consciousness back into one piece. What happened in Fantasy #3? Could she even remember? It had been months since she wrote and submitted her desires to the site. Two men . . . silk ropes . . . unfeasible number of orgasms . . . double penetration . . . was that it?

'After all, this is what you asked for,' Master reminded her as the taxi stood still, indicator clicking, outside the façade of a large hotel.

'We are here to please you.' Sir smiled, fussing with her blouse until it was buttoned back up. 'And you are here to please us.'

'It's all too good to be true,' mumbled Charlotte, trying to reconfigure her body into something she recognised, allowing Master to pull her to her feet and yank her skirt back down over her soaked thighs.

'I'm not sure good is the word,' he said, and he winked. The strict taskmaster of the train journey actually winked. He was human, somewhere inside the granite.

Charlotte giggled, her heart suddenly light and optimistic. Here she was outside an exclusive hotel, with two attractive men who meant to ravish her until she could be ravished no more. This was exactly the kind of story she wanted to follow.

'Shall we?' she said, offering an elbow each to her distinguished escorts.

'We'd be delighted,' they replied in unison. The cab driver was tipped, the door opened and the three stepped out onto the bustling pavements of the capital, drawing a small wave of attention from the passers-by as they paraded along the marble concourse, past the doormen and into the Hotel Luxe Noir.

Please turn the page for

Office Sex

A short story
by Justine Elyot

Office Sex
Justine Elyot

Why, when the time accurate to a millisecond ticks away on the screen before me, do I still find myself watching the clock? Something about the stiff vibration of the minute hand compels my eyes, or maybe it's the effect of years spent at school in the same pursuit. Is it habit, or do I prefer the clock to the screen?

Who cares anyway? Usually he has been into the office by now. This is the latest he's left it by a good ten minutes, and I'm beginning to feel antsy. I keep clicking the screen, refreshing it for no good reason, so it looks as if I'm doing something productive, but really I'm wondering whether I could phone or email him on some pathetic pretext, just to make sure he's in the building.

But then, that would make him think I care, and I don't want him to think that. I don't want him to realise that this daily ration of furtive eye contact and quasi-accidental touching is at all important to me, because then it would probably stop, and I'd have to think about getting a life. Or a 'normal' boyfriend.

I chuckle under my breath at the concept of 'normal' and tip my half-cup of paperclips onto the desk. Time for some Clip Art. I link them together to make two rough stick-figure shapes and flatten them out on the veneered wood. What shall it be today? Doggy style perhaps. Paperclip figure 1 bends gracefully, clinky metal arms hanging down, while Paperclip figure 2 (extra clip for height) stands behind. I think his arms can cross in a diagonal, so that they rest on figure 1's back. Ah, primitive but surprisingly pretty to look at. I try to cross my legs, which is hard work in the progressively shorter and tighter skirts I have been favouring lately. Before the left and right limbs can cross, there is a low rumble in my ear which makes me leap off my chair, sending it skittering on its castors across the office.

It is *him*, clearing his throat behind me. The bastard has come in through the fire escape door at the back of the office.

He has a hand lightly on my back, preventing my impulse – to flee to the Ladies' and beyond – from taking effect.

'If that isn't flagrant misuse of company property, I don't know what is,' he says, his voice perfectly mingling amusement and disapproval in that uniquely come-hither-but-only-if-you-can-handle-it way.

I just glance at him from under radically lowered eyelashes and curl a bit of lip. Should I apologise or flirt? I'm not sure, so I wait for his next signal. The other four desk jockeys in my bank of workstations are trying their best not to rubberneck blatantly, but I know what the water-cooler conversation will be today.

At that very moment, my bloody screensaver chooses to make its appearance; usually I can hastily return it to the default setting whenever anyone important crosses the threshold, but the boss's sneaky entrance has thrown me into confusion. 'MR MORRELL IS HOTTER THAN HELL' ambles across the screen, in no hurry to pass by and spare my blushes. Childish, I know, but I've only been here three weeks and nothing wittier has occurred to me yet.

I shut my eyes and await my P45.

Instead, I am told that the stationery cupboard needs re-organising, and I seem to be just the person for the job.

I open my eyes and stare blankly at Mr Hotter-Than-Hell Morrell. It's true though. He is almost impossible to look in the eye without salivating. I want to put out a hand and grab him by the tie, drawing him into a passionate lambada across the beige expanse of the office. The only reason I watch *Strictly Come Dancing* is so I can imagine it is Morrell spinning me around the floor in thrall to his body, our eyes locked, our pelvises conjoined. Also because I like the use of the word 'Strictly' in the title. Kinky!

'You know the way, I assume?' he says, raising an eyebrow and gesturing to me to turn around and march. My route will take me through the office, past the vending machine, lifts and toilets, to the other side of the landing. Just a short hop on an ordinary day, but in this alternative reality it seems like the London Marathon. At least I get a chance to practise the Marilyn Monroe wiggle I read about in some magazine. I put each high-heeled foot in front of the other, forcing my arse to sway and strain against the constricting seams of my inappropriately short skirt. The thought of him following me, watching my bottom, is arousing and I can feel my nipples start to chafe against my scratchy lace bra.

Once we are out on the landing, my heels echo clickily on the shiny floor; I have to slow down to make sure I don't go arse over tit. One of my fellow temps emerges from the Ladies' and looks us both up and down curiously before scurrying back into the office.

The door of the stationery cupboard looms towards me; I turn the handle and lead us inside, flicking on the light. It is the size of a small room, carpeted, with banks of metal shelves covering three of the walls.

I hear Mr Morrell shut the door, then take a quick breath when I hear a sound like a key turning in a lock.

'Turn around and face me,' he says. He is standing, arms

folded, a pinstriped sex god with a key dangling from the fingers of one hand. He puts the key into a pocket, withdraws a BlackBerry and, with total deliberation, switches it off before replacing it.

It seems I have become Priority Number One, marked 'urgent'.

Oh, what on Earth is in store for me, in the stores?

'That's a very short skirt you're wearing,' he remarks. 'I'm not sure it's entirely appropriate for the workplace.'

'Oh . . . aren't you?' My conversational faculties have taken an early coffee break.

'I'll give you a choice, Hannah. You can go home, get changed and come back here in a longer skirt. Or . . .' The pause is just long enough for me to wonder if my heart is still beating. '. . . you can take it off. Here. Now. Which do you choose?'

Oh, I *hate* choices. It takes me half my lunch break to pick a sandwich filling. This, though, is one of the easier decisions I have faced in life. The set of his jaw, the angle of his eyebrow, make it for me.

Fumbling fingers unclip and unzip; the brief strip of charcoal flannel slides over my hips and down to the floor, the nylon lining crackling static against my stockings as it falls.

'Plucky,' he says, smirking slightly. 'I like that. I like it a lot.'

Only now does the implication of what I am doing sink in. I am standing in front of Morrell – my boss – in my tarty underwear. In a stationery cupboard. A *cold* stationery cupboard. My hands reach down to cover my goose-pimpled thighs, but he tuts and shakes his head. He swirls a finger in the air, the circular motion suggesting that I am to give him a twirl.

I remove my hands and perform a slow 360-degree turn. The knickers I am wearing are sheer and black with a red bow on the front. While not as revealing as a thong, they are cut high at the back, the filmy lace shearing away up to my hips so that most of my bottom cheeks elude coverage.

'Good,' he says eventually, then after another excruciating pause, 'Shall we make a start then?'

I laugh nervously. 'A start?'

'This stock inventory I have in mind. Why don't you count the scissors in that box and then bring a pair to me.'

This was *not* what I had been expecting him to say. Wrong-footed, suspecting trickery of some kind, I go over to the box of scissors and count nineteen pairs, conscious all the time of his eyes upon my bum cheeks, then take the nineteenth gleaming pair of stainless steel snippers and hand them to him, nonplussed.

'Didn't anyone tell you to offer the handle, not the blade?' he tuts. 'Stay there. I want to make sure these are in full working order.'

He reaches down to the top button of my white work shirt, tugs on it and then, heartstoppingly, snips it off.

'Hmm,' he says, putting the button in his top pocket. 'It seems fine . . . but we have to make sure . . . we can't do things by halves at Morrell & Co . . . yes, I think I'm satisfied now.'

With each murmured phrase he shears another button away from the placket until my shirt hangs open, revealing my bra in its gauzy glory.

'You might as well take that off,' he observes, handing me the scissors. 'And put these back.'

Reduced to my wisps of underwear, I retreat to the shelving, pressing my back to it for rickety support, feeling like a small animal, vole or something, cornered by a fox.

'Now then, Miss,' he says, folding his arms and switching his stern look to its highest setting. 'Somebody here needs a lesson in the proper use of my time and my property. I don't tolerate wastefulness or clock-watching here. Do you have anything to say for yourself?'

His tone is making me feel weak; I lean back, hoping my heels will support me as they dig into the carpet, and half-whisper, 'I'm willing to learn, Sir.'

He approves of the reply, smiling broadly, before returning to boss mode. 'I'm sure you are. Now is the time to prove your commitment to the company, and your loyalty to your manager. But first there is a small matter of correction for your misdemeanours . . . and how better to correct an employee than with . . . correction fluid.'

For a second I'm not sure what he means, and wonder if he is making an obscure reference to his sperm. I am all set to give the man a spectacular blow job, dithering by the shelves, but he shakes his head and indicates a clutter of liquid paper bottles behind me.

'Oh! You want one of these?' I can't quite believe it, but he nods and holds out his hand.

'Yes. Now stay there, quite still.' He approaches me, unscrewing the cap. I have nowhere to run, pressed up there against the metal struts, bars of coldness against my naked back. I breathe in sharply as he applies the brush to my right breast, just above the cup of my bra. He is . . . writing something. It is ticklish, and I squirm a little. The fluid chills my skin in a room that is already unheated, and I am conscious of my nipples, hardened to soreness in their sheer casing.

'I need a little more space to fit the full message,' notes Morrell, and he yanks down the cup, chafing the crimson crest of the nipple so that I emit a quick 'ooh'. I look down and read, upside down and backwards, the word BAD, underneath which he is painstakingly tracing out a G and then an I and then an R and finally an L.

'Judging by the state of these,' he says, pinching slightly at the nipple before running the pad of his thumb across it, 'I'm not far wrong. Am I?'

'No, Sir,' I wheeze, shutting my eyes and throwing my head back, rolling my neck against the metal, while he repeats the procedure with my left breast.

He must be able to smell me, I think desperately, conscious of how my knickers are flooding with my arousal juices. He must know he can do what he likes to me.

'Now then,' he says, giving my tits a tactile examination. 'While we're waiting for that to dry, let's move to the next stage of your punishment, shall we?'

Yikes! Punishment? I cast my eyes around the room, noticing several types of stationery I would not want much to do with. Hole punchers. Staple guns. Drawing pins.

He does not ask me to fetch anything though. Instead he instructs me to turn around, facing away from him, and bend over so that my hands are on the lowest shelf.

Oh, those words . . . *bend over* . . . taking me back to one of my oldest fascinations. Though corporal punishment in school was outlawed by the time I reached secondary age, I had often imagined how it must have been to be called up to the teacher's desk and ordered over for a taste of the slipper or the strap or even the cane. The ritual, the humiliation, the idea that everybody would *know* – oh yes, that had been a fantasy to be savoured, slowly, drawing out the detail, on many a long night.

I swallow, then slowly lower myself, pivoting at the waist, until my hands reach for the lowest sheet of metal and grip it. My spine is sloping downwards, creating maximum upthrust of arse, and although my knickers are still scantily on, I imagine he can see the clenched nutmeg shape of my mound through the filmy material.

'Spread your legs a little,' he commands, and then he *definitely* can – and not so clenched either. I jump and almost lose a shoe when he unexpectedly twangs a suspender strap against my thigh. 'Keep still,' he growls.

There is a hand, two hands, large and warm, on my goose-pimpled bum cheeks. They feel good, cupping the globes, brushing the skin like one of those anti-cellulite mitts but much, much better, tugging at the frilly edge of the knickers, pinching and kneading. I am gushing, the scrap of fabric sodden, and I try to push myself back towards his touch, greedy for as much of it as I can get.

His hands fly away from me, then I feel the top of my knickers pulled ruthlessly taut – a wedgie, no less! – so that the black material disappears into the crack of my bum. I yelp at that, and then I yelp louder as his hand returns, no longer the giver of pleasure but of pain. It deals a sharp smack to my right side then my left. The sensation is intense, but brief, the burn dying down almost immediately, outlived by the shame of my position.

'Do you think you deserve this?' asks Morrell, his tone making it clear how he thinks I should answer.

'Yes, Sir,' I quiver dutifully.

'Yes, Sir. I should think you do. Ask me for it then.'

Oooh, the *bastard!* I want to feel more of this tingling, but I'm not sure I can frame the words he expects from me.

'Ohhh . . . Sir!' I protest.

'Ask me.'

'I can't.'

'You can and you will. Tell me what you deserve.'

My mouth fits itself reluctantly around the words, muttering them. 'I deserve a . . . a good spanking, Sir.' *A good spanking*, a phrase I have often heard in my imaginings, sounds weird and foreign in my actual voice. It makes me want to giggle with mortification.

'Indeed you do,' he says, and there is a hint of smile in his voice amid the grimness.

I grit my teeth, bracing myself for the next strike, but it is slow in coming. Not until I have finally unclenched my buttock muscles and tried to look back does the stinging onslaught resume. His technique blends speed and accuracy to a degree that finds me hopping and hissing in very short order. My cheeks and upper thighs are peppered with the fast-falling smacks, their pattern unpredictable but their impact never less than yelp-provoking.

Somewhere between the sharp report of each smack and my own yowls of surprised pain, I am expected also to listen to some kind of lecture taking place above and behind me.

'My property is to be respected,' is one phrase that does not drown in the crack-smack-ouch filling the air. 'You will learn that I do not tolerate slapdash work or lax attitudes,' is another. Periodically I am expected to contribute a 'Yes, Sir' or 'No, Sir' and I am vaguely grateful that no more verbose expressions of contrition are called for. I am far too busy concentrating on the slow heating up of my rear; like an electric hob ring I imagine it beginning to glow, first faintly, then a vibrant orange, then an unbearable beacon red. Oddly enough, the same effect seems to be transferring to my crotch. Hot and swollen, though mercifully missing the soreness, it is making its presence felt quite insistently.

When he stops I miss the size and weight and heat of his chastising hand immediately, and even push my bum out in a silent plea for more.

'You blatant little tart,' he says, pressing a fingertip to my throbbing flesh, no doubt admiring his handiwork. 'You enjoyed that, didn't you?'

'Mmm, of course I didn't, Sir,' I murmur, swivelling my hips a little in invitation. 'I've learnt my lesson, honest.'

One finger drifts down the line of my bunched-up knickers in the crack of my arse, stopping at the puddle of lust between my legs.

'You're very wet down here, aren't you? Eh?'

'Er, yes, Sir.'

'Why is that, do you think?'

'I . . . not sure, Sir.' I know he is going to make me say it. I really don't want to.

'I need an answer, Hannah. Why are you so wet between the legs?'

Oh, for God's sake, I wanted a shag, not a bloody interrogation. I hunch my shoulders sulkily and say, 'No idea, Sir.'

'Oh dear. I don't think you have learnt your lesson, have you, Hannah? You need to brush up your communication skills. Well, let's see . . . Hand me one of those rulers from the top shelf.'

I stare at him, biting my lip. My arse is sore enough as it is – does he really mean to . . . ?

'A traditional six of the best might prove sufficient incentive to untie your tongue,' he clarifies.

Wow. The full-on schoolgirl fantasy. My curiosity is stronger than my fear, and my arousal stronger than both together, so I reach up and take one of the rulers. It is thirty centimetres long and about half a centimetre thick, made of Perspex. 'Shatterproof' is proudly proclaimed across the centre.

I hand it to Morrell and he slaps it rather terrifyingly in his palm a few times, then bends it backwards and lets it flick back into place.

'Oh yes,' he says, 'this will do nicely. Firm but flexible, and capable of producing a serious sting. A little like me.' He grins demonically. This is almost too exciting; my heart is bumping about my ribcage like a pinball. 'Back into position please.'

My bottom, still hot from the spanking, resumes its vulnerable pose. I try to work on my breathing – keep it even, keep it regular.

'You will have to count these, Hannah,' says Morrell. 'I have been known to miscount . . . I can get carried away . . .' So he has plenty of practice at this kind of thing then. I suppose you could say that that's a good thing.

The wait is almost more excruciating than the first blow, when it comes. He takes his time preparing, flipping the ruler through the air, then tapping it lightly against my bottom, testing it for resilience perhaps.

The first stroke shocks me; it falls hard and loud across the broadest part of my bottom, a white stripe of exquisite pain. I wonder if the people in the distant office can hear my howl of outrage, which ends in a broken, 'One, Sir.'

'Felt that, did you?' His voice drips with sadistic glee. 'There's plenty more where that came from.'

The ruler whaps down again, directly beneath the first line of fire. I rock back and forth on my legs a little, wondering if I can keep position for the next four. If they are all as hard as this, I don't think I'll be able to do it.

'I didn't hear your count.' Morrell's voice seems disembodied, a distant thing now.

'Oh . . . two, Sir.'

'Hmm, well, just for that . . .' He flicks the ruler, lightly but sharply, between my legs, stinging the insides of my thighs. Their dampness accentuates the pain. 'Don't forget again,' he warns me.

On the next stroke I almost pull the shelving over, so fiercely do I have to cling to it to maintain my humbling stance. It falls directly on the tender spot between bum cheek and thigh top, searing like a brand, making me wonder how long the marks will last.

'Oh lordy lordy Lord. Three, Sir,' I wail. Are we really only halfway through?

He takes a break to pull my knickers down to my knees, where they are stretched so tight their elastic digs into my skin, cancelling out the relief to my scratchy rear cleft. I wince in anticipation of the fourth stroke, but it is slow in coming. Instead, Morrell places the flat of his hand beneath my pussy lips and slowly moves it up and down, rubbing against my swollen clitoris in a way that is teasingly gentle until I have to jam myself down into his palm, desperate for a firmer touch.

At once he withdraws his hand, tutting, and puts it to my nose.

'What do you smell?' he asks.

'Myself,' I hedge.

'More specifically, Hannah, or I shall have to add to your punishment.'

'My . . . juices.'

'Juices? What sort of juices?'

'Oh, oh, sexual lubrication juices,' I fluster.

He laughs. 'Why would your body be producing sexual lubrication juices, as you call them, when I am whipping you? Do you have an explanation?'

'No, Sir.'

'Think about it. I might let you off a stroke if I like your answer. Or would that disappoint you?'

It makes sense now that Morrell would be hotter than hell. Because he lives there. He is the devil.

'Because . . . oh, because I suppose it must be turning me on.'

'I suppose it must be,' he muses. He moves his hand down so that it rests against my lips. 'Lick it. Tell me what it tastes like.'

Obediently, I slip out my tongue and lap at his lifeline for a few seconds.

'It tastes pretty much the way it smells,' I report. 'A little salty, but that could just be the natural flavour of your hand.'

He laughs again, and is still laughing when the ruler cracks its fourth wicked blow, catching me completely off guard so that I leap up, shrieking and clutching my bottom.

'Four, Sir!' My count has an indignant tone. He pushes me right back down and is swift with the fifth, laying it on the top of my thighs for maximum ouch effect.

At last, the final stroke; relief tinged with disappointment and excitement about where we might be heading next floods my head, until the pain drives all other emotions out again. His hardest, cruellest blow, back across the spot where the first was laid, breaks the ruler in half.

'Aaaaaaaaaaargh, six, Sir,' I yowl, my knuckles whiter than white, my legs trembling.

'Good girl,' says Morrell. 'Your debt is paid. And those rulers really are shatterproof, if not unbreakable. You'll have to order a new box. No, don't move. Stay there. I'm enjoying the view.'

One fingertip travels the scorched terrain of my well-thrashed bum, climbing the raised strips and descending into the less reddened valleys, tracing patterns. It feels sore, but nice, and much nicer still when the finger reaches my wide-open slit. More fingers are called into service, exploring each fold and crevice, rubbing and flicking my longing clit, circling the hole that I hope to have filled before long. One digit spears it with a luscious sucking sound.

The man who is fingering me chuckles and says, 'I think you enjoyed that almost as much as I did. Didn't you, Hannah?'

'Yes, Sir,' I sigh, pushing down on him, lost in the swirl of sensation his other fingers are producing with their clitoral manipulations, drowning sweetly, feeling the pressure build and build and build and then . . .

He takes them away.

'Not yet, dirty girl,' he says. 'You haven't thanked me properly for your punishment.'

'Right. Oh. Thank you, Sir.'

'That isn't what I meant. Kneel down in front of me.'

A little dizzy from breaking position, I do so, grateful that the cupboard is carpeted, although it is that rough, scratchy kind of office covering that produces the worst carpet burns. From this position, Morrell looms high above me, a towering inferno of sex, still impeccably suited and booted in contrast to my nakedness.

I reach up and unbuckle his belt, wondering how that would feel on the tender flesh of my whipped bottom, then wondering why I even want to know. I unbutton his fly, push the waist of the trousers down, steering wide of the substantial lump in front, letting them drop to his ankles. That really is a bulge and a half. I reach wondering hands up to feel its steely weight inside the silk boxers, which are tellingly stained, before pulling them down too.

Now I have a problem. I cannot get his cock – which is pretty similar in length to the late-lamented ruler – into my mouth from this position. He is too tall. The most I can hope for is to give his balls a tongue wash. So this is what I begin to do, approaching my task with reverence.

'I need a chair,' he says, taking a red plastic number from a stack in the corner and sitting astride it. 'You can kneel between my knees, come on.'

I proceed to give him the first blow job I have ever given my full concentration; his magnificent tool demands no less. Nothing quick or perfunctory about this; no back-of-the-mind shopping lists. I do everything the magazines recommend, from massaging his perineum to flicking my tongue against his frenulum; I even hazard a deep-throat, but I don't think there is a throat deep enough for him.

His legs twitch; he moans and clutches at my hair and I feel rewarded, his pleasure my prize. I have already decided to swallow, but before the crisis approaches, he yanks me off his cock by the roots of my hair and whispers, 'No. I want to fuck you. I want to make you come. I want to hear you beg for mercy.'

'Mercy,' I whisper, mesmerised by his low-spoken words.

'Yes, like that. Now go and get that box of OHP transparencies. And a roll of parcel tape.'

What? Is there no end to this man's fiendish imagination? I hope not.

I'm guessing that the parcel tape presages a spot of bondage, but I can't figure out why he could need OHP transparencies. In the event, he doesn't – he just needs the box, a large, flattish square. He puts it in front of the chair.

'That should do it,' he says, eyeing me and the chair in a trigonometric kind of way. 'Now stand on the box and bend over so your hands are at the top corners of the seat. Good.'

He tapes my wrists to the chair legs, repeating the process with my ankles. Up on the box with my red arse sticking out, my sleeve is now at the ideal height to take his cock. He will need to keep a good hold of my hips, though, if he doesn't want to push the chair over. That would be the highlight of the Accident Book, for sure.

'Perhaps I'll tether you with this next time,' he says, pulling the tie from around his neck and dangling it in front of my nose. Next time. I like that. His jacket and tie drop to the floor, but he does not remove his shirt, opting only to unbutton the collar. He has those bands round the elbows; I always find that strangely sexy. Lovely cufflinks as well.

Now he is moving around behind me; one hand travels slowly up a captive thigh while another brushes my dangling tits. He pinches at the nipples, coming closer, fingering my clitoris, and now his hard cock is between my thighs, rocking back and forth, getting wetter and thicker. My position, head hanging down, forehead on the chair seat, means that I can see through my legs. I can see the head of his cock, slipping and sliding between my swollen lips; I can see his hand squeezing my breasts. Oh, put it in, put it in, put it in, I silently beg, and then I remember what kind of man he is – silent begging is no good to him.

'Please put it in, Sir,' I gasp.

'Put what in, Hannah?'

'Your cock, Sir. Please put it in. Please fuck me.'

'Put it in? Here?' His thumb prods my startled arsehole and I squeal.

'No! Well, not now.' I have never done that before, and I'm not sure I want to try it while gaffer-taped to an office chair until I'm a bit more used to the idea.

'So where do you want me to . . . put it in? You'll have to tell me. We need all communications to be clear and unambiguous, Hannah, don't we?'

The swine is directly quoting something I said at the Monday meeting. I would laugh if I wasn't so insanely horny.

'In my, oh, my pussy, or my cunt, or my vagina, or whatever,' I blither.

'Yes, that was suitably unambiguous,' he approves. 'Good. Now prepare yourself for a good, hard shag. You aren't going to be walking straight until the weekend.'

Yikes, it's only Tuesday. With one clean smooth thrust, his shaft is embedded deep inside, stretching me as I've never been stretched before. He stays in up to the hilt for a little while, waiting for me to habituate to the unfamiliar girth, jiggling and swivelling. His hands are clamped to my hips and his abdomen presses against my lower bottom and thighs, heating them up again where they had begun to cool off.

He draws back, slowly, very, very, slowly, so that I feel every inch travelling down the tunnel. He almost pulls out, and I voice an inarticulate protest, but then he slams back all the way, knocking the breath out of me for a second. And we're off!

His pace is measured at first, nothing too wild, a languid see-sawing accompanied by plenty of little finger-dances across my nipples and clit, but he has to cut down on those when the tempo increases. Soon each thrust is vividly felt, pounding broad and hard, causing the chair to wobble and my breasts to swing like out-of-control pendulums. The friction is divine and intense; his cock seems to get ever thicker, stretching me, splitting me, owning and controlling me. He wraps an iron arm around my stomach, keeping me and chair in place, while he uses the other hand to prise apart my bum cheeks, opening me impossibly further, gaining the angle he needs and I crave.

'One day,' he tells me, his voice strained with effort, 'I'm going to bugger you. I'm going to bend you over, tie you up, strap your arse till it's sunset red and then give it a good reaming. Would you like that, Hannah?'

'Nnrgh,' I say.

He slaps my bottom. 'I didn't hear you.'

'Yes, Sir,' I pant.

'I thought so. I've always thought . . .' He punctuates each phrase with a ragged breath. '. . . Ever since you joined the company . . . that there's a girl . . . who needs a good seeing-to . . . by a man like me . . .'

'Have you?' I ask, enthralled at the idea, pushing back on his hard rod, sucking him all up.

'Oh yes, Hannah . . . your tight skirts . . . your high heels . . . your "fuck me" eyes . . . you little trollop . . . you need it, don't you? . . . and now you're getting it . . .'

I can hardly contradict him. I am, in just about every sense, 'getting it'. His nails are digging into my hips now, his speed increasing. Between my legs, the scene is blurring; I see the root of his cock whipping in and out, feel the slap of his skin against mine, hear the slicking noise his thrusts provoke, smell the warm, heady scent of our combined juices. My legs are starting to give way; one heel has punctured the cardboard of the box I am standing on and is making an indentation in the plastic transparencies within; I am hot and sticky and sweaty with exertion, even though I am taped into immobility.

He finds the spot and I scream, bucking the chair back and forth, alight with orgasmic electricity, then he roars, pinches my hips so hard I fear his nails will break off in them, sends one final body-shattering stroke to the target and then collapses limply over my sloping back. My legs want to melt but they can't because of the tape that secures them to the chair, so I flop sideways, hoping he will catch me. He does, skilfully managing to turn the chair on to its side on the floor, where we lie, spent and exhausted, in a spoons position.

Then there is a knock at the door.

We ignore it, lying silently. I know the door is locked, but I can feel Morrell's heart thumping against my back.

A cough. A trying of the handle.

'Is everything all right? Is there anyone in there?'

It is Sharon, one of the girls from the office. She knocks again.

'Maybe something fell off a shelf,' says another voice. Her friend.

'It was people, I'm sure,' says Sharon's muffled voice. 'Sounded like they were in pain.'

'Maybe it was coming from the loos?'

'Well . . . I don't know. Maybe. Where's Hannah got to?'

'Dunno; Morrell marched her off. Maybe he's given her the boot.'

'Or he's giving her one . . . ooh! Do you think . . . ?'

'Shit! Let's get back to the office.'

Their heels scuttle clickily off and I exhale again. As does Morrell. And then he kisses me.

'Unfortunately, we do need to get back to work,' he says into my ear, his voice low and caressing. 'Perhaps next time we'll use my office. That could be just as much fun. I have a very big desk, you know.'

'Next time, eh?' I sigh, then I suck in my breath when he starts untaping my wrists. You could wax your pubes with that stuff. I am examining the red cuffs of sore skin above my hands as he talks.

'Oh yes, I think so. I might have it written into your Job Description. Personal services to the manager, no fewer than three times weekly.'

'That could come under "Other Duties As Required", I suppose.' Damn it, my stockings are laddered now.

'Yes. And instead of Dress Down Friday, we could have Get Undressed Friday.'

I giggle. 'Are there any tissues in here?' I ask, squinting at the dark shelves.

'No tissues,' he says. 'I want you sitting at your desk – if you can still sit – in sticky knickers for the rest of the day. I want the other girls to smell it on you.'

'You pervert.'

He raises an eyebrow. 'Is that any way to talk to your manager?' he asks. 'Do I need to test another of these rulers to destruction?'

'Maybe not today, Sir,' I concede. I pull my knickers back up, but he stops me, placing a Post-it note on each pink bum cheek.

He leans over and writes on them in green felt tip pen. 'What does it say?' I ask, craning my neck to read.

'"Spank me",' he says. 'Keep those there until you get home.'

'Oh, OK.' I pull the knickers carefully over the notes, making sure not to detach them from my skin, picturing the tasteful colour contrast they must make. My skirt is next, up over my laddered stockings, then I try to button my shirt up over the hardened correction fluid message on my breasts. Except . . . no buttons. Morrell chuckles, then reaches for a stapler, tacking the shirt together haphazardly. I stare at him wildly – surely he can't expect me to wear this in the office? – but he simply smirks and nods.

'Don't forget to order those rulers,' he says, as I turn to him, uncertain how to end this strange interlude. 'And I want to see you in my office at close of play. I want to check that Post-its, stained knickers and Tippexed tits are all still intact. Do you understand?'

'Yes, Sir.' I grin blushingly.

'Good. Now get back to work, and no more slacking.' He sends me on my way with a light pat to the seat of my skirt that still manages to make me wince.

What a long work day it proves to be.

I can barely sit on my swivel chair; my bum throbs, and rustles every time I shift; my knickers are cold and slimy against my sore and swollen pussy and I have to avoid crossing the office for fear that the spunk has stained my skirt. My laddered stockings would be bound to draw comment too.

Inferences are made around the workstations; I often catch heads bowed behind screens in muttered conversation, then raised to look at me. Sharon, sitting opposite, comments loudly to her neighbour that she might buy an air freshener at lunchtime.

I soldier on, working harder than I ever have before. Morrell's unusual management techniques are certainly improving my productivity.

They haven't cured my clock-watching though.

Want more sexy fiction?

September 2012 saw the re-launch of the iconic erotic fiction series *Black Lace* with a brand new look and even steamier fiction. We're also re-visiting some of our most popular titles in our *Black Lace Classics* series.

First launched in 1993, *Black Lace* was the first erotic fiction imprint written by women for women and quickly became the most popular erotica imprint in the world.

To find out more, visit us at:
www.blacklace.co.uk

And join the *Black Lace* community:

🐦 @blacklacebooks

f BlackLaceBooks

BLACK
LACE

The leading imprint of women's sexy fiction is back – and it's better than ever!

Also available from Black Lace:

The Dark Garden
Eden Bradley

Surrender has its own rewards...

Rowan Cassidy likes to be in charge – especially in her personal life. At Club Privé, the most exclusive S&M club on the West Coast, she can live out her dominant fantasies safely, and with complete control.

Then she meets Christian Thorne. Self-confidant and sophisticated, he's a natural dominant and makes it clear he wants to be Rowan's master. He makes Rowan a daring proposition: she must give herself over to him for thirty days and discover her true nature . . .

Also available from Black Lace:

The Ninety Days of Genevieve
Lucinda Carrington

He is an arrogant, worldly entrepreneur who always gets
what he wants.

And what he wants is for Genevieve to spend the next
ninety days submitting to his every desire...

*A dark, sensual tale of love and obsession, featuring a
very steamy relationship between an inexperienced
heroine and a masterful and rich older man.*

Praise for *The Ninety Days of Genevieve*

'This month's essential reading . . . For fans of
the renaissance of erotic fiction comes
Lucinda Carrington's tale of love
and obsession'
Stylist

'sizzling ...It's full of expertly written sex scenes
that will appeal to any woman who has ever fantasised
about bondage, lust, exhibitionism and voyeurism! . . .
an excellent plot, well written characters
and heaps of charm'
Handbag.com

In Too Deep
Portia Da Costa

Lust among the stacks . . .

Librarian Gwendolyne Price starts finding indecent proposals and sexy stories in her suggestion box. Shocked that they seem to be tailored specifically to her own deepest sexual fantasies, she begins a tantalising relation - ship with a man she's never met.

But pretty soon, erotic letters and toe-curlingly sensual emails just aren't enough. She has to meet her mysterious correspondent in the flesh . . .

Praise for Portia Da Costa

'Imaginative, playful and a lot of fun'
For Women

Also available from Black Lace:

All You Can Eat
Emma Holly

Sex, lies and murder…

Frankie Smith is having a bad day: her boyfriend has just dumped her and she's just found a dead body behind her café.

Still, things look up when sexy local detective, Jack West, turns up to investigate. And when stranger turns up at the diner looking for work, Frankie soon finds herself juggling two men and an increasingly kinky sex life…

Explicit, erotic fiction from the bestselling author of Ménage

Also available from Black Lace:

The Stranger
Portia Da Costa

Once she had got over the initial shock of the young man's nudity, Claudia allowed herself to breathe properly again...

When Claudia finds a sexy stranger on the beach near her home she discovers that he has lost his memory along with his clothes.

Having turned her back on relationships since the death of her husband, Claudia finds herself scandalising her friends by inviting the stranger into her home and into her bed...

Black Lace Classics – **our best erotic fiction ever from our leading authors**

Also available from Black Lace:

I Kissed a Girl
Edited by Regina Perry

Everyone's heard the Katy Perry song, but have you ever been tempted...?

If so, you're not alone: most heterosexual women have had same-sex fantasies, and this diverse collection of short erotic fiction takes us way beyond kissing.

An anthology featuring kinky girl stories from around the globe and women from every walk of life and culture who are curious and eager to explore their full sexuality...with each other.

Black Lace Books: **the leading imprint of erotic fiction by women for women**

Also available from Black Lace:

Wedding Games
Karen S. Smith

Emma is not looking forward to her cousin's wedding: the usual awkward guests, the endless small talk, the bad dancing...But a chance encounter with Kit, a very sexy stranger, leaves her breathless.

Without a chance to say goodbye, Emma resigns herself to the fact their incredibly hot encounter will be just sexy memory, but then she meets Kit at another wedding...

Also available from Black Lace:

Hot Ménage
Edited by Lori Perkins

**A super-hot short story collection
about threesomes.**

In this delightfully wicked anthology, you'll find
threesomes of all types ranging from historical to contemporary, with even a touch of the paranormal. Whether it's
two men and a woman, two women and a man, or same-sex threesomes, these groups find interesting and inspiring
ways to get it on. From sexed-up cowboys to an all male
medieval threesome, hot vintage Hollywood to a triple
lesbian story right out of *Mad Men*, *Hot Ménage* has a
story for everyone.

Contributors include: Jen Bluekissed, Kristabel Reed,
Em Brown, K.T. Grant, Janet Post, Jo Atkinson, Courtney
Sheets, Cathleen Ross, Rebecca Leigh, Melanie Thompson,
Elizabeth Coldwell, Cynthia Gentry, Mercy Loomis,
Laura Neilsen, Reno Lark and Brit M.

And available digitally, a brand new collection in our best-selling **'Quickies'** series: short erotic fiction anthologies

QUICKIES: GIRLS ON TOP
Emma Hawthorne

This new collection of sensational, sexy stories will arouse and, occasionally, even shock you. This volume contains brand new stories from women who ignore the rules, unleash their sexual fantasies and find out just how wildly delicious sex can be when you take it to the limit – and, sometimes, beyond….

Includes:

Darkroom – Jen and her boyfriend explore group sex

Doctor in the house – Debbie's visit to A&E results in a romp with a doctor which gives a whole new meaning to the term 'bedside manner'….

Mistress Millie – when Millie meets fit farmhand Jake she knows exactly how to put him in his place...

Juicy – Samantha is about to discover her husband and his best friend are hiding a sexy secret...

Festival Fever – Leanna shares a tent with her friends Dee and Mar. And they get up close and very personal...

Top Brass – She's the boss's wife and Cindy knows she shouldn't say no to any of her demands...